Margaret Fuller

Life without and life within

Margaret Fuller

Life without and life within

ISBN/EAN: 9783744737258

Printed in Europe, USA, Canada, Australia, Japan

Cover: Foto ©Andreas Hilbeck / pixelio.de

More available books at **www.hansebooks.com**

LIFE WITHOUT AND LIFE WITHIN;

OR,

Reviews, Narratives, Essays, and Poems,

BY

MARGARET FULLER OSSOLI,

AUTHOR OF "WOMAN IN THE NINETEENTH CENTURY," "AT HOME AND
ABROAD," "ART, LITERATURE, AND THE DRAMA," ETC.

EDITED BY HER BROTHER,

ARTHUR B. FULLER.

BOSTON:

BROWN, TAGGARD AND CHASE.

NEW YORK: SHELDON & CO. PHILADELPHIA: J. B. LIPPINCOTT & CO.

LONDON: SAMPSON LOW, SON & CO.

1860.

STEREOTYPED AT THE
BOSTON STEREOTYPE FOUNDRY.

RIVERSIDE, CAMBRIDGE:
PRINTED BY H. O. HOUGHTON AND COMPANY.

PREFACE.

EVERY person, who can be said to really live at all, leads two lives during this period of mortal existence. The one life is outward; it is passed in reading the thoughts of others; in contemplating the struggles, the defeats, the victories, the virtues, the sins, in fine, all things which make the history of those who surround us; and in gazing upon the structures which Art has reared, or paintings which she hath inscribed on the canvas; or looking upon the grand temple of the material universe, and beholding scenes painted by a hand more skilled, more wondrous, in its creative power, than ever can be human hand. The life passed in examining what other minds have produced, or living other men's lives by looking at their deeds, or in any way discerning what addresses the bodily eye or the physical ear, — this is often wise and well; essential, indeed, to any inner life; but it is outward, not self-centred, not the product of our own individual natures.

But the thought of others suggests or develops

thought of our own — the history of other men, as it is
writing itself imperishably every day upon their souls,
or already has written itself in letters of living light or
lines of gloomy blackness — gives rise to internal sympathy or abhorrence on the part of us who look on and
read what is thus writing and written. Our own spirits
are stirred within us: our passions, which have been
sleeping lions, our affections and aspirations, before
angels with folded wings, — these are awakened by what
others are doing, and then we struggle with the bad or
yield to it; we obey or disobey the good, and our internal moral life begins; the outward universe or the
Great Spirit in our hearts speaks to our souls, leading
first to inward dissatisfaction, then to aspiration for
and attainment of holiness, and now the inner spiritual
life, which shall transfigure all outward life, and throw
its own light and give its own hue to all the outward
universe, has begun. These two lives are parallel
streams; often they mingle their waters, and each imparts its own hue and characteristic to the other.
Sometimes the outer life is the main stream; men live
only in other men's thoughts and deeds — look only
upon the material universe, and retire but seldom
within: the inner life is but a silver thread — a little
rill, scarce discoverable save by the eye of God. Again,
with many the outer life is but little; the passing
scene, the din of the battle which humanity is ever
waging, the one scarce is gazed upon or the other heard

by those who retire much from the outward world, and live almost exclusively upon their own thoughts, and in an ideal realm of fancy, or a real one of internal conflict, which is hidden from the outer vision. Better is it when the stream of outward and inner life are both full and broad — when the glories of the material universe attract the gaze, the realm of literature and learning invite the willing feet to wander in paths where poetry has planted many flowers, philosophy many a sturdy oak of truth, which centuries cannot overthrow — and when, on the other hand, men do not forget to retire often within, and find their own minds kingdoms, where many a noble thought spontaneously grows; their own souls heavens, where, the busy world withdrawn, they commune much with their own aspirations, fight many a noble battle with whatever hinders their spiritual peace, and where they commune yet more with that Comforter, the Divine Spirit, and Christ, that Friend and Helper of all who are seeking to make the life of thought and desire, as well as outward word and deed, high and holy.

It is not a brother's part to pass critical judgment upon a sister's literary attainments, or mental and spiritual gifts, nor is it needful in reference to Madame Ossoli. The world never has questioned her great learning or rich and varied culture; these have been ‚uniformly acknowledged. As a keen and sagacious critic of literature, as an admirer of whatever was noble, an

1 *

abhorrer of all low and mean, this she was early, and is, so far as we know, without any question regarded. That her judgments have always been acquiesced in is far from true; but the public has ever believed them alike sincere and fearless. The life without, — that of culture and intelligent, careful observation, — all know *that* stream to have been full to overflowing.

More and more, too, every year, the public are beginning to recognize and appreciate the richness and the beauty of her inner life. The very keenness of her critical acumen, — the very boldness of her rebuke of all she deemed petty and base — the very truthfulness of her conformity to her own standard — her very abhorrence of all cant and mere conformity, long prevented, and even yet somewhat hinder, many from adequately recognizing the loving spirit, the sympathetic nature, the Christian faith, and spiritual devoutness which made her domestic and social life, her action amid her own kindred and nation, and in Rome, for those not allied to her by birth and lineage, at once kindly, noble, and full of holy self-sacrifice. Yet continually the world is learning these things: the history of her life, as her memoirs reveal it, the testimony of so many witnesses here and in other lands, a more careful study and a wider reading of her works, are leading, perhaps rapidly enough, to a true appreciation of the spiritual beauty of her soul, and men see that the waters of her inner life form a stream at once clear and pure, deep and broad.

In presenting to the public the last volume of Margaret Fuller's works, the Editor is encouraged to hope for them a candid, cordial reception. It has been a work of love on his part, for which he has ever felt inadequate, and from it for a time shrunk. But each volume has had a wider and more cordial welcome than its predecessor, and works received by the great public almost with coldness when first published, have, when republished, had a large and cheering circulation, and, what is far better, a kindly appreciation not only by the few, but even by the many. This is evidence enough that the progress of time has brought the public and my sister into closer sympathy and agreement, and a better understanding on its part of her true views and character.

The present volume is less than any of its predecessors a republication. *Only one of its articles has ever appeared before in book form.* As a book, it is, then, essentially new, though some of its reviews and essays have appeared in the columns of the Tribune and Dial. A large portion of it has never appeared at all in print, especially its poetical portions. The work of collecting these essays, reviews, and poems has been a difficult one, much more than attended the preparation of the previous volumes. Unable, of course, to consult

their author as to any of them, the revision I have
given is doubtless very imperfect, and requires large
allowance. It is even possible that among the poems
one or more written by friends and sent her, or copied
from some other author, may have crept in unawares ;
but this all possible pains have been taken to prevent.
Such as it is, the volume is now before the public ; it
truly reveals her inner and outer life, and is doubtless
the last of the volumes containing the writings of
MARGARET FULLER OSSOLI.

CONTENTS.

PART I.—REVIEWS.

PART II.—MISCELLANEOUS.

PART III.—POEMS.

Life without and Life within.

PART I.

REVIEWS.

MENZEL'S VIEW OF GŒTHE.

Menzel's view of Gœthe is that of a Philistine, in the least opprobrious sense of the term. It is one which has long been applied in Germany to petty cavillers and incompetent critics. I do not wish to convey a sense so disrespectful in speaking of Menzel. He has a vigorous and brilliant mind, and a wide, though imperfect, culture. He is a man of talent, but talent cannot comprehend genius. He judges of Gœthe as a Philistine, inasmuch as he does not enter into Canaan, and read the prophet by the light of his own law, but looks at him from without, and tries him by a rule beneath which he never lived. That there *was* something Menzel saw; what that something was *not* he saw, but *what* it *was* he could not see; none could *see;* it was something to be felt and known at the time of its apparition, but the clear sight of it was reserved to a day far enough removed from its sphere to get a commanding point of view. Has that day come? A little while ago it seemed so; certain features of Gœthe's person-

2   (13)

ality, certain results of his tendency, had become so manifest.
But as the plants he planted mature, they shed a new seed
for a yet more noble growth. A wider experience, a deeper
insight, make rejected words come true, and bring a more refined perception of meaning already discerned. Like all his
elder brothers of the elect band, the forlorn hope of humanity,
he obliges us to live and grow, that we may walk by his side ;
vainly we strive to leave him behind in some niche of the
hall of our ancestors ; a few steps onward and we find him
again, of yet serener eye and more towering mien than on
his other pedestal. Former measurements of his size have,
like the girdle bound by the nymphs round the infant Apollo,
only served to make him outgrow the unworthy compass.
The still rising sun, with its broader light, shows us it is not
yet noon. In him is soon perceived a prophet of our own
age, as well as a representative of his own ; and we doubt
whether the revolutions of the century be not required to interpret the quiet depths of his *Saga*.

Sure it is that none has yet found Goethe's place, as sure
that none can claim to be his peer, who has not some time,
ay, and for a long time, been his pupil !

Yet much truth has been spoken of him in detail, some by
Menzel, but in so superficial a spirit, and with so narrow a
view of its bearings, as to have all the effect of falsehood.
Such denials of the crown can only fix it more firmly on the
head of the " Old Heathen." To such the best answer may be
given in the words of Bettina Brentan : " The others criticise
thy works ; I only know that they lead us on and on till we
live in them." And thus will all criticism end in making
more men and women read these works, and " on and on,"
till they forget whether the author be a patriot or a moralist,
in the deep humanity of the thought, the breathing nature of
the scene. While words they have accepted with immediate
approval fade from memory, these oft-denied words of keen,
cold truth return with ever new force and significance.

Men should be true, wise, beautiful, pure, and aspiring. This man was true and wise, capable of all things. Because he did not in one short life complete his circle, can we afford to lose him out of sight? Can we, in a world where so few men have in any degree redeemed their inheritance, neglect a nature so rich and so manifestly progressive?

Historically considered, Gœthe needs no apology. His so-called faults fitted him all the better for the part he had to play. In cool possession of his wide-ranging genius, he taught the imagination of Germany, that the highest flight should be associated with the steady sweep and undazzled eye of the eagle. Was he too much the connoisseur, did he attach too great an importance to the cultivation of taste, where just then German literature so much needed to be refined, polished, and harmonized? Was he too sceptical, too much an experimentalist, — how else could he have formed himself to be the keenest, and, at the same time, most nearly universal of observers, teaching theologians, philosophers, and patriots that nature comprehends them all, commands them all, and that no one development of life must exclude the rest? Do you talk, in the easy cant of the day, of German obscurity, extravagance, pedantry, and bad taste, — and will you blame this man, whose Greek, English, Italian, German mind steered so clear of these rocks and shoals, clearing, adjusting, and calming on each side, wherever he turned his prow? Was he not just enough of an idealist, just enough of a realist, for his peculiar task? If you want a moral enthusiast, is not there Schiller? If piety, of purest, mystic sweetness, who but Novalis? Exuberant sentiment, that treasures each withered leaf in a tender breast, look to your Richter. Would you have men to find plausible meaning for the deepest enigma, or to hang up each map of literature, well painted and dotted on its proper roller, — there are the Schlegels. Men of ideas were numerous as migratory crows in autumn, and Jacobi wrote the heart into philosophy, as well as he could. Who could fill Gœthe's place to Germany, and to the world, of which she is now the teacher? His much-reviled aristocratic turn was at that time a reconciling element. It is plain why he was what he was, for his country and his age.

Whoever looks into the history of his youth, will be struck by a peculiar force with which all things worked together to prepare him for his office of artist-critic to the then chaotic world of thought in his country. What an unusually varied scene of childhood and of youth! What endless change and contrast of circumstances and influences! Father and mother, life and literature, world and nature, — playing into one another's hands, always by antagonism! Never was a child so carefully guarded by fate against prejudice, against undue bias, against any engrossing sentiment. Nature having given him power of poetical sympathy to know every situation, would not permit him to make himself at home in any. And how early what was most peculiar in his character manifested itself, may be seen in these anecdotes related by his mother to Bettina.

Of Gœthe's childhood. — "He was not willing to play with other little children, unless they were very fair. In a circle he began suddenly to weep, screaming, ' Take away the black, ugly child; I cannot bear to have it here.' He could not be pacified; they were obliged to take him home, and there the mother could hardly console him for the child's ugliness. He was then only three years old."

" His mother was surprised, that when his brother Jacob died, who had been his playmate, he shed no tear, but rather seemed annoyed by the lamentations of those around him. But afterwards, when his mother asked whether he had not loved his brother, he ran into his room and brought from under his bed a bundle of papers, all written over, and said he had done all this for Jacob."

Even so in later years, had he been asked if he had not

loved his country and his fellow-men, he would not have answered by tears and vows, but pointed to his works.

In the first anecdote is observable that love of symmetry in external relations which, in manhood, made him give up the woman he loved, because she would not have been in place among the old-fashioned furniture of his father's house; and dictated the course which, at the crisis of his life, led him to choose an outward peace rather than an inward joy. In the second, he displays, at the earliest age, a sense of his vocation as a recorder, the same which drew him afterwards to write his life into verse, rather than clothe it in action. His indirectness, his aversion to the frankness of heroic meetings, is repulsive and suspicious to generous and flowing natures; yet many of the more delicate products of the mind seem to need these sheaths, lest bird and insect rifle them in the bud.

And if this subtlety, isolation, and distance be the dictate of nature, we submit, even as we are not vexed that the wild bee should hide its honey in some old moss-grown tree, rather than in the glass hives of our gardens. We believe it will repay the pains we take in seeking for it, by some peculiar flavor from unknown flowers. Was Gœthe the wild bee? We see that even in his boyhood he showed himself a very Egyptian, in his love for disguises; forever expressing his thought in roundabout ways, which seem idle mummery to a mind of Spartan or Roman mould. Had he some simple thing to tell his friend, he read it from the newspaper, or wrote it into a parable. Did he make a visit, he put on the hat or wig of some other man, and made his bow as Schmidt or Schlosser, that they might stare, when he spoke as Gœthe. He gives as the highest instance of passionate grief, that he gave up for one day watching the tedious ceremonies of the imperial coronation. In daily life many of these carefully recorded passages have an air of platitude, at which no wonder the Edinburgh Review laughed. Yet, on examination, they are full of meaning. And when we see the same propensity

2 *

writing itself into Ganymede, Mahomet's song, the Bayadere, and Faust, telling all Goethe's religion in Mignon and Makana, all his wisdom in the Western-Eastern Divan, we respect it, accept, all but love it.

This theme is for a volume, and I must quit it now. A brief summary of what Goethe was suffices to vindicate his existence, as an agent in history and a part of nature, but will not meet the objections of those who measure him, as they have a right to do, by the standard of ideal manhood.

Most men, in judging another man, ask, Did he live up to our standard?

But to me it seems desirable to ask rather, Did he live up to his own?

So possible is it that our consciences may be more enlightened than that of the Gentile under consideration. And if we can find out how much was given him, we are told, in a pure evangelium, to judge thereby how much shall be required.

Now, Goethe has given us both his own standard and the way to apply it. "To appreciate any man, learn first what object he proposed to himself; next, what degree of earnestness he showed with regard to attaining that object."

And this is part of his hymn for man made in the divine image, "THE GODLIKE."

> "Hail to the Unknown, the
>   Higher Being
>   Felt within us!
>
>   "Unfeeling
>   As nature,
>   Still shineth the sun
>   Over good and evil;
>   And on the sinner,
>   Smile as on the best,

Moon and stars.
Fate too, &c.

" There can none but man
Perform the Impossible.
He understandeth,
Chooseth, and judgeth;
He can impart to the
Moment duration.

" He alone may
The good reward,
The guilty punish,
Mend and deliver;
All the wayward, anomalous
Bind in the useful.

" And the Immortals,
Them we reverence
As if they were men, and   .
Did, on a grand scale,
What the best man in little
Does, or fain would do.

" Let noble man
Be helpful and good;
Ever creating
The Right and the Useful;
Type of those loftier
Beings of whom the heart whispers."

This standard is high enough.   It is what every man should express in action, the poet in music!

And this office of a judge, who is of purer eyes than to behold iniquity, and of a sacred oracle, to whom other men may go to ask when they should choose a friend, when face a foe, this great genius does not adequately fulfil. Too often has the priest left the shrine to go and gather simples by the aid of spells whose might no pure power needs. Glimpses are found in his works of the highest spirituality, but it is blue sky seen through chinks in a roof which should never have been builded. He has used life to excess. He is too rich for his nobleness, too judicious for his inspiration, too humanly wise for his divine mission. He might have been a priest ; he is only a sage.

An Epicurean sage, say the multitude. This seems to me unjust. He is also called a debauchee. There may be reason for such terms, but it is partial, and received, as they will be, by the unthinking, they are as false as Menzel's abuse, in the impression they convey. Did Gœthe value the present too much? It was not for the Epicurean aim of pleasure, but for use. He, in this, was but an instance of reaction, in an age of painful doubt and restless striving as to the future. Was his private life stained by profligacy? That far largest portion of his life, which is ours, and which is expressed in his works, is an unbroken series of efforts to develop the higher elements of our being. I cannot speak to private gossip on this subject, nor even to well-authenticated versions of his private life. Here are sixty volumes, by himself and others, which contain sufficient evidence of a life of severe labor, steadfast forbearance, and an intellectual growth almost unparalleled. That he has failed of the highest fulfilment of his high vocation is certain, but he was neither Epicurean nor sensualist, if we consider his life as a whole.

Yet he had failed to reach his highest development ; and how was it that he was so content with this incompleteness, nay, the serenest of men? His serenity alone, in such a time of scepticism and sorrowful seeking, gives him a claim to all our study. See how he rides at anchor, lordly, rich in freight, every white sail ready to be unfurled at a moment's warning!

And it must be a very slight survey which can confound this calm self-trust with selfish indifference of temperament. Indeed, he, in various ways, lets us see how little he was helped in this respect by temperament. But we need not his declaration, — the case speaks for itself. Of all that perpetual accomplishment, that unwearied constructiveness, the basis must be sunk deeper than in temperament. He never halts, never repines, never is puzzled, like other men; that tranquillity, full of life, that ceaseless but graceful motion, "without haste, without rest," for which we all are striving, he has attained. And is not his love of the noblest kind? Reverence the highest, have patience with the lowest. Let this day's performance of the meanest duty be thy religion. Are the stars too distant, pick up that pebble that lies at thy foot, and from it learn the all. Go out like Saul, the son of Kish, look earnestly after the meanest of thy father's goods, and a kingdom shall be brought thee. The least act of pure self-renunciation hallows, for the moment, all within its sphere. The philosopher may mislead, the devil tempt, yet innocence, though wounded and bleeding as it goes, must reach at last the holy city. The power of sustaining himself and guiding others rewards man sufficiently for the longest apprenticeship. Is not this lore the noblest?

Yes, yes, but still I doubt. 'Tis true, he says all this in a thousand beautiful forms, but he does not warm, he does not inspire me. In his certainty is no bliss, in his hope no love, in his faith no glow. How is this?

A friend, of a delicate penetration, observed, "His atmosphere was so calm, so full of light, that I hoped he would teach me his secret of cheerfulness. But I found, after long search, that he had no better way, if he wished to check emotion or clear thought, than to go to work. As his mother tells us, 'My son, if he had a grief, made it into a poem, and so got rid of it.' This mode is founded in truth, but does not involve the whole truth. I want the method which is indicated by the phrase, ' Perseverance of the saints.' "

This touched the very point. Gœthe attained only the perseverance of a man. He was true, for he knew that nothing can be false to him who is true, and that to genius nature has pledged her protection. Had he but seen a little farther, he would have given this covenant a higher expression, and been more deeply true to a diviner nature.

In another article on Gœthe, I shall give some account of that period, when a too determined action of the intellect limited and blinded him for the rest of his life ; I mean only in comparison with what he should have been. Had it been otherwise, what would he not have attained, who, even thus self-enchained, rose to Ulyssean stature. Connected with this is the fact, of which he spoke with such sarcastic solemnity to Eckermann — " My works will never be popular."

I wish, also, to consider the Faust, Elective Affinities, Apprenticeship and Pilgrimages of Wilhelm Meister, and Iphigenia, as affording indications of the progress of his genius here, of its wants and prospects in future spheres of activity. For the present I bid him farewell, as his friends always have done, in hope and trust of a better meeting.

GŒTHE.

"Nemo contra Deum nisi Deus ipse."

"Wer Grosses will muss sich zusammen raffen;
In der Beschrankung zeigt sich erst der Meister,
Und der Gesetz nur Kann uns Freikeit geben." *

THE first of these mottoes is that prefixed by Gœthe to the last books of "Dichtung und Wahrheit." These books record the hour of turning tide in his life, the time when he was called on for a choice at the "Parting of the Ways." From these months, which gave the sun of his youth, the crisis of his manhood, date the birth of Egmont, and of Faust too, though the latter was not published so early. They saw the rise and decline of his love for Lili, apparently the truest love he ever knew. That he was not himself dissatisfied with the results to which the decisions of this era led him, we may infer from his choice of a motto, and from the calm beauty with which he has invested the record.

The Parting of the Ways! The way he took led to court-favor, wealth, celebrity, and an independence of celebrity. It led to large performance, and a wonderful economical management of intellect. It led Faust, the Seeker, from the heights of his own mind to the trodden ways of the world. There, indeed, he did not lose sight of the mountains, but he never breathed their keen air again.

* "He who would do great things must quickly draw together his forces. The master can only show himself such through limitation, and the law alone can give us freedom."

After this period we find in him rather a wide and deep Wisdom, than the inspiration of Genius. His faith, that all *must* issue well, wants the sweetness of piety, and the God he manifests to us is one of law or necessity, rather than of intelligent love. As this God makes because he must, so Goethe, his instrument, observes and re-creates because he must, observing with minutest fidelity the outward exposition of Nature; never blinded by a sham, or detained by a fear, he yet makes us feel that he wants insight to her sacred secret. The calmest of writers does not give us repose, because it is too difficult to find his centre. Those flame-like natures, which he undervalues, give us more peace and hope, through their restless aspirations, than he with his hearth-enclosed fires of steady fulfilment. For, true as it is, that God is every where, we must not only see him, but see him acknowledged. Through the consciousness of man, "shall not Nature interpret God?" We wander in diversity, and with each new turning of the path, long anew to be referred to the One.

Of Goethe, as of other natures, where the intellect is too much developed in proportion to the moral nature, it is difficult to speak without seeming narrow, blind, and impertinent. For such men *see* all that others *live*, and, if you feel a want of a faculty in them, it is hard to say they have it not, lest, next moment, they puzzle you by giving some indication of it. Yet they are not, nay, *know* not; they only discern. The difference is that between sight and life, prescience and being, wisdom and love. Thus with Goethe. Naturally of a deep mind and shallow heart, he felt the sway of the affections enough to appreciate their workings in other men, but never enough to receive their inmost regenerating influence.

How this might have been had he ever once abandoned himself entirely to a sentiment, it is impossible to say. But the education of his youth seconded, rather than balanced, his natural tendency. His father was a gentlemanly martinet; dull, sour, well-informed, and of great ambition as to externals.

His influence on the son was wholly artificial. He was always turning his powerful mind from side to side in search of information, for the attainment of what are called accomplishments. The mother was a delightful person in her way; open, genial, playful, full of lively talent, but without earnestness of soul. She was one of those charming, but not noble persons, who take the day and the man as they find them, seeing the best that is there already, but never making the better grow in its stead. His sister, though of graver kind, was social and intellectual, not religious or tender. The mortifying repulse of his early love checked the few pale buds of faith and tenderness that his heart put forth. His friends were friends of the intellect merely; altogether, he seemed led by destiny to the place he was to fill.

Pardon him, World, that he was too worldly. Do not wonder, Heart, that he was so heartless. Believe, Soul, that one so true, as far as he went, must yet be initiated into the deeper mysteries of Soul. Perhaps even now he sees that we must accept limitations only to transcend them; work in processes only to detect the organizing power which supersedes them; and that Sphinxes of fifty-five volumes might well be cast into the abyss before the single word that solves them all.

Now, when I think of Gœthe, I seem to see his soul, all the variegated plumes of knowledge, artistic form "und so weiter," burnt from it by the fires of divine love, wingless, motionless, unable to hide from itself in any subterfuge of labor, saying again and again, the simple words which he would never distinctly say on earth — God beyond Nature — Faith beyond Sight — the Seeker nobler than the *Meister.*

For this mastery that Gœthe prizes seems to consist rather in the skilful use of means than in the clear manifestation of ends. His Master, indeed, makes acknowledgment of a divine order, but the temporal uses are always uppermost in

3

the mind of the reader.   But of this, more at large in reference to his works.

Apart from this want felt in his works, there is a littleness
in his aspect as a character.   Why waste his time in Weimar
court entertainments?   His duties as minister were not unworthy of him, though it would have been, perhaps, finer, if
he had not spent so large a portion of that prime of intellectual
life, from five and twenty to forty, upon them.

But granted that the exercise these gave his faculties, the
various lore they brought, and the good they did to the community, made them worth his doing, — why that perpetual
dangling after the royal family?   Why all that verse-making
for the albums of serene highnesses, and those pretty poetical
entertainments for the young princesses, and that cold setting
himself apart from his true peers, the real sovereigns of
Weimar — Herder, Wieland, and the others?   The excuse
must be found in circumstances of his time and temperament,
which made the character of man of the world and man of
affairs more attractive to him than the children of nature can
conceive it to be in the eyes of one who is capable of being a
consecrated bard.

The man of genius feels that literature has become too
much a craft by itself.   No man should live by or for his pen.
Writing is worthless except as the record of life; and no
great man ever was satisfied thus to express all his being.
His book should be only an indication of himself.   The obe-
lisk should point to a scene of conquest.   In the present state
of division of labor, the literary man finds himself condemned
to be nothing else.   Does he write a good book? it is not
received as evidence of his ability to live and act, but rather
the reverse.   Men do not offer him the care of embassies, as
an earlier age did to Petrarca; they would be surprised if he
left his study to go forth to battle like Cervantes.   We have
the swordsman, and statesman, and penman, but it is not considered that the same mind which can rule the destiny of a poem,

may as well that of an army or an empire.* Yet surely it should be so. The scientific man may need seclusion from the common affairs of life, for he has his materials before him; but the man of letters must seek them in life, and he who cannot act will but imperfectly appreciate action.

The literary man is impatient at being set apart. He feels that monks and troubadours, though in a similar position, were brought into more healthy connection with man and nature, than he who is supposed to look at them merely to write them down. So he rebels; and Sir Walter Scott is prouder of being a good sheriff and farmer, than of his reputation as the Great Unknown. Byron piques himself on his skill in shooting and swimming. Sir H. Davy and Schlegel would be admired as dandies, and Gœthe, who had received an order from a publisher " for a dozen more dramas in the same style as Gœtz von Berlichingen," and though (in sadder sooth) he had already Faust in his head asking to be written out, thought it no degradation to become premier in the little Duchy of Weimar.

" Straws show which way the wind blows," and a comment may be drawn from the popular novels, where the literary man is obliged to wash off the ink in a violet bath, attest his courage in the duel, and hide his idealism beneath the vulgar nonchalance and coxcombry of the man of fashion.

If this tendency of his time had some influence in making Gœthe find pleasure in tangible power and decided relations with society, there were other causes which worked deeper. The growth of genius in its relations to men around must always be attended with daily pain. The enchanted eye turns from the far-off star it has detected to the short-sighted bystander, and the seer is mocked for pretending to see what others cannot. The large and generalizing mind infers the whole from a single circumstance, and is reproved by all

* Except in "La belle France."

around for its presumptuous judgment. Its Ithuriel temper pierces shams, creeds, covenants, and chases the phantoms which others embrace, till the lovers of the false Florimels hurl the true knight to the ground. Little men are indignant that Hercules, yet an infant, declares he has strangled the serpent; they demand a proof; they send him out into scenes of labor to bring thence the voucher that his father is a god. What the ancients meant to express by Apollo's continual disappointment in his loves, is felt daily in the youth of genius. The sympathy he seeks flies his touch, the objects of his affection sneer at his sublime credulity, his self-reliance is arrogance, his far sight infatuation, and his ready detection of fallacy fickleness and inconsistency. Such is the youth of genius, before the soul has given that sign of itself which an unbelieving generation cannot controvert. Even then he is little benefited by the transformation of the mockers into worshippers. For the soul seeks not adorers, but peers; not blind worship, but intelligent sympathy. The best consolation even then is that which Gœthe puts into the mouth of Tasso: "To me gave a God to tell what I suffer." In "Tasso" Gœthe has described the position of the poetical mind in its prose relations with equal depth and fulness. We see what he felt must be the result of entire abandonment to the highest nature. We see why he valued himself on being able to understand the Alphonsos, and meet as an equal the Antonios of every-day life.

But, you say, there is no likeness between Gœthe and Tasso. Never believe it; such pictures are not painted from observation merely. That deep coloring which fills them with light and life is given by dipping the brush in one's own life-blood. Gœthe had not from nature that character of self-reliance and self-control in which he so long appeared to the world. It was wholly acquired, and so highly valued because he was conscious of the opposite tendency. He was by nature as impetuous, though not as tender, as Tasso, and the

disadvantage at which this constantly placed him was keenly
felt by a mind made to appreciate the subtlest harmonies in
all relations. Therefore was it that when he at last cast
anchor, he was so reluctant again to trust himself to wave
and breeze.

I have before spoken of the antagonistic influences under
which he was educated. He was driven from the severity of
study into the world, and then again drawn back, many times
in the course of his crowded youth. Both the world and the
study he used with unceasing ardor, but not with the sweetness of a peaceful hope. Most of the traits which are considered to mark his character at a later period were wanting
to him in youth. He was very social, and continually per-
turbed by his social sympathies. He was deficient both in
outward self-possession and mental self-trust. "I was always,"
he says, "either *too volatile or too infatuated*, so that those
who looked kindly on me did by no means always honor me
with their esteem." He wrote much and with great freedom.
The pen came naturally to his hand, but he had no confidence in the merit of what he wrote, and much inferior persons to Merck and Herder might have induced him to throw
aside as worthless what it had given him sincere pleasure to
compose. It was hard for him to isolate himself, to console
himself, and, though his mind was always busy with important
thoughts, they did not free him from the pressure of other
minds. His youth was as sympathetic and impetuous as any
on record.

The effect of all this outward pressure on the poet is
recorded in Werther — a production that he afterwards under-
valued, and to which he even felt positive aversion. It was
natural that this should be. In the calm air of the cultivated
plain he attained, the remembrance of the miasma of sentimentality was odious to him. Yet sentimentality is but sentiment diseased, which to be cured must be patiently observed
by the wise physician; so are the morbid desire and despair

3 *

of Werther, the sickness of a soul aspiring to a purer, freer state, but mistaking the way.

The best or the worst occasion in man's life is precisely that misused in Werther, when he longs for more love, more freedom, and a larger development of genius than the limitations of this terrene sphere permit. Sad is it indeed if, persisting to grasp too much at once, he lose all, as Werther did. He must accept limitation, must consent to do his work in time, must let his affections be baffled by the barriers of convention. Tantalus-like, he makes this world a Tartarus, or, like Hercules, rises in fires to heaven, according as he knows how to interpret his lot. But he must only use, not adopt it. The boundaries of the man must never be confounded with the destiny of the soul. If he does not decline his destiny, as Werther did, it is his honor to have felt its unfitness for his eternal scope. He was born for wings; he is held to walk in leading-strings; nothing lower than faith must make him resigned, and only in hope should he find content — a hope not of some slight improvement in his own condition or that of other men, but a hope justified by the divine justice, which is bound in due time to satisfy every want of his nature.

Schiller's great command is, " Keep true to the dream of thy youth." The great problem is how to make the dream real, through the exercise of the waking will.

This was not exactly the problem Gœthe tried to solve. To *do* somewhat, became too important, as is indicated both by the second motto to this essay, and by his maxim, " It is not the knowledge of what *might be*, but what *is*, that forms us."

Werther, like his early essays now republished from the Frankfort Journal, is characterized by a fervid eloquence of Italian glow, which betrays a part of his character almost lost sight of in the quiet transparency of his later productions, and may give us some idea of the mental conflicts through which he passed to manhood.

The acting out the mystery into life, the calmness of sur-

vey, and the passionateness of feeling, above all the ironical
baffling at the end, and want of point to a tale got up with
such an eye to effect as he goes along, mark well the man that
was to be. Even so did he demand in Werther; even so res-
olutely open the door in the first part of Faust; even so seem
to play with himself and his contemporaries in the second
part of Faust and Wilhelm Meister.

Yet was he deeply earnest in his play, not for men, but for
himself. To himself as a part of nature it was important to
grow, to lift his head to the light. In nature he had all confidence; for man, as a part of nature, infinite hope; but in
him as an individual will, seemingly, not much trust at the
earliest age.

The history of his intimacies marks his course; they were entered into with passionate eagerness, but always ended in an observation of the intellect, and he left them on his road, as the
snake leaves his skin. The first man he met of sufficient
force to command a large share of his attention was Herder,
and the benefit of this intercourse was critical, not genial.
Of the good Lavater he soon perceived the weakness.
Merck, again, commanded his respect; but the force of Merck
also was cold.

But in the Grand Duke of Weimar he seems to have met
a character strong enough to exercise a decisive influence
upon his own. Gœthe was not so politic and worldly that a
little man could ever have become his Mæcenas. In the
Duchess Amelia and her son he found that practical sagacity,
large knowledge of things as they are, active force, and genial
feeling, which he had never before seen combined.

The wise mind of the duchess gave the first impulse to
the noble course of Weimar. But that her son should have
availed himself of the foundation she laid is praise enough, in
a world where there is such a rebound from parental influence that it generally seems that the child makes use of the
directions given by the parent only to avoid the prescribed

path. The duke availed himself of guidance, though with a perfect independence in action. The duchess had the unusual wisdom to know the right time for giving up the reins, and thus maintained her authority as far as the weight of her character was calculated to give it.

Of her Goethe was thinking when he wrote, " The admirable woman is she, who, if the husband dies, can be a father to the children."

The duke seems to have been one of those characters which are best known by the impression their personal presence makes on us, resembling an elemental and pervasive force, rather than wearing the features of an individuality. Goethe describes him as " *Dämonische*," that is, gifted with an instinctive, spontaneous force, which at once, without calculation or foresight, chooses the right means to an end. As these beings do not calculate, so is their influence incalculable. Their repose has as much influence over other beings as their action, even as the thunder cloud, lying black and distant in the summer sky, is not less imposing than when it bursts and gives forth its quick lightnings. Such men were Mirabeau and Swift. They had also distinct talents, but their influence was from a perception in the minds of men of this spontaneous energy in their natures. Sometimes, though rarely, we see such a man in an obscure position; circumstances have not led him to a large sphere; he may not have expressed in words a single thought worth recording; but by his eye and voice he rules all around him.

He stands upon his feet with a firmness and calm security which make other men seem to halt and totter in their gait. In his deep eye is seen an infinite comprehension, an infinite reserve of power. No accent of his sonorous voice is lost on any ear within hearing; and, when he speaks, men hate or fear perhaps the disturbing power they feel, but never dream of disobeying. But hear Goethe himself.

" The boy believed in nature, in the animate and inanimate,

the intelligent and unconscious, to discover somewhat which manifested itself only through contradiction, and therefore could not be comprehended by any conception, much less defined by a word. It was not divine, for it seemed without reason; not human, because without understanding; not devilish, because it worked to good; not angelic, because it often betrayed a petulant love of mischief. It was like chance, in that it proved no sequence; it suggested the thought of Providence, because it indicated connection. To this all our limitations seem penetrable; it seemed to play at will with all the elements of our being; it compressed time and dilated space. Only in the impossible did it seem to delight, and to cast the possible aside with disdain.

" This existence which seemed to mingle with others, sometimes to separate, sometimes to unite, I called the Dämonische, after the example of the ancients, and others who have observed somewhat similar." — *Dichtung und Wahrheit.*

" The Dämonische is that which cannot be explained by reason or understanding; it lies not in my nature, but I am subject to it.

" Napoleon was a being of this class, and in so high a degree that scarce any one is to be compared with him. Also our late grand duke was such a nature, full of unlimited power of action and unrest, so that his own dominion was too little for him, and the greatest would have been too little. Demoniac beings of this sort the Greeks reckoned among their demigods." — *Conversations with Eckermann.**

This great force of will, this instinctive directness of action, gave the duke an immediate ascendency over Gœthe which no other person had ever possessed. It was by no means mere sycophancy that made him give up the next ten years,

[* Eckermann's Conversations with Gœthe, translated from the German by my sister, form one volume of the "Specimens of Foreign Literature," edited by Rev. George Ripley, and published in 1839. This volume has been republished by James Munroe & Co., Boston, within a few years.— ED.]

the prime of his manhood, to accompanying the grand duke in his revels, or aiding him in his schemes of practical utility, or to contriving elegant amusements for the ladies of the court. It was a real admiration for the character of the genial man of the world and its environment.

Whoever is turned from his natural path may, if he will, gain in largeness and depth what he loses in simple beauty; and so it was with Gœthe. Faust became a wiser if not a nobler being. Werther, who must die because life was not wide enough and rich enough in love for him, ends as the Meister of the Wanderjahre, well content to be one never inadequate to the occasion, "help-full, comfort-full."

A great change was, during these years, perceptible to his friends in the character of Gœthe. From being always "either too volatile or infatuated," he retreated into a self-collected state, which seemed at first even icy to those around him. No longer he darted about him the lightnings of his genius, but sat Jove-like and calm, with the thunderbolts grasped in his hand, and the eagle gathered to his feet. His freakish wit was subdued into a calm and even cold irony; his multiplied relations no longer permitted him to abandon himself to any; the minister and courtier could not expatiate in the free regions of invention, and bring upon paper the signs of his higher life, without subjecting himself to an artificial process of isolation. Obliged to economy of time and means, he made of his intimates not objects of devout tenderness, of disinterested care, but the crammers and feeders of his intellect. The world was to him an arena or a studio, but not a temple.

"Ye cannot serve God and Mammon."

Had Gœthe entered upon practical life from the dictate of his spirit, which bade him not be a mere author, but a living, loving man, that had all been well. But he must also be a man of the world, and nothing can be more unfavorable to true manhood than this ambition. The citizen, the hero, the general, the poet, all these are in true relations; but what is called being a man of the world is to truckle to it, not truly to serve it.

Thus fettered in false relations, detained from retirement upon the centre of his being, yet so relieved from the early pressure of his great thoughts as to pity more pious souls for being restless seekers, no wonder that he wrote, —

" Es ist dafür gesorgt dass die Bäume nicht in den Himmel wachsen."

"Care is taken that the trees grow not up into the heavens." Ay, Gœthe, but in proportion to their force of aspiration is their height.

Yet never let him be confounded with those who sell all their birthright.   He became blind to the more generous virtues, the nobler impulses, but ever in self-respect was busy to develop his nature.   He was kind, industrious, wise, gentlemanly, if not manly.   If his genius lost sight of the highest aim, he is the best instructor in the use of means; ceasing to be a prophet poet, he was still a poetic artist.   From this time forward he seems a listener to nature, but not himself the highest product of nature, — a priest to the soul of nature.   His works grow out of life, but are not instinct with the peculiar life of human resolve, as are Shakspeare's or Dante's.

Faust contains the great idea of his life, as indeed there is but one great poetic idea possible to man — the progress of a soul through the various forms of existence.

All his other works, whatever their miraculous beauty of execution, are mere chapters to this poem, illustrative of particular points.   Faust, had it been completed in the spirit in which it was begun, would have been the Divina Commedia of its age.

But nothing can better show the difference of result between a stern and earnest life, and one of partial accommodation, than a comparison between the Paridiso and that of the second

part of Faust. In both a soul, gradually educated **and led
back** to God, is received at last not through merit, but grace.
But O the difference between the grandly humble reliance of
old Catholicism, and the loophole redemption of modern
sagacity! Dante was a *man*, of vehement passions, many
prejudices, bitter as much as sweet. His knowledge was
scanty, his sphere of observation narrow, the objects of his
active life petty, compared with those of Goethe. But, constantly retiring to his deepest self, clearsighted to the limitations of man, but no less so to the illimitable energy of the
soul, the sharpest details in his work convey a largest sense,
as his strongest and steadiest flights only direct the eye to
heavens yet beyond.

Yet perhaps he had not so hard a battle to wage, as this
other great poet. The fiercest passions are not so dangerous
foes to the soul as the cold scepticism of the understanding.
The Jewish demon assailed the man of Uz with physical ills ,
the Lucifer of the middle ages tempted his passions ; but the
Mephistopheles of the eighteenth century bade the finite
strive to compass the infinite, and the intellect attempt to
solve all the problems of the soul.

This path Faust had taken: it is that of modern necro-
mancy. Not willing to grow into God by the steady worship
of a life, men would enforce his presence by a spell ; not willing to learn his existence by the slow processes of their own,
they strive to bind it in a word, that they may wear it about
the neck as a talisman.

Faust, bent upon reaching the centre of the universe through
the intellect alone, naturally, after a length of trial, which has
prevented the harmonious unfolding of his nature, falls into
despair. He has striven for one object, and that object eludes
him. Returning upon himself, he finds large tracts of his
nature lying waste and cheerless. He is too noble for apathy,
too wise for vulgar content with the animal enjoyments of
life. Yet the thirst he has been so many years increasing is

not to be borne. Give me, he cries, but a drop of water to cool my burning tongue. Yet, in casting himself with a wild recklessness upon the impulses of his nature yet untried, there is a disbelief that any thing short of the All can satisfy the immortal spirit. His first attempt was noble, though mistaken, and under the saving influence of it, he makes the compact, whose condition cheats the fiend at last.

> Kannst du mich schmeichelnd je belügen
> Dass ich mir selbst gefallen mag,
> Kannst du mich mit Genuss betrügen:
> Das sey für mich der letzte Tag.

> Werd ich zum Augenblicke sagen:
> Verweile doch! du bist so schön!
> Dann magst du mich in Fesseln schlagen,
> Dann will ich gern zu Grunde gehen.

> Canst thou by falsehood or by flattery
> Make me one moment with myself at peace,
> Cheat me into tranquillity? Come then
> And welcome, life's last day.
> Make me but to the moment say,
> O fly not yet, thou art so fair,
> Then let me perish, &c.

But this condition is never fulfilled. Faust cannot be content with sensuality, with the charlatanry of ambition, nor with riches. His heart never becomes callous, nor his moral and intellectual perceptions obtuse. He is saved at last.

With the progress of an individual soul is shadowed forth that of the soul of the age; beginning in intellectual scepticism; sinking into license; cheating itself with dreams of perfect bliss, to be at once attained by means no surer than a spurious paper currency; longing itself back from conflict between the

4

spirit and the flesh, induced by Christianity, to the Greek era
with its harmonious development of body and mind; striving
to reëmbody the loved phantom of classical beauty in the
heroism of the middle age; flying from the Byron despair of
those who die because they cannot soar without wings, to
schemes however narrow, of practical utility, — redeemed at
last through mercy alone.

The second part of Faust is full of meaning, resplendent
with beauty; but it is rather an appendix to the first part
than a fulfilment of its promise. The world, remembering
the powerful stamp of individual feeling, universal indeed in
its application, but individual in its life, which had conquered
all its scruples in the first part, was vexed to find, instead of
the man Faust, the spirit of the age, — discontented with the
shadowy manifestation of truths it longed to embrace, and,
above all, disappointed that the author no longer met us face
to face, or riveted the ear by his deep tones of grief and
resolve.

When the world shall have got rid of the still overpower-
ing influence of the first part, it will be seen that the funda-
mental idea is never lost sight of in the second. The change
is that Goethe, though the same thinker, is no longer the same
person.

The continuation of Faust in the practical sense of the
education of a man is to be found in Wilhelm Meister. Here
we see the change by strongest contrast. The mainspring of
action is no longer the impassioned and noble seeker, but a
disciple of circumstance, whose most marked characteristic is
a *taste* for virtue and knowledge. Wilhelm certainly prefers
these conditions of existence to their opposites, but there is
nothing so decided in his character as to prevent his turning
a clear eye on every part of that variegated world-scene
which the writer wished to place before us.

To see all till he knows all sufficiently to put objects into
their relations, then to concentrate his powers and use his

knowledge under recognized conditions, — such is the progress of man from Apprentice to Master.

'Tis pity that the volumes of the Wanderjahre have not been translated entire, as well as those of the Lehrjahre, for many, who have read the latter only, fancy that Wilhelm becomes a master in that work. Far from it; he has but just become conscious of the higher powers that have ceaselessly been weaving his fate. Far from being as yet a Master, he but now begins to be a Knower. In the Wanderjahre we find him gradually learning the duties of citizenship, and hardening into manhood, by applying what he has learned for himself to the education of his child. He converses on equal terms with the wise and beneficent; he is no longer duped and played with for his good, but met directly mind to mind.

Wilhelm is a master when he can command his actions, yet keep his mind always open to new means of knowledge; when he has looked at various ways of living, various forms of religion and of character, till he has learned to be tolerant of all, discerning of good in all; when the astronomer imparts to his equal ear his highest thoughts, and the poor cottager seeks his aid as a patron and counsellor.

To be capable of all duties, limited by none, with an open eye, a skilful and ready hand, an assured step, a mind deep, calm, foreseeing without anxiety, hopeful without the aid of illusion, — such is the ripe state of manhood. This attained, the great soul should still seek and labor, but strive and battle never more.

The reason for Gœthe's choosing so negative a character as Wilhelm, and leading him through scenes of vulgarity and low vice, would be obvious enough to a person of any depth of thought, even if he himself had not announced it. He thus obtained room to paint life as it really is, and bring forward those slides in the magic lantern which are always known to exist, though they may not be spoken of to ears polite.

Wilhelm cannot abide in tradition, nor do as his fathers did
before him, merely for the sake of money or a standing in
society. The stage, here an emblem of the ideal life as it
gleams before unpractised eyes, offers, he fancies, opportunity
for a life of thought as distinguished from one of routine.
Here, no longer the simple citizen, but Man, all Men, he will
rightly take upon himself the different aspects of life, till
poet-wise, he shall have learned them all.

No doubt the attraction of the stage to young persons of a
vulgar character is merely the brilliancy of its trappings; but
to Wilhelm, as to Gœthe, it was this poetic freedom and daily
suggestion which seemed likely to offer such an agreeable
studio in the greenroom.

But the ideal must be rooted in the real, else the poet's life
degenerates into buffoonery or vice. Wilhelm finds the characters formed by this would-be ideal existence more despicable
than those which grew up on the track, dusty and bustling
and dull as it had seemed, of common life. He is prepared
by disappointment for a higher ambition.

In the house of the count he finds genuine elegance, genuine sentiment, but not sustained by wisdom, or a devotion to
important objects. This love, this life, is also inadequate.

Now, with Teresa he sees the blessings of domestic peace.
He sees a mind sufficient for itself, finding employment and
education in the perfect economy of a little world. The lesson is pertinent to the state of mind in which his former experiences have left him, as indeed our deepest lore is won
from reaction. But a sudden change of scene introduces him
to the society of the sage and learned uncle, the sage and beneficent Natalia. Here he finds the same virtues as with
Teresa, and enlightened by a larger wisdom.

A friend of mine says that his ideal of a friend is a worthy
aunt, one who has the tenderness without the blindness of a
mother, and takes the same charge of the child's mind as the
mother of its body. I don't know but this may have a foun-

dation in truth, though, if so, auntism, like other grand professions, has sadly degenerated. At any rate, Gœthe seems to be possessed with a similar feeling. The Count de Thorane, a man of powerful character, who made a deep impression on his childhood, was, he says, "reverenced by me as an uncle." And the ideal wise man of this common life epic stands before us as " The Uncle."

After seeing the working of just views in the establishment of the uncle, learning piety from the Confessions of a Beautiful Soul, and religious beneficence from the beautiful life of Natalia, Wilhelm is deemed worthy of admission to the society of the Illuminati, that is, those who have pierced the secret of life, and know what it is to be and to do.

Here he finds the scroll of his life "drawn with large, sharp strokes," that is, these truly wise read his character for him, and "mind and destiny are but two names for one idea."

He now knows enough to enter on the Wanderjahre.

Gœthe always represents the highest principle in the feminine form. Woman is the Minerva, man the Mars. As in the Faust, the purity of Gretchen, resisting the demon always, even after all her faults, is announced to have saved her soul to heaven; and in the second part she appears, not only redeemed herself, but by her innocence and forgiving tenderness hallowed to redeem the being who had injured her.

So in the Meister, these women hover around the narrative, each embodying the spirit of the scene. The frail Philina, graceful though contemptible, represents the degradation incident to an attempt at leading an exclusively poetic life. Mignon, gift divine as ever the Muse bestowed on the passionate heart of man, with her soft, mysterious inspiration, her pining for perpetual youth, represents the high desire that leads to this mistake, as Aurelia, the desire for excitement; Teresa, practical wisdom, gentle tranquillity, which seem most desirable after the Aurelia glare. Of the beautiful soul and Natalia we have already spoken. The former embodies

4 *

what was suggested to Gœthe by the most spiritual person he knew in youth — Mademoiselle von Klettenberg, over whom, as he said, in her invalid loneliness the Holy Ghost brooded like a dove.

Entering on the Wanderjahre, Wilhelm becomes acquainted with another woman, who seems the complement of all the former, and represents the idea which is to guide and mould him in the realization of all the past experience.

This person, long before we see her, is announced in various ways as a ruling power. She is the last hope in cases of difficulty, and, though an invalid, and living in absolute retirement, is consulted by her connections and acquaintance as an unerring judge in all their affairs.

All things tend towards her as a centre; she knows all, governs all, but never goes forth from herself.

Wilhelm at last visits her. He finds her infirm in body, but equal to all she has to do. Charity and counsel to men who need her are her business, astronomy her pleasure.

After a while, Wilhelm ascertains from the Astronomer, her companion, what he had before suspected, that she really belongs to the solar system, and only appears on earth to give men a feeling of the planetary harmony. From her youth up, says the Astronomer, till she knew me, though all recognized in her an unfolding of the highest moral and intellectual qualities, she was supposed to be sick at her times of clear vision. When her thoughts were not in the heavens, she returned and acted in obedience to them on earth; she was then said to be well.

When the Astronomer had observed her long enough, he confirmed her inward consciousness of a separate existence and peculiar union with the heavenly bodies.

Her picture is painted with many delicate traits, and a gradual preparation leads the reader to acknowledge the truth; but, even in the slight indication here given, who does not recognize thee, divine Philosophy, sure as the planetary orbits, and inexhaustible as the fountain of light, crowning the faithful Seeker at last with the privilege to possess his own soul.

In all that is said of Macaria,* we recognize that no thought is too religious for the mind of Gœthe. It was indeed so; you can deny him nothing, but only feel that his works are not instinct and glowing with the central fire, and, after catching a glimpse of the highest truth, are forced again to find him too much afraid of losing sight of the limitations of nature to overflow you or himself with the creative spirit.

While the apparition of the celestial Macaria seems to announce the ultimate destiny of the soul of man, the practical application of all Wilhelm has thus painfully acquired is not of pure Delphian strain. Gœthe draws, as he passes, a dart from the quiver of Phœbus, but ends as Æsculapius or Mercury. Wilhelm, at the school of the Three Reverences, thinks out what can be done for man in his temporal relations. He learns to practise moderation, and even painful renunciation. The book ends, simply indicating what the course of his life will be, by making him perform an act of kindness, with good judgment and at the right moment.

Surely the simple soberness of Gœthe should please at least those who style themselves, preëminently, people of common sense.

The following remarks are by the celebrated Rahel von Ense, whose discernment as to his works was highly prized by Gœthe.

" Don Quixote and Wilhelm Meister!

" Embrace one another, Cervantes and Gœthe!

" Both, using their own clear eyes, vindicated human nature. They saw the champions through their errors and follies, looking down into the deepest soul, seeing there the

---

* The name of Macaria is one of noblest association. It is that of the daughter of Hercules, who devoted herself a voluntary sacrifice for her country. She was adored by the Greeks as the true Felicity.

true form. *Respectable* people call the Don as well as
Meister a fool, wandering hither and thither, transacting
no business of real life, bringing nothing to pass, scarce even
knowing what he ought to think on any subject, very unfit for
the hero of a romance. Yet has our sage known how to paint
the good and honest mind in perpetual toil and conflict with
the world, as it is embodied; never sharing one moment the
impure confusion; always striving to find fault with and im-
prove itself, always so innocent as to see others far better
than they are, and generally preferring them to itself, learning
from all, indulging all except the manifestly base; the more
you understand, the more you respect and love this character.
Cervantes has painted the knight, Gœthe the culture of the
entire man, — both their own time."

But those who demand from him a life-long continuance of
the early ardor of Faust, who wish to see, throughout his
works, not only such manifold beauty and subtle wisdom, but
the clear assurance of divinity, the pure white light of Macaria, wish that he had not so variously unfolded his nature, and
concentred it more. They would see him slaying the serpent
with the divine wrath of Apollo, rather than taming it to his
service, like Æsculapius. They wish that he had never gone
to Weimar, had never become a universal connoisseur and
dilettante in science, and courtier as " graceful as a born nobleman," but had endured the burden of life with the suffering
crowd, and deepened his nature in loneliness and privation.
till Faust had conquered, rather than cheated the devil, and
the music of heavenly faith superseded the grave and mild
eloquence of human wisdom.

The expansive genius which moved so gracefully in its self
imposed fetters, is constantly surprising us by its content with
a choice low, in so far as it was not the highest of which the
mind was capable. The secret may be found in the second
motto of this slight essay.

" He who would do great things must quickly draw together his forces. The master can only show himself such through limitation, and the law alone can give us freedom."

But there is a higher spiritual law always ready to supersede the temporal laws at the call of the human soul. The soul that is too content with usual limitations will never call forth this unusual manifestation.

If there be a tide in the affairs of men, which must be taken at the right moment to lead on to fortune, it is the same with inward as with outward life. He who, in the crisis hour of youth, has stopped short of himself, is not likely to find again what he has missed in one life, for there are a great number of blanks to a prize in each lottery.

But the pang we feel that " those who are so much are not more," seems to promise new spheres, new ages, new crises to enable these beings to complete their circle.

Perhaps Gœthe is even now sensible that he should not have stopped at Weimar as his home, but made it one station on the way to Paradise; not stopped at humanity, but regarded it as symbolical of the divine, and given to others to feel more distinctly the centre of the universe, as well as the harmony in its parts. It is great to be an Artist, a Master, greater still to be a Seeker till the Man has found all himself.

What Gœthe meant by self-collection was a collection of means for work, rather than to divine the deepest truths of being. Thus are these truths always indicated, never declared; and the religious hope awakened by his subtle discernment of the workings of nature never gratified, except through the intellect.

He whose prayer is only work will not leave his treasure in the secret shrine.

One is ashamed when finding any fault with one like Gœthe, who is so great. It seems the only criticism should be to do all he omitted to do, and that none who cannot is entitled to say a word. Let that one speak who was all Gœthe

was not, — noble, true, virtuous, but neither wise nor subtle in
his generation, a divine ministrant, a baffled man, ruled and
imposed on by the pygmies whom he spurned, an heroic artist,
a democrat to the tune of Burns:

> "The rank is but the guinea's stamp;
> The man's the gowd for a' that."

Hear Beethoven speak of Gœthe on an occasion which
brought out the two characters in strong contrast.

Extract from a letter of Beethoven to Bettina Brentano,
Töplitz, 1812.

" Kings and princes can indeed make professors and privy
councillors, and hang upon them titles; but great men they
cannot make; souls that rise above the mud of the world,
these they must let be made by other means than theirs, and
should therefore show them respect. When two such as I
and Gœthe come together, then must great lords observe what
is esteemed great by one of us. Coming home yesterday we
met the whole imperial family. We saw them coming, and
Gœthe left me and insisted on standing one side; let me say
what I would, I could not make him come on one step. I
pressed my hat upon my head, buttoned my surtout, and
passed on through the thickest crowd. Princes and parasites
made way; the Archduke Rudolph took off his hat; the
empress greeted me first. Their highnesses KNOW ME. I
was well amused to see the crowd pass by Gœthe. At the
side stood he, hat in hand, low bowed in reverence till all
had gone by. Then I scolded him well; I gave no pardon,
but reproached him with all his sins, most of all those towards you, dearest Bettina; we had just been talking of
you."

If Beethoven appears, in this scene, somewhat arrogant and
bearish, yet how noble his extreme compared with the opposite! Gœthe's friendship with the grand duke we respect,
for Karl August was a strong man. But we regret to see at

the command of any and all members of the ducal family, and their connections, who had nothing but rank to recommend them, his time and thoughts, of which he was so chary to private friends. Beethoven could not endure to teach the Archduke Rudolph, who had the soul duly to revere his genius, because he felt it to be " hofdienst," court service. He received with perfect nonchalance the homage of the sovereigns of Europe. Only the Empress of Russia and the Archduke Karl, whom he esteemed as individuals, had power to gratify him by their attentions. Compare with Gœthe's obsequious pleasure at being able gracefully to compliment such high personages, Beethoven's conduct with regard to the famous Heroic Symphony. This was composed at the suggestion of Bernadotte, while Napoleon was still in his first glory. He was then the hero of Beethoven's imagination, who hoped from him the liberation of Europe. With delight the great artist expressed in his eternal harmonies the progress of the Hero's soul. The symphony was finished, and even dedicated to Bonaparte, when the news came of his declaring himself Emperor of the French. The first act of the indignant artist was to tear off his dedication and trample it under foot; nor could he endure again even the mention of Napoleon until the time of his fall.

Admit that Gœthe had a natural taste for the trappings of rank and wealth, from which the musician was quite free, yet we cannot doubt that both saw through these externals to man as a nature; there can be no doubt on whose side was the simple greatness, the noble truth. We pardon thee, Gœthe, — but thee, Beethoven, we revere, for thou hast maintained the worship of the Manly, the Permanent, the True !

The clear perception which was in Gœthe's better nature of the beauty of that steadfastness, of that singleness and simple melody of soul, which he too much sacrificed to become " the many-sided One," is shown most distinctly in his two surpassingly beautiful works, The Elective Affinities and Iphigenia.

Not Werther, not the Nouvelle Héloise, have been assailed with such a storm of indignation as the first-named of these works, on the score of gross immorality.

The reason probably is the subject; any discussion of the validity of the marriage vow making society tremble to its foundation; and, secondly, the cold manner in which it is done. All that is in the book would be bearable to most minds if the writer had had less the air of a spectator, and had larded his work here and there with ejaculations of horror and surprise.

These declarations of sentiment on the part of the author seem to be required by the majority of readers, in order to an interpretation of his purpose, as sixthly, seventhly, and eighthly were, in an old-fashioned sermon, to rouse the audience to a perception of the method made use of by the preacher.

But it has always seemed to me that those who need not such helps to their discriminating faculties, but read a work so thoroughly as to apprehend its whole scope and tendency, rather than hear what the author says it means, will regard the Elective Affinities as a work especially what is called moral in its outward effect, and religious even to piety in its spirit. The mental aberrations of the consorts from their plighted faith, though in the one case never indulged, and though in the other no veil of sophistry is cast over the weakness of passion, but all that is felt expressed with the openness of one who desires to legitimate what he feels, are punished by terrible griefs and a fatal catastrophe. Ottilia, that being of exquisite purity, with intellect and character so harmonized in feminine beauty, as they never before were found in any portrait of woman painted by the hand of man, perishes, on finding she has been breathed on by unhallowed passion, and led to err even by her ignorant wishes against what is held sacred. The only personage whom we do not pity is Edward, for he is the only one who stifles the voice of conscience.

There is indeed a sadness, as of an irresistible fatality, brooding over the whole. It seems as if only a ray of angelic truth could have enabled these men to walk wisely in this twilight, at first so soft and alluring, then deepening into blind horror.

But if no such ray came to prevent their earthly errors, it seems to point heavenward in the saintly sweetness of Ottilia. Her nature, too fair for vice, too finely wrought even for error, comes lonely, intense, and pale, like the evening star on the cold, wintry night. It tells of other worlds, where the meaning of such strange passages as this must be read to those faithful and pure like her, victims perishing in the green garlands of a spotless youth to atone for the unworthiness of others.

An unspeakable pathos is felt from the minutest trait of this character, and deepens with every new study of it. Not even in Shakspeare have I so felt the organizing power of genius. Through dead words I find the least gestures of this person, stamping themselves on my memory, betraying to the heart the secret of her life, which she herself, like all these divine beings, knew not. I feel myself familiarized with all beings of her order. I see not only what she was, but what she might have been, and live with her in yet untrodden realms.

Here is the glorious privilege of a form known only in the world of genius. There is on it no stain of usage or calculation to dull our sense of its immeasurable life. What in our daily walk, mid common faces and common places, fleets across us at moments from glances of the eye, or tones of the voice, is felt from the whole being of one of these children of genius.

This precious gem is set in a ring complete in its enamel. I cannot hope to express my sense of the beauty of this book as a work of art. I would not attempt it if I had elsewhere met any testimony to the same. The perfect picture, always before the mind, of the chateau, the moss hut, the park, the garden, the lake, with its boat and the landing beneath the platan trees; the gradual manner in which both localities and persons grow upon us, more living than life, inasmuch as we are, unconsciously, kept at our best temperature by the atmosphere of genius, and thereby more delicate in our perceptions than amid our customary fogs; the gentle unfolding of the central thought, as a flower in the morning sun; then the conclusion, rising like a cloud, first soft and white, but darkening as it comes, till with a sudden wind it bursts above our heads; the ease with which we every where find points of view all different, yet all bearing on the same circle, for, though we feel every hour new worlds, still before our eye lie the same objects, new, yet the same, unchangeable, yet always changing their aspects as we proceed, till at last we find we ourselves have traversed the circle, and know all we overlooked at first, — these things are worthy of our highest admiration.

For myself, I never felt so completely that very thing which genius should always make us feel — that I was in its circle, and could not get out till its spell was done, and its last spirit permitted to depart. I was not carried away, instructed, delighted more than by other works, but I was *there*, living there, whether as the platan tree, or the architect, or any other observing part of the scene. The personages live too intensely to let us live in them; they draw around themselves circles within the circle; we can only see them close, not be themselves.

Others, it would seem, on closing the book, exclaim, " What an immoral book ! " I well remember my own thought, " It is a work of art ! " At last I understood that world within a world, that ripest fruit of human nature, which is called art. With each perusal of the book my surprise and delight at this

wonderful fulfilment of design grew. I understood why
Gœthe was well content to be called Artist, and his works,
works of Art, rather than revelations. At this moment, remembering what I then felt, I am inclined to class all my
negations just written on this paper as stuff, and to look upon
myself, for thinking them, with as much contempt as Mr. Carlyle, or Mrs. Austin, or Mrs. Jameson might do, to say nothing of the German Gœtheans.

Yet that they were not without foundation I feel again
when I turn to the Iphigenia — a work beyond the possibility
of negation; a work where a religious meaning not only
pierces but enfolds the whole; a work as admirable in art,
still higher in significance, more single in expression.

There is an English translation (I know not how good) of
Gœthe's Iphigenia. But as it may not be generally known, I
will give a sketch of the drama. Iphigenia, saved, at the
moment of the sacrifice made by Agamemnon in behalf of
the Greeks, by the goddess, and transferred to the temple at
Tauris, appears alone in the consecrated grove. Many
years have passed since she was severed from the home of
such a tragic fate, the palace of Mycenæ. Troy had fallen,
Agamemnon been murdered, Orestes had grown up to avenge
his death. All these events were unknown to the exiled
Iphigenia. The priestess of Diana in a barbarous land, she
had passed the years in the duties of the sanctuary, and in
acts of beneficence. She had acquired great power over the
mind of Thoas, king of Tauris, and used it to protect strangers, whom it had previously been the custom of the country
to sacrifice to the goddess.

She salutes us with a soliloquy, of which I give a rude
translation : —

> Beneath your shade, living summits
> Of this ancient, holy, thick-leaved grove,
> As in the silent sanctuary of the Goddess,

Still I walk with those same shuddering feelings,
As when I trod these walks for the first time.
My spirit cannot accustom itself to these places;
Many years now has kept me here concealed
A higher will, to which I am submissive;
Yet ever am I, as at first, the stranger;
For ah! the sea divides me from my beloved ones,
And on the shore whole days I stand,
Seeking with my soul the land of the Greeks,
And to my sighs brings the rushing wave only
Its hollow tones in answer.
Woe to him who, far from parents, and brothers, and sisters,
Drags on a lonely life.   Grief consumes
The nearest happiness away from his lips;
His thoughts crowd downwards —
Seeking the hall of his fathers, where the Sun
First opened heaven to him, and kindred-born
In their first plays knit daily firmer and firmer
The bond from heart to heart — I question not the Gods,
Only the lot of woman is one of sorrow;
In the house and in the war man rules,
Knows how to help himself in foreign lands,
Possessions gladden and victory crowns him,
And an honorable death stands ready to end his days.
Within what narrow limits is bounded the luck of woman!
To obey a rude husband even is duty and comfort; how sad
When, instead, a hostile fate drives her out of her sphere!
So holds me Thoas, indeed a noble man, fast
In solemn, sacred, but slavish bonds.   .
O, with shame I confess that with secret reluctance
I serve thee, Goddess, thee, my deliverer.

   My life should freely have been dedicate to thee,
But I have always been hoping in thee, O Diana,
Who didst take in thy soft arms me, the rejected daughter
Of the greatest king!   Yes, daughter of Zeus,

I thought if thou gavest such anguish to him, the high hero,
The godlike Agamemnon ;
Since he brought his dearest, a victim, to thy altar,
That, when he should return, crowned with glory, from Ilium,
At the same time thou would'st give to his arms his other
     treasures,
His spouse, Electra, and the princely son ;
Me also, thou would'st restore to mine own,
Saving a second time me, whom from death thou didst save,
From this worse death, — the life of exile here.

These are the words and thoughts ; but how give an idea of the sweet simplicity of expression in the original, where every word has the grace and softness of a flower petal ?

She is interrupted by a messenger from the king, who prepares her for a visit from himself of a sort she has dreaded. Thoas, who has always loved her, now left childless by the calamities of war, can no longer resist his desire to reanimate by her presence his desert house. He begins by urging her to tell him the story of her race, which she does in a way that makes us feel as if that most famous tragedy had never before found a voice, so simple, so fresh in its naïveté is the recital.

Thoas urges his suit undismayed by the fate that hangs over the race of Tantalus.

THOAS.

Was it the same Tantalus,
Whom Jupiter called to his council and banquets,
In whose talk so deeply experienced, full of various learning,
The Gods delighted as in the speech of oracles ?

IPHIGENIA.

It is the same, but the Gods should not
Converse with men, as with their equals.
The mortal race is much too weak
Not to turn giddy on unaccustomed heights.

He was not ignoble, neither a traitor,
But for a servant too great, and as a companion
Of the great Thunderer only a man.   So was
His fault also that of a man, its penalty
Severe, and poets sing — Presumption
And faithlessness cast him down from the throne of Jove,
Into the anguish of ancient Tartarus;
Ah, and all his race bore their hate.

THOAS.

Bore it the blame of the ancestor, or its own?

IPHIGENIA.

Truly the vehement breast and powerful life of the Titan
Were the assured inheritance of son and grandchild;
But the Gods bound their brows with a brazen band,
Moderation, counsel, wisdom, and patience
Were hid from their wild, gloomy glance,
Each desire grew to fury,
And limitless ranged their passionate thoughts.

Iphigenia refuses with gentle firmness to give to gratitude what was not due.   Thoas leaves her in anger, and, to make her feel it, orders that the old, barbarous custom be renewed, and two strangers just arrived be immolated at Diana's altar.

Iphigenia, though distressed, is not shaken by this piece of tyranny.   She trusts her heavenly protectress will find some way for her to save these unfortunates without violating her truth.

The strangers are Orestes and Pylades, sent thither by the oracle of Apollo, who bade them go to Tauris and bring back "The Sister;" thus shall the heaven-ordained parricide of Orestes be expiated, and the Furies cease to pursue him.

The Sister they interpret to be Dian, Apollo's sister; but Iphigenia, sister to Orestes, is really meant.

The next act contains scenes of most delicate workmanship, first between the light-hearted Pylades, full of worldly resource and ready tenderness, and the suffering Orestes, of far nobler, indeed heroic nature, but less fit for the day and more for the ages. In the first scene the characters of both are brought out with great skill, and the nature of the bond between "the butterfly and the dark flower," distinctly shown in few words.

The next scene is between Iphigenia and Pylades. Pylades, though he truly answers the questions of the priestess about the fate of Troy and the house of Agamemnon, does not hesitate to conceal from her who Orestes really is, and manufactures a tissue of useless falsehoods with the same readiness that the wise Ulysses showed in exercising his ingenuity on similar occasions.

It is said, I know not how truly, that the modern Greeks are Ulyssean in this respect, never telling straightforward truth, when deceit will answer the purpose ; and if they tell any truth, practising the economy of the King of Ithaca, in always reserving a part for their own use. The character which this denotes is admirably hit off with few strokes in Pylades, the fair side of whom Iphigenia thus paints in a later scene.

> Bless, ye Gods, our Pylades,
> And whatever he may undertake ;
> He is the arm of the youth in battle,
> The light-giving eye of the aged man in the council.
> For his soul is still ; it preserves
> The holy possession of Repose unexhausted,
> And from its depths still reaches
> Help and advice to those tossed to and fro.

Iphigenia leaves him in sudden agitation, when informed of the death of Agamemnon. Returning, she finds in his place

Orestes, whom she had not before seen, and draws from him
by her artless questions the sequel to this terrible drama
wrought by his hand.   After he has concluded his narrative,
in the deep tones of cold anguish, she cries, —

Immortals, you who through your bright days
Live in bliss, throned on clouds ever renewed,
Only for this have you all these years
Kept me separate from men, and so near yourselves,
Given me the child-like employment to cherish the fires on
        your altars,
That my soul might, in like pious clearness,
Be ever aspiring towards your abodes,
That only later and deeper I might feel
The anguish and horror that have darkened my house.
                                    O Stranger,
Speak to me of the unhappy one, tell me of Orestes.

ORESTES.

            O, might I speak of his death !
Vehement flew up from the reeking blood
His Mother's Soul !
And called to the ancient daughters of Night,
Let not the parricide escape ;
Pursue that man of crime ; he is yours !
They obey, their hollow eyes
Darting about with vulture eagerness ;
They stir themselves in their black dens,
From corners their companions
Doubt and Remorse steal out to join them :
Before them roll the mists of Acheron ;
In its cloudy volumes rolls
The eternal contemplation of the irrevocable.
Permitted now in their love of ruin they tread
The beautiful fields of a God-planted earth,

From which they had long been banished by an early curse,
Their swift feet follow the fugitive,
They pause never except to gather more power to dismay.

IPHIGENIA.

Unhappy man, thou art in like manner tortured,
And feelest truly what he, the poor fugitive, suffers !

ORESTES.

What sayest thou? what meanest by "like manner"?

IPHIGENIA.

Thee, too, the weight of a fratricide crushes to earth; the tale
I had from thy younger brother.

ORESTES.

I cannot suffer that thou, great soul,
Shouldst be deceived by a false tale;
A web of lies let stranger weave for stranger
Subtle with many thoughts, accustomed to craft,
Guarding his feet against a trap.
      But between us
Be Truth ; —
I am Orestes, — and this guilty head
Bent downward to the grave seeks death ;
In any shape were he welcome.
Whoever thou art, I wish thou mightst be saved,
Thou and my friend ; for myself I wish it not.
Thou seem'st against thy will here to remain ;
Invent a way to fly and leave me here.

Like all pure productions of genius, this may be injured by
the slightest change, and I dare not flatter myself that the
English words give an idea of the heroic dignity expressed in
the cadence of the original, by the words

" Twischen uns
 Seg Wahrheit !
 Ich bin Orest ! "

where the Greek seems to fold his robe around him in the
full strength of classic manhood, prepared for worst and best,
not like a cold Stoic, but a hero, who can feel all, know all,
and endure all. The name of two syllables in the German
is much more forcible for the pause, than the three-syllable
Orestes.

" Between us
 Be Truth,"

is fine to my ear, on which our word Truth also pauses with
a large dignity.

The scenes go on more and more full of breathing beauty.
The lovely joy of Iphigenia, the meditative softness with
which the religiously educated mind perpetually draws the
inference from the most agitating events, impress us more
and more. At last the hour of trial comes. She is to keep
off Thoas by a cunningly devised tale, while her brother and
Pylades contrive their escape. Orestes has received to his
heart the sister long lost, divinely restored, and in the embrace the curse falls from him, he is well, and Pylades more
than happy. The ship waits to carry her to the palace home
she is to free from a century's weight of pollution ; and
already the blue heavens of her adored Greece gleam before
her fancy.

But, O, the step before all this can be obtained ; — to deceive Thoas, a savage and a tyrant indeed, but long her pro-
tector, — in his barbarous fashion, her benefactor! How can
she buy life, happiness, or even the safety of those dear ones
at such a price ?

" Woe,
O Woe upon the lie ! It frees not the breast,
Like the true-spoken word ; it comforts not, but tortures

Him who devised it, and returns,
An arrow once let fly, God-repelled, back,
On the bosom of the Archer!"

O, must I then resign the silent hope
Which gave a beauty to my loneliness?
Must the curse dwell forever, and our race
Never be raised to life by a new blessing?
All things decay, the fairest bliss is transient,
The powers most full of life grow faint at last;
And shall a curse alone boast an incessant life?

Then have I idly hoped that here kept pure,
So strangely severed from my kindred's lot,
I was designed to come at the right moment,
And with pure hand and heart to expiate
The many sins that stain my native home.
To lie, to steal the sacred image!
Olympians, let not these vulture talons
Seize on the tender breast. O, save me,
And save your image in my soul!

Within my ears resounds the ancient lay, —
I had forgotten it, and would so gladly, —
The lay of the Parcæ, which they awful sung;
As Tantalus fell from his golden seat
They suffered with the noble friend. Wrathful
Was their heart, and fearful was the song.
In our childhood the nurse was wont to sing it
To me, and my brother and sister. I marked it well.

Then follows the sublime song of the Parcæ, well known
through translations.

But Iphigenia is not a victim of fate, for she listens steadfastly to the god in her breast. Her lips are incapable of
subterfuge. She obeys her own heart, tells all to the king,

calls up his better nature, wins, hallows, and purifies all
around her, till the heaven-prepared way is cleared by the
obedient child of heaven, and the great trespass of Tantalus
cancelled by a woman's reliance on the voice of her innocent soul.

If it be not possible to enhance the beauty with which such
ideal figures as the Iphigenia and the Antigone appeared to
the Greek mind, yet Gœthe has unfolded a part of the life
of this being, unknown elsewhere in the records of literature.
The character of the priestess, the full beauty of virgin
womanhood, solitary, but tender, wise and innocent, sensitive
and self-collected, sweet as spring, dignified as becomes the
chosen servant of God, each gesture and word of deep and
delicate significance, — where else is such a picture to be
found ?

It was not the courtier, nor the man of the world, nor the
connoisseur, nor the friend of Mephistopheles, nor Wilhelm
the Master, nor Egmont the generous, free liver, that saw
Iphigenia in the world of spirits, but Gœthe, in his first-born
glory; Gœthe, the poet; Gœthe, designed to be the brightest
star in a new constellation. Let us not, in surveying his
works and life, abide with him too much in the suburbs and
outskirts of himself. Let us enter into his higher tendency,
thank him for such angels as Iphigenia, whose simple truth
mocks at all his wise " Beschrankungen," and hope the hour
when, girt about with many such, he will confess, contrary to
his opinion, given in his latest days, that it *is* well worth
while to live seventy years, if only to find that they are nothing in the sight of God.

Now almost the last light has gone out of the galaxy that made the first thirty years of this age so bright. And the dynasty that now reigns over the world of wit and poetry is poor and pale, indeed, in comparison.

We are anxious to pour due libations to the departed; we need not economize our wine; it will not be so often needed now.

Hood has closed the most fatiguing career in the world — that of a professed wit; and we may say with deeper feeling than of others who shuffle off the load of care, May he rest in peace! The fatigues of a conqueror, a missionary preacher, even of an active philanthropist, like Howard, are nothing to those of a professed wit. Bad enough is it when he is only a man of society, by whom every one expects to be enlivened and relieved; who can never talk gravely in a corner, without those around observing that he must have heard some bad news to be so out of spirits; who can never make a simple remark, while eating a peaceful dinner, without the table being set in a roar of laughter, as when Sheridan, on such an occasion, opened his lips for the first time to say that "he liked currant jelly." For these unhappy men there are no intervals of social repose, no long silences fed by the mere feeling of sympathy or gently entertained by observation, no warm quietude in the mild liveries of green or brown, for the world has made up its mind that motley is their only wear, and teases them to jingle their bells forever.

But far worse is it when the professed wit is also by profession a writer, and finds himself obliged to coin for bread those

6

jokes which, in the frolic exuberance of youth, he so easily coined for fun. We can conceive of no existence more cruel, so tormenting, and at the same time so dull. We hear that Hood was forever behindhand with his promises to publishers; no wonder! But when we hear that he, in consequence, lost a great part of the gains of his hard life, and was, as a result, harassed by other cares, we cannot mourn to lose him, if,

> " After life's fitful fever, he sleeps well ; "

or if, as our deeper knowledge leads us to hope, he is now engaged in a better life, where his fancies shall take their natural place, and flicker like light on the surface of a profound and full stream flowing betwixt rich and peaceful shores, such as, no less than the drawbacks upon his earthly existence, are indicated in the following

SONNET.

The curse of Adam, the old curse of all,
   Though I inherit in this feverish life
   Of worldly toil, vain wishes, and hard strife,
And fruitless thought in care's eternal thrall,
Yet more sweet honey than of bitter gall
   I taste through thee, my Eva, my sweet wife.
   Then what was Man's lost Paradise? how rife
Of bliss, since love is with him in his fall!
   Such as our own pure passion still might frame
Of this fair earth and its delightful bowers,
   If no fell sorrow, like the serpent, came
To trail its venom o'er the sweetest flowers;
But, O! as many and such tears are ours
   As only should be shed for guilt and shame.

In Hood, as in all true wits, the smile lightens on the verge of a tear. True wit and humor show that exquisite sensibility to the relations of life, that fine perception as to slight tokens of its fearful, hopeless mysteries, which imply pathos to a still higher degree than mirth.

Hood knew and welcomed the dower which nature gave him at his birth, when he wrote thus : —

> All things are touched with melancholy
>   Born of the secret soul's mistrust,
> To feel her fair ethereal wings
>   Weighed down with vile, degraded dust.
> Even the bright extremes of joy
>   Bring on conclusions of disgust,
> Like the sweet blossoms of the May,
>   Whose fragrance ends in must.
> O, give her, then, her tribute just,
>   Her sighs and tears and musings holy ;
> There is no music in the life
>   That sounds with idiot laughter solely ;
> There's not a string attuned to mirth,
>   But has its chord in melancholy.

Hood was true to this vow of acceptance. He vowed to accept willingly the pains as well as joys of life for what they could teach. Therefore, years expanded and enlarged his sympathies, and gave to his lightest jokes an obvious harmony with a great moral design, not obtrusively obvious, but enough so to give a sweetness and permanent complacency to our laughter. Indeed, what is written in his gayer mood has affected us more, as spontaneous productions always do, than what he has written of late with grave design, and which has been so much lauded by men too obtuse to discern a latent meaning, or to believe in a good purpose unless they are formally told that it exists.

The later serious poems of Hood are well known ; so are his jest books and novel. We have now in view to speak rather of a little volume of poems published by him some years since, republished here, but never widely circulated.

When a book or a person comes to us in the best possible circumstances, we judge — not too favorably, for all that the book or person can suggest is a part of its fate, and what is not seen under the most favorable circumstances is never quite truly seen either as to promise or performance — but we form a judgment above what can be the average sense of the world in general as to its merits, which may be esteemed, after time enough has elapsed, a tolerably fair estimate of performance, though not of promise or suggestion.

We became acquainted with these poems in one of those country towns which would be called, abroad, the most provincial of the province. The inhabitants had lost the simplicity of farmers' habits, without gaining in its place the refinement, the variety, the enlargement of civic life. Their industry had received little impulse from thought; their amusement was gossip. All men find amusement from gossip — literary, artistic, or social; but the degrees in it are almost infinite. They were at the bottom of the scale; they scrutinized their neighbors' characters and affairs incessantly, impertinently, and with minds unpurified by higher knowledge; consequently the bitter fruits of envy and calumny abounded.

In this atmosphere I was detained two months, and among people very uncongenial both to my tastes and notions of right. But I had a retreat of great beauty. The town lay on the bank of a noble river; behind it towered a high and rocky hill. Thither every afternoon went the lonely stranger, to await the fall of the sunset light on the opposite bank of the full and rapid stream. It fell like a smile of heavenly joy; the white sails on the stream glided along like angel thoughts; the town itself looked like a fair nest, whence virtue and happiness might soar with sweetest song. So looked the scene *from above;* and that hill was the scene of many an aspiration and many an effort to attain as high a point of view for the mental prospect, in the hope that little discrepancies, or what seemed so when on a level with them, might also, from above, be softened into beauty and found subservient to a noble design on the whole.

This town boasted few books, and the accident which threw Hood's poems in the way of the watcher from the hill, was a very fortunate one. They afforded a true companionship to hours which knew no other, and, perhaps, have since been overrated from association with what they answered to or suggested.

Yet there are surely passages in them which ought to be generally known and highly prized. And if their highest value be for a few individuals with whom they are especially in concord, unlike the really great poems which bring something to all, yet those whom they please will be very much pleased.

Hood never became corrupted into a hack writer. This shows great strength under his circumstances. Dickens has fallen, and Sue is falling; for few men can sell themselves by inches without losing a cubit from their stature. But Hood resisted the danger. He never wrote when he had nothing to say, he stopped when he had done, and never hashed for a second meal old thoughts which had been drained of their choicest juices. His heart is truly human, tender, and brave. From the absurdities of human nature he argues the possibility of its perfection. His black is admirably contrasted with his white, but his love has no converse of hate. His descriptions of nature, if not accurately or profoundly evidencing insight, are unstudied, fond, and reverential. They are fine reveries about nature.

He has tried his powers on themes where he had great rivals — in the " Plea of the Midsummer Fairies," and " Hero and Leander." The latter is one of the finest subjects in the world, and one, too, which can never wear out as long as each mind shall have its separate ideal of what a meeting would be

6 *

between two perfect lovers, in the full bloom of beauty and youth, under circumstances the most exalting to passion, because the most trying, and with the most romantic accompaniments of scenery. There is room here for the finest expression of love and grief, for the wildest remonstrance against fate. Why are they made so lovely and so beloved? Why was a flower brought to such perfection, and then culled for no use? One of the older English writers has written an exquisite poem on this subject, painting a youthful pair, fitted to be not only a heaven but a world to one another. Hood had not power to paint or conceive such fulness of character; but, in a lesser style, he has written a fine poem. The best part of it, however, is the innocent cruelty and grief of the Sea Siren.

"Lycus the Centaur" is also a poem once read never to be forgotten. The hasty trot of the versification, unfit for any other theme, on this betokens well the frightened horse. Its mazy and bewildered imagery, with its countless glancings and glimpses, expressed powerfully the working of the Circean spell, while the note of human sadness, a yearning and condemned human love, thrills through the whole and gives it unity.

The Sonnets, "It is not death," &c., and that on Silence, are equally admirable. Whoever reads these poems will regard Hood as something more than a great wit, — as a great poet also.

To express this is our present aim, and therefore we shall leave to others, or another time, the retrospect of his comic writings. But having, on the late promptings of love for the departed, looked over these, we have been especially amused with the "Schoolmistress Abroad," which was new to us. Miss Crane, a "she Mentor, stiff as starch, formal as a Dutch ledge, sensitive as a daguerreotype, and so tall, thin, and upright, that supposing the Tree of Knowledge to have been a poplar, she was the very Dryad to have fitted it," was left, with a sister little better endowed with the pliancy and power of adaptation which the exigencies of this varied world-scene demand, in attendance upon a sick father, in a foreign inn, where she cannot make herself understood, because her French is not " French French, but English French," and no two things in nature or art can be more unlike. Now look at the position of the sisters.

" The younger, Miss Ruth, was somewhat less disconcerted. She had by her position the greater share in the active duties of Lebanon House, and under ordinary circumstances would not have been utterly at a loss what to do for the comfort or relief of her parent. But in every direction in which her instinct and habits would have prompted her to look, the *materials* she sought were deficient. There was no easy chair — no fire to wheel it to — no cushion to shake up — no cupboard to go to — no female friend to consult — no Miss Parfitt — no cook — no John to send for the doctor — no English — no French — nothing but that dreadful ' Gefullig,' or ' Ja Wohl,' and the equally incomprehensible ' Gnadige Frau !'

" ' Der herr,' said the German coachman, ' ist sehr krank,' (the gentleman is very sick.)

" The last word had occurred so frequently on the organ of the Schoolmistress, that it had acquired in her mind some important significance.

" ' Ruth, what is krank ?'

" ' How should I know?' retorted Ruth, with an asperity apt to accompany intense excitement and perplexity. ' In English, it's a thing that helps to pull the bell. But look at papa — do help to support him — you're good for nothing.'

" ' I am, indeed,' murmured poor Miss Priscilla, with a gentle shake of her head, and a low, slow sigh of acquiescence. Alas ! as she ran over the catalogue of her accomplishments, the more she remembered what she *could* do for her sick parent, the more helpless and useless she appeared. For

instance, she could have embroidered him a night-cap — or
knitted him a silk purse — or plaited him a guard-chain —
or cut him out a watch-paper — or ornamented his braces
with bead-work — or embroidered his waistcoat — or worked
him a pair of slippers — or openworked his pocket handkerchief. She could even, if such an operation would have been
comforting or salutary, have roughcasted him with shell-work
— or coated him with red or black seals — or encrusted him
with blue alum — or stuck him all over with colored wafers
— or festooned him.

" But alas! what would it have availed her poor dear papa
in the spasmodics, if she had even festooned him, from top to
toe, with little rice-paper roses ? "

The comments of the female chorus, as the author reads
aloud the sorrows of Miss Crane, are droll as Hood's drollest.
Who can say more?

So farewell, gentle, generous, inventive, genial, and most
amusing friend. We thank thee for both tears and laughter;
tears which were not heart-breaking, laughter which was
never frivolous or unkind. In thy satire was no gall, in the
sting of thy winged wit no venom, in the pathos of thy sorrow
no enfeebling touch! Thou hadst faults as a writer, we know
not whether as a man; but who cares to name or even to
note them? Surely there is enough on the sunny side of
the peach to feed us and make us bless the tree from which
it fell.

THIS is a very pleasing book, and if the "Essays of Summer Hours" resemble it, we are not surprised at the favor with which they have been received, not only in this country, but in England.

The writer is, we believe, very young, and as these Essays have awakened in us a friendly expectation which he has time and talent to fulfil, we will, at this early hour, proffer our counsel on two points.

First. Avoid details, so directly personal, of emotion. A young and generous mind, seeing the deceit and cold reserve which so often palsy men who write, no less than those who act, may run into the opposite extreme. But frankness must be tempered by delicacy, or elevated into the region of poetry. You may tell the world at large what you please, if you make it of universal importance by transporting it into the field of general human interest. But your private griefs, merely *as* yours, belong to yourself, your nearest friends, to Heaven and to nature. There is a limit set by good taste, or the sense of beauty, on such subjects, which each, who seeks, may find for himself.

Second. Be more sparing of your praise: above all, of its highest terms. We should have a sense of mental as well as moral honor, which, while it makes us feel the baseness of uttering merely hasty and ignorant censure, will also forbid that hasty and extravagant praise which strict truth will not justify. A man of honor wishes to utter no word to which he cannot adhere. The offices of Poet — of Hero-worship — are sacred,

* "By the Author of Essays of Summer Hours."

and he who has a heart to appreciate the excellent should call nothing excellent which falls short of being so.   Leave yourself some incense worthy of the *best ;* do not lavish it on the merely *good.*   It is better to be too cool than extravagant in praise ; and though mediocrity may be elated if it can draw to itself undue honors, true greatness shrinks from the least exaggeration of its claims.   The truly great are too well aware how difficult is the attainment of excellence, what labors and sacrifices it requires, even from genius, either to flatter themselves as to their works, or to be otherwise than grieved at idolatry from others ; and so, with best wishes, and a hope to meet again, we bid farewell to the " Landscape Painter."

BEETHOVEN.*

THIS book bears on its outside the title, "Life of Beetho-ven, by Moscheles." It is really only a translation of Schin-dler, and it seems quite unfair to bring Moscheles so much into the foreground, merely because his name is celebrated in England. He has only contributed a few notes and a short introduction, giving a most pleasing account of his own devo-tion to the Master. Schindler was the trusty friend of Beethoven, and one whom he himself elected to write his biography. Inadequate as it is, there is that fidelity in the col-lection of materials which makes it serviceable to our knowl-edge of Beethoven, and we wish it might be reprinted in America. Though there is little knowledge of music here, yet so far as any exists in company with a free development of mind, the music of Beethoven is *the* music which delights, which awakens, which inspires, an infinite hope.

This influence of these most profound, bold, original and sin-gular compositions, even upon the uninitiated, above those of a simpler construction and more obvious charms, we have ob-served with great pleasure. For we think its cause lies deep, far beneath fancy, taste, fashion, or any accidental cause.

It is because there is a real and steady unfolding of cer-tain thoughts which pervade the civilized world. They strike their roots through to us beneath the broad Atlantic; and these roots shoot stems upward to the light wherever the soil allows them free course.

* The Life of Beethoven, including his Correspondence with his Friends, numerous characteristic Traits, and Remarks on his Musical Works. Edited by Ignace Moscheles, Pianist to His Royal Highness Prince Albert.

Our era, which permits of freer inquiry, of bolder experiment, than ever before, and a firmer, broader basis, may also, we sincerely trust, be depended on for nobler discovery and a grander scope of thought.

Although we sympathize with the sadness of those who lament the decay of forms and methods round which so many associations have wound their tendrils, and understand the sufferings which gentle, tender natures undergo from the forlorn homelessness of a period of doubt, speculation, reconstruction in every way, yet we cannot disjoin ourselves, by one moment's fear or regret, from the advance corps. That body, leagued by an invisible tie, has received too deep an assurance that the spirit is not dead nor sleeping, to look back to the past, even if they must advance uniformly through scenes of decay and the rubbish of falling edifices.

But how far it is from being so! How many developments, in various ways, of truth! How manifold the aspirations of love! In the church the attempt is now to reconstruct on the basis proposed by its founder — "Love one another;" in the philosophy of mind, if completeness of system is, as yet, far from being attained, yet mistakes and vain dogmas are set aside, and examinations conducted with intelligence and an enlarged discernment of what is due both to God and man. Science advances, in some route with colossal strides; new glimpses are daily gained into the arcana of natural history, and the mysteries attendant on the modes of growth, are laid open to our observation; while in chemistry, electricity, magnetism, we seem to be getting nearer to the law of life which governs them, and in astronomy "fathoming the heavens," to use the sublime expression of Herschel, daily to greater depths, we find ourselves admitted to a perception of the universal laws and causes, where harmony, permanence and perfection leave us no excuse for a moment of despondency, while under the guidance of a Power who has ordered all so well.

Then, if the other arts suffer a temporary paralysis, and notwithstanding the many proofs of talent and genius, we consider that is the case with architecture, painting, and sculpture, music is not only thoroughly vital, but in a state of rapid development. The last hundred years have witnessed a succession of triumphs in this art, the removal of obstructions, the transcending of limits, and the opening new realms of thought, to an extent that makes the infinity of promise and hope very present with us. And take notice that the prominent means of excellence now are not in those ways which give form to thought already existent, but which open new realms to thought. Those who live most with the life of their age, feel that it is one not only beautiful, positive, full of suggestion, but vast, flowing, of infinite promise. It is dynamics that interest us now, and from electricity and music we borrow the best illustrations of what we know.

Let no one doubt that these grand efforts at synthesis are capable of as strict analysis. Indeed, it is wonderful with what celerity and precision the one process follows up the other.

Of this great life which has risen from the stalk and the leaf into bud, and will in the course of this age be in full flower, Beethoven is the last and greatest exponent. His music is felt, by every soul whom it affects, to be the explanation of the past and the prophecy of the future. It contains the thoughts of the time. A dynasty of great men preceded him, each of whom made conquests and accumulated treasures which prepared the way for his successor. Bach, Handel, Hadyn, Mozart, were corner-stones of the glorious temple. Who shall succeed Beethoven? A host of musicians, full of talent, even of genius, live now he is dead; but the greatest among them is confessed by all men to be but of Lilliputian size compared with this demigod. Indeed, it should be so! As copious draughts of soul have been given to the earth, as she can quaff for a century or more. Disciples and critics must follow, to gather up the gleanings of the golden grain.

It is observable as an earnest of the great Future which opens for this country, that such a genius is so easily and so much appreciated here, by those who have not gone through the steps that prepared the way for him in Europe. He is felt, because he expresses, in full tones, the thoughts that lie at the heart of our own existence, though we have not found means to stammer them as yet. To those who have obtained some clew to all this, — and their number is daily on the increase,— this biography of Beethoven will be very interesting. They will here find a picture of the great man, as he looked and moved in actual life, though imperfectly painted, — as by one who saw the figure from too low a stand-point.

It will require the united labors of a constellation of minds to paint the portrait of Beethoven. That of his face, as seen in life, prefixed to these volumes, is better than any we have seen. It bears tokens of the force, the grandeur, the grotesqueness of his genius, and at the same time shows the melancholy that came to him from the great misfortune of his life — his deafness ; and the affectionateness of his deep heart.

Moscheles thus gives a very pleasing account of his first cognizance of Beethoven : —

"I had been placed under the guidance and tuition of Dionysius Weber, the founder and present director of the Prague Musical Conservatory ; and he, fearing that in my eagerness to read new music, I might injure the systematic development of my piano-forte playing, prohibited the library, a circulating musical library, and in a plan for my musical education which he laid before my parents. made it an express condition that for three years I should study no other authors but Mozart, Clemente, and S. Bach. I must confess, however, that in spite of such prohibition, I visited the library, gaining access to it through my pocket money. It was about this time that I learned from some schoolfellows that a young composer had appeared in Vienna, who wrote the oddest stuff possible, such as no one could either play or understand — crazy music, in opposition to all rule; and that this composer's name was Beethoven. On repairing to the library to satisfy my curiosity as to this so-called eccentric genius, I found there Beethoven's 'Sonate Pathetique.' This was in the year 1804. My pocket money would not suffice for the purchase of it, so I secretly copied it. The novelty of its style was so attractive to me, and I became so enthusiastic in my admiration of it, that I forgot myself so far as to mention my new acquisition to my master, who reminded me of his injunction, and warned me not to play or study any eccentric productions until I had based my style upon more solid models. Without, however, minding his injunction, I seized upon the piano-forte works of Beethoven as they successively appeared, and in them found a solace and delight such as no other composer afforded me.

"In the year 1809, my studies with my master, Weber, closed; and being then also fatherless, I chose Vienna for my residence, to work out my future musical career. Above all, I longed to see and become acquainted with that man who had exercised so powerful an influence over my whole being; whom, though I scarcely understood, I blindly worshipped. I learned that Beethoven was most difficult of access, and would admit no pupil but Ries; and for a long time my anxiety to see him remained ungratified. In the year 1810, however, the longed-for opportunity presented itself. I happened to be one morning in the music shop of Domenico Artaria, who had just been publishing some of my early attempts at composition, when a man entered with short and hasty steps, and gliding through the circle of ladies and professors assembled on business, or talking over musical matters, without looking up, as though he wished to pass unnoticed, made his way direct for Artaria's private office at the bottom of the

shop. Presently Artaria called me in, and said, 'This is
Beethoven,'—and to the composer, 'This is the youth of
whom I have been speaking to you.' Beethoven gave me a
friendly nod, and said he had just been hearing a favorable
account of me. To some modest and humble expressions
which I stammered forth he made no reply, and seemed to
wish to break off the conversation. I stole away with a
greater longing for that which I had sought, than before this
meeting, thinking to myself, 'Am I then, indeed, such a nobody that he could not put one musical question to me? nor
express one wish to know who had been my master, or
whether I had any acquaintance with his works?' My only
satisfactory mode of explaining the matter, and comforting
myself for the omission, was in Beethoven's tendency to deafness; for I had seen Artaria speaking close to his ear. But
I made up my mind that the more I was excluded from the
private intercourse which I so earnestly coveted, the closer
I would follow Beethoven in all the productions of his
mind."

If Moscheles had never seen more of Beethoven, how re-
joiced he would have been on reading his pathetic expressions recorded in those volumes, as to the misconstructions
he knew his fellow-men must put on conduct caused by his
calamity, at having detected the true cause of coldness in
his own instance, and that no mean suggestions of offended
vanity made him false to the genius, because repelled by the
man!

Moscheles did see him further, and learned a great deal
from this intercourse, though it never became intimate. He
closes with these excellent remarks : —

"My feelings with respect to Beethoven's music have
undergone no variation, save to become warmer. In my first
half score of years of acquaintance with his works, he was
repulsive to me, as well as attractive. In each of them, while
I felt my mind fascinated by the prominent idea, and my en-

thusiasm kindled by the flashes of his genius, his unlooked-for episodes, shrill dissonances, and bold modulations, gave me an unpleasant sensation. But how soon did I become reconciled to them ! all that had appeared hard I soon found indispensable. The gnome-like pleasantries, which at first appeared too distorted, the stormy masses of sound which I found too chaotic, I have in after times learned to love. But while retracting my early critical exceptions, I must still maintain as my creed that eccentricities like those of Beethoven are reconcilable with his works alone, and are dangerous models to other composers, many of whom have been wrecked in their attempts at imitation."

No doubt the peculiarities of Beethoven are inimitable, though as great would be as welcome in a mind of equal greatness. The natural office of such a genius is to rouse others to a use and knowledge of their own faculties; never to induce imitation of its own individuality.

As an instance of the justice and undoubting clearness of such a mind, as to its own methods, take the following anecdote from Beethoven's " Pupil Ries " : —

" All the initiated must be interested in the striking fact which occurred respecting one of Beethoven's last solo sonatas, (in B major, with the great fugue, Op. 106,) a sonata which has *forty-one pages of print*. Beethoven had sent it to me, to London, for sale, that it might appear there at the same time as in Germany. The engraving was completed, and I in daily expectation of the letter naming the day of publication. This arrived at last, but with this extraordinary request : ' Prefix the following two notes, as a first bar, to the beginning of the adagio.' This adagio has from nine to ten pages of print. I own the thought struck me involuntarily that all might not be right with my dear old master, a rumor to that effect having often been spread. What! add *two notes* to a composition already worked out and out, and completed six months ago? But my astonishment was yet to be height-

7 *

ened by the *effect* of these two notes. Never could such be found again — so striking — so important; no, not even if contemplated at the very beginning of the composition. I would advise every true lover of the art to play this adagio first *without,* and then with these two notes which now form the first bar, and I have no doubt he will share in my opinion."

No instance could more forcibly show how in the case of Beethoven, as in that of other transcendent geniuses, the cry of insanity is raised by vulgar minds on witnessing extraordinary manifestations of power. Such geniuses perceive results so remote, are alive to combinations so subtle, that common men cannot rise high enough to see why they think or do as they do, and settle the matter easily to their own satisfaction, crying, " He is mad " — " He hath a devil." Genius perceives the efficacy of slight signs of thought, and loves best the simplest symbols ; coarser minds demand coarse work, long preparations, long explanations.

But genius heeds them not, but fills the atmosphere with irresistible purity, till they also are pervaded by the delicate influence, which, too subtle for their ears and eyes, enters with the air they breathe, or through the pores of the skin.

The life of a Beethoven is written in his works; and all that can be told of his life beside, is but as marginal notes on that broad page. Yet since we have these notes, it is pleasant to have them in harmony with the page. The acts and words of Beethoven are what we should expect, — noble, leonine, impetuous, — yet tender. His faults are the faults of one so great that he found few paths wide enough for his tread, and knew not how to moderate it. They are not faults in themselves, but only in relation to the men who surrounded him. Among his peers he would not have had faults. As it is, they hardly deserve the name. His acts were generally great and benignant ; only in transports of sudden passion at what he thought base did he ever injure any one. If he found himself mistaken, he could not humble himself enough, — but far outwent, in his contrition, what was due to those whom he had offended. So it is apt to be with magnanimous and tender natures; they will humble themselves in a way that those of a coarser or colder make think shows weakness or want of pride. But they do so because a little discord and a little wrong is as painful to them as a great deal to others.

In one of his letters to a young friend, Beethoven thus magnanimously confesses his errors: —

"I could not converse with you and yours with that peace of mind which I could have desired, for the late wretched altercation was hovering before me, showing me my own despicable conduct. But so it was; and what would I not give could I obliterate from the page of my life this last action, so degrading to my character, and so unlike my usual proceedings!"

It seems this action of his was not of importance in the eyes of others. Of the causes which acted upon him at such times he gives intimations in another letter.

"I had been wrought into this burst of passion by many an unpleasant circumstance of an earlier date. I have the gift of concealing and restraining my irritability on many subjects; but if I happen to be touched at any time when I am more than usually susceptible of anger, I burst forth more violently than any one else. B. has doubtless most excellent qualities, but he thinks himself utterly without faults, and yet is most open to blame for those for which he censures others. He has a littleness of mind which I have held in contempt since my infancy."

As a correspondent example of the manner in which true greatness apologizes for its errors, we must quote a letter, lately made public, from Sir Isaac Newton to Mr. Locke.

"Sir: Being of opinion that you endeavored to embroil me with women, and by other means, I was so much affected

with it as that, when one told me you were sickly, and would
not live, I answered, ''Twere better if you were dead.' I
desire you to forgive me this uncharitableness, for I am now
satisfied that what you have done is just, and I beg your pardon for having had hard thoughts of you for it, and for representing that you struck at the root of morality in a principle you laid down in your book of ideas, and designed to pursue
in another book, and that I took you for a Hobbist. I beg your
pardon also for saying or thinking that there was a design to
sell me an office, or to embroil me.

"I am your most humble and unfortunate servant,

"ISAAC NEWTON."

And this letter, observe, was quoted as proof of insanity in
Newton. Locke, however, shows by his reply that *he* did not
think the power of full sincerity and elevation above self-love
proved a man to be insane.

At a happy period Beethoven thus unveils the generous
sympathies of his heart.

"My compositions are well paid, and I may say I have
more orders than I can well execute; six or seven publishers,
and more, being ready to take any of my works. I need no
longer submit to being bargained with; I ask my terms, and
am paid. You see this is an excellent thing; as, for instance,
I see a friend in want, and my purse does not at the moment
permit me to assist him; I have but to sit down and write,
and my friend is no longer in need."

Some additional particulars are given, in the letters collected by Moscheles, of the struggles of his mind during the
coming on of deafness. This calamity, falling upon the greatest genius of his time, in the prime of manhood, — a calamity
which threatened to destroy not only all enjoyment of life,
but the power of using the vast treasure with which he had
been endowed for the use of all men, — casts common ills so
into the shade that they can scarcely be seen. Who dares

complain, since Beethoven could resign himself, to such an ill at such a time as this?

"This beautiful country of mine, what was my lot in it? The hope of a happy futurity. This might now be realized if I were freed from my affliction. O, freed from that, I should compass the world! I feel it — my youth is but beginning; have I not been hitherto but a sickly creature? My physical powers have for some time been materially increasing — those of my mind likewise. I feel myself nearer and nearer the mark; I feel but cannot describe it; this alone is the vital principle of your Beethoven. No rest for me: I know of none but in sleep, and I grieve at having to sacrifice to that more time than I have hitherto deemed necessary. Take but one half of my disease from me, and I will return to you a matured and accomplished man, renewing the ties of our friendship; for you shall see me as happy as I may be in this sublunary world; not as a sufferer; no, that would be more than I could bear; I will blunt the sword of fate; it shall not utterly destroy me. How beautiful it is to live a thousand lives in one! No; I am not made for a retired life — I feel it."

He *did* blunt the sword of fate; he *did* live a thousand lives in one; but that sword had power to inflict a deep and poisoned wound; those thousand lives cost him the pangs of a thousand deaths. He, born for perpetual conquest, was condemned through life to "resignation." Let any man, disposed to complain of his own ills, read the "Will" of Beethoven; and see if he dares speak of himself above a whisper, after.

The matter of interest new to us in this English book is in notes and appendix. Schindler's biography, whose plain and *naïve* style is fit for the subject, is ironed out and plaited afresh to suit the "genteel" English, in this translation. Elsewhere we have given in brief the strong lineaments and

piquant anecdotes from this biography; * here there is not
room: smooth and shorn as it is, we wish the translation
might be reprinted here.

We may give, at parting, two directions for the study of
Beethoven's genius and the perusal of his biography in two
sayings of his own. For the biography, "The limits have
never yet been discovered which genius and industry could
not transcend." For the music, "From the depths of the
soul brought forth, she (Poesy) can only by the depths of
the soul be received or understood."

[* See article on Beethoven, in Margaret's volume, entitled " Art, Literature, and the Drama." — Ed.]

BROWN'S NOVELS.*

WE rejoice to see these reprints of Brown's novels, as we have long béen ashamed that one who ought to be the pride of the country, and who is, in the higher qualities of the mind, so far in advance of our other novelists, should have become almost inaccessible to the public.

It has been the custom to liken Brown to Godwin. But there was no imitation, no second hand in the matter. They were congenial natures, and whichever had come first might have lent an impulse to the other. Either mind might have been conscious of the possession of that peculiar vein of ore, without thinking of working it for the mint of the world, till the other, led by accident, or overflow of feeling, showed him how easy it was to put the reveries of his solitary hours into words, and upon paper, for the benefit of his fellow-men.

> "My mind to me a kingdom is."

Such a man as Brown or Godwin has a right to say that. Their mind is no scanty, turbid rill, rejoicing to be daily fed from a thousand others, or from the clouds. Its plenteous source rushes from a high mountain between bulwarks of stone. Its course, even and full, keeps ever green its banks, and affords the means of life and joy to a million gliding shapes, that fill its deep waters, and twinkle above its golden sands.

Life and Joy! Yes, Joy! These two have been called the dark Masters, because they disclose the twilight recesses of

* Ormond, or the Secret Witness; Wieland, or the Transformation; by Charles Brockden Brown.

the human heart. Yet the gravest page in the history of such men is joy, compared with the mixed, shallow, uncertain pleasures of vulgar minds. Joy! because they were all alive, and fulfilled the purposes of being. No sham, no imitation, no convention deformed or veiled their native lineaments, or checked the use of their natural force. All alive themselves, they understood that there is no happiness without truth, no perception of it without real life. Unlike most men, existence was to them not a tissue of words and seemings, but a substantial possession.

Born Hegelians, without the pretensions of science, they sought God in their own consciousness, and found him. The heart, because it saw itself so fearfully and wonderfully made, did not disown its Maker. With the highest idea of the dignity, power, and beauty of which human nature is capable, they had courage to see by what an oblique course it proceeds, yet never lose faith that it would reach its destined aim. Thus their darkest disclosures are not hobgoblin shows, but precious revelations.

Brown is great as ever human writer was in showing the self-sustaining force of which a lonely mind is capable. He takes one person, makes him brood like the bee, and extract from the common life before him all its sweetness, its bitterness, and its nourishment.

We say makes *him*, but it increases our own interest in Brown, that, a prophet in this respect of a better era, he has usually placed this thinking, royal mind in the body of a woman. This personage, too, is always feminine, both in her character and circumstances, but a conclusive proof that the term *feminine* is not a synonyme for *weak*. Constantia, Clara Wieland, have loving hearts, graceful and plastic natures, but they have also noble, thinking minds, full of resource, constancy, courage. The Marguerite of Godwin, no less, is all refinement and the purest tenderness; but she is also the soul of honor, capable of deep discernment, and of acting in conformity with the inferences she draws. The Man of Brown and Godwin has not eaten of the fruit of the tree of knowledge, and been driven to sustain himself by the sweat of his brow for nothing, but has learned the structure and laws of things, and become a being, natural, benignant, various, and desirous of supplying the loss of innocence by the attainment of virtue. So his Woman need not be quite so weak as Eve, the slave of feeling or of flattery; she also has learned to guide her helm amid the storm across the troubled waters.

The horrors which mysteriously beset these persons, and against which, so far as outward facts go, they often strive in vain, are but a representation of those powers permitted to work in the same way throughout the affairs of this world. Their demoniacal attributes only represent a morbid state of the intellect, gone to excess from want of balance with the other powers. There is an intellectual as well as a physical drunkenness, and which, no less, impels to crime. Carwin, urged on to use his ventriloquism till the presence of such a strange agent wakened the seeds of fanaticism in the breast of Wieland, is in a state no more foreign to nature than that of the wretch executed last week, who felt himself drawn as by a spell to murder his victim, because he had thought of her money and the pleasures it might bring him, till the feeling possessed his brain that hurls the gamester to ruin. The victims of such agency are like the soldier of the Rio Grande, who, both legs shot off, and his life-blood rushing out with every pulse, replied serenely to his pitying comrades, that " he had now that for which the soldier enlisted." The end of the drama is not in this world, and the fiction which rounds off the whole to harmony and felicity before the curtain falls, sins against truth, and deludes the reader. The Nelsons of the human race are all the more exposed to the assaults of Fate, that they are decorated with the badges of well-earned glory. Who but feels as they fall in death, or rise again to a mutilated existence, that the end is not yet? Who, that thinks, but must feel that the recompense is, where Brown

places it, in the accumulation of mental treasure, in the severe
assay by fire that leaves the gold pure to be used some time
— somewhere ?

Brown, — man of the brooding eye, the teeming brain, the
deep and fervent heart, — if thy country prize thee not, and
had almost lost thee out of sight, it is because her heart is made
shallow and cold, her eye dim, by the pomp of circumstance,
the love of gross outward gain. She cannot long continue
thus, for it takes a great deal of soul to keep a huge body
from disease and dissolution. As there is more soul, thou
wilt be more sought ; and many will yet sit down with thy
Constantia to the meal and water on which she sustained
her full and thoughtful existence, who could not endure the
ennui of aldermanic dinners, or find any relish in the imitation of French cookery. To-day many will read the
words, and some have a cup large enough to receive the
spirit, before it is lost in the sand on which their feet are
planted.

Brown's high standard of the delights of intellectual communion and of friendship, correspond with the fondest hopes
of early days. But in the relations of real life, at present,
there is rarely more than one of the parties ready for such
intercourse as he describes. On the one side there will be
dryness, want of perception, or variety, a stupidity unable to
appreciate life's richest boon when offered to its grasp; and
the finer nature is doomed to retrace its steps, unhappy as
those who, having force to raise a spirit, cannot retain or
make it substantial, and stretch out their arms only to bring
them back empty to the breast.

We were glad to see these reprints, but sorry to see them
so carelessly done. Under the cheap system, the carelessness in printing and translating grows to a greater excess day
by day. Please, Public, to remonstrate ; else very soon all
your books will be offered for two shillings apiece, and none
of them in a fit state to be read.

EDGAR A. POE.*

Mr. Poe throws down the gauntlet in his preface by what he says of "the paltry compensations, or more paltry commendations, of mankind." Some champion might be expected to start up from the "somewhat sizable" class embraced, or, more properly speaking, boxed on the ear, by this defiance, who might try whether the sting of Criticism was as indifferent to this knight of the pen as he professes its honey to be.

Were there such a champion, gifted with acumen to dissect, and a swift-glancing wit to enliven the operation, he could find no more legitimate subject, no fairer game, than Mr. Poe, who has wielded the weapons of criticism without relenting, whether with the dagger he rent and tore the garment in which some favored Joseph had pranked himself, secure of honor in the sight of all men, or whether with uplifted tomahawk he rushed upon the new-born children of some hapless genius, who had fancied, and persuaded his friends to fancy, that they were beautiful, and worthy a long and honored life. A large band of these offended dignitaries and aggrieved parents must be on the watch for a volume of "Poems by Edgar A. Poe," ready to cut, rend, and slash in turn, and hoping to see his own Raven left alone to prey upon the slaughter of which it is the herald.

Such joust and tournament we look to see, and, indeed, have some stake in the matter, so far as we have friends whose wrongs cry aloud for the avenger. Natheless we could not

---

* The Raven and other Poems, by Edgar A. Poe, 1845.

take part in the *mêlée*, except to join the crowd of lookers-on in the cry " heaven speed the right ! "

Early we read that fable of Apollo who rewarded the critic, who had painfully winnowed the wheat, — with the chaff for his pains.   We joined the gentle Affirmative School, and have confidence that if we indulge ourselves chiefly with the appreciation of good qualities, Time will take care of the faults.   For Time holds a strainer like that used in the diamond mines — have but patience and the water and gravel will all pass through, and only the precious stones be left.   Yet we are not blind to the uses of severe criticism, and of just censure, especially in a time and place so degraded by venal and indiscriminate praise as the present.   That unholy alliance ; that shameless sham, whose motto is,

> " Caw me
> And I'll caw thee ; "

that system of mutual adulation and organized puff which was carried to such perfection in the time, and may be seen drawn to the life in the correspondence, of Miss Hannah More, is fully represented in our day and generation.   We see that it meets a counter-agency, from the league of Truth-tellers, few, but each of them mighty as Fingal or any other hero of the sort.   Let such tell the whole truth, as well as nothing but the truth, but let their sternness be in the spirit of Love.   Let them seek to understand the purpose and scope of an author, his capacity as well as his fulfilments, and how his faults are made to grow by the same sunshine that acts upon his virtues, for this is the case with talents no less than with character.   The rich field requires frequent and careful weeding ; frequent, lest the weeds exhaust the soil ; careful, lest the flowers and grain be pulled up along with the weeds.

It has often been our lot to share the mistake of Gil Blas with regard to the Archbishop.   We have taken people at their word, and while rejoicing that women could bear

neglect without feeling mean pique, and that authors, rising
above self-love, could show candor about their works, and
magnanimously meet both justice and injustice, we have been
rudely awakened from our dream, and found that chanticleer,
who crowed so bravely, showed himself at last but a dunghill
fowl. Yet Heaven grant we never become too worldly-wise
thus to trust a generous word, and we surely are not so yet,
for we believe Mr. Poe to be sincere when he says, —

" In defence of my own taste, it is incumbent upon me to
say that I think nothing in this volume of much value to the
public or very creditable to myself. Events not to be con-
trolled have prevented me from making, at any time, any
serious effort, in what, under happier circumstances, would
have been the field of my choice."

We believe Mr. Poe to be sincere in this declaration; if
he is, we respect him; if otherwise, we do not. Such things
should never be said unless in hearty earnest. If in earnest,
they are honorable pledges; if not, a pitiful fence and foil of
vanity. Earnest or not, the words are thus far true; the productions in this volume indicate a power to do something far
better. With the exception of the Raven, which seems intended chiefly to show the writer's artistic skill, and is in its
way a rare and finished specimen, they are all fragments —
fyttes upon the lyre, almost all of which leave a something
to desire or demand. This is not the case, however, with
these lines : —

To one in Paradise.

Thou wast all that to me, love,
    For which my soul did pine —
A green isle in the sea, love,
    A fountain and a shrine,
All wreathed with fairy fruits and flowers,
    And all the flowers were mine.

8 *

Ah, dream too bright to last!
   Ah, starry Hope! that didst arise
But to be overcast!
   A voice from out the Future cries,
"On! on!"—but o'er the Past
   (Dim gulf!) my spirit hovering lies
Mute, motionless, aghast!

For, alas! alas! with me
   The light of life is o'er!
No more — no more — no more
(Such language holds the solemn sea
   To the sands upon the shore)
Shall bloom the thunder-blasted tree,
   Or the stricken eagle soar!

And all my days are trances,
   And all my nightly dreams
Are where thy dark eye glances,
   And where thy footstep gleams —
In what ethereal dances,
   By what eternal streams.

The poems breathe a passionate sadness, relieved sometimes by touches very lovely and tender : —

   " Amid the earnest woes
     That crowd around my earthly path
   (Drear path, alas! where grows
     Not even one lonely rose.")   *   *   *

     *   *   *   *

" For her, the fair and debonair, that now so lowly lies,
The life upon her yellow hair, but not within her eyes —
The life still there, upon her hair — the death upon her eyes."

This kind of beauty is especially conspicuous, even rising into dignity, in the poem called the Haunted Palace.

The imagination of this writer rarely expresses itself in pronounced forms, but rather in a sweep of images, thronging and distant like a procession of moonlight clouds on the horizon, but like them characteristic and harmonious one with another, according to their office.

The descriptive power is greatest when it takes a shape not unlike an incantation, as in the first part of the Sleeper, where

> " I stand beneath the mystic moon ;
> An opiate vapor, dewy, dim,
> Exhales from out a golden rim,
> And, softly dripping, drop by drop,
> Upon the quiet mountain top,
> Steals drowsily and musically
> Into the universal valley."

Why *universal ?* — " resolve me that, Master Moth."

And farther on, " the lily *lolls* upon the wave."

This word *lolls*, often made use of in these poems, presents a vulgar image to our thought ; we know not how it is to that of others.

The lines which follow, about the open window, are highly poetical. So is the Bridal Ballad in its power of suggesting a whole tribe and train of thoughts and pictures, by few and simple touches.

The poems' written in youth, written, indeed, we understand, in childhood, before the author was ten years old, are a great psychological curiosity. Is it the delirium of a prematurely excited brain that causes such a rapture of words ? What is to be gathered from seeing the future so fully anticipated in the germ ? The passions are not unfrequently *felt* in their full shock, if not in their intensity, at eight or nine years old, but here they are *reflected upon* : —

" Sweet was their death — with them to die was rife
   With the last ecstasy of satiate life."

The scenes from Politian are done with clear, sharp
strokes ; the power is rather metaphysical than dramatic.
We must repeat what we have heretofore said, that we could
wish to see Mr. Poe engaged in a metaphysical romance.
He needs a sustained flight and far range to show what his
powers really are.   Let us have from him the analysis of the
Passions, with their appropriate Fates ; let us have his specu-
lations clarified ; let him intersperse dialogue or poem, as the
occasion prompts, and give us something really good and
strong, firmly wrought, and fairly blazoned.

THESE two publications have come to hand during the last month — a cheering gleam upon the winter of our discontent, as we saw the flood of bad translations of worse books which swelled upon the country.

We love our country well. The many false deeds and low thoughts; the devotion to interest; the forgetfulness of principle; the indifference to high and noble sentiment, which have, in so many ways, darkened her history for some years back, have not made us despair of her yet fulfilling the great destiny whose promise rose, like a star, only some half a century ago upon the hopes of the world.

Should that star be forsaken by its angel, and those hopes set finally in clouds of shame, the church which we had built out of the ruins of the ancient time must fall to the ground. This church seemed a model of divine art. It contained a labyrinth which, when threaded by aid of the clew of Faith, presented, re-viewed from its centre, the most admirable harmony and depth of meaning in its design, and comprised in its decorations all the symbols of permanent interest of which the mind of man has made use for the benefit of man. Such was to be our church, a church not made with hands, catholic, universal, all whose stones should be living stones, its officials the cherubim of Love and Knowledge, its worship wiser and purer action than has before been known to men. To such a church men do indeed constitute the state, and men indeed

---

* The Autobiography of Alfieri, translated by C. E. Lester. Memoirs of Benvenuto Cellini, translated by Roscoe.

we hoped from the American church and state, men so truly human that they could not live while those made in their own likeness were bound down to the condition of brutes.

Should such hopes be baffled, should such a church fall in the building, such a state find no realization except to the eye of the poet, God would still be in the world, and surely guide each bird, that can be patient, on the wing to its home at last.   But expectations so noble, which find so broad a basis in the past, which link it so harmoniously with the future, cannot lightly be abandoned.   The same Power leads by a pillar of cloud as by a pillar of fire — the Power that deemed even Moses worthy only of a distant view of the Promised Land.

And to those who cherish such expectations rational education, considered in various ways and bearings, must be the one great topic of interest; an enterprise in which the humblest service is precious and honorable to any who can inspire its soul.   Our thoughts anticipate with eager foresight the race that may grow up from this amalgamation of all races of the world which our situation induces.   It was the pride and greatness of ancient nations to keep their blood unmixed; but it must be ours to be willing to mingle, to accept in a generous spirit what each clime and race has to offer us.

It is, indeed, the case that much diseased substance is offered to form this new body; and if there be not in ourselves a nucleus, a heart of force and purity to assimilate these strange and various materials into a very high form of organic life, they must needs induce one distorted, corrupt, and degraded beyond the example of other times and places. There will be no medium about it.   Our grand scene of action demands grandeur and purity; lacking these, one must suffer from so base failure in proportion to the success that should have been.

. It would be the worthiest occupation of mind to ascertain

the conditions propitious for this meeting of the nations in their new home, and to provide preventions for obvious dangers that attend it. It would be occupation for which the broadest and deepest knowledge of human nature in its mental, moral, and bodily relations, the noblest freedom from prejudice, with the finest discrimination as to differences and relations, directed and enlightened by a prophetic sense as to what Man is designed by God to become, would all be needed to fit the thinker. Yet some portion of these qualities, or of some of these qualities, if accompanied by earnestness and aspiration, may enable any one to offer useful suggestions. The mass of ignorance and selfishness is such, that no grain of leaven must be despised.

And as the men of all countries come hither to find a home, and become parts of a new life, so do the books of all countries gravitate towards this new centre. Copious infusions from all quarters mingle daily with the new thought which is to grow into American mind, and develop American literature.

As every ship brings us foreign teachers, a knowledge of living contemporary tongues must in the course of fifty years become the commonest attainment. There exists no doubt in the minds of those who can judge, that the German, French, Italian, Spanish, and Portuguese tongues might, by familiar instruction and *an intelligent method*, be taught with perfect ease during the years of childhood, so that the child would have as distinct a sense of their several natures, and nearly as much expertness in their use, as in his own. The higher uses of such knowledge can, of course, be expected only in a more advanced state of the faculties ; but it is pity that the acquaintance with the medium of thought should be deferred to a period when the mind is sufficiently grown to bend its chief attention on the thoughts themselves. Much of the most precious part of short human lives is now wasted from an ignorance of what might easily be done for children, and without taking from them the time they need for common life, play, and bodily growth, more than at present.

Meanwhile the English begins to vie with the German and French literature in the number, though not in the goodness, of the translations from other languages. The indefatigable Germans can translate, and do other things too ; so that geniuses often there apply themselves to the work as an amusement : even the all-employed Gœthe has translated one of the books before us, (Memoirs of Cellini.) But in English we know but of one, Coleridge's Wallenstein, where the reader will feel the electric current undiminished by the medium through which it comes to him. And then the profligate abuse of the power of translation has been unparalleled, whether in the choice of books or the carelessness in disguising those that were good in a hideous mask. No falsehood can be worse than this of deforming the expression of a great man's thoughts, of corrupting that form which he has watched, and toiled and suffered to make beautiful and true. We know no falsehood that should call a more painful blush to the check of one engaged in it.

We have no narrowness in our view of the contents of such books. We are not afraid of new standards and new examples. Only give enough of them, variety enough, and from well-intentioned, generous minds. America can choose what she wants, if she has sufficient range of choice ; and if there is any real reason, any deep root in the tastes and opinions she holds at present, she will not lightly yield them. Only give her what is good of its kind. Her hope is not in ignorance, but in knowledge. We are, indeed, very fond of range, and if there is check, there should be countercheck ; and in this view we are delighted to see these great Italians domesticated here. We have had somewhat too much of the French and Germans of late. We value unchangeably our sparkling and rapid French friend ; still more the searching, honest, and, in highest sense, visionary German genius. · But there is not on earth, and, we dare to say it, will not be again, genius *like* that of Italy, or that can compare with it, in its own way.

Italy and Greece were alike in this; those sunny skies ripened their fruits perfectly. The oil and honey of Greece, the wine of Italy, not only suggest, but satisfy. *There* we find fulfilment, elsewhere great achievement only.

O, acute, cautious, calculating Yankee; O, graceful, witty, hot-blooded, flimsy Southron; and thou, man of the West, going ahead too fast to pick up a thought or leave a flower upon thy path, — look at these men with their great fiery passions, but will and intellect still greater and stronger, perfectly sincere, from a contempt of falsehood. If they had acted wrong, they said and felt that they had, and that it was base and hateful in them. They were sagacious, as children are, not from calculation, but because the fine instincts of nature were unspoiled in them. I speak now of Alfieri and Cellini. Dante had all their instinctive greatness and deep-seated fire, with the reflective and creative faculties besides, to an extent of which they never dreamed.

He who reads these biographies may take them from several points of view. As pictures of manners, as sincere transcripts of the men and their times, they are not and could not be surpassed. That truth which Rousseau sought so painfully and vainly by self-brooding, subtle analysis, they attained without an effort. *Why* they felt they cared little, but *what* they felt they surely knew; and where a fly or worm has injured the peach, its passage is exactly marked, so that you are sure the rest is fair and sound. Both as physiological and psychical histories, they are full of instruction. In Alfieri, especially, the nervous disease generated in the frame by any uncongenial tension of the brain, the periodical crises in his health, the manner in which his accesses of passion came upon him, afford infinite suggestion to one who has an eye for the circumstances which fashion the destiny of man.

9

Let the physician compare the furies of Alfieri with the silent rages of Byron, and give the mother and pedagogue the light in which they are now wholly wanting, showing how to treat such noble plants in the early stages of growth. We think the "hated cap" would not be put a second time on the head so easily diseased.

The biography of Cellini, it is commonly said, is more interesting than any romance. It *is* a romance, with the character of the hero fully brought out. Cellini lived in all the fulness of inward vigor, all the variety of outward adventure, and passed through all the signs of the Zodiac, in his circling course, occasionally raising a little vapor from the art magic. He was really the Orlando Furioso turned Goldsmith, and Angelicas and all the Peers of France joined in the show. However, he never lived deeply; he had not time; the creative energy turned outward too easily, and took those forms that still enchant the mind of Europe. Alfieri was very different in this. He was like the root of some splendid southern plant, buried beneath a heap of rubbish. Above him was a glorious sky, fit to develop his form and excite his colors; but he was compelled to a long and terrible struggle to get up where he could be free to receive its influence. Institutions, language, family, modes of education, — all were unfit for him; and perhaps no man was ever called to such efforts, after he had reached manly age, to unmake and remake himself before he could become what his inward aspiration craved. All this deepened his nature, and it *was* deep. It is his great force of will and the compression of Nature within its iron grasp, where Nature was so powerful and impulsive, that constitutes the charm of his writings. It is the man Alfieri who moves, nay, overpowers us, and not his writings, which have no flow nor plastic beauty. But we feel the vital dynamics, and imagine it all.

By us Americans, if ever such we really are to be, Alfieri

should be held sacred as a godfather and holy light. He
was a harbinger of what most gives this time its character and value. He was the friend of liberty, the friend
of man, in the sense that Burns was — of the native nobleness of man. Soiled and degraded men he hated. He
was, indeed, a man of pitiless hatred as of boundless love,
and he had bitter prejudices too, but they were from antipathies too strongly intertwined with his sympathies for
any hand less powerful than that of Death to rend them
away.

But our space does not permit us to do any justice to such
a life as Alfieri's. Let others read it, not from their habitual,
but an eternal point of view, and they cannot mistake its
purport. Some will be most touched by the storms of his
youth, others by the exploits and conquests of his later
years; but all will find him, in the words of his friend
Casella, "sculptured just as he was, lofty, strange, and extreme, not only in his natural characteristics, but in every
work that did not seem to him unworthy of his generous
affections. And where he went too far, it is easy to perceive his excesses always flowed from some praiseworthy
sentiment."

Among a crowd of thoughts suggested to the mind by re-
perusal of this book, to us a friend of many years standing,
we hastily note the following : —

Alfieri knew how to be a friend, and had friends such as
his masculine and uncompromising temper fitted him to endure and keep. He had even two or three of these noble
friends. He was a perfect lover in delicacy of sentiment, in
devotion, in a desire for constancy, in a high ideal, growing
always higher, and he was, at last, happy in love. Many
geniuses have spoken worthily of women in their works, but
he speaks of woman as she wishes to be spoken of, and declares that he met the desire of his soul realized in life. This,
almost alone, is an instance where a great nature was perma-

nently satisfied, and the claims of man and woman equally
met, where one of the parties had the impatient fire of genius.
His testimony on this subject is of so rare a sort, we must
copy it : —

"My fourth and last passion, fortunately for me, showed
itself by symptoms entirely different from the three first.   In
the former, my intellect had felt little of the fires of passion ;
but now my heart and my genius were both equally kindled,
and if my passion was less impetuous, it became more profound and lasting.   Such was the flame which by degrees
absorbed every affection and thought of my being, and it will
never fade away except with my life.   Two months satisfied
me that I had now found the *true woman ;* for, instead of
encountering in her, as in all common women, an obstacle to
literary glory, a hinderance to useful occupations, and a damper
to thought, she proved a high stimulus, a pure solace, and an
alluring example to every beautiful work.   Prizing a treasure so rare, I gave myself away to her irrevocably.   And
I certainly erred not.   More than twelve years have passed,
and while I am writing this chit-chat, having reached that
calm season when passion loses its blandishments, I cherish
her more tenderly than ever; and I love her just in proportion as glide from her in the lapse of time those little-es-
teemed toll-gatherers of departing beauty.   In her my soul
is exalted, softened, and made better day by day; and I
will dare to say and believe she has found in me support
and consolation."

We have spoken of the peculiarities in Alfieri's physical
condition.   These naturally led him to seek solace in violent
exercise ; and as in the case of Beckford and Byron, horses
were his best friends in the hour of danger.   This sort of
man is the modern Achilles, "the tamer of horses."   In what
degree the health of Alfieri was improved, and his sympathies awakened by the society and care of these noble animals, is very evident.   Almost all persons, perhaps all that

are in a natural state, need to stand in patriarchal relations with the animals most correspondent with their character. We have the highest respect for this instinct and sincere belief in the good it brings; if understood, it would be cherished, not ridiculed.

9 *

TRANSLATING Dante is indeed a labor of love. It is one in which even a moderate degree of success is impossible. No great Poet can be well translated. The form of his thought is inseparable from his thought. The births of his genius are perfect beings: body and soul are in such perfect harmony that you cannot at all alter the one without veiling the other. The variation in cadence and modulation, even where the words are exactly rendered, takes not only from the form of the thought, but from the thought itself, its most delicate charm. Translations come to us as a message to the lover from the lady of his love through the lips of a confidante or menial — we are obliged to imagine what was most vital in the utterance.

These difficulties, always insuperable, are accumulated a hundred-fold in the case of Dante, both by the extraordinary depth and subtlety of his thought, and his no less extraordinary power of concentrating its expression, till every verse is like a blade of thoroughly tempered steel. You might as well attempt to translate a glance of fire from the human eye into any other language — even music cannot do that.

We think, then, that the use of Cary's translation, or any other, can never be to diffuse a knowledge of Dante. This is not in its nature diffusible; he is one of those to whom others must draw near; he cannot be brought to them. He has no superficial charm to cheat the reader into a belief that he knows him, without entrance into the same sphere.

These translations can be of use only to the translators, as a means of deliberate study of the original, or to others who

are studying the original, and wish to compare their own version of doubtful passages with that of an older disciple, highly
qualified, both by devotion and mental development, for the
study.

We must say a few words as to the pedantic folly with
which this study has been prosecuted in this country, and, we
believe, in England. Not only the tragedies of Alfieri and
the Faust of Gœthe, but the Divina Commedia of Dante, — a
work which it is not probable there are upon earth, at any
one time, a hundred minds able to appreciate, — are turned into
school books for little girls who have just left their hoops and
dolls, and boys whose highest ambition it is to ride a horse
that will run away, and brave the tutor in a college frolic.

This is done from the idea that, in order to get acquainted
with a foreign language, the student must read books that have
attained the dignity of classics, and also which are "hard."
Hard indeed it must be for the Muses to see their lyres turned
into gridirons for the preparation of a school-girl's lunch;
harder still for the younglings to be called to chew and digest
thunderbolts, in lieu of their natural bread and butter.

Are there not "classics" enough which would not suffer by
being put to such uses? In Greek, Homer is a book for a
boy; must you give him Plato because it is harder? Is there
no choice among the Latins? Are all who wrote in the Latin
tongue equally fit for the appreciation of sixteen Yankee
years? In Italian, have you not Tasso, Ariosto, and other
writers who have really a great deal that the immature mind
can enjoy, without choking it with the stern politics of Alfieri,
or piling upon a brain still soft the mountainous meanings of
Dante? Indeed, they are saved from suffering by the perfect ignorance of all meaning in which they leave these great
authors, fancying, to their life-long misfortune, that they have
read them. I have been reminded, by the remarks of my
young friends on these subjects, of the Irish peasant, who,
having been educated on a book prepared for his use, called

" Reading made easy," blesses through life the kindness that taught him his " Radamadasy ; " and of the child who, hearing her father quote Horace, observed *she* "thought Latin was even sillier than French."

No less pedantic is the style in which the grown-up, in stature at least, undertake to become acquainted with Dante. They get the best Italian Dictionary, all the notes they can find, amounting in themselves to a library, for his countrymen have not been less external and benighted in their way of regarding him. Painfully they study through the book, seeking with anxious attention to know who Signor This is, and who was the cousin of Signora That, and whether any deep papal or anti-papal meaning was couched by Dante under the remark that Such-a-one wore a great-coat. A mind, whose small chambers look yet smaller by being crowded with furniture from all parts of the world, bought by labor, not received from inheritance or won by love, asserts that he must understand Dante well, better than any other person probably, because he has studied him through in this way thirty or forty times. As well declare you have a better ap preciation of Shakspeare than any one else because you have identified the birthplace of Dame Quickly, or ascertained the churchyard where the ghost of the royal Dane hid from the sight of that far more celestial spirit, his son.

O, painstaking friends ! Shut your books, clear your minds from artificial nonsense, and feel that only by spirit can spirit be discerned. Dante, like each other great one, took the stuff that lay around him, and wove it into a garment of light. It is not by ravelling that you will best appreciate its tissue or design. It is not by studying out the petty strifes or external relations of his time, that you can become acquainted with the thought of Dante. To him these things were only soil in which to plant himself — figures by which to dramatize and evolve his ideas. Would you learn him, go listen in the forest of human passions to all the terrible voices he heard with a tormented but never-to-be-deafened ear; go down into the hells, where each excess that mars the harmony of nature is punished by the sinner finding no food except from his own harvest; pass through the purgatories of speculation, of struggling hope, and faith, never quite quenched, but smouldering often and long beneath the ashes. Soar if thou canst, but if thou canst not, clear thine eye to see this great eagle soar into the higher region where forms arrange themselves for stellar dance and spheral melody, — and thought, with costly-accelerated motion, raises itself a spiral which can only end in the heart of the Supreme.

He who finds in himself no fitness to study Dante in this way, should regard himself as in the position of a candidate for the ancient mysteries, when rejected as unfit for initiation. He should seek in other ways to purify, expand, and strengthen his being, and, when he feels that he is nobler and stronger, return and try again whether he is "grown up to it," as the Germans say.

"The difficulty is in the thoughts;" and this cannot be obviated by the most minute acquaintance with the history of the times. Comparison of one edition with another is of use, as a guard against obstructions through mistake. Still more useful will be the method recommended by Mr. Cary, of comparing the Poet with himself; this belongs to the intellectual method, and is the way in which to study our intellectual friend.

The versions of Cary and Lyell will be found of use to the student, if he wants to compare his ideas with those of accomplished fellow-students. The poems in the London book would aid much in a full appreciation of the comedy; they ought to be read in the original, but copies are not easily to be met here, unless in the great libraries. The Vita Nuova is the noblest expression extant of the inward life of Love, the best preface and comment to every thing else that Dante did.

'Tis pity that the designs of Flaxman are so poorly reproduced in this American book. It would have been far better
to have had it a little dearer, and thus better done. The
designs of Flaxman were really a noble comment upon Dante,
and might help to interpret him; and we are sorry that those
who can see only a few of them should see them so imperfectly. But in some, as in that of the meeting with Farinata,
the expression cannot be destroyed while one line of the
original remained. The "lost portrait" we do not like as
preface to "La Divina Comedia." To that belongs our
accustomed object of reverence, the head of Dante, such as
the Florentine women saw him, when they thought his hair
and beard were still singed, his face dark and sublime with
what he had seen *below*.

Prefixed to the other book is a head "from a cast taken
after death at Ravenna, A. D. 1321." It has the grandeur
which death sometimes puts on; the fulness of past life is
there, but made sacred in Eternity. It is also the only front
view of Dante we have seen. It is not unworthy to mark
the point

> " When vigor failed the towering fantasy,
> But yet the will rolled onward, like a wheel
> In even motion by the love impelled
> That moves the sun in heaven, and all the stars."

We ought to say, in behalf of this publication, that whosoever wants Cary's version will rejoice, at last, as do we, to
possess it in so fair and legible guise.

Before leaving the Italians, we must mourn over the misprints of our homages to the great tragedian in the preceding review. Our manuscripts being as illegible as if we were
a great genius, we never complain of these errata, except
when we are made to reverse our meaning on some vital
point. We did not say that Alfieri was perfect *in person*,

nor sundry other things that are there; but we do mourn at seeming to say of our friends, " *Why* they felt they care little, but *what* they felt they *scarcely* knew," when in fact we asserted, " what they felt they *surely* knew."

In the article on the Celestial Empire we had made this assertion of the Chinese music: " Like *their* poetry, the music is of the narrowest monotony;" in place of which stands this assertion: " Like *true* poetry, their music is of the narrowest monotony." But we trust the most careless reader would not think the merely human mind capable of so original a remark, and will put this blasphemy to account of that little demon who has so much to answer for in the sufferings of poor writers before they can get their thoughts to the eyes of their fellow-creatures, in print, that there seems scarcely a chance of his being redeemed as long as there is one author in existence to accuse him.*

[* Although the errors here specially referred to by my sister have been corrected in this volume, I let her statement remain as explanation of any other errors which may possibly have crept into type, in this volume, through the illegibility of some of her manuscripts from which I have been compelled to copy for this work. — ED.]

AMERICAN FACTS.

SUCH is the title of a volume just issued from the press; a grand title, which suggests the epic poet or the philosopher. The purpose of the work, however, is modest. It is merely a compilation, from which those who have lived at some distance from the great highway may get answers to their questions, as to events and circumstances which may have escaped them. It is one of those books which will be valued in the back-woods.

It would be a great book indeed, and one that would require the eye and heart of a great man, — great as a judge, great as a seer, and great as a prophet, — that should select for us and present in harmonious outline the true American facts. To choose the right point of view supposes command of the field.

Such a man must be attentive, a quiet observer of the slighter signs of growth. But he must not be one to dwell superstitiously on details, nor one to hasten to conclusions. He must have the eye of the eagle, the courage of the lion, the patience of the worm, and faith such as is the prerogative of man alone, and of man in the highest phase of his culture.

We doubt not the destiny of our country — that she is to accomplish great things for human nature, and be the mother of a nobler race than the world has yet known. But she has been so false to the scheme made out at her nativity, that it is now hard to say which way that destiny points. We can hardly exhibit the true American facts without some idea of the real character of America. Only one thing seems clear — that the energy here at work is very great, though the men employed in carrying out its purposes may have generally no

(108)

more individual ambition to understand those purposes, or cherish noble ones of their own, than the coral insect through whose restless working new continents are upheaved from ocean's breast.

Such a man, passing in a boat from one extremity of the Mississippi to another, and observing every object on the shore as he passed, would yet learn nothing of universal or general value, because he has no principles, even in hope, by which to classify them. American facts! Why, what has been done that marks individuality? Among men there is Franklin. He is a fact, and an American fact. Niagara is another, in a different style. The way in which newspapers and other periodicals are managed is American; a go-ahead, fearless adroitness is American; so is *not*, exclusively, the want of strict honor. But we look about in vain for traits as characteristic of what may be individually the character of the nation,.as we can find at a glance in reference to Spain, England, France, or Turkey. America is as yet but a European babe; some new ways and motions she has, consequent on a new position; but that soul that may shape her mature life scarce begins to know itself yet. One thing is certain; we live in a large place, no less morally than physically: woe to him who lives meanly here, and knows the exhibitions of selfishness and vanity as the only American facts.

10

As we pass the old Brick Chapel our eye is sometimes arrested by placards that hang side by side. On one is advertised "the Lives of the Apostles," on the other "Napoleon and his Marshals."

Surely it is the most monstrous thing the world ever saw, that eighteen hundred years' profound devotion to a religious teacher should not preclude flagrant and all but universal violation of his most obvious precepts ; that Napoleon and his Marshals should be some of the best ripened fruit of our time ; that our own people, so unwearied in building up temples of wood and stone to the Prince of Peace, should be at this era mad with boyish exultation at the winning of battles, and in a bad cause too.

In view of such facts we cannot wonder that Dr. Channing, the editor of the Tribune, and others who make Christianity their standard, should find little savor in glowing expositions of the great French drama, and be disgusted at words of defence, still more of admiration, spoken in behalf of its leading actor.

We can easily admit at once that the whole French drama was anti-Christian, just as the political conduct of every nation of Christendom has been thus far, with rare and brief exceptions. Something different might have been expected from our own, because the world has now attained a clearer consciousness of right, and in our case our position would have made obedience easy. We have not been led into

* Napoleon and his Marshals, by J. T. Headley.

temptation; we sought it. It is greed, and not want, that has impelled this nation to wrong. The paths of peace would have been for her also the paths of wisdom and of pleasantness, but she would not, and has preferred the path of the beast of prey in the uncertain forest, to the green pastures where "walks the good Shepherd, his meek temples crowned with roses red and white."

Since the state of things is such, we see no extremity of censure that should fall upon the great French leader, except that he was like the majority. He was ruthless and selfish on a larger scale than most monarchs; but we see no difference in grain, nor in principles of action.

Admit, then, that he was not a good man, and never for one moment acted disinterestedly. But do not refuse to do homage to his genius. It is well worth your while to learn to appreciate *that*, if you wish to understand the work that the spirit of the time did, and is still doing, through him; for his mind is still upon the earth, working here through the tributary minds it fed. We must say, for our own part, we cannot admit the right of men severely to criticise Napoleon, till they are able to appreciate what he was, as well as see what he was not. And we see no mind of sufficient grasp, or high-placed enough to take this estimate duly, nor do we believe this age will furnish one. Many problems will have to be worked out first.

We reject the exclusively moral no less than the exclusively intellectual view, and find most satisfaction in those who, aiming neither at apology nor attack, make their observations upon the great phenomenon as partial, and to be received as partial.

Mr. Headley, in his first surprise at finding how falsely John Bull, rarely liberal enough to be fully trusted in evidence on any topic, has spoken of the acts of a hated and dreaded foe, does indeed rush too much on the other side. He mistakes the touches of sentiment in Napoleon for genuine feeling.

Now we know that Napoleon loved to read Ossian, and could appreciate the beauty of tenderness : but we do not believe that he had one particle of what is properly termed heart ; — that is, he could always silence sentiment at once when his projects demanded it.   Then Mr. Headley finds apologies for acts where apology is out of place.   They characterize the ruthless nature of the man, and that is all that can be said of them.   He moved on, like the Juggernaut car, to his end, and spilled the blood that was needed for this, whether that blood were "ditch-water" or otherwise.   Neither is this supposing him to be a monster.   The human heart is very capable of such uncontrolled selfishness, just as it is of angelic love.   "'Tis but the first step that costs" — *much*.   Yet some compassionate hand strewed flowers on Nero's grave, and the whole world cried shame when Bonaparte's Mameluke forsook his master.

Mr. Headley does not seem to be aware that there is no trust to be put in Napoleon's own account of his actions. He seems to have been almost incapable of speaking sincerely to those about him.   We doubt whether he could have forgotten with the woman he loved, that she might become his historiographer.

But granting the worst that can be said of ruthless acts in the stern Corsican, are we to reserve our anathema for him alone?   He is no worse than the other crowned ones, against whom he felt himself continually in the balance.   He has shed a greater quantity of blood, and done mightier wrongs, because he had more power, and followed with more fervor a more dazzling lure.   We see no other difference between his conduct and that of the great Frederic of Prussia.   He never did any thing so meanly wicked as has just been done in stirring up the Polish peasants to assassinate the nobles.   He never did any thing so atrocious as has been done by Nicholas of Russia, who, just after his hypocritical intercourse with that "venerable man," the Pope, when he so zealously defended himself against the charge of scourging nuns to convert them to the Greek church, administers the knout to a noble and beautiful lady because she had given shelter for an hour to the patriot Dembinski. Why then so zealous against Napoleon only? He is but a specimen of what man must become when he *will* be king over the bodies, where he cannot over the souls, of his fellow-men. We doubt if it is any worse in the sight of God to drain France of her best blood by the conscription, than to tear the flower of Genius from the breast of Italy to perish in a dungeon, leaving her overwhelmed and broken-hearted. Leaving all this aside, and granting that Napoleon might have done more and better, had his heart been pure from ambition, which gave it such electric power to animate a vast field of being, there is no reason why we should not prize what he did do. And here we think Mr. Headley's style the only one in place. We honor him for the power he shows of admiring the genius which, in ploughing its gigantic furrow, broke up every artificial barrier that hid the nations of Europe one from the other — that has left the " career open to talent," by a gap so broad that no " Chinese alliance " can ever close it again, and in its vast plans of civic improvement half-anticipated Fourier. With him all *thoughts* became *things;* it has been spoken in blame, it has been spoken in praise; for ourselves we see not how this most practical age and country can refuse to apprehend the designs, and study the instincts of this wonderful practical genius.

The characters of the marshals are kept up with the greatest spirit, and that power of seizing leading traits that gives these sketches the greatness of dramatic poetry. The marshals are majestic figures; men vulgar and undeveloped on many sides, but always clear and strong in their own way. One mind animates them, and of that mind Napoleon is the culminating point. He did not choose them; they were a part of himself, a part of the same thought of which he was

10 *

the most forcible expression. If sometimes inclined to disparage them, it was as a man might disparage his hand by saying it was not his head. He truly felt that he was the central force, though some of them were greater in the details of action than himself. Attempts have often been made to darken even the military fame of Napoleon and his generals — attempts disgraceful enough from a foe whom they so long held in terror. But to any unprejudiced mind there is evident in the conduct of their battles, the development of the instincts of genius in mighty force, and to inevitable results.

With all the haste of hand and inequality of touch they show, these sketches are full of strength and brilliancy, an honor to the country that produced them. There is no got-up harmony, no attempt at originality or acuteness; all is living, — the overflow of the mind; we like Mr. Headley; even in his faults he is a most agreeable contrast to the made men of the day.

In the sketches of the Marshals we have the men before us, a living reality. Massena, at the siege of Genoa, is represented with a great deal of simple force. The whole personality of Murat, with his "Oriental nature" and Oriental dress, is admirably depicted. Why had nobody ever before had the clearness of perception to see just this, *and no more*, in the "theatrical" Murat? Of his darling hero, Ney, the writer has implied so much all along, that he lays less stress on what he says of him directly. He thinks it is all understood, and it is.

Take this book for just what it is; do not look for cool discussion, impartial criticism, but take it as a vivacious and feeling representation of events and actors in a great era: you will find it full of truth, such as only sympathy could teach, and will derive from it a pleasure and profit lively and genuine as itself. As to denying or correcting its statements, it is very desirable that those who are able should do that part of the work; but, in doing it, let them be grateful for what *is* done, and what *they* could not do; grateful for reproduction such as he who throws himself into the genius and the persons of the time may hope for; but he never can who keeps himself composed in critical distance and self-possession. You cannot have all excellences combined in one person; let us then cheerfully work together to complete the beautiful whole, — beautiful in its unity, — no less beautiful in its variety.

PHYSICAL EDUCATION.*

THIS lecture of Dr. Warren is printed in a form suitable for popular distribution, while the high reputation of its author insures it respect. Readers will expect to find here those rules for daily practice taught by that plain common-sense which men possess from nature, but strangely lose sight of, amid their many inventions, and are obliged to rediscover by aid of experience and science.

Here will be found those general statements as to modes of exercise, care of the skin, choice of food, and time, and circumstances required for its digestion, which might furnish the ounce of prevention that is worth so many pounds of cure. And how much are these needed in this country, where the most barbarous ignorance prevails on the sub-ject of cleanliness, sleeping accommodations, &c.! On these subjects improvement would be easy; that of diet is far more complicated, and is, unfortunately, one which requires great knowledge of the ways in which the human frame is affected by the changes of climate and various other influences, even wisely to discuss. If it is difficult where a race, mostly indige-nous to the soil, feed upon what Mother Nature has prepared expressly for their use, and where excess or want of judgment in its use produces disease, it must be far more so where men come from all latitudes to live under new circumstances, and need a judicious adaptation of the old to the new. The dogmatism and proscription that prevail on this topic amuse

* Physical Education and the Preservation of Health, by John C. Warren.

the observer and distress the patient. "Touch no meat for your life," says one. "It is not meat, but sugar, that is your ruin," cries another. "No, salt is the destruction of the world," sadly and gravely declares a third. Milk, which once conciliated all regards, has its denunciators. "Water," say some, "is the bliss that shall dissolve all bane. Drink; wash — take to yourself all the water you can get." "That is madness — is far worse than useless," cry others, "unless the water be pure. You must touch none that has not been tested by a chemist." "Yes, you may at any rate drink it," say others, "and in large quantities, for the power of water to aid digestion is obvious to every observer."

"No," says Dr. Warren, "animals do not drink at the time they eat, but some hours after; and they generally take very small quantities of liquid, compared with that which is used by man. The savage, in his native wilds, takes his solid food, when he can obtain it, to satiety, reposes afterwards, and then resuming his chase through the forest, stops at the rivulet to allay his thirst. The disadvantage of taking a large quantity of liquid must be obvious to all those who consider that the digesting liquid is diluted and weakened in proportion to the quantity of drink."

What wonder is it, if even the well-disposed among the multitude, seeing such dissension among the counsellors, gathering just enough from their disputes to infer that they have no true philosophical basis for their opinions, and seeing those who would set the example in practice of this art without science of dietetics generally among the most morbid and ill-developed specimens of humanity, just throw aside all rule upon the subject, partake of what is set before them, trust to air, exercise, and good intentions to ward off the worst effects of the promiscuous fare?

Yet, while hopeless at present of selecting the right articles, and building up, so far as hereditary taint will permit, a pure and healthful body from feeding on congenial substances, we

know at least this much, that stimulants and over-eating —
not food — are injurious, and may take care enough of ourselves to avoid these.

The other branches we can really act wisely in, Dr. Warren, after giving the usual directions (rarely followed as yet)
for airing beds and sleeping-rooms, adds, —

"The manner in which children sleep will readily be acknowledged to be important; yet very little attention is paid
to this matter.   Children are crowded together in small, un-
ventilated rooms, often two or three in a bed, and on beds
composed of half prepared feathers, from which issues a
noxious effluvia, infecting the child at a period when he is
least able to resist its influence; so that in the morning,
instead of feeling the full refreshment and vigor natural to
his age, he is pale, languid, and for some time indisposed
to exertion.

"The rooms in which children are brought up should be
well aired, by having a fireplace, which should be kept open
the greater part of the year.   There never should be more
than one in the same bed; and this remark may be applied
with equal propriety to adults.   The substance on which they
lie should be hair, thoroughly prepared, so that it should have
no bad smell.   In winter it may be of cotton, or of hair and
cotton.   It would be very desirable, however, to place children in separate apartments, as well as in separate beds.

"It has been justly said that adults as well as children had
better employ single instead of double beds; this remark is
intended to apply universally.   The use of double beds has
been very generally adopted in this country, perhaps in part
as a matter of economy; but this practice is objectionable, for
more reasons than can be stated here."

On the subject of exercise, he mentions particularly the
triangle, and we copy what he says, because of the perfect
ease and convenience with which one could be put up and
used in every bed-chamber.

"The exercising the upper limbs is too much neglected; and it is important to provide the means of bringing them into action, as well to develop their powers as to enlarge and invigorate the chest, with which they are connected, and which they powerfully influence. The best I know of is the use of the triangle. This admirably exerts the upper limbs and the muscles of the chest, and, indeed, when adroitly employed, those of the whole body. The triangle is made of a stick of walnut wood, four feet long, and an inch and a half in diameter. To each end is connected a rope, the opposite extremities of which being confined together at such height as to allow the motion of swinging by the hands."

We have ourselves derived the greatest benefit from this simple means. Gymnastic exercises, and if possible in the open air, are needed by every one who is not otherwise led to exercise all parts of the body by various kinds of labor. Some, though only partial provision, is made for boys by gymnasia and riding-schools. In wiser nations, such have been the care of the state. And in despotic governments, the jealousy of a tyrant was never more justly awakened than when the youth of the land, by a devotion to gymnastic exercises, showed their aspiration to reach the healthful stature of manhood. For every one who possesses a strong mind in a sane body is heir presumptive to the kingdom of this world; he needs no external credentials, but has only to appear and make clear his title. But for such a princely form the eye searches the street, the mart, and the council-chamber, in vain.

Those who feel that the game of life is so nearly up with them that they cannot devote much of the time that is left to the care of wise living in their own persons, should, at least, be unwilling to injure the next generation by the same ignorance which has blighted so many of us in our earliest year. Such should attend to the work of Mr. Combe,* among other

* Physiological and Moral Management of Infancy, by Andrew Combe, M. D.

good books.   Mr. Combe has done much good already in this
country, and this book should be circulated every where, for
many of its suggestions are too obviously just not to be
adopted as soon as read.

Dr. Warren bears his testimony against the pernicious
effects that follow upon the use of tobacco, and we cannot
but hope that what he says of its tendency to create cancer
will have weight with some who are given to the detesta-
ble habit of chewing.   This practice is so odious to women,
that we must regard its prevalence here as a token of the
very light regard in which they are held, and the consequent
want of refinement among men.   Dr. Warren seems to favor
the practice of hydropathy to some extent, but must needs
bear his testimony in full against homœopathy.   No matter;
the little doses will insinuate their way, and cure the ills that
flesh is heir to,

> "For a' that, and a' that,
>   And mickle mair for a' that."

FREDERICK DOUGLASS.*

FREDERICK DOUGLASS has been for some time a prominent member of the abolition party. He is said to be an
excellent speaker — can speak from a thorough personal experience — and has upon the audience, besides, the influence
of a strong character and uncommon talents. In the book
before us he has put into the story of his life the thoughts, the
feelings, and the adventures that have been so affecting
through the living voice ; nor are they less so from the printed
page. He has had the courage to name persons, times,
and places, thus exposing himself to obvious danger, and setting the seal on his deep convictions as to the religious need
of speaking the whole truth. Considered merely as a narrative, we have never read one more simple, true, coherent, and
warm with genuine feeling. It is an excellent piece of writing, and on that score to be prized as a specimen of the powers of the black race, which prejudice persists in disputing.
We prize highly all evidence of this kind, and it is becoming
more abundant. The cross of the Legion of Honor has just
been conferred in France on Dumas and Soulié, both celebrated in the paths of light literature. Dumas, whose father
was a general in the French army, is a mulatto; Soulié, a
quadroon. He went from New Orleans, where, though to the
eye a white man, yet, as known to have African blood in his
veins, he could never have enjoyed the privileges due to a
human being. Leaving the land of freedom, he found himself free to develop the powers that God had given.

* Narrative of the Life of Frederick Douglass, an American Slave, written by himself.

11   (121)

Two wise and candid thinkers — the Scotchman Kinmont, prematurely lost to this country, of which he was so faithful and generous a student, and the late Dr. Channing, — both thought that the African race had in them a peculiar element, which, if it could be assimilated with those imported among us from Europe, would give to genius a development, and to the energies of character a balance and harmony, beyond what has been seen heretofore in the history of the world. Such an element is indicated in their lowest estate by a talent for melody, a ready skill at imitation and adaptation, an almost indestructible elasticity of nature. It is to be remarked in the writings both of Soulié and Dumas, full of faults, but glowing with plastic life and fertile in invention. The same torrid energy and saccharine fulness may be felt in the writings of this Douglass, though his life, being one of action or resistance, has been less favorable to *such* powers than one of a more joyous flow might have been.

The book is prefaced by two communications — one from Garrison, and one from Wendell Phillips. That from the former is in his usual over-emphatic style. His motives and his course have been noble and generous; we look upon him with high respect; but he has indulged in violent invective and denunciation till he has spoiled the temper of his mind. Like a man who has been in the habit of screaming himself hoarse to make the deaf hear, he can no longer pitch his voice on a key agreeable to common ears. Mr. Phillips's remarks are equally decided, without this exaggeration in the tone. Douglass himself seems very just and temperate. We feel that his view, even of those who have injured him most, may be relied upon. He knows how to allow for motives and influences. Upon the subject of religion, he speaks with great force, and not more than our own sympathies can respond to. The inconsistencies of slaveholding professors of religion cry to Heaven. We are not disposed to detest, or refuse communion with them. Their blindness is but one form of that prevalent fallacy which substitutes a creed for a faith, a ritual for a life. We have seen too much of this system of atonement not to know that those who adopt it often began with good intentions, and are, at any rate, in their mistakes worthy of the deepest pity. But that is no reason why the truth should not be uttered, trumpet-tongued, about the thing. " Bring no more vain oblations ; " sermons must daily be preached anew on that text. Kings, five hundred years ago, built churches with the spoils of war ; clergymen to-day command slaves to obey a gospel which they will not allow them to read, and call themselves Christians amid the curses of their fellow-men. The world ought to get on a little faster than this, if there be really any principle of improvement in it. The kingdom of heaven may not at the beginning have dropped seed larger than a mustard-seed, but even from that we had a right to expect a fuller growth than we can believe to exist, when we read such a book as this of Douglass. Unspeakably affecting is the fact that he never saw his mother at all by daylight.

" I do not recollect of ever seeing my mother by the light of day. She was with me in the night. She would lie down with me, and get me to sleep, but long before I waked she was gone."

The following extract presents a suitable answer to the hackneyed argument drawn by the defender of slavery from the songs of the slave, and is also a good specimen of the powers of observation and manly heart of the writer. We wish that every one may read his book, and see what a mind might have been stifled in bondage — what a man may be subjected to the insults of spendthrift dandies, or the blows of mercenary brutes, in whom there is no whiteness except of the skin, no humanity except in the outward form, and of whom the Avenger will not fail yet to demand, " Where is thy brother ? "

" The Home Plantation of Colonel Lloyd wore the appear-

ance of a country village.   All the mechanical operations for
all the farms were performed here.   The shoemaking and
mending, the blacksmithing, cartwrighting, coopering, weaving, and grain-grinding, were all performed by the slaves on
the Home Plantation.   The whole place wore a business-like
aspect very unlike the neighboring farms.   The number of
houses, too, conspired to give it advantage over the neighboring farms.   It was called by the slaves the *Great House
Farm*.   Few privileges were esteemed higher, by the slaves
of the out-farms, than that of being selected to do errands at
the Great House Farm.   It was associated in their minds
with greatness.   A representative could not be prouder of his
election to a seat in the American Congress, than a slave on
one of the out-farms would be of his election to do errands at
the Great House Farm.   They regarded it as evidence of
great confidence reposed in them by their overseers ; and it
was on this account, as well as a constant desire to be out of
the field, from under the driver's lash, that they esteemed it a
high privilege, one worth careful living for.   He was called
the smartest and most trusty fellow who had this honor conferred upon him the most frequently.   The competitors for
this office sought as diligently to please their overseers as the
office-seekers in the political parties seek to please and deceive the people.   The same traits of character might be seen
in Colonel Lloyd's slaves, as are seen in the slaves of the
political parties.

   " The slaves selected to go to the Great House Farm, for
the monthly allowance for themselves and their fellow-slaves,
were peculiarly enthusiastic.   While on their way, they would
make the dense old woods, for miles around, reverberate with
their wild songs, revealing at once the highest joy and the
deepest sadness.   They would compose and sing as they went
along, consulting neither time nor tune.   The thought that
came up came out, — if not in the word, in the sound, — and
as frequently in the one as in the other.   They would some-

times sing the most pathetic sentiment in the most rapturous tone, and the most rapturous sentiment in the most pathetic tone. Into all their songs they would manage to weave something of the Great House Farm. Especially would they do this when leaving home. They would then sing most exultingly the following words: —

> 'I am going away to the Great House Farm!
> O, yea! O, yea! O!'

This they would sing as a chorus to words which to many would seem unmeaning jargon, but which, nevertheless, were full of meaning to themselves. I have sometimes thought that the mere hearing of those songs would do more to impress some minds with the horrible character of slavery, than the reading of whole volumes of philosophy on the subject could do.

"I did not, when a slave, understand the deep meaning of those rude and apparently incoherent songs. I was myself within the circle; so that I neither saw nor heard as those without might see and hear. They told a tale of woe which was then altogether beyond my feeble comprehension; they were tones loud, long, and deep; they breathed the prayer and complaint of souls boiling over with the bitterest anguish. Every tone was a testimony against slavery, and a prayer to God for deliverance from chains. The hearing of those wild notes always depressed my spirit, and filled me with ineffable sadness. I have frequently found myself in tears while hearing them. The mere recurrence to those songs, even now, afflicts me; and while I am writing these lines, an expression of feeling has already found its way down my cheek. To those songs I trace my first glimmering conception of the dehumanizing character of slavery. I can never get rid of that conception. Those songs still follow me, to deepen my hatred of slavery, and quicken my sympathies for my brethren in bonds. If any one wishes to be impressed with the soul-kill-

11 *

ing effects of slavery, let him go to Colonel Lloyd's plantation, and, on allowance day, place himself in the deep pine woods, and there let him, in silence, analyze the sounds that shall pass through the chambers of his soul; and if he is not thus impressed, it will only be because 'there is no flesh in his obdurate heart.'

"I have often been utterly astonished, since I came to the north, to find persons who could speak of the singing among slaves as evidence of their contentment and happiness. It is impossible to conceive of a greater mistake. Slaves sing most when they are most unhappy. The songs of the slave represent the sorrows of his heart; and he is relieved by them only as an aching heart is relieved by its tears. At least, such is my experience. I have often sung to drown my sorrow, but seldom to express my happiness. Crying for joy and singing for joy were alike uncommon to me while in the jaws of slavery. The singing of a man cast away upon a desolate island might be as appropriately considered as evidence of contentment and happiness, as the singing of a slave; the songs of the one and of the other are prompted by the same emotion."

THESE volumes have met with as warm a reception "as ever unripe author's quick conceit," to use Mr. Taylor's own language, could hope or wish; and so deservedly, that the critic's happy task, in examining them, is to point out, not what is most to be blamed, but what is most to be praised.

With joy we hail a new poet. Star after star has been withdrawn from our firmament, and when that of Coleridge set, we seemed in danger of being left, at best, to a gray and confounding twilight; but, lo! a "ray of pure white light" darts across the obscured depths of ether, and allures our eyes and hearts towards the rising orb from which it emanates. Let us tremble no more lest our summer pass away without its roses, but receive our present visitor as the harbinger of a harvest of delights.

The natural process of the mind in forming a judgment is comparison. The office of sound criticism is to teach that this comparison should be made, not between the productions of differently-constituted minds, but between any one of these and a fixed standard of perfection. Nevertheless it is not contrary to the canon to take a survey of the labors of many artists with reference to one, if we value them, not according to the degree of pleasure we have experienced from them, which must always depend upon our then age, the state of the passions and relations with life, but according to the success of the artist in attaining the object he himself had in view. To illustrate: In the same room hang two pictures, Raphael's

---

* Philip van Artevelde, A Dramatic Romance, by Henry Taylor.

Madonna and Martin's Destruction of Nineveh. A person enters, capable of admiring both, but young, excitable; he is delighted with the Madonna, but probably far more so with the other, because his imagination is at that time more developed than the pure love for beauty which is the characteristic of a taste in a higher state of cultivation. He prefers the Martin, because it excites in his mind a thousand images of sublimity and terror, recalls the brilliancy of Oriental history, and the stern pomp of the old prophetic day, and rouses his mind to a high state of action, *then* as congenial with its wants as at a later day would be the feeling of contented absorption, of perfect satisfaction with a production of the human soul, which one of Raphael's calmly beautiful creations is fitted to cause. Now, it would be very unfair for this person to pronounce the Martin superior to the Raphael, because it then gave him more pleasure. But if he said, the one is intended to excite the imagination, the other to gratify the taste, that which fulfils its object most completely must be the best, whether it give me most pleasure or no; he would be on the right ground, and might consider the two pictures relatively to one another, without danger of straying very far from the truth.

This is the ground we would assume in a hasty sketch, which will not, we hope, be deemed irrelevant, of the most prominent essays to which the last sixty years have given rise in the department of the work now before us, previous to stating our opinion of its merits. Many, we are aware, ridicule the idea of filling reviews with long dissertations, and say they only want brief accounts of such books as are coming out, by way of saving time. With such we cannot agree. We think the office of the reviewer is, indeed, in part, to point out to the public attention deserving works, which might otherwise slumber too long unknown on the bookseller's shelves, but still more to present to the reader as large a cluster of objects round one point as possible, thus, by suggestion, stimulating him to take a broader or more careful view of the subject than his indolence or his business would have permitted.

The terms Classical and Romantic, which have so long divided European critics, and exercised so powerful an influence upon their decisions, are not much known or heeded among us, — as, indeed, *belles-lettres* cannot, generally, in our busy state of things, be important or influential, as among a less free and more luxurious people, to whom the more important truths are proffered through those indirect but alluring mediums. Here, where every thing may be spoken or written, and the powers that be, abused without ceremony on the very highway, the Muse has nothing to do with dagger or bowl; hardly is the censor's wand permitted to her hand. Yet is her lyre by no means unheeded, and if it is rather by refining our tastes than by modelling our opinions that she influences us, yet is that influence far from unimportant. And the time is coming, perhaps in our day, we may (if war do not untimely check the national progress) even see and temper its beginning, when the broad West shall swarm with an active, happy, and cultivated population ; when the South, freed from the incubus which now oppresses her best energies, shall be able to do justice to the resources of her soil and of her mind; when the East, gathering from every breeze the riches of the old world, shall be the unwearied and loving agent to those regions which lie far away from the great deep, our bulwark and our minister. Then will the division of labor be more complete; then will a surplus of talent be spared from the mart, the forum, and the pulpit; then will the fine arts assume their proper dignity, as the expression of what is highest and most ethereal in the mind of a people. Then will our quarries be thoroughly explored, and furnish materials for stately fabrics to adorn the face of all the land, while our ports shall be crowded with foreign artists flocking to take lessons in the school of American architecture.

Then will our floral treasures be arranged into harmonious gardens, which, environing tasteful homes, shall dimple all the landscape. Then will our Allstons and our Greenoughs preside over great academies, and be raised far above any need, except of giving outward form to the beautiful ideas which animate them; and ornament from the exhaustless stores of genius the marble halls where the people meet to rejoice, or to mourn, or where dwell those wise and good whom the people delight to honor. Then shall music answer to and exalt the national spirit, and the poet's brows shall be graced with the civic as well as the myrtle crown. Then shall we have an American mind, as well as an American system, and, no longer under the sad necessity of exchanging money for thoughts, traffic on perfectly equal terms with the other hemisphere. Then — ah, not yet! — shall our literature make its own laws, and give its own watchwords; till then we must learn and borrow from that of nations who possess a higher degree of cultivation though a much lower one of happiness.

The term Classical, used in its narrow sense, implies a servile adherence to the Unities, but in its wide and best sense, it means such a simplicity of plan, selection of actors and events, such judicious limitations on time and range of subject, as may concentrate the interest, perfect the illusion, and make the impression most distinct and forcible. Although no advocates for the old French school, with its slavish obedience to rule, which introduces follies greater than those it would guard against, we lay the blame, not on their view of the drama, but on the then bigoted nationality of the French mind, which converted the Mussulman prophet into a De Retz, the Roman princess into a French grisette, and infected the clear and buoyant atmosphere of Greece with the vapors of the Seine. We speak of the old French Drama: with the modern we do not profess to be acquainted, having met with scarcely any specimens in our own bookstores or libraries; but if it has been revolutionized with the rest of their literature, it is probably as unlike as possible to the former models.

We shall speak of productions in the classical spirit first; because Mr. Taylor is a disciple of the other school, though otherwise we should have adopted a contrary course.

The most perfect specimens of this style with which we are acquainted are the Filippo, the Saul, and the Myrrha of Alfieri; the Wallenstein of Schiller; the Tasso and the Iphigenia of Gœthe. England furnishes nothing of the sort. She is thoroughly Shakspearian.

There is no higher pleasure than to see a genius of a wild, impassioned, many-sided eagerness, restraining its exuberance by its sense of fitness, taming its extravagance beneath the rule its taste approves, exhibiting the soul within soul, and the force of the will over all that we inherit. The *abandon* of genius has its beauty — far more beautiful its voluntary submission to wise law. A picture, a description, has beauty, the beauty of life; these pictures, these descriptions, arranged upon a plan, made subservient to a purpose, have a higher beauty — that of the mind of man acting upon life. Art is nature, but nature new-modelled, condensed, and harmonized. We are not merely like mirrors, to reflect our own times to those more distant. The mind has a light of its own, and by it illumines what it re-creates.

This is the ground of our preference for the classical school, and for Alfieri beyond all pupils of that school. We hold that if a vagrant bud of poesy here and there be blighted by conforming to its rules, our loss is more than made up to us by our enjoyment of plan, of symmetry, of the triumph of genius over multiplied obstacles.

It has been often said that the dramas of Alfieri contrast directly with his character. This is, perhaps, not true; we do but see the depths of that volcano which in early days boiled over so fiercely. The wild, infatuated youth often becomes the stern, pitiless old man. Alfieri did but bend his surplus strength upon literature, and became a despot to his own haughty spirit, instead of domineering over those of others.

We have selected his three masterpieces, though he, to himself an inexorable critic, has shown no indulgence to his own works, and the least successful of those which remain to us, Maria Stuarda, is marked by great excellence.

Filippo has been so ably depicted in a work now well known, " Carlyle's Life of Schiller," that we need not dwell upon it. All the light of the picture, the softer feelings of the hapless Carlos and Elizabeth, is so cast, as to make more visible the awing darkness of the tyrant's perverted mind, deadened to all virtue by a false religion, cold and hopeless as the dungeons of his own Inquisition, and relentless as death. Forced by the magic wand of genius into the stifling precincts of this mind, horror-struck that we must sympathize with such a state as possible to humanity, we rush from the contemplation of the picture, and would gladly curtain it over in our hall of imagery forever. Yet stigmatize not our poet as a dark master, courting the shade, and hating the glad lights which love and hope cast upon human nature. The drama has a holy meaning, a patriot moral, and we, above all, should reverence him, the aristocrat by birth, by education, and by tastes, whose love of liberty could lead him to such conclusions.

In " Saul," a bright rainbow rises, by the aid of the Sun of Righteousness, above the commotion of the tempest. David, the faithful, the hopeful, combining the æsthetic culture, the winged inspiration of the poet with the noble pride of Israel's chosen warrior, contrasts finely with the unfortunate Saul, his mind darkened and convulsed by jealousy, vain regrets, and fear of the God he has forgotten how to love. The other three actors shade in the picture without attracting our attention from the two principal personages. The Hebrew spirit breathes through the whole. The beauty of the lyric effusions is so generally felt, that encomium is needless; we shall only observe that in them Alfieri's style, usually so severe, becomes flexible, melodious, and glowing; thus we may easily perceive what he might have done, had not the simplicity of his genius disdained the foreign aid of ornament upon its Doric proportions.

Myrrha is, however, the highest exertion of his genius. The remoteness of time and manners, the subject, at once so hackneyed and so revolting, these great obstacles he seizes with giant grasp, and moulds them to his purpose. Our souls are shaken to the foundation; all every-day barriers fall with the great convulsion of passion. We sorrow, we sicken, we die with the miserable girl, so pure under her involuntary crime of feeling, pursued by a malignant deity in her soul's most sacred recesses, torn from all communion with humanity, and the virtue she was framed to adore. The perfection of plan, the matchless skill with which every circumstance is brought out! The agonizing rapidity with which her misery "va camminando al fine"! No! never was higher tragic power exhibited; never were love, terror, pity, fused into a more penetrating draught! Myrrha is a favorite acting-play in Italy — a fact inconceivable to an English or American mind; for (to say nothing of other objections) we should think such excess of emotion unbearable. But in those meridian climes they drink deep draughts of passion too frequently to taste them as we do.

We pass to works of far inferior power, but of greater beauty. We have selected Iphigenia and Tasso as the most finished results of their author's mature views of art. On his plays in the Romantic style, we shall touch in another place. If any one ask why we do not class Faust with either, we reply, *that* is a work without a parallel; one of those few originals which have their laws within themselves, and should always be discussed singly.

The unity of plan in Iphigenia is perfect. There is one

12

pervading idea. The purity of Iphigenia's mind must be kept unsullied, that she may be a fit intercessor to the gods in behalf of her polluted family. Gœthe, in his travels through Italy, saw a picture of a youthful Christian saint — Agatha, we think ; struck by the radiant purity of her expression, he resolved his heathen priestess should not have one thought which could revolt the saint of the true religion. This idea is wonderfully preserved throughout a drama so classic in its coloring and manners. The happiest development of' character, an interest in the denouement which is only so far tempered by our trust in the lovely heroine, as to permit us to enjoy all the minuter beauties on our way, (this the breathless interest of Alfieri's dramas hardly allows, on a fourth or fifth reading,) exquisite descriptive touches, and expressions of sentiment, unequalled softness and harmony of style, distinguish a drama not to be surpassed in its own department. Torquato Tasso * is of inferior general, but greater particular beauty. The two worldly, the two higher characters, with that of Alphonso halting between, are shaded with equal delicacy and distinctness. The inward-turning imagination of the ill-fated bard, and the fantastic tricks it plays with life, are painted as only a poet's soul of equal depth, of greater versatility, could have painted them. In analysis of the passions, and eloquent descriptions of their more hidden workings, some parts may vie with Rousseau ; while several effusions of feeling are worthy of Tasso's own lyre, with its "breaking heartstring's tone." The conduct of the piece being in perfect accordance with the plan, gives the satisfaction we have mentioned in speaking of Raphael's Madonna.

Schiller's Wallenstein does not strictly belong to this class, yet we are disposed to claim it as observing the unities of

---

[* For a translation by my sister of this Drama, see Part III. of her "Art, Literature, and the Drama," where it is now, for the first time, published, simultaneously with the appearance of this volume. — ED.]

time and interest; the latter especially is entire, notwithstanding the many actors and side-scenes which are introduced. Numberless touches of nature arrest our attention, bright lights are flashed across many characters, but our interest, momently increasing, is for Wallenstein — for the perversion, the danger, the ruin of that monarch soul, that falling son of the morning. Even that we feel in Max, with his celestial bloom of heart, in Thekla's sweet trustfulness, is subsidiary. This work, generally known to the reader through Mr. Coleridge's translation, affords an imperfect illustration of our meaning. Miss Baillie's plays on the passions hold a middle place. Unity of purpose there is — no unity of plan or conduct. Bold, fine outline — very bad coloring. Profound, beautifully-expressed reflections on the passions — utter want of skill in showing them out; a thorough feeling, indeed, of the elements of tragedy, — had but the vitalizing energy been added. Her plays are failures; but since she has given us nothing else, we cannot but rejoice in having these. 'Tis great pity that the authoress of De Montfort and Basil should not have attempted a narrative poem.

Coleridge and Byron are signal instances how peculiar is the kind of talent required for the drama; one a philosopher, both men of great genius and uncommon mastery over language, both conversant with each side of human nature, both considering the drama in its true light as one of the highest departments of literature, both utterly wanting in simplicity, pathos, truth of passion and liveliness of action — in that thrilling utterance of heart to heart, whose absence *here*, no other excellence can atone for. Of Maturin and Knowles we do not speak, because theirs, though very good acting plays, are not, like Mr. Taylor's, written for the closet; of Milman, because not sufficiently acquainted with his plays. We would here pay a tribute to our countryman Hillhouse, whose Hadad, read at a very early age, we remember with much delight. Probably our judgment now might be different ; but a work which could make so deep an impression on any age, must have genius. We are sorry we have never since met it in any library or parlor, and are not competent to speak of it more particularly.

It will be seen that Mr. Taylor has not attempted the sort of dramatic poetry which we consider the highest, but has labored in that which the great wizard of Avon adopted, because it lay nearest at hand to clothe his spells withal, and consecrated it, with his world-embracing genius, to the (in our judgment) no small detriment of his country's taste. Having thus declared that we cannot grant him our very highest meed of admiration, (though we will not say that he might not win it if he made the essay,) we hasten to meet him on his own ground. "Dramatica Poesis est veluti Historia spectabilis," is his motto, taken from Bacon, who formed his taste on Shakspeare. We would here mention that Gœthe's earlier works, Gœtz von Berlichingen and Egmont are of this school — brilliant fragments of past days, ballads acted out, historical scenes and personages clustered round a hero ; and we have seen that his ripened taste preferred the form of Iphigenia and Tasso.

We cannot too strongly express our approbation of the opinions maintained in his short preface to this work. We rejoice to see a leader coming forward who is likely to un-Hemansize and un-Cornwallize literature. We too have been sick, we too have been intoxicated with *words* till we could hardly appreciate thoughts ; perhaps our present writing shows traces of this Lower-Empire taste ; but we have sense enough left to welcome the English Phocion, who would regenerate public feeling. The candor and modest dignity with which these opinions are offered charm us. The remarks upon Shelley, whom we have loved, and do still love passing well. brought truth home to us in a definite shape. With regard to the lowness of Lord Byron's standard of character, every thing indeed has been said which could be, but not as Mr. Taylor has said it; and we opine that his refined and gentle remarks will find their way to ears which have always been deaf to the harsh sarcasms unseasoned by wit, which have been current on this topic.

Our author too, notwithstanding his modest caveat, has acted upon his principles, and furnished a forcible illustration of their justice. For dignity of sentiment, for simplicity of manner, for truth to life, never infringing upon respect for the ideal, we look to such a critic, and we are *not* disappointed.

The scene is laid in Ghent, in the fourteenth century. The Flemish mobocracy are brought before us with a fidelity and animation surpassing those displayed in Egmont. Their barbarism, and the dissimilar, but not inferior barbarism of their would-be lords, the bold, bad men, the shameless crime and brainless tumult of those days, live before us. Amid these clashing elements moves Philip Van Artevelde, with the presence, not of a god, but of a great man, too superior to be shaken, too wise to be shocked by their rude jarrings. He becomes the leader of his people, and despite pestilence, famine, and their own untutored passions, he leads them on to victory and power.

In the second part we follow Van Artevelde from his zenith of glory to his decline. The tarnishing influence of prosperity on his spirit, and its clear radiance again in adversity, are managed as the noble and well-defined conception of the character deserves.

The boy king and his courtly, intriguing counsellors are as happily portrayed as Vauclaire and the fierce commonalty he ruled, or resisted with rope or sword, as the case might demand.

The two loves of Van Artevelde are finely imagined, as types of the two states of his character. Both are lovely; the one how elevated! the other how pity-moving in her loveliness! On the interlude of Elena we must be allowed to linger fondly, though the author's self condemn our taste.

We are no longer partial to the machinery of portents and presentiments. Wallenstein's were the last we liked, but Van Artevelde's make good poetry, and have historical vouchers. They remind us of those of Fergus Mac Ivor.

We shall extract a speech of Van Artevelde's, in which a leading idea of the work is expressed.

Father, —

So ! with the chivalry of Christendom
I wage my war, — no nation for my friend,
Yet in each nation having hosts of friends.
The bondsmen of the world, that to their lords   ·
Are bound with chains of iron, unto me
Are knit by their affections. Be it so.
From kings and nobles will I seek no more
Aid, friendship, or alliance. With the poor
I make my treaty ; and the heart of man
Sets the broad seal of its allegiance there,
And ratifies the compact. Vassals, serfs,
Ye that are bent with unrequited toil,
Ye that have whitened in the dungeon's darkness,
Through years that know not change of night nor day,
Tatterdemalions, lodgers in the hedge,
Lean beggars with raw backs, and rumbling maws,
Whose poverty was whipped for starving you, —
I hail you my auxiliars and allies,
The only potentates whose help I crave !
Richard of England, thou hast slain Jack Straw,
But thou hast left unquenched the vital spark
That set Jack Straw on fire. The spirit lives ;
And as when he of Canterbury fell,
His seat was filled by some no better clerk,
So shall John Ball, that slew him, be replaced.

Fain would we extract Van Artevelde's reply to the French envoy — the oration of the dying Van den Bosch in the market-place of Ypres, the last scene between the hero and the double-dyed dastard and traitor, Sir Heurant of Heurlée, and many, many more, had we but space enough.

We have purposely avoided telling the story, as is usual in an article of this kind, because we wish that every one should buy and read Van Artevelde, instead of resting content with the canvas side of the carpet.

A few words more, and we shall conclude these, we fear, already too prolonged remarks. We would compare Mr. Taylor with the most applauded of living dramatists, the Italian Alessandro Manzoni.

To wide and accurate historical knowledge, to purity of taste, to the greatest elevation of sentiment, Manzoni unites uncommon lyric power, and a beautiful style in the most beautiful language of the modern world. The conception of both his plays is striking, the detached beauties of thought and imagery are many; but where are the life, the glow, the exciting march of action, the thorough display of character which charm us in Van Artevelde? We *live* at Ghent and Senlis; we *think* of Italy. Van Artevelde dies, — and our hearts die with him. When Elena says, "The body, — O!" we could echo that "long, funereal note," and weep as if the sun of heroic nobleness were quenched from our own horizon. "Carmagnola, Adelchis die," — we calmly shut the book, and think how much we have enjoyed it. Manzoni can deeply feel goodness and greatness, but he cannot localize them in the contours of life before our eyes. His are capital sketches, poems of a deep meaning, — but this, yes! this *is* a drama.

We cannot conclude more fitly, nor inculcate a precept on the reader more forcibly, than in Mr. Taylor's own words, with a slight alteration: "To say that I admire him is to admit that I owe him much; for admiration is never thrown away upon the mind of him who feels it, except when it is misdirected or blindly indulged. There is perhaps nothing which more enlarges or enriches the mind than the disposition to lay it genially open to impressions of pleasure, from the exercise of every species of talent; nothing by which it is more impoverished than the habit of undue depreciation. What is puerile, pusillanimous, or wicked, it can do us no good to admire; but let us admire all that can be admired without debasing the dispositions or stultifying the understanding."

SLIGHT as the intercourse held by the Voyager with the South Sea Islands is, his narrative is always more prized by us than those of the missionary and traders, who, though they have better opportunity for full and candid observation, rarely use it so well, because their minds are biased towards their special objects. It is deeply interesting to us to know how much and how little God has accomplished for the various nations of the larger portion of the earth, before they are brought into contact with the civilization of Europe and the Christian religion. To suppose it so little as most people do, is to impugn the justice of Providence. We see not how any one can contentedly think that such vast multitudes of living souls have been left for thousands of years without manifold and great means of instruction and happiness. To appreciate justly how much these have availed them, to know how far they are competent to receive new benefits, is essential to the philanthropist as a means of aiding them, no less than it is important to the philosopher who wishes to see the universe as God made it, not as some men think he *ought to* have made it.

The want of correct knowledge, and a fair appreciation of the uncultivated man as he stands, is a cause why even the good and generous fail to aid him, and contact with Europe has proved so generally more of a curse than a blessing. It is easy enough to see why our red man, to whom the white extends the Bible or crucifix with one hand, and the rum-bottle with the other, should look upon Jesus as only one more Manitou, and learn nothing from his precepts or the

civilization connected with them.   The Hindoo, the South
American Indian, who knew their teachers first as powerful
robbers, and found themselves called upon to yield to violence
not only their property, personal freedom, and peace, but also
the convictions and ideas that had been rooted and growing in
their race for ages, could not be otherwise than degraded and
stupefied by a change effected through such violence and convulsion.   But not only those who came with fire and sword,
crying, " Believe or die ; " " Understand or we will scourge
you ; " " Understand *and* we will only plunder and tyrannize
over you," — not only these ignorant despots, self-deceiving
robbers, have failed to benefit the people they dared esteem
more savage than themselves, but the worthy and generous
have failed from want of patience and an expanded intelligence.   Would you speak to a man ? first learn his language.
Would you have the tree grow ? learn the nature of the soil
and climate in which you plant it.   Better days are coming,
we do hope, as to these matters — days in which the new
shall be harmonized with the old, rather than violently rent
asunder from it ; when progress shall be accomplished by
gentle evolution, as the stem of the plant grows up, rather
than by the blasting of rocks, and blindness or death of the
miners.

The knowledge which can lead to such results must be collected, as all true knowledge is, from the love of it.   In the
healthy state of the mind, the state of elastic youth, which
would be perpetual in the mind if it were nobly disciplined
and animated by immortal hopes, it likes to learn just how the
facts are, seeking truth for its own sake, not doubting that the
design and cause will be made clear in time.   A mind in such
a state will find many facts ready for its use in these volumes
relative to the South Sea Islanders, and other objects of
interest.

Does any shame still haunt the age of bronze — a shame, the lingering blush of an heroic age, at being caught in doing any thing merely for amusement? Is there a public still extant which needs to excuse its delinquencies by the story of a man who liked to lie on the sofa all day and read novels, though he could, at time of need, write the gravest didactics? Live they still, those reverend seigniors, the object of secret smiles to our childish years, who were obliged to apologize for midnight oil spent in conning story-books by the "historic bearing" of the novel, or the "correct and admirable descriptions of certain countries, with climate, scenery, and manners therein contained," wheat, for which they, industrious students, were willing to winnow bushels of frivolous love-adventures? We know not, but incline to think the world is now given over to frivolity so far as to replace by the novel the minstrel's ballad, the drama, and even those games of agility and strength in which it once sought pastime. For, indeed, *mere* pass-time is sometimes needed; the nursery legend comprised a primitive truth of the understanding and the wisdom of nations in the lines, —

> " All play and no work makes Jack a mere toy,
> But all work and no play makes Jack a dull boy."

We have reversed the order of arrangement to suit our present purpose. For we, O useful reader! being ourselves so far of the useful class as to be always wanted somewhere, have also to fight a good fight for our amusements, either with the foils of excuse, like the reverend seigniors above

mentioned, or with the sharp weapons of argument, or main-
tenance of a view of our own without argument, which we
take to be the sharpest weapon of all.

Thus far do we defer to the claims of the human race, with
its myriad of useful errands to be done, that we read most of
our novels in the long sunny days, which call all beings to
chirp and nestle, or fly abroad as the birds do, and permit the
very oxen to ruminate gently in the just-mown fields.

On such days it was well, we think, to read " Sybil, or the
Two Worlds." We have always felt great interest in D'Israeli. He is one of the many who share the difficulty of our
era, which Carlyle says, quoting, we believe, from his Master,
consists in unlearning the false in order to arrive at the true.
We think these men, when they have once taken their degree,
can be of far greater use to their brethren than those who
have always kept their instincts unperverted.

, In " Vivian Grey," the young D'Israeli, an educated Englishman, but with the blood of sunnier climes glowing and
careering in his veins, gave us the very flower and essence of
factitious life. That book sparkled and frothed like cham-
pagne ; like that, too, it produced no dull and imbecile state
by its intoxication, but one witty, genial, spiritual even. A
deep, soft melancholy thrilled through its gay mockeries ; the
eyes of nature glimmered through the painted mask, and a
nobler ambition was felt beneath the follies of petty success
and petty vengeance. Still, the chief merit of the book, as a
book, was the light and decided touch with which its author
took up the follies and poesies of the day, and brought them
all before us. The excellence of the foreign part, with its
popular superstitions, its deep passages in the glades of the
summer woods, and above all, the capital sketch of the prime
minister with his original whims and secret history of romantic sorrows, were beyond the appreciation of most readers.

Since then, D'Israeli has never written any thing to be
compared with this first jet of the fountain of his mind in the

sunlight of morning. The "Young Duke" was full of brilliant sketches, and showed a soul struggling, blinded by the gaudy mists of fashion, for realities. The "Wondrous Tale of Alroy" showed great power of conception, though in execution it is a failure. "Henrietta Temple" Mr. Willis, with his usual justness of perception, has praised, as containing a collection of the best love-letters ever written; and which show that excellence, signal and singular among the literary tribe, of which D'Israeli never fails, of daring to write a thing down exactly as it rises in his mind.

Now he has come to be a leader of Young England, and a rooted plant upon her soil. If the performance of his prime do not entirely correspond with the brilliant lights of its dawn, it is yet aspiring, and with a large kernel of healthy nobleness in it. D'Israeli shows now not only the heart, but the soul of a man. He cares for all men; he wishes to care wisely for all.

"Coningsby" was full of talent, yet its chief interest lay in this aspiration after reality, and the rich materials taken from contemporary life. There is nothing in it good after the original manner of D'Israeli, except the sketches of Eton, and above all, the noble schoolboy's letter. The picture of the Jew, so elaborately limned, is chiefly valuable as affording keys to so many interesting facts.

"Sybil" is an attempt to do justice to the claims of the laboring classes, and investigate the duties of those in whose hands the money is at present, towards the rest. It comes to no result: it only exhibits some truths in a more striking light than heretofore. D'Israeli shows the taint of old prejudice in the necessity he felt to marry the daughter of the people to one *not* of the people. Those worthy to be distinguished must still have good blood, or rather old blood, for what is called good needs now to be renovated from a homelier source. But his leaders must have *old* blood; the fresh ichor, the direct flow from heaven, is not enough to animate their lives to the deeds now needed.

13

D'Israeli is another of those who give testimony in behalf of our favorite idea that a leading feature of the new era will be in new and higher developments of the feminine character. He looks at women as a man does who is truly in love. He does not paint them well, that is, not with profound fidelity to nature. But, ideally, he sees them well, for they are to him the inspirers and representatives of what is holy, tender, and simply great.

There are good sketches of the manufacturers at home, not the overseers, but the real makers.

Sue is a congenial activity with D'Israeli, but with clearer notions of what he wants. His " De Rohan " is a poor book, though it contains some things excellent. But it is faulty, — even more so than is usual with him, in heavy exaggerations, and is less redeemed by brilliant effects, good schemes, and lively strains of feeling. The wish to unmask Louis XIV. is defeated by the hatred with which the character inspired him, the liberal of the nineteenth century. The Grand Monarque was really brutally selfish and ignorant, as Sue represents him ; but then there *was* a native greatness which justified, in some degree, the illusion he diffused, and which falsifies all Sue's representation. It is not by an inventory of facts or traits that what is most vital in character, and which makes its due impression on contemporaries, can be apprehended or depicted. " De Rohan " is worth reading for particulars of an interesting period, put together with accuracy and with a sense of physiological effects, if not of the spiritual realities that they represented.

" Self, by the Author of Cecil," is one of the worst of a paltry class of novels — those which aim at representing the very dregs in a social life, now at its lowest ebb. If it has produced a sensation, that only shows the poverty of life among those who can be interested in it. I have known more life lived in a day among factory girls, or in a village school, than informs these volumes, with all their great pretension and affected vivacity.   It is not worth our while to read this class of English novels; they are far worse than the French, morally as well as mentally.   This has no merits as to the development of character or exposition of motives; it is a poor, external, lifeless thing.

"Dashes at Life," by N. P. Willis.   The life of Mr. Willis is too European for him to have a general or permanent fame in America.   We need a life of our own, and a literature of our own.   Those writers who are dearest to us, and really most interesting, are those who are at least rooted to the soil. If they are not great enough to be the prophets of the new era, they at least exhibit the features of their native clime, and the complexion given by its native air.   But Mr. Willis is a son of Europe, and his writings can interest only the fashionable world of this country, which, by imitating Europe, fails entirely of a genius, grace, and invention of its own. Still, in their way, they are excellent.   They are most lively pictures, showing the fine natural organization of the writer, on whom none, the slightest symptom of what he is looking for, is thrown away; sparkling with bold, light wit, succinct, and colored with glow, and for a full light.   Some of them were new to us, and we read them through, missing none of the words, and laughed with a full heart, and without one grain of complaisance, which is much, very much, to say in these days.   We said these sketches would not have a permanent fame, and yet we may be wrong.   The new, full, original, radiant, American life may receive them as an heirloom from this transition state we are in now, and future generations may stare at the mongrel products of Saratoga, and maidens still laugh till they cry at the " Letter of Jane S. to her Spirit-Bridegroom."

All these story-books show, even to the languor of the hottest day, the solemn signs of revolution.   Life has become too factitious; it has no longer a leg left to stand upon, and cannot be carried much farther in this way.   England — ah! who can resist visions of phalansteries in every park, and tho treasures of art turned into public galleries for the use of the artificers who will no longer be unwashed, but raised and educated by the refinements of sufficient leisure, and the instructions of genius. England must glide, or totter, or fall into revolution; there is not room for such selfish elves, and unique young dukes, in a country so crowded with men, and with those who ought to be women, and are turned into work tools. There are very impressive hints on this last topic in " Sybil, or the Two Worlds," (of the rich and poor.) God has time to remember the design with which he made this world also.

WE are very glad to see this handsome copy of Shelley ready for those who have long been vainly inquiring at all the bookstores for such a one.

In Europe the fame of Shelley has risen superior to the clouds that darkened its earlier days, hiding his true image from his fellow-men, and from his own sad eyes oftentimes the common light of day. As a thinker, men have learned to pardon what they consider errors in opinion for the sake of singular nobleness, purity, and love in his main tendency or spirit. As a poet, the many faults of his works having been acknowledged, there are room and place to admire his far more numerous and exquisite beauties.

The heart of the man, few, who have hearts of their own, refuse to reverence, and many, even of devoutest Christians, would not refuse the book which contains Queen Mab as a Christmas gift. For it has been recognized that the founder of the Christian church would have suffered one to come unto him, who was in faith and love so truly what he sought in a disciple, without regard to the form his doctrine assumed.

The qualities of his poetry have often been analyzed, and the severer critics, impatient of his exuberance, or unable to use their accustomed spectacles in the golden mist that broods over all he has done, deny him high honors; but the soul of aspiring youth, untrammelled by the canons of taste, and untamed by scholarly discipline, swells into rapture at his lyric sweetness, finds ambrosial refreshment from his plenteous

* The Poetical Works of Percy Bysche Shelley. First American edition, (complete.) With a Biographical and Critical Notice, by G. G. Foster.

13 *   (149)

fancies, catches fire at his daring thought, and melts into boundless weeping at his tender sadness — the sadness of a soul betrothed to an ideal unattainable in this present sphere.

For ourselves, we dispute not with the *doctrinaires* or the critics. We cannot speak dispassionately of an influence that has been so dear to us. Nearer than the nearest companions of life actual has Shelley been to us. Many other great ones have shone upon us, and all who ever did so shine are still resplendent in our firmament, for our mental life has not been broken and contradictory, but thus far we " see what we foresaw." But Shelley seemed to us an incarnation of what was sought in the sympathies and desires of instinctive life, a light of dawn, and a foreshowing of the weather of this day.

When still in childish years, the " Hymn to Intellectual Beauty " fell in our way. In a green meadow, skirted by a rich wood, watered by a lovely rivulet, made picturesque by a mill a little farther down, sat a party of young persons gayer than, and almost as inventive, as those that told the tales recorded by Boccaccio. They were passing a few days in a scene of deep seclusion, there uncared for by tutor or duenna, and with no bar of routine to check the pranks of their gay, childish fancies. Every day they assumed parts which through the waking hours must be acted out. One day it was the characters in one of Richardson's novels ; and most solemnly we " my deared " each other with richest brocade of affability, and interchanged in long, stiff phrase our sentimental secrets and prim opinions. But to-day we sought relief in personating birds or insects ; and now it was the Libellula who, tired of wild flitting and darting, rested on the grassy bank and read aloud the " Hymn to Intellectual Beauty," torn by chance from the leaf of a foreign magazine.

It was one of those chances which we ever remember as the interposition of some good angel in our fate. Solemn tears marked the change of mood in our little party, and with the words

" Have I not kept my vow ? "

began a chain of thoughts whose golden links still bind the years together.

Two or three years passed. The frosty Christmas season came; the trees cracked with their splendid burden of ice, the old wooden country house was banked up with high drifts of the beautiful snow, and the Libellula became the owner of Shelley's Poems. It was her Christmas gift, and for three days and three nights she ceased not to extract its sweets; and how familiar still in memory every object seen from the chair in which she sat enchanted during those three days, memorable to her as those of July to the French nation! The fire, the position of the lamp, the variegated shadows of that alcoved room, the bright stars up to which she looked with such a feeling of congeniality from the contemplation of this starry soul, —O, could but a De Quincey describe those days in which the bridge between the real and ideal rose unbroken! He would not do it, though, as *Suspiria de Profundis,* but as sighs of joy upon the mountain height.

The poems we read then are what every one still reads, the " Julian and Maddalo," with its profound revelations of the inward life; " Alastor," the soul sweeping like a breeze through nature; and some of the minor poems. " Queen Mab," the " Prometheus," and other more formal works we have not been able to read much. It was not when he tried to express opinions which the wrongs of the world had put into his head, but when he abandoned himself to the feelings which nature had implanted in his own breast, that Shelley seemed to us so full of inspiration, and it is so still.

In reply to all that can be urged against him by people of whom we do not wish to speak ill, — for surely " they know not what they do," — we are wont simply to refer to the fact that he was the only man who redeemed the human race from suspicion to the embittered soul of Byron. " Why," said Byron, " he is a man who would willingly die for others. *I am sure of it.*"

Yes! balance that against all the ill you can think of him.

that he was a man able to live wretched for the sake of speaking sincerely what he supposed to be truth, willing to die for the good of his fellows !

Mr. Foster has spoken well of him as a man: "Of Shelley's personal character it is enough to say that it was wholly pervaded by the same unbounded and unquestioning love for his fellow-men — the same holy and fervid hope in their ultimate virtue and happiness — the same scorn of baseness and hatred of oppression — which beam forth in all his writings with a pure and constant light. The theory which he wrote was the practice which his whole life exemplified. Noble, kind, generous, passionate, tender, with a courage greater than the courage of the chief of warriors, for it could *endure* — these were the qualities in which his life was embalmed."

FESTUS.*

WE are right glad to see this beloved stranger domesticated among us. Yet there are queer little circumstances that herald the introduction. The poet is a barrister at law!—well! it is always worthy of note when a man is not hindered by study of human law from knowledge of divine; which last is all that concerns the poet. Then the preface to the American edition closes with this discreet remark: "It is perfectly SAFE to pronounce it (the poem) one of the most powerful and splendid productions of the age." Dear New England! how purely that was worthy thee, region where the tyranny of public opinion is carried to a perfection of minute scrutiny beyond what it ever was before in any age or place, though the ostracism be administered with the mildness and refinement fit for this age. Dear New England! yes! it is *safe* to say that the poem is good; whatever Mrs. Grundy may think, she will not have it burned by the hangman if it is not. But it may not be *discreet*, because she can, if she sees fit, exile its presence from bookstores, libraries, centre tables, and all mention of its existence from lips polite, and of thine also, who hast dared to praise it, on peril of turning all surrounding eyes to lead by its utterance. This kind of gentle excommunication thou mayst not be prepared to endure, O preface-writer! And we should greatly fear that thou wert deceived in thy fond security, for "Festus" is a bold book—in respect of freedom of words, a boldest book—also it reveals the solitudes of hearts with unexampled sincerity, and

* Festus: A Poem, by Philip James Bailey. First American edition, Boston.

remorselessly lays bare human nature in its naked truth —
but for the theology of the book. That may save it, and
none the less for all it shows of the depravity of human nature. It is through many pages and leaves what is technically praised as "a serious book." A friend went into a
bookstore to select presents for persons with whom she was
about to part, and among other things requested the shopman
to "show her some serious books in handsome binding." He
looked into several, and then, struck by passages here and
there, offered her the "Letters of Lady M. W. Montague."
She assuring him that it would not be safe to make use
of this work, he offered her a miniature edition of Shakspeare, as "a book containing many excellent things, though
you had to wade through a great deal of rubbish to get at
them."

We fear the reader will have to wade through a great deal of
"rubbish" in "Festus" before he gets at the theology. However, there it is, in sufficient quantities to give dignity to any
book. In seriousness, it may compete with Pollok's "Course
of Time." In "splendor and power," we feel ourselves safe
in saying that, as sure as the sun shines, it cannot be outdone
in the English tongue, thus far, short of Milton. So there is
something for all classes of readers, and we hope it will get
to their eyes, albeit Boston books are not likely to be detected
by all eyes to which they belong.

To ourselves the theology of this writer, and the conscious
design of the poem, have little interest. They seem to us, like
the color of his skin and hair, the result of the circumstances
under which he was born. Certain opinions came in his way
early, and became part of the body of his thought. But what
interests us is not these, but what is deepest, universal — the
soul of that body. To us the poem is

" . . . full of great dark meanings like the sea ; "

and it is these, the deep experiences and inspirations of the immortal man, that engage us.

Even the proem shows how large is his nature — its most careless utterance full of grandeur, its tamest of bold nobleness. This, that truly engages us, he spoke of more forcibly when the book first went forth to the world : —

> "Read this, world. He who writes is dead to thee,
> But still lives in these leaves. He spake inspired ;
> Night and day, thought came unhelped, undesired,
> Like blood to his heart. The course of study he
> Went through was of the soul-rack. The degree
> He took was high ; it was wise wretchedness.
> He suffered perfectly, and gained no less
> A prize than, in his own torn heart, to see
> A few bright seeds ; he sowed them, hoped them truth.
> The autumn of that seed is in these pages."

Such is, in our belief, the true theologian, the learner of God, who does not presumptuously expect at this period of growth to bind down all that is to be known of divine things in a system, a set of words, but considers that he is only spelling the first lines of a work, whose perusal shall last him through eternity. Such a one is not in a hurry to declare that the riddles of Fate and of Time are solved, for he knows it is not calling them so that will make them so. His soul does not decline the great and persevering labors that are to develop its energies. He has faith to study day by day. Such is the practice of the author of Festus, whenever he is truly great. When he shows to us the end and plan of all things, we feel that he only hides them from us. He speaks only his wishes. But when he tells us of what he does really know, the moods and aspirations of fiery youth to which all things are made present in foresight and foretaste, — when he shows us the temptations of the lonely soul pining for knowl-

edge, but unable to feel the love that alone can bestow it, —
then he is truly great, and the strings of life thrill oftentimes
to their sublimest, sweetest music.

We admire in this author the unsurpassed force and distinctness with which he casts out single thoughts and images.
Each is thrown before us fresh, deep in its impress as if just
snatched from the forge. We admire not less his vast flow,
his sustained flight. His is a rich and spacious genius; it
gives us room; it is a palace home; we need not economize our joys; blessed be the royalty that welcomes us so
freely.

In simple transposition of the thought from the mind to the
paper, that wonder, even rarer than perfect,— that is, simple
expression, through the motions of the body, of the motions
of the soul, — we dare to say *no* writer excels him. Words
are no veil between us and him, but a luminous cloud that
upbears us both together.

So in touches of nature, in the tones of passion; he is absolute. There is nothing better, where it is good; we have the
very thing itself.

We are told by the critics that he has no ear, and, indeed,
when we listen for such, we perceive blemishes enough in the
movement of his line. But we did not perceive it before,
more than, when the Æolian was telling the secrets of that
most spirit-like minister of Nature that bloweth where it
listeth, and no man can trace it, we should attempt to divide
the tones and pauses into regular bars, and be disturbed when
we could not make a tune.

England has only two poets now that can be named near
him : these two are Tennyson and the author of "Philip Van
Artevelde." Tennyson is all that Bailey is not in melody and
voluntary finish, having no less than a Greek moderation in
declining all undertakings he is not sure of completing. Taylor, noble, an earnest seer, a faithful narrator of what he sees,
firm and sure, sometimes deep and exquisite, but in energy

and grandeur no more than Tennyson to be named beside the
author of Festus. In inspiration, in prophecy, in those flashes
of the sacred fire which reveal the secret places where Time
is elaborating the marvels of Nature, he stands alone. It is
just true what Ebenezer Elliott says, that "Festus contains
poetry enough to set up fifty poets," — ay ! even such poets,
so far as richness of thought and imagery are concerned, as
the two noble bards we have named.

But we need call none less to make him greater, whose
liberal soul is alive to every shade of beauty, every token of
greatness, and whose main stress is to seek a soul of goodness in things evil. The book is a precious, even a sacred
book, and we could say more of it, had we not years ago
vented our enthusiasm when it was in first full flow.

14

WE hear much lamentation among good people at the introduction of so many French novels among us, corrupting, they say, our youth by pictures of decrepit vice and prurient crime, such as would never, otherwise, be dreamed of here, and corrupting it the more that such knowledge is so precocious — for the same reason that a boy may be more deeply injured by initiation into wickedness than a man, for he is not only robbed of his virtue, but prevented from developing the strength that might restore it. But it is useless to bewail what is the inevitable result of the movement of our time. Europe must pour her corruptions, no less than her riches, on our shores, both in the form of books and of living men. She cannot, if she would, check the tide which bears them hitherward; no defences are possible, on our vast extent of shore, that can preclude their ingress. We have exulted in premature and hasty growth; we must brace ourselves to bear the evils that ensue. Our only hope lies in rousing, in our own community, a soul of goodness, a wise aspiration, that shall give us strength to assimilate this unwholesome food to better substance, or cast off its contaminations. A mighty sea of life swells within our nation, and, if there be salt enough, foreign bodies shall not have power to breed infection there.

We have had some opportunity to observe that the worst works offered are rejected. On the steamboats we have seen translations of vile books, bought by those who did not know

* Balzac, Eugene Sue, De Vigny.

from the names of their authors what to expect, torn, after a cursory glance at their contents, and scattered to the winds. Not even the all but all-powerful desire to get one's money's worth, since it had once been paid, could contend against the blush of shame that rose on the cheek of the reader.

It would be desirable for our people to know something of these writers, and of the position they occupy abroad ; for the nature of their circulation, rather than its extent, might be the guide both to translator and buyer. The object of the first is generally money ; of the last, amusement. But the merest mercenary might prefer to pass his time in translating a good book, and our imitation of Europe does not yet go so far that the American milliner can be depended on to copy any thing from the Parisian grisette, except her cap.

We have just been reading " Le Père Goriot," Balzac's most celebrated work ; a remarkable production, to which Paris alone, at the present day, could have given birth.

In other of his works, I have admired his skill in giving the minute traits of passion, and his intrepidity, not inferior to that of Le Sage and Cervantes, in facing the dark side of human nature. He reminds one of the Spanish romancers in the fearlessness with which he takes mud into his hands, and dips his foot in slime. We cannot endure this when done, as by most Frenchmen, with an air of recklessness and gayety ; but Balzac does it with the stern manliness of a Spaniard.

But the conception of this work is so sublime, that, though the details are even more revolting than in his others, you can bear it, and would not have missed your walk through the Catacombs, though the light of day seems stained afterwards with the mould of horror and dismay.

Balzac, we understand, is one of that wretched class of writers who live by the pen. In Paris they count now by thousands, and their leaves fall from the press thick-rustling

like the November forest.   I had heard of this class not without envy, for I had been told pretty tales of the gay poverty
of the Frenchman — how he will live in garrets, on dry bread,
salad, and some wine, and spend all his money on a single
good suit of clothes, in which, when the daily labor of copy-
ing music, correcting the press, or writing poems or novels, is
over, he sallies forth to enjoy the theatre, the social soirée, or
the humors of the streets and cafés, as gay, as keenly alive to
observation and enjoyment, as if he were to return to a well-
stocked table and a cheerful hearth, encompassed by happy
faces.

I thought the intellectual Frenchman, in the extreme of
want, never sunk into the inert reverie of the lazzaroni, nor
hid the vulture of famine beneath the mantle of pride with
the bitter mood of a Spaniard.   But Balzac evidently is
familiar with that which makes the agony of poverty — its
vulgarity.

Dirt, confusion, shabby expedients, living to live, — these
are what make poverty terrible and odious, and in these Balzac
would seem to have been steeped to the very lips.

These French writers possess the art of plunging at once
in medias res, and Balzac places you, in the twinkling of an
eye, in one of the lowest boarding-houses of Paris.   At first
all is dirt, hubbub, and unsavory odors; but from the vapors
of the caldron evolves a web of many-colored life, of terrible
pathos, and original humor, not unenlivened by pale golden
threads of beauty, which had better never been.

All the characters are excellently drawn : the harpy mistress of the house ; Mlle. Michonnet the spy, and her imbecile
lover ; Mme. Coutuner, with her purblind strivings after
virtue, and her real, though meagre respectability ; Vautrim,
the disguised galley-slave, with his cynical philosophy and ·
Bonaparte character ; and the young students of medicine,
cheering the dense fog with the scintillations of their wit, and

the joyousness and petulance with which their age meets the most adverse circumstances, at least in France !

The connection between this abject poverty and the highest luxury of Parisian life is made naturally by Eugene, connected to his misfortune with a noble family, of which his own is a poor and young branch, studying a profession and sighing to live like a duke, and *Le Père Goriot*, who has stripped himself of all his wealth for his daughters, who are more naturally unnatural than those of Lear. The transitions are made with as much swiftness as a curtain is drawn upon the stage, yet with no feeling of abruptness, so skilfully are the incidents woven into one another.

And be it recorded to the credit of Balzac, that, much as he appears to have suffered from the want of wealth, the vices which pollute it are represented with as terrible force as those of poverty.

The book affords play for similar powers, and brings a similar range of motives into action with Scott's " Fortunes of Nigel." If less rich than that work, it is more original, and has a force of pencil all its own.

Insight and a master's hand are admirable throughout; but the product of genius is *Le Père Goriot*. And, wonderful to relate, this character is as much ennobled, made as poetical by abandonment to a single instinct, as others by the force of will. Prometheus, chained on his rock, and giving his heart to the birds of prey for aims so majestic, is scarcely a more affecting, a more reverent object, than the rich confectioner whose intellect has never been awakened at all, except in the way of buying and selling, and who gives up his acuteness even there, and commits such unspeakable follies through paternal love ; a *blind* love too, nowise superior to that of the pelican !

Analyze it as you will, see the difference between this and the instinct of the artist or the philanthropist, and it produces on your mind the same impression of a present divinity. And

14 *

scarce any tears could be more sacred than those which choke the breath at the death-bed of this man, who forgot that he was a man, to be wholly a father, this poor, mad, stupid. father Goriot. I know nothing in fiction to surpass the terrible, unpretending pathos of this scene, nor the power with which the mistaken benediction given to the two medical students whom he takes for his daughters, is redeemed from burlesque.

The scepticism as to *virtue* in this book is fearful, but the love for innocence and beautiful instincts casts a softening tint over the gloom. We never saw any thing sweeter or more natural than the letters of the mother and sisters of Eugene, when they so delightfully sent him the money of which he had been wicked enough to plunder them. These traits of domestic life are given with much grace and delicacy of sentiment.

How few writers can paint *abandon*, without running into exaggeration! and here the task was one of peculiar difficulty. It seemed as if the writer were conscious enough of his power to propose to himself the most difficult task he could undertake.

A respectable reviewer in "Les Deux Mondes" would wish us to think that there is no life in Paris like what Balzac paints; but we can never believe that: evidently it is "too true," though we doubt not there is more redemption than he sees.

But this book was too much for our nerves, and would be, probably, for those of most people accustomed to breathe a healthier atmosphere.

Balzac has been a very fruitful writer, and, as he is fond of jugglers' tricks of every description, and holds nothing earnest or sacred, he is vain of the wonderful celerity with which some of his works, and those quite as good as any, have been written. They seem to have been conceived, composed, and written down with that degree of speed with which it is possible to lay pen to paper. Indeed, we think he cannot be surpassed in the ready and sustained command of his resources. His almost unequalled quickness and fidelity of eye, both as to the disposition of external objects, and the symptoms of human passion, combined with a strong memory, have filled his mind with materials, and we doubt not that if his thoughts could be put into writing with the swiftness of thought, he would give us one of his novels every week in the year.

Here end our praises of Balzac; what he is, as a man, in daily life, we know not. He must originally have had a heart, or he could not read so well the hearts of others; perhaps there are still private ties that touch him. But as a writer, never was the modern Méphistopheles, " the spirit that denieth," more worthily represented than by Balzac.

He combines the spirit of the man of science with that of the amateur collector. He delights to analyze, to classify; there is no anomaly too monstrous, no specimen too revolting, to insure his ardent but passionless scrutiny. But then he has taste and judgment to know what is fair, rare, and exquisite. He takes up such an object carefully, and puts it in a good light. But he has no hatred for what is loathsome, no contempt for what is base, no love for what is lovely, no faith in what is noble. To him there is no virtue and no vice; men and women are more or less finely organized; noble and tender conduct is more agreeable than the reverse, because it argues better health; that is all.

Nor is this from an intellectual calmness, nor from an unusual power of analyzing motives, and penetrating delusions merely; neither is it mere indifference. There is a touch of the demon, also, in Balzac, the cold but gayly familiar demon; and the smile of the amateur yields easily to a sneer, as he delights to show you on what foul juices the fair flower was fed. He is a thorough and willing materialist. The trance of religion is congestion of the brain; the joy of the poet the thrilling of the blood in the rapture of sense; and every good not only rises from, but hastens back into, the jaws of death and nothingness; a rainbow arch above a pestilential chaos!

Thus Balzac, with all his force and fulness of talent, never rises one moment into the region of genius. For genius is, in its nature, positive and creative, and cannot exist where there is no heart to believe in realities. Neither can he have a permanent influence on a nature which is not thoroughly corrupt. He might for a while stagger an ingenuous mind which had not yet thought for itself. But this could not last. His unbelief makes his thought too shallow. He has not that power which a mind, only in part sophisticated, may retain, where the heart still beats warmly, though it sometimes beats amiss. Write, paint, argue, as you will, where there is a sound spot in any human being, he cannot be made to believe that this present bodily frame is more than a temporary condition of his being, though one to which he may have become shamefully enslaved by fault of inheritance, education, or his own carelessness.

Taken in his own way, we know no modern tragedies more powerful than Balzac's "Eugenie Grandet," "Sweet Pea," "Search after the Absolute," "Father Goriot." See there goodness, aspiration, the loveliest instincts, stifled, strangled by fate, in the form of our own brute nature. The fate of the ancient Prometheus was happiness to that of these, who must pay, for ever having believed there was divine fire in heaven, by agonies of despair, and conscious degradation, unknown to those who began by believing man to be the most richly endowed of brutes — no more!

Balzac is admirable in his description of look, tone, gesture. He has a keen sense of whatever is peculiar to the individual. Nothing in modern romance surpasses the death-scene of Father Goriot, the Parisian Lear, in the almost immortal life with which the parental instincts are displayed. And with equal precision and delicacy of shading he will paint the slightest by-play in the manners of some young girl.

" Seraphitus " is merely a specimen of his great powers of intellectual transposition. Amid his delight at the botanical riches of the new and elevated region in which he is travelling, we catch, if only by echo, the hem and chuckle of the French materialist.

No more of him ! — We leave him to his suicidal work.

It is cheering to know how great is the influence such a writer as Sue exerts, from his energy of feeling on some subjects of moral interest. It is true that he has also much talent and a various experience of life ; but writers who far surpass him here, as we think Balzac does, wanting this heart of faith, have no influence, except merely on the tastes of their readers.

We observe, in a late notice of Sue, that he began to write at quite mature age, at the suggestion of a friend. We should think it was so ; that he was by nature intended for a practical man, rather than a writer. He paints all his characters from the practical point of view.

As an observer, when free from exaggeration, he has as good an eye as Balzac, but he is far more rarely thus free, for, in temperament, he is unequal and sometimes muddy. But then he has the heart and faith that Balzac wants, yet is less enslaved by emotion than Sand ; therefore he has made more impression on his time and place than either. We refer now to his later works ; though his earlier show much talent, yet his progress, both as a writer and thinker, has been so considerable that those of the last few years entirely eclipse his earlier essays.

These latter works are the " Mysteries of Paris," " Matilda," and the " Wandering Jew," which is now in course of publication. In these, he has begun, and is continuing, a crusade against the evils of a corrupt civilization which are inflicting such woes and wrongs upon his contemporaries.

Sue, however, does not merely assail, but would build up. His anatomy is not intended to injure the corpse, or, like that

of Balzac, to entertain the intellectual merely.   Earnestly he
hopes to learn from it the remedies for disease and the conditions of health.   Sue is a Socialist.   He believes he sees the
means by which the heart of mankind may be made to beat
with one great hope, one love ; and instinct with this thought,
his tales of horror are not tragedies.

This is the secret of the deep interest he has awakened in
this country, that he shares a hope which is, half unconsciously
to herself, stirring all her veins.   It is not so warmly out-
spoken as in other lands, both because no such pervasive ills
as yet call loudly for redress, and because private conserva-
tism is here great, in proportion to the absence of authorized
despotism.   We are not disposed to quarrel with this ; it is
well for the value of new thoughts to be tested by a good deal
of resistance.   Opposition, if it does not preclude free discussion, is of use in educating men to know what they want.
Only by intelligent men, exercised by thought and tried in
virtue, can such measures as Sue proposes be carried out ;
and when such associates present themselves in sufficient
numbers, we have no fear but the cause of association, in its
grander forms, will have fair play in America.

As a writer, Sue shows his want of a high kind of imagination by his unshrinking portraiture of physical horrors.   We
do not believe any man could look upon some things he describes and live.   He is very powerful in his description of
the workings of animal nature ; especially when he speaks
of them in animals merely, they have the simplicity of the
lower kind with the more full expression of human nature.
His pictures of women are of rare excellence, and it is observable that the more simple and pure the character is, the more
justice he does to it.   This shows that, whatever his career
may have been, his heart is uncontaminated.   Men he does
not describe so well, and fails entirely when he aims at one
grand and simple enough for a great moral agent.   His con-
ceptions are strong, but in execution he is too melodramatic.

Just compare *his* "Wandering Jew" with that of Beranger. The latter is as diamond compared with charcoal. Then, like all those writers who write in numbers that come out weekly or monthly, he abuses himself and his subject; he often *must;* the arrangement is false and mechanical.

The attitude of Sue is at this moment imposing, as he stands, pen in hand, — this his only weapon against an innumerable host of foes, — the champion of poverty, innocence, and humanity, against superstition, selfishness, and prejudice. When his works are forgotten, — and for all their strong points and brilliant decorations, they may ere long be forgotten, — still the writer's name shall be held in imperishable honor as the teacher of the ignorant, the guardian of the weak, a true tribune for the people of his own time.

One of the most unexceptionable and attractive writers of modern France is De Vigny. His life has been passed in the army; but many years of peace have given him time for literary culture, while his acquaintance with the traditions of the army, from the days of its dramatic achievements under Bonaparte, supply the finest materials both for narrative and reflection. His tales are written with infinite grace, refined sensibility, and a dignified view. His treatment of a subject shows that closeness of grasp and clearness of sight which are rarely attained by one who is not at home in active as well as thoughtful life. He has much penetration, too, and has touched some of the most delicate springs of human action. His works have been written in hours of leisure; this has diminished their number, but given him many advantages over the thousands of professional writers that fill the coffee-houses of Paris by day, and its garrets by night. We wish he were more read here in the original; with him would be found good French, and the manners, thoughts, and feelings of a cosmopolitan gentleman.

To sum up this imperfect account of the merits of these Novelists: I see De Vigny, a retiring figure, the gentleman, the solitary

thinker, but, in his way, the efficient foe of false honor and super-
stitious prejudice ; Balzac is the heartless surgeon, probing the
wounds and describing the delirium of suffering men for the
amusement of his students ; Sue, a bold and glittering crusader,
with endless ballads jingling in the silence of the night before
the battle. They are all much right and a good deal wrong ; for
instance, all who would lay down their lives for the sake of truth,
yet let their virtuous characters practise stratagems, falsehood,
and violence ; in fact, do evil for the sake of good.   They still
show this taint of the old régime, and no wonder!   La belle
France has worn rouge so long that the purest mountain air
will not, at once, or soon, restore the natural hues to her complexion.   But they are fine figures, and all ruled by the
onward spirit of the time.   Led by that spirit, I see them
moving on the troubled waters ; they do not sink, and I trust
they will find their way to the coasts where the new era will
introduce new methods, in a spirit of nobler activity, wiser
patience, and holier faith, than the world has yet seen.

Will Balzac also see that shore, or has he only broken away
the bars that hindered others from setting sail?   We do not
know.   When we read an expression of such lovely innocence
as the letter of the little country maidens to their Parisian
brother, (in Father Goriot,) we hope ; but presently we see
him sneering behind the mask, and we fear.   Let Frenchmen
speak to this question.   They know best what disadvantages a
Frenchman suffers under, and whether it is possible Balzac
be still alive, except in his eyes.   Those, we know, are quite
alive.

To read these, or any foreign works fairly, the reader must
understand the national circumstances under which they were
written.   To use them worthily, he must know how to interpret them for the use of the universe.

THE NEW SCIENCE, OR THE PHILOSOPHY OF MESMERISM OR ANIMAL MAGNETISM.*

MAN is always trying to get charts and directions for the super-sensual element in which he finds himself involuntarily moving. Sometimes, indeed, for long periods, a life of continual activity in supplying bodily wants or warding off bodily dangers will make him inattentive to the circumstances of this other life. Then, in an interval of leisure, he will start to find himself pervaded by the power of this more subtle and searching energy, and will turn his thoughts, with new force, to scrutinize its nature and its promises.

At such times a corps is formed of workmen, furnished with various implements for the work. Some collect facts from which they hope to build up a theory; others propose theories by whose light they hope to detect valuable facts; a large number are engaged in circulating reports of these labors; a larger in attempting to prove them invalid and absurd. These last are of some use by shaking the canker-worms from the trees; all are of use in elucidating truth.

Such a course of study has the civilized world been engaged in for some years back with regard to what is called Animal Magnetism. We say the civilized world, because, though a large portion of the learned and intellectual, to say nothing of the thoughtless and the prejudiced, view such researches as folly, yet we believe that those prescient souls, those minds more deeply alive, which are the life of this

---

* Etherology, or the Philosophy of Mesmerism and Phrenology: Including a New Philosophy of Sleep and of Consciousness, with a Review of the Pretensions of Neurology and Phreno-Magnetism. By J. Stanley Grimes.

15

and the parents of the next era, all, more or less, consciously or unconsciously, share the belief in such an agent as is understood by the largest definition of animal magnetism; that is, a means by which influence and thought may be communicated from one being to another, independent of the usual organs, and with a completeness and precision rarely attained through these.

For ourselves, since we became conscious at all of our connection with the two forms of being called the spiritual and material, we have perceived the existence of such an agent, and should have no doubts on the subject, if we had never heard one human voice in correspondent testimony with our perceptions. The reality of this agent we know, have tested some of its phenomena, but of its law and its analysis find ourselves nearly as ignorant as in earliest childhood. And we must confess that the best writers we have read seem to us about equally ignorant. We derive pleasure and profit in very unequal degrees from their statements, in proportion to their candor, clearness of perception, severity of judgment, and largeness of view. If they possess these elements of wisdom, their statements are valuable as affording materials for the true theory; but theories proposed by them affect us, as yet, only as partially sustained hypotheses. Too many among them are stained by faults which must prevent their coming to any valuable results, sanguine haste, jealous vanity, a lack of that profound devotion which alone can win Truth from her cold well, careless classification, abrupt generalizations. We see, as yet, no writer great enough for the patient investigation, in a spirit liberal yet severely true, which the subject demands. We see no man of Shakspearian, Newtonian incapability of deceiving himself or others.

However, no such man is needed, and we believe that it is pure democracy to rejoice that, in this department as in others, it is no longer some one great genius that concentrates within himself the vital energy of his time. It is many working together who do the work. The waters spring up in every direction, as little rills, each of which performs its part. We see a movement corresponding with this in the region of exact science, and we have no doubt that in the course of fifty years a new spiritual circulation will be comprehended as clearly as the circulation of the blood is now. •

In metaphysics, in phrenology, in animal magnetism, in electricity, in chemistry, the tendency is the same, even when conclusions seem most dissonant. The mind presses nearer home to the seat of consciousness the more intimate law and rule of life, and old limits, become fluid beneath the fire of thought. We are learning much, and it will be a grand music, that shall be played on this organ of many pipes.

With regard to Mr. Grimes's book, in the first place, we do not possess sufficient knowledge of the subject to criticise it thoroughly; and secondly, if we did, it could not be done in narrow limits. To us his classification is unsatisfactory, his theory inadequate, his point of view uncongenial. We disapprove of the spirit in which he criticises other disciples in this science, who have, we believe, made some good observations, with many failures, though, like himself, they do not hold themselves sufficiently lowly as disciples. For we do not believe there is any man, *yet*, who is entitled to give himself the air of having taken a degree on this subject. We do not want the tone of qualification or mincing apology. We want no mock modesty, but its reality, which is the almost sure attendant on greatness. What a lesson it would be for this country if a body of men could be at work together in that harmony which would not fail to ensue on a *disinterested* love of discovering truth, and with that patience and exactness in experiment without which no machine was ever invented worthy a patent! The most superficial, go-ahead, hit-or-miss American knows that no machine was ever perfected without this patience and exactness; and let no one hope to achieve victories in the realm of mind at a cheaper rate than in that of matter.

In speaking thus of Mr. Grimes's book, we can still cordially recommend it to the perusal of our readers. Its statements are full and sincere. The writer has abilities which only need to be used with more thoroughness and a higher aim to guide him to valuable attainments.

In this connection we will relate a passage from personal experience, to us powerfully expressive of the nature of this higher agent in the intercourse of minds.

Some years ago I went, unexpectedly, into a house where a blind girl, thought at that time to have attained an extraordinary degree of clairvoyance, lay in a trance of somnambulism. I was not invited there, nor known to the party, but accompanied a gentleman who was.

The somnambulist was in a very happy state. On her lips was the satisfied smile, and her features expressed the gentle elevation incident to the state. At that time I had never seen any one in it, and had formed no image or opinion on the subject. I was agreeably impressed by the somnambulist, but on listening to the details of her observations on a distant place, I thought she had really no vision, but was merely led or impressed by the mind of the person who held her hand.

After a while I was beckoned forward, and my hand given to the blind girl. The latter instantly dropped it with an expression of pain, and complained that she should have been brought in contact with a person so sick, and suffering at that moment under violent nervous headache. This really was the case, but no one present could have been aware of it.

After a while the somnambulist seemed penitent and troubled. She asked again for my hand which she had rejected, and, while holding it, attempted to magnetize the sufferer. She seemed touched by profound pity, spoke most intelligently of the disorder of health and its causes, and gave advice, which, if followed at that time, I have every reason to believe would have remedied the ill.

Not only the persons present, but the person advised also,

had no adequate idea then of the extent to which health was affected, nor saw fully, till some time after, the justice of what was said by the somnambulist. There is every reason to believe that neither she, nor the persons who had the care of her, knew even the name of the person whom she so affectionately wished to help.

Several years after, in visiting an asylum for the blind, I saw this same girl seated there. She was no longer a somnambulist, though, from a nervous disease, very susceptible to magnetic influences. I went to her among a crowd of strangers, and shook hands with her as several others had done. I then asked, " Do you not not know me?" She answered, " No." " Do you not remember ever to have met me?" She tried to recollect, but still said, "No." I then addressed a few remarks to her about her situation there, but she seemed preoccupied, and, while I turned to speak with some one else, wrote with a pencil these words, which she gave me at parting : —

> "The ills that Heaven decrees
> The brave with courage bear."

Others may explain this as they will ; to me it was a token that the same affinity that had acted before, gave the same knowledge; for the writer was at the time ill in the same way as before. It also seemed to indicate that the somnambulic trance was only a form of the higher development, the sensibility to more subtle influences — in the terms of Mr. Grimes, a susceptibility to etherium. The blind girl perhaps never knew who I was, but saw my true state more clearly than any other person did, and I have kept those pencilled lines, written in the stiff, round character proper to the blind, as a talisman of " Credenciveness," as the book before me styles it, Credulity as the world at large does, and. to my own mind, as one of the clews granted, during this earthly life, to the mysteries of future states of being, and more rapid and complete modes of intercourse between mind and mind.

DEUTSCHE SCHNELLPOST.*

THE publishers of this interesting and spirited journal have, this year, begun to issue a weekly paper in addition to their former arrangement. We regret not to have been able earlier to take some notice of their prospectus, but an outline of it will be new to most of our readers.

Their journal has hitherto been intended for German readers in this country, and has been devoted to topics of European interest, but by the addition of the Weekly, it hopes to discuss with some fulness those of American interest also ; thus becoming "an organ of communication between Germans of the old and new home, as to their wants, interests, and thoughts." These judicious remarks follow : —

" The editors do not coincide with those who believe it the vocation of the immigrant German, by systematic separation from the people who offer him a new home, by voluntary withdrawal from the unaccustomed, and, perhaps, for him too vehement stream of their life, in a word, by obstinate adhesion to the old, to keep inviolate the stamp of his nationality.

" Rather is it their faith that it should be the most earnest desire of the immigrant, not merely to appropriate in form, but to *deserve* the rights of a citizen here — rights which we confide in the healthy mind of the nation to sustain him in, all fanatical opposition to the contrary notwithstanding. And he must deserve them by becoming an American, not merely

* A German newspaper.

(174)

in name, but in deed, not merely by assuming claims, but by appreciating duties.

" But while we renounce this narrow and one-sided isolation, desiring to integrate ourselves, fairly and truly, with the great family that receives us to its hospitality, we will hold so much the more firmly to the higher traits of our own race. We hold to the noble jewel of our native tongue ; the memories of our nation's ancient glory ; the sympathy with its future, as yet only glimmering in the dusk ; our old, true, domestic manners ; dear inherited customs, that give to the tranquillities of home their sanctity — to the intercourse between men a fresh, glad life.

" So much for our position in general."

They promise, as to American affairs, " to be just as far as in them lies, and independent, certainly."

We think the tone of these remarks truly honorable and right-minded. It is such a tone that each division of our adopted citizens needs to hear from those of their compatriots able to guide and enlighten them. We do want that each nation should preserve what is valuable in its parent stock. We want all the elements for the new people of the new world. We want the prudence, the honor, the practical skill of the English ; the fun, the affectionateness, the generosity of the Irish ; the vivacity, the grace, the quick intelligence of the French ; the thorough honesty, the capacity for philosophic view, and deep enthusiasm of the German Biedermann ; the shrewdness and romance of the Scotch,— but we want none of their prejudices. We want the healthy seed to develop itself into a different plant in the new climate. We have reason to hope a new and generous race, where the Italian meets the German, the Swede, the Jew. Let nothing be obliterated, but all be regenerated ; let each leader say in like manner to his band, Apply the old loyalty to a study of new duties. Examine yourself whether you are worthy of the new rights so freely bestowed upon you, and recognize that only intelligent action, and not mere bodily presence, can make you really a citizen on any soil. It is a glorious boon offered you to be a founder of the new dynasty in the new world; but it would have been better for you to have died a thousand deaths beneath the factory wheels of England, or in the prisons of Russia, than to sell this great privilege for selfish or servile ends. Here each man has before him the choice of Esau — each may defraud a long succession of souls of their princely inheritance.

Do those whose bodies were born upon this soil reject you, and claim for themselves the name of natives? You may be natives, in another sort, for the soul may be re-born here. Cast for yourselves a new nativity, and invoke the starry influences that do not fail to shine into the life of a good man, whose heart is kept open daily to truth in every new form, whose heart is strengthened by a desire to do his duty valiantly to every brother of the human family. Offer upon the soil a libation of worthy feelings in gratitude for the bread it so willingly yields you, and it is true that the "healthy mind of the nation" cannot long fail to greet you with joy, and hail your endowment with civic rights.

We must think there is a deep root, in fact, for the late bitter expressions of prejudice, however unworthy the mode of exhibiting them, against the foreign element in our population. We want all this new blood, but we want it purified, assimilated, or it will take all form of comeliness from the growing nation. Our country is a willing foster mother, but her children need wise tutors to prevent them from playing, willingly or unwillingly, the viper's part.

There is a little poem in the Schnellpost, by Mority Hartmann, called the "Three,"— which would be a forcible appeal, if any were needed, in behalf of all who are exiled from their native soil. We translate it into prose, and this will not spoil it, as its poetry lies in the situation.

"In a tavern of Hungary are sitting together Three who

have taken refuge there from storm and darkness — in Hungary, where the wind of chance drives together the children of many a land.

"Their eyes glow with fires of various light; their locks are unlike in their flow; but their hearts — their wounded hearts — are urns filled with the tears of a common grief.

"One cries, ' Silent companions! Shall we have no toast to cheer our meeting? I offer you one which you cannot fail to pledge — Freedom and greatness to the Fatherland!

" ' To the fatherland! But I am one that knows not where is his; I am a Gypsy; my fatherland lies in the realm of tradition — in the mournful tone of the violin swelled by grief and storm.

" ' I pass musing over heath and moor, and think of my painful losses. Yet long since was I weaned from desire of a home, and think of Egypt but as the cymbal sounds.'

"The second says, ' This toast of fatherland I will not drink; mine own shame should I pledge. For the seed of Jacob flies like the dried leaf, and takes no root in the dust of slavery.'

"The lips of the third seem frozen at the edge of his goblet. He asks himself in silence, ' Shall *I* drink to the fatherland? Lives Poland yet, or is all life departed, and am I, like these, a motherless son?'"

To those and others who, if they still had homes, could not live there, without starving body and soul, may our land be a fatherland; and may they seek and learn to act as children in a father's house!

A foreign correspondent of the Schnellpost, having, it seems, been reproved by some friends on the safe side of the water for the violence of his attack on crowned heads, and other dilettanti, defends himself with great spirit, and argues his case well from his own point of view. We do not agree with him as to the use of methods, but cannot fail to sympathize in his feeling.

Anecdotes of Russian proceedings towards delinquents are well associated with one anecdote quoted of Peter, who yet was truly the Great. In a foreign city, seeing the gallows, he asked the use of that three-cornered thing. Being told, to hang people on, he requested that one might be hung for him, directly. Being told this, unfortunately, could not be done, as there was no criminal under sentence, he desired that one of his own retinue might be made use of. Probably he did this with no further thought than the Empress Catharine bestowed, on having a ship of the line blown up, as a model for the painter who was to adorn her palace with pictures of naval battles. Disregard for human life and human happiness is not confined to the Russian snows, or the eastern hemisphere; it may be found on every side, though, indeed, not on a scale so imperial.

A LONG expectation is rewarded at last by the appearance of this book. We cannot wonder that it should have been long, when Mr. Carlyle shows us what a world of ill-arranged and almost worthless materials he has had to wade through before achieving any possibility of order and harmony for his narrative.

The method which he has chosen of letting the letters and speeches of Cromwell tell the story when possible, only himself doing what is needful to throw light where it is most wanted and fill up gaps, is an excellent one. Mr. Carlyle, indeed, is a most peremptory showman, and with each slide of his magic lantern informs us not only of what is necessary to enable us to understand it, but *how* we must look at it, under peril of being ranked as "imbeciles," "canting scep-tics," "disgusting rose-water philanthropists," and the like. And aware of his power of tacking a nickname or ludicrous picture to any one who refuses to obey, we might perhaps feel ourselves, if in his neighborhood, under such constraint and fear of deadly laughter, as to lose the benefit of having under our eye to form our judgment upon the same materials on which he formed his.

But the ocean separates us, and the showman has his own audience of despised victims, or scarce less despised pupils; and we need not fear to be handed down to posterity as "a little gentleman in a gray coat" "shrieking" unutterable "im-becilities," or with the like damnatory affixes, when we profess

* Letters and Speeches of Oliver Cromwell, by Thomas Carlyle.

that, having read the book, and read the letters and speeches thus far, we cannot submit to the showman's explanation of the lantern, but must, more than ever, stick to the old " Philistine," " Dilettante," " Imbecile," and what not view of the character of Cromwell.

We all know that to Mr. Carlyle greatness is well nigh synonymous with virtue, and that he has shown himself a firm believer in Providence by receiving the men of destiny as always entitled to reverence. Sometimes a great success has followed the portraits painted by him in the light of such faith, as with regard to Mahomet, for instance. The natural autocrat is his delight, and in such pictures as that of the monk in " Past and Present," where the geniuses of artist and subject coincide, the result is no less delightful for us.

But Mr. Carlyle reminds us of the man in a certain parish who had always looked up to one of its squires as a secure and blameless idol, and one day in church, when the minister asked " all who felt in concern for their souls to rise," looked to the idol and seeing him retain his seat, (asleep perchance!) sat still also. One of his friends asking him afterwards how he could refuse to answer such an appeal, he replied, " he thought it safest to stay with the squire."

Mr. Carlyle's squires are all Heaven's justices of peace or war, (usually the latter;) they are beings of true energy and genius, and so far, as he describes them, " genuine men." But in doubtful cases, where the doubt is between them and principles, he will insist that the men must be in the right. On such occasions he favors us with such doctrine as the following, which we confess we had the weakness to read with " sibylline execration " and extreme disgust.

Speaking of Cromwell's course in Ireland : —

" Oliver's proceedings here have been the theme of much loud criticism, sibylline execration, into which it is not our plan to enter at present. We shall give these fifteen letters of his in a mass, and without any commentary whatever. To those who think that a land overrun with sanguinary quacks can be healed by sprinkling it with rose-water, these letters must be very horrible. Terrible surgery this; but *is* it surgery and judgment, or atrocious murder merely? This is a question which should be asked; and answered. Oliver Cromwell did believe in God's judgments; and did not believe in the rose-water plan of surgery, — which, in fact, is this editor's case too! Every idle lie and piece of empty bluster this editor hears, he too, like Oliver, has to shudder at it; has to think, 'Thou, idle bluster, not true, thou also art shutting men's minds against God's fact; thou wilt issue as a cleft crown to some poor man some day; thou also wilt have to take shelter in bogs, whither cavalry cannot follow!' But in Oliver's time, as I say, there was still belief in the judgments of God; in Oliver's time, there was yet no distracted jargon of 'abolishing capital punishments,' of Jean-Jacques philanthropy, and universal rose-water in this world still so full of sin. Men's notion was, not for abolishing punishments, but for making laws just. God the Maker's laws, they considered, had not yet got the punishment abolished from them! Men had a notion that the difference between good and evil was still considerable — equal to the difference between heaven and hell. It was a true notion, which all men yet saw, and felt, in all fibres of their existence, to be true. Only in late decadent generations, fast hastening toward radical change or final perdition, can such indiscriminate mashing up of good and evil into one universal patent treacle, and most unmedical electuary, of Rousseau sentimentalism, universal pardon and benevolence, with dinner and drink and one cheer more, take effect in our earth. Electuary very poisonous, as sweet as it is, and very nauseous; of which Oliver, happier than we, had not yet heard the slightest intimation even in dreams.

*   *   *

" In fact, Oliver's dialect is rude and obsolete; the phrases

16

of Oliver, to him solemn on the perilous battle field as voices
of God, have become to us most mournful when spouted as
frothy cant from Exeter Hall.   The reader has, all along, to
make steady allowance for that.   And on the whole, clear
recognition will be difficult for him.   To a poor slumberous
canting age, mumbling to itself every where, Peace, peace,
when there is no peace, — such a phenomena as Oliver, in
Ireland or elsewhere, is not the most recognizable in all its
meanings.   But it waits there for recognition, and can wait
an age or two.   The memory of Oliver Cromwell, as I count,
has a good many centuries in it yet; and ages of very varied
complexion to apply to, before all end.   My reader, in this
passage and others, shall make of it what he can.

" But certainly, at lowest, here is a set of military despatches of the most unexampled nature !   Most rough, un-
kempt; shaggy as the Numidian lion.   A style rugged as
crags; coarse, drossy: yet with a meaning in it, an energy,
a depth; pouring on like a fire torrent; perennial *fire* of it
visible athwart all drosses and defacements; not uninteresting
to see !   This man has come into distracted Ireland with a
God's truth in the heart of him, though an unexpected one;
the first such man they have seen for a great while indeed.
He carries acts of Parliament, laws of earth and heaven, in
one hand; drawn sword in the other.   He addresses the bewildered Irish populations, the black ravening coil of sanguinary blustering individuals at Tredah and elsewhere: ' Sanguinary, blustering individuals, whose word is grown worthless as the barking of dogs; whose very thought is false, representing no fact, but the contrary of fact — behold, I am
come to speak and to do the truth among you.   Here are acts
in Parliament, methods of regulation and veracity, emblems
the nearest we poor Puritans could make them of God's law-
book, to which it is and shall be our perpetual effort to make
them correspond nearer and nearer.   Obey them, help us to
perfect them, be peaceable and true under them, it shall be

well with you. Refuse to obey them, I will not let you continue living! As articulate speaking veracious orderly men,
not as a blustering, murderous kennel of dogs run rabid, shall
you continue in this earth. Choose!' They chose to disbe-
lieve him ; could not understand that he, more than the others,
meant any truth or justice to them. They rejected his sum-
mons and terms at Tredah ; he stormed the place; and, according to his promise, put every man of the garrison to death.
His own soldiers are forbidden to plunder, by paper proclama-
tion ; and in ropes of authentic hemp, they are hanged when
they do it. To Wexford garrison, the like terms as at Tredah ; and, failing these, the like storm. Here is a man whose
word represents a thing! Not bluster this, and false jargon
scattering itself to the winds ; what this man speaks out of
him comes to pass as a fact ; speech with this man is accurately prophetic of deed. This is the first king's face poor
Ireland ever saw ; the first friend's face, *little as it recognizes
him* — poor Ireland ! "

Yes, Cromwell had force and sagacity to get that done
which he had resolved to get done ; and this is the whole truth
about your admiration, Mr. Carlyle. Accordingly, at Drog-
heda quoth Cromwell, —

" I believe we put to sword the whole number of the defend-
ants. * * Indeed, being in the heat of action, I forbade
them to spare any that were in arms in the town ; and I think
that night they put to the sword about two thousand men,
divers of the officers and soldiers being fled over the bridge
into the other part of the town ; and where about one hundred of them possessed St. Peter's Church, steeple, &c.
These, being summoned to yield to mercy, refused. Where-
upon I ordered the steeple of St. Peter's Church to be fired ;
when one of them was heard to say, in the midst of the flames,
God confound me ! I burn, I burn !'

" I am persuaded that this is a righteous judgment of God

upon these barbarous wretches who have imbrued their hands
in so much innocent blood ; and that it will tend to prevent
the effusion of blood for the future.   Which are the satisfactory grounds to such actions, which otherwise cannot but work
remorse and regret.   *   *   This hath been an exceeding
great mercy."

Certainly one not of the rose-water or treacle kind.   Mr.
Carlyle says such measures "cut to the heart of the war,"
and brought peace.   Was there *then* no crying of Peace,
Peace, when there was no peace ?   Ask the Irish peasantry
why they mark that period with the solemn phrase of "Cromwell's Curse ! "

For ourselves, though aware of the mistakes and errors in
particulars that must occur, we believe the summing up of a
man's character in the verdict of his time, is likely to be correct.   We believe that Cromwell was "a curse," as much as
a blessing, in these acts of his.   We believe him ruthless,
ambitious, half a hypocrite, (few men have courage or want
of soul to bear being wholly so,) and we think it is rather too
bad to rave at us in our time for canting, and then hold up
the prince of canters for our reverence in his "dimly seen
nobleness."   Dimly, indeed, despite the rhetoric and satire
of Mr. Carlyle !

In previous instances where Mr. Carlyle has acted out his
predeterminations as to the study of a character, we have seen
circumstances favor him, at least sometimes.   There were fine
moments, fine lights upon the character that he would seize
upon.   But here the facts look just as they always have.   He
indeed ascertains that the Cromwell family were not mere
brewers or plebeians, but "substantial gentry," and that there
is not the least ground for the common notion that Cromwell lived at any time a dissolute life.   But with the exception of these emendations, still the history looks as of old.
We see a man of strong and wise mind, educated by the pres-

sure of great occasions to station of command; we see him wearing the religious garb which was the custom of the times, and even preaching to himself as well as to others — for well can we imagine that his courage and his pride would have fallen without keeping up the illusion; but we never see Heaven answering his invocations in any way that can interfere with the rise of his fortunes or the accomplishment of his plans. To ourselves, the tone of these religious holdings-forth is sufficiently expressive; they all ring hollow; we have never read any thing of the sort more repulsive to us than the letter to Mr. Hammond, which Mr. Carlyle thinks such a noble contrast to the impiety of the present time. Indeed, we cannot recover from our surprise at Mr. Carlyle's liking these letters; his predetermination must have been strong indeed. Again, we see Cromwell ruling with the strong arm, and carrying the spirit of monarchy to an excess which no Stuart could surpass. Cromwell, indeed, is wise, and the king he had punished with death is foolish; Charles is faithless, and Cromwell crafty; we see no other difference. Cromwell does not, in power, abide by the principles that led him to it; and we can't help — so rose-water imbecile are we! — admiring those who do: one Lafayette, for instance — poor chevalier so despised by Mr. Carlyle — for abiding by his principles, though impracticable, more than Louis Philippe, who laid them aside, so far as necessary, "to secure peace to the kingdom;" and to us it looks black for one who kills kings to grow to be more kingly than a king.

The death of Charles I. was a boon to the world, for it marked the dawn of a new era, when kings, in common with other men, are to be held accountable by God and mankind for what they do. Many who took part in this act which *did* require a courage and faith almost unparalleled, were, no doubt, moved by the noblest sense of duty. We doubt not this had its share in the bosom counsels of Cromwell. But

16 *

we cannot sympathize with the apparent satisfaction of Mr. Carlyle in seeing him engaged, two days after the execution, in marriage treaty for his son. This seems more ruthlessness than calmness. One who devoted so many days to public fasting and prayer, on less occasions, might well make solemn pause on this. Mr. Carlyle thinks much of some pleasant domestic letters from Cromwell. What brigand, what pirate, fails to have some such soft and light feelings?

In short, we have no time to say all we think; but we stick to the received notions of Old Noll, with his great, red nose, hard heart, long head, and crafty ambiguities. Nobody ever doubted his great abilities and force of will; neither doubt we that he was made an "instrument" just as he professeth. But as to looking on him through Mr. Carlyle's glasses, we shall not be sneered or stormed into it, unless he has other proof to offer than is shown yet. And we resent the violence he offers both to our prejudices and our perceptions. If he has become interested in Oliver, or any other pet hyena, by studying his habits, is that any reason we should admit him to our Pantheon? No! our imbecility shall keep fast the door against any thing short of proofs that in the hyena a god is incarnated. Mr. Carlyle declares that he sees it, but we really cannot. The hyena is surely not out of the kingdom of God, but as to being the finest emblem of what is divine — no, no!

In short, we can sympathize with the words of John Maidstone: —

"He [Cromwell] was a strong man in the dark perils of war; in the high places of the field, hope shone in him like a pillar of fire, when it had gone out in the others" — a poetic and sufficient account of the secret of his power.

But Mr. Carlyle goes on to gild the refined gold thus: —

"A genuine king among men, Mr. Maidstone! The divinest

sight this world sees, when it is privileged to see such, and not be sickened with the unholy apery of such."

We know you do with all your soul love kings and heroes, Mr. Carlyle, but we are not sure you would always know the Sauls from the Davids. We fear, if you had the disposal of the holy oil, you would be tempted to pour it on the head of him who is taller by the head than all his brethren, without sufficient care as to purity of inward testimony.

Such is the impression left on us by the book thus far, as to the view of its hero; but as to what difficulties attended the writing the history of Cromwell, the reader will like to see what Mr. Carlyle himself says : —

"These authentic utterances of the man Oliver himself — I have gathered them from far and near; fished them up from the foul Lethean quagmires where they lay buried; I have washed, or endeavored to wash, them clean from foreign stupidities, (such a job of buck-washing as I do not long to repeat;) and the world shall now see them in their own shape."

For the rest, this book is of course entertaining, witty, dramatic, picturesque; all traits that are piquant, many that have profound interest, are brought out better than new. The "letters and speeches" are put into readable state, and this alone is a great benefit. They are a relief after Mr. Carlyle's high-seasoned writing; and this again is a relief after their long-winded dimnesses. Most of the heroic anecdotes of the time had been used up before, but they lose nothing in the hands of Carlyle; and pictures of the scenes, such as of Naseby fight, for instance, it was left to him to give. We have passed over the hackneyed ground attended by a torch-bearer, who has given a new animation to the procession of events, and cast a ruddy glow on many a striking physiognomy. That any truth of high value has been brought to light, we do not perceive — certainly nothing has been added to our own sense of the greatness of the times, nor any new view presented that we can adopt, as to the position and character of the agents.

We close with the only one of Cromwell's letters that we really like. Here his religious words and his temper seem quite sincere.

" To my loving Brother, Colonel Valentine Walton : These.
July, 1644.

"DEAR SIR : It's our duty to sympathize in all mercies; and to praise the Lord together in chastisements or trials, so that we may sorrow together.

"Truly England and the church of God hath had a great favor from the Lord, in this great victory given unto us, such as the like never was since this war began. It had all the evidences of an absolute victory obtained by the Lord's blessing upon the godly party principally. We never charged but we routed the enemy. The left wing, which I commanded, being our own horse, saving a few Scots in our rear, beat all the prince's horse. God make them as stubble to our swords. We charged their regiments of foot with our horse, and routed all we charged. The particulars I cannot relate now ; but I believe, of twenty thousand, the prince hath not four thousand left. Give glory, all the glory, to God.

"Sir, God hath taken away your eldest son by a cannon-shot. It brake his leg. We were necessitated to have it cut off, whereof he died.

"Sir, you know my own trials this way ;* but the Lord supported me with this, that the Lord took him into the happiness we all pant for and live for. There is your precious child, full of glory, never to know sin or sorrow any more. He was a gallant young man, exceedingly gracious. God give you his comfort. Before his death he was so full of

---

* I conclude the poor boy Oliver has already fallen in these wars ; none of *us* knows where, though his father well knew.

comfort, that to Frank Russel and myself he could not express it, 'it was so great above his pain.' This he said to us. Indeed it was admirable. A little after, he said one thing lay upon his spirit. I asked him what that was. He told me it was, that God had not suffered him to be any more the executioner of his enemies. At his fall, his horse being killed with the bullet, and, as I am informed, three horses more, I am told he bid them open to the right and left, that he might see the rogues run. Truly he was exceedingly beloved in the army, of all that knew him. But few knew him; for he was a precious young man, fit for God. You have cause to bless the Lord. He is a glorious saint in heaven; wherein you ought exceedingly to rejoice. Let this drink up your sorrow; seeing these are not feigned words to comfort you, but the thing is so real and undoubted a truth. You may do all things by the strength of Christ. Seek that, and you shall easily bear your trial. Let this public mercy to the church of God make you to forget your private sorrow. The Lord be your strength; so prays

"Your truly faithful and loving brother,

"OLIVER CROMWELL."

And add this noble passage, in which Carlyle speaks of the morbid affection of Cromwell's mind : —

"In those years it must be that Dr. Simcott, physician in Huntingdon, had to do with Oliver's hypochondriac maladies. He told Sir Philip Warwick, unluckily specifying no date, or none that has survived, 'he had often been sent for at midnight;' Mr. Cromwell for many years was very 'splenetic,' (spleen-struck,) often thought he was just about to die, and also 'had fancies about the Town Cross.' * Brief intimation, of which the reflective reader may make a great deal. Samuel Johnson too had hypochondrias; all great souls are apt to

* Sir Philip Warwick's Memoirs, (London, 1701,) p. 249.

have; and to be in thick darkness generally, till the eternal ways and the celestial guiding stars disclose themselves, and the vague abyss of life knit itself up into firmaments for them. The temptations in the wilderness, choices of Hercules, and the like, in succinct or loose form, are appointed for every man that will assert a soul in himself and be a man. Let Oliver take comfort in his dark sorrows and melancholies. The quantity of sorrow he has, does it not mean withal the quantity of *sympathy* he has, the quantity of faculty and victory he shall yet have? 'Our sorrow is the inverted image of our nobleness.' The depth of our despair measures what capability, and height of claim, we have to hope. Black smoke as of Tophet filling all your universe, it can yet by true heart-energy become *flame*, and brilliancy of heaven. Courage!"

Were the flame but a pure as well as a bright flame! Sometimes we know the black phantoms change to white angel forms; the vulture is metamorphosed into a dove. Was it so in this instance? Unlike Mr. Carlyle, we are willing to let each reader judge for himself; but perhaps we should not be so generous if we had studied ourselves sick in wading through . all that mass of papers, and had nothing to defend us against the bitterness of biliousness, except a growing enthusiasm about our hero.

At the distance of three years this volume follows the first series of Essays, which have already made to themselves a circle of readers, attentive, thoughtful, more and more intelligent; and this circle is a large one if we consider the circumstances of this country, and of England also, at this time.

In England it would seem there are a larger number of persons waiting for an invitation to calm thought and sincere intercourse than among ourselves. Copies of Mr. Emerson's first published little volume called "Nature," have there been sold by thousands in a short time, while one edition has needed seven years to get circulated here. Several of his orations and essays from the "Dial" have also been republished there, and met with a reverent and earnest response.

We suppose that while in England the want of such a voice is as great as here, a larger number are at leisure to recognize that want; a far larger number have set foot in the speculative region, and have ears refined to appreciate these melodious accents.

Our people, heated by a partisan spirit, necessarily occupied in these first stages by bringing out the material resources of the land, not generally prepared by early training for the enjoyment of books that require attention and reflection, are still more injured by a large majority of writers and speakers, who lend all their efforts to flatter corrupt tastes and mental indolence, instead of feeling it their prerogative and their duty to admonish the community of the danger and

---

* Essays, Second Series, by Ralph Waldo Emerson.

arouse it to nobler energy. The plan of the popular writer or lecturer is not to say the best he knows in as few and well-chosen words as he can, making it his first aim to do justice to the subject. Rather he seeks to beat out a thought as thin as possible, and to consider what the audience will be most willing to receive.

The result of such a course is inevitable. Literature and art must become daily more degraded; philosophy cannot exist. A man who feels within his mind some spark of genius, or a capacity for the exercises of talent, should consider himself as endowed with a sacred commission. He is the natural priest, the shepherd of the people. He must raise his mind as high as he can towards the heaven of truth, and try to draw up with him those less gifted by nature with ethereal lightness. If he does not so, but rather employs his powers to flatter them in their poverty, and to hinder aspiration by useless words, and a mere seeming of activity, his sin is great; he is false to God, and false to man.

Much of this sin indeed is done ignorantly. The idea that literature calls men to the genuine hierarchy is almost forgotten. One, who finds himself able, uses his pen, as he might a trowel, solely to procure himself bread, without having reflected on the position in which he thereby places himself.

Apart from the troop of mercenaries, there is one, still larger, of those who use their powers merely for local and temporary ends, aiming at no excellence other than may conduce to these. Among these rank persons of honor and the best intentions; but they neglect the lasting for the transient, as a man neglects to furnish his mind that he may provide the better for the house in which his body is to dwell for a few years.

At a period when these sins and errors are prevalent, and threaten to become more so, how can we sufficiently prize and honor a mind which is quite pure from such? When, as in the

present case, we find a man whose only aim is the discernment
and interpretation of the spiritual laws by which we live, and
move, and have our being, all whose objects are permanent,
and whose every word stands for a fact.

If only as a representative of the claims of individual culture in a nation which is prone to lay such stress on artificial
organization and external results, Mr. Emerson would be in-
valuable here. History will inscribe his name as a father of
his country, for he is one who pleads her cause against herself.

If New England may be regarded as a chief mental focus
to the New World, — and many symptoms seem to give her this
place, — as to other centres belong the characteristics of heart
and lungs to the body politic ; if we may believe, as we
do believe, that what is to be acted out, in the country at
large, is, most frequently, first indicated there, as all the phenomena of the nervous system are in the fantasies of the brain,
we may hail as an auspicious omen the influence Mr. Emerson has there obtained, which is deep-rooted, increasing, and,
over the younger portion of the community, far greater than
that of any other person.

His books are received there with a more ready intelligence than elsewhere, partly because his range of personal
experience and illustration applies to that region ; partly because he has prepared the way for his books to be read by
his great powers as a speaker.

The audience that waited for years upon the lectures, a
part of which is incorporated into these volumes of Essays,
was never large, but it was select, and it was constant. Among
the hearers were some, who, though, attracted by the beauty
of character and manner, they were willing to hear the speaker
through, yet always went away discontented. They were accustomed to an artificial method, whose scaffolding could easily
be retraced, and desired an obvious sequence of logical inferences. They insisted there was nothing in what they had
heard, because they could not give a clear account of its

course and purport. They did not see that Pindar's odes might be very well arranged for their own purpose, and yet not bear translating into the methods of Mr. Locke.

Others were content to be benefited by a good influence, without a strict analysis of its means. " My wife says it is about the elevation of human nature, and so it seems to me," was a fit reply to some of the critics. Many were satisfied to find themselves excited to congenial thought and nobler life, without an exact catalogue of the thoughts of the speaker.

Those who believed no truth could exist, unless encased by the burrs of opinion, went away utterly baffled. Sometimes they thought he was on their side; then presently would come something on the other. He really seemed to believe there were two sides to every subject, and even to intimate higher ground, from which each might be seen to have an infinite number of sides or bearings, an impertinence not to be endured! The partisan heard but once, and returned no more.

But some there were, — simple souls, — whose life had been, perhaps, without clear light, yet still a-search after truth for its own sake, who were able to receive what followed on the suggestion of a subject in a natural manner, as a stream of thought. These recognized, beneath the veil of words, the still small voice of conscience, the vestal fires of lone religious hours, and the mild teachings of the summer woods.

The charm of the elocution, too, was great. His general manner was that of the reader, occasionally rising into direct address or invocation in passages where tenderness or majesty demanded more energy. At such times both eye and voice called on a remote future to give a worthy reply, — a future which shall manifest more largely the universal soul as it was then manifest to this soul. The tone of the voice was a grave body tone, full and sweet rather than sonorous, yet flexible, and haunted by many modulations, as even instruments of wood and brass seem to become after they have been long played on with skill and taste; how much more so the human voice! In the more expressive passages it uttered notes of silvery clearness, winning, yet still more commanding. The words uttered in those tones floated a while above us, then took root in the memory like winged seed.

In the union of an even rustic plainness with lyric inspirations, religious dignity with philosophic calmness, keen sagacity in details with boldness of view, we saw what brought to mind the early poets and legislators of Greece — men who taught their fellows to plough and avoid moral evil, sing hymns to the gods, and watch the metamorphoses of nature. Here in civic Boston was such a man — one who could see man in his original grandeur and his original childishness, rooted in simple nature, raising to the heavens the brow and eyes of a poet.

And these lectures seemed not so much lectures as grave didactic poems, theogonies, perhaps, adorned by odes when some power was in question whom the poet had best learned to serve, and with eclogues wisely portraying in familiar tongue the duties of man to man and "harmless animals."

Such was the attitude in which the speaker appeared to that portion of the audience who have remained permanently attached to him. They value his words as the signets of reality; receive his influence as a help and incentive to a nobler discipline than the age, in its general aspect, appears to require; and do not fear to anticipate the verdict of posterity in claiming for him the honors of greatness, and, in some respects, of a master.

In New England Mr. Emerson thus formed for himself a class of readers who rejoice to study in his books what they already know by heart. For, though the thought has become familiar, its beautiful garb is always fresh and bright in hue.

A similar circle of "like-minded" persons the books must and do form for themselves, though with a movement less directly powerful, as more distant from its source.

The Essays have also been obnoxious to many charges;

to that of obscurity, or want of perfect articulation; of
" euphuism," as an excess of fancy in proportion to imagination, and an inclination, at times, to subtlety at the expense of
strength, have been styled. The human heart complains of
inadequacy, either in the nature or experience of the writer,
to represent its full vocation and its deeper needs. Sometimes it speaks of this want as " under development," or a
want of expansion which may yet be remedied; sometimes
doubts whether " in this mansion there be either hall or portal
to receive the loftier of the passions." Sometimes the soul is
deified at the expense of nature, then again nature at that of
man ; and we are not quite sure that we can make a true harmony by balance of the statements. This writer has never
written one good work, if such a work be one where the
whole commands more attention than the parts, or if such a
one be produced only where, after an accumulation of materials, fire enough be applied to fuse the whole into one new
substance. This second series is superior in this respect to
the former; yet in no one essay is the main stress so obvious
as to produce on the mind the harmonious effect of a noble
river or a tree in full leaf. Single passages and sentences engage our attention too much in proportion. These Essays, it
has been justly said, tire like a string of mosaics or a house
built of medals. We miss what we expect in the work of the
great poet, or the great philosopher — the liberal air of all the
zones; the glow, uniform yet various in tint, which is given
to a body by free circulation of the heart's blood from the
hour of birth. Here is, undoubtedly, the man of ideas; but
we want the ideal man also — want the heart and genius of
human life to interpret it; and here our satisfaction is not so
perfect. We doubt this friend raised himself too early to the
perpendicular, and did not lie along the ground long enough to
hear the secret whispers of our parent life. We could wish
he might be thrown by conflicts on the lap of mother earth,
to see if he would not rise again with added powers.

All this we may say, but it cannot excuse us from benefiting by the great gifts that have been given, and assigning them their due place.

Some painters paint on a red ground. And this color may be supposed to represent the groundwork most immediately congenial to most men, as it is the color of blood, and represents human vitality. The figures traced upon it are instinct with life in its fulness and depth.

But other painters paint on a gold ground. And a very different, but no less natural, because also a celestial beauty, is given to their works who choose for their foundation the color of the sunbeam, which Nature has preferred for her most precious product, and that which will best bear the test of purification — gold.

If another simile may be allowed, another no less apt is at hand. Wine is the most brilliant and intense expression of the powers of earth. It is her potable fire, her answer to the sun. It exhilarates, it inspires, but then it is liable to fever and intoxicate, too, the careless partaker.

Mead was the chosen drink of the northern gods. And this essence of the honey of the mountain bee was not thought unworthy to revive the souls of the valiant who had left their bodies on the fields of strife below.

Nectar should combine the virtues of the ruby wine, the golden mead, without their defects or dangers.

Two high claims on the attention of his contemporaries our writer can vindicate. One from his sincerity. You have his thought just as it found place in the life of his own soul. Thus, however near or relatively distant its approximation to absolute truth, its action on you cannot fail to be healthful. It is a part of the free air.

Emerson belongs to that band of whom there may be found a few in every age, and who now in known human history may be counted by hundreds, who worship the one God only, the God of Truth. They worship, not saints, nor creeds, nor churches, nor reliques, nor idols in any form. The mind is kept open to truth, and life only valued as a tendency towards it. This must be illustrated by acts and words of love, purity and intelligence. Such are the salt of the earth; let the minutest crystal of that salt be willingly by us held in solution.

The other claim is derived from that part of his life, which, if sometimes obstructed or chilled by the critical intellect, is yet the prevalent and the main source of his power. It is that by which he imprisons his hearer only to free him again as a "liberating God," (to use his own words.) But, indeed, let us use them altogether, for none other, ancient or modern, can more worthily express how, making present to us the courses and destinies of nature, he invests himself with her serenity and animates us with her joy.

" Poetry was all written before time was; and whenever we are so finely organized that we can penetrate into that region where the air is music, we hear those primal warblings, and attempt to write them down, but we lose ever and anon a word or a verse, and substitute something of our own, and thus miswrite the poem. The men of more delicate ear write down these cadences more faithfully, and these transcripts, though imperfect, become the songs of the nations."

Thus have we, in a brief and unworthy manner, indicated some views of these books. The only true criticism of these or any good books may be gained by making them the companions of our lives. Does every accession of knowledge or a juster sense of beauty make us prize them more? Then they are good, indeed, and more immortal than mortal. Let that test be applied to these Essays which will lead to great and complete poems — somewhere.

CAPITAL PUNISHMENT.*

WE have had this book before us for several weeks, but the task of reading it has been so repulsive that we have been obliged to get through it by short stages, with long intervals of rest and refreshment between, and have only just reached the end. We believe, however, we are now possessed of its substance, so far as it is possible to admit into any mind matter wholly uncongenial with its structure, its faith, and its hope.

Meanwhile others have shown themselves more energetic in the task, and notices have appeared that express, in part, our own views. Among others an able critic has thus summed up his impressions : —

"Of the whole we will say briefly, that its premises are monstrous, its reasoning sophistical, its conclusions absurd, and its spirit diabolic."

We know not that we can find a better scheme of arrangement for what we have to say than by dividing it into sections under these four heads : —

1st. The premises are monstrous. Here we must add the qualification, they are monstrous *to us*. The God of these writers is not the God we recognize ; the views they have of human nature are antipodal to ours. We believe in a Creative Spirit, the essense of whose being is Love. He has created men in the spirit of love, intending to develop them to

* A Defence of Capital Punishment, and an Essay on the Ground and Reason of Punishment, with Special Reference to the Penalty of Death. New York, 1846.

perfect harmony with himself.   He has permitted the temporary existence of evil as a condition necessary to bring out in
them free agency and individuality of character.   Punishment
is the necessary result of a bad choice in them; it is not
meant by him as vengeance, but as an admonition to choose
better.   Man is not born totally evil; he is born capable both
of good and evil, and the Holy Spirit in working on him only
quickens the soul already there to know its Father.   To one
who takes such views the address of Jesus becomes intelligi-
ble — " Be ye therefore merciful, as your Father also is
merciful."   " For with the same measure that ye mete withal,
it shall be measured to you again."

Those who take these views of the relation between God
and man must naturally tend to have punishment consist as
much as possible in the inward spiritual results of faults,
rather than a violent outward enforcement of penalty.   They
must, so far as possible, seek to revere God by showing themselves brotherly to man; and if they wish to obey Christ,
will not forget that he came especially to call *sinners* to repentance.

The views of these writers are the opposite of all this.   We
need not state them; they are sufficiently indicated in each
page of their own.   Their conclusions are the natural result
of such premises.   We could say nothing about either, except
to express dissent from beginning to end.   Yet would it be
sweet and noble, and worthy of this late period of human
progress, if their position had been stated in a spirit of religious, of manly courtesy; if they had had the soul to say,
" We differ from you, but we know that so wide and full a
stream of thought and emotion as you are moved by could
not, under the providential rule in which we believe, have
arisen in vain.   The object of every such manifestation of life
must be to bring out truth; come, let us seek it together.
Let us show you our view, compare it with yours, and let us
see which is the better.   If, as we think, the truth lie with us,

what joy will it be for us to cast the clear light on the object of your aspirations ! "

Of this degree of liberality we have known some, even, who served the same creed as these writers to be capable. There is, indeed, a higher spirit, which, believing all forms of opinion which we hold in the present stage of our growth can be but approximations to truth, and that God has permitted to the multitude of men a multitude of ways by which they may approach one common goal, looks with reverence on all modes of faith sincerely held and acted upon, and while it rejoices in those souls which have reached the higher stages of spiritual growth, has no despair as to those which still grope in a narrow path and by a glimmering light. Such liberality is, of course, out of the question with such writers as the present. Their faith binds them to believe that they have absolute truth, and that all who do not believe as they do are wretched heretics. Those whose creed is of narrower scope are to them hateful bigots ; but also those with whom it is of wider are latitudinarians or infidels. The spot of earth on which they stand is the only one safe from the conflagration, and only through spectacles and spyglasses such as are used by them can the sun and stars be seen. Yet, as we said before, some such, though incapacitated for an intellectual, are not so for a spiritual tolerance. With them the heart, more Christ-like than the creed, urges to a spirit of love and reverence even towards convictions opposed to their own The sincere man is always respectable in their eyes, and they cannot help feeling that, wherever there is a desire for truth, there is the spirit of God, and his true priests will approach with gentleness, and do their ministry with holy care. Unhappily, it is very different with the persons before us.

We let go the first two counts of the indictment. Their premises are, as we have said, such as we totally dissent from, and their conclusions such as naturally flow from those premises. Yet they are those of a large body of men, and there must, no doubt, be temporary good in this state of things, or it would not be permitted. When these writers say, that to them moral and penal are coincident terms, they display a state of mind which prefers basing virtue on the fear of punishment, rather than the love of right. If this be sincerely their state, if the idea of morality is with them entirely dependent on the retributions upon vice, rather than the loveliness and joys of goodness, it is impossible for those who are in a different state of mind to say what they *do* need. It may seem to us, indeed, that, if the strait jacket was taken off, they might recover the natural energy of their frames, and do far better without it; or that, if no longer hurried along the road by the impending lash behind, they might uplift their eyes, and find sufficient cause for speed in the glory visible before, though at a distance; however, it is not for us to say what their wants are. Let them choose their own principles of action, and if they lead to purity of life, and benevolence, and humanity of heart, we will not say a word against them.

But in the instance before us, they do not produce these good fruits, but the contrary; and therefore we have something to say on the other part of the criticism, to wit: that "the reasoning is sophistical, and the spirit diabolic;" for, indeed, in the sense of pride by which the angels fell, arrogance of judgment, malice, and all uncharitableness, we have never looked on printed pages more deeply sinful. We love an honest lover; but next best, we, with Dr. Johnson, know how to respect an honest hater. But even he would scarce endure so bitter and ardent haters as these, and with so many and inconsistent objects of hatred — who hate Catholics and thorough Protestants, hate materialists, and hate spiritualists. Their list is really too large for *human* sympathy.

We wish, however, to make all due allowance for incapacity in these writers to do better; and their disqualifications for their task, apart from a form of belief which inclines them rather to cling to the past, than to seek progress for the future, seem to be many.

The "reasoning is sophistical," and it would need the patience of a Socrates to unravel the weary web, and convince these sophists, against their will, that they are exactly in the opposite region to what they suppose. For the task we have not space, skill, or patience ; but we can give some hints by which readers may be led to examine whether it is so or not.

These writers profess to occupy the position of defence ; surely never was one sustained so in the spirit of offence.

1st. They appeal either to the natural or regenerate man, as suits their purpose. Sometimes all traditions and their literal interpretations are right; sometimes it is impossible to interpret them aright, unless according to some peculiar doctrine, and the natural inference of the common mind would be an error.

2d. They strain, but vainly, to show the New Testament no improvement on the Old, and themselves in harmonious relations to both. On this subject we would confidently leave the arbitration to a mind — could such a one be found — sufficiently disciplined to examine the subject, and new both to the New Testament and this volume, as that of Rammohun Roy might have been, whether its views are not of the same strain that Jesus sought to correct and enlighten among the Jews, and whether the writers do not treat the teachings of the new dispensation most unfairly, in their desire to wrest them into the service of the old.

3d. Wherever there is a weak place in the argument, it is filled up by abuse of the opposite party. The words "absurd," "infidel," "blasphemous," "shallow philosophy," "sickly sentimentalism," and the like, are among the favorite missiles of these *defenders* of the truth. They are of a sort whose frequent use is generally supposed to argue the want of a shield of reason and a heart of faith.

And this brings us to a more close consideration of the *spirit* of this book, characterized by our contemporary as "diabolic." And we, also, cannot excuse ourselves from marking it as, in this respect, one of the worst books we have ever seen.

It is not merely bitter intolerance, arrogance, and want of spiritual perception, which we have to condemn in these writers. It is a want of fairness and honor, of which we think they must be conscious. We fear they are of those who hold the opinion that the end sanctifies the means, and who, by pretending to serve the God of truth by other means than strict truth, have drawn upon the "ministers of religion" the frequent obloquy of "priestcraft." How else are we to construe the artful use of the words "dishonest" and "infidel," wherever they are likely to awaken the fears and prejudices of the ignorant?

Of as bad a stamp as any is the part of this book headed "Spurious Public Opinion." Here, as in the insinuations against Charles Burleigh, we are unable to believe the writers to be sincere. Where we think they are, however poor and narrow we may esteem their statement, we can respect it, but here we cannot.

Who can believe that such passages as the following stand for any thing real in the mind of the writer?

"Indeed, there is nothing that can possibly check the spirit of murder, but the fear of death. That was all that Cain feared; he did not say, People will put me in prison, but, They will put me to death ; *and how many other murders he may have committed, when released from that fear, the sacred writer does not tell us !* "

Why does not the writer of this passage draw the inference, and accuse God of mistake, as he says his opponents accuse Him, whenever they attempt to get beyond the Jewish ideas of vengeance. He plainly thinks death was the only safe penalty in this case of Cain.

"The reasoning from these drivellings of depravity in malefactors is to the last degree wretched and absurd. Hard pushed indeed must he be in argument who can consent to dive down into the polluted heart of a Newgate criminal, in order to fish up, from the confessions of his monstrous, unnatural obduracy, an argument in that very obduracy against the fit punishment of his own crimes."

We can only wish for such a man, that the vicissitudes of life may break through the crust of theological arrogance and Phariseeism, and force him to "dive down" into the depths of his own nature. We should see afterwards whether he would be so forward to throw stones at malefactors, so eager to hurry souls to what he regards as a final account.

But we have said enough as to the spirit and tendency of this book. We shall only add a few words as to the unworthy use of the word "infidel," in the attempt to fix a stigma upon opponents. We feel still more contempt than indignation at the desire to work in this way on the unthinking and ignorant.

We ourselves are of the number stigmatized by these persons as sharing an infidel tendency, as are all not enlisted under their own sectarian banner. They, on their side, seem to us unbelievers in all that is most pure and holy, and in the saving grace of love. They do not believe in God, as we believe; they seem to us utterly deficient in the spirit of Christ, and to be of the number of those who are always calling, "Lord, Lord," yet never have known him. We find throughout these pages the temper of "Lord, I thank thee that I am not as other men are" — hatred of those whom they deem Gentiles, and a merciless spirit towards the sinner; yet we do not take upon ourselves to give them the name of infidels, and we solemnly call them to trial before the bar of the Only Wise and Pure, the Searcher of hearts, to render an account of this daring assumption. We ask them in that presence, if they are not of the class threatened with "retri-

18

bution" for saying to their brother, "Thou fool;" and that
not merely in the heat of anger, but coolly, pertinaciously,
and in a thousand ways.

We call to sit in council the spirits of our Puritan fathers,
and ask if such was the right of individual judgment, of private conscience, they came here to vindicate. And we solicit
the verdict of posterity as to whether the spirit of mercy or
of vengeance be the more divine, and whether the denuncia-
tory and personal mode chosen by these writers for carrying
on this inquiry be the true one.

We wish most sincerely this book had been a wise and
noble one. To ascertain just principles, it is necessary that
the discussion should be full and fair, and both sides ably
argued. After this has been done, the sense of the world
can decide. It would be a happiness for which it might seem
that man at this time of day is ripe. that the opposing parties
should meet in open lists as brothers, believing each that the
other desired only that the truth should triumph, and able to
clasp hands as men of different structure and ways of thinking, but fellow-students of the divine will. O, had we but
found such an adversary, above the use of artful abuse, or
the feints of sophistry, able to believe in the noble intention
of a foe as of a friend, how cheerily would the trumpets ring
out while the assembled world echoed the signal words, " GOD
SPEED THE RIGHT!" The tide of progress rolls onward,
swelling more and more with the lives of those who would
fain see all men called to repentance. It must be a strong
arm, indeed, that can build a dam to stay it even for a moment. None such do we see yet; but we should rejoice in a
noble and strong opponent, putting forth all his power for
conscience's sake. God speed the Right!

PART II.

MISCELLANIES.

FIRST OF JANUARY.

THE new year dawns, and its appearance is hailed by a flutter of festivity. Men and women run from house to house, scattering gifts, smiles, and congratulations. It is a custom that seems borrowed from a better day, unless indeed it be a prophecy that such must come.

For why so much congratulation? A year has passed; we are nearer by a twelvemonth to the term of this earthly probation. It is a solemn thought; and though the consciousness of having hallowed the days by our best endeavor, and of having much occasion to look to the Ruling Power of all with grateful benediction, must, in cases where such feelings are unalloyed, bring joy, one would think it must even then be a grave joy, and one that would disincline to this loud gayety in welcoming a new year; another year — in which we may, indeed, strive forward in a good spirit, and find our strivings blest, but must surely expect trials, temptations, and disappointments from without; frailty, short-coming, or convulsion in ourselves.

If it be appropriate to a reflective habit of mind to ask with

each night-fall the Pythagorean questions, how much more so
at the close of the year!

> "What hast thou done that's worth the doing?
> And what pursued that's worth pursuing?
> What sought thou knewest thou shouldst shun?
> What done thou shouldst have left undone?"

The intellectual man will also ask, What new truths have
been opened to me, or what facts presented that will lead to
the discovery of truths? The poet and the lover, — What
new forms of beauty have been presented for my delight, and
as memorable illustrations of the divine presence — unceasing,
but oftentimes unfelt by our sluggish natures.

Are there many men who fail sometimes to ask themselves questions to this depth? who do not care to know
whether they have done right, or forborne to do wrong;
whether their spirits have been enlightened by truth, or
kindled by beauty?

Yes, strange to say, there are many who, despite the natural aspirations of the soul and the revelations showered upon
the world, think only whether they have made money; whether the world thinks more highly of them than it did in bygone
years; whether wife and children have been in good bodily
health, and what those who call to pay their respects and
drink the new year's coffee, will think of their carpets,
new also.

How often is it that the rich man thinks even of that proposed by Dickens as the noblest employment of the season,
making the poor happy in the way he likes best for himself,
by distribution of turkey and plum-pudding! Some, indeed,
adorn the day with this much grace, though we doubt whether
it be oftenest those who could each, with ease, make that one
day a glimpse of comfort to a thousand who pass the other
winter days in shivering poverty. But some such there are

who go about to the dark and frosty dwellings, giving the
"mite" where and when it is most needed. We knew a lady,
all whose riches consisted in her good head and two hands.
Widow of an eminent lawyer, but-keeping boarders for a live-
lihood; engaged in that hardest of occupations, with her house
full and her hands full, she yet found time to make and bake
for new year's day a hundred pies — and not the pie from
which, being cut, issued the famous four-and-twenty black-
birds, gave more cause for merriment, or was a fitter "dish
to set before the king."

God bless his majesty, the *good* king, who on such a day
cares for the least as much as the greatest; and like Henry
IV., proposes it as a worthy aim of his endeavor that "every
poor man shall have his chicken in the pot." This does not
seem, on superficial survey, such a wonderful boon to crave
for creatures made in God's own likeness, yet is it one that
no king could ever yet bestow on his subjects, if we except
the king of Cockaigne. Our maker of the hundred pies
is the best prophet we have seen, as yet, of such a blissful
state.

But mostly to him who hath is given in material as well
as in spiritual things, and we fear the pleasures of this day
are arranged almost wholly in reference to the beautiful, the
healthy, the wealthy, the witty, and that but few banquets are
prepared for the halt, the blind, and the sorrowful. But where
they are, of a surety water turns to wine by inevitable Christ-
power; no aid of miracle need be invoked. As for thoughts
which should make an epoch of the period, we suppose the
number of these to be in about the same proportion to the
number of minds capable of thought, that the pearls now existent bear to the oysters still subsistent.

Can we make pearls from our oyster-bed? At least, let us
open some of the shells and try.

Dear public and friends! we wish you a happy new year.
We trust that the year past has given earnest of such a one

18 *

in so far as having taught you somewhat how to deserve and
to appreciate it.

For ourselves, the months have brought much, though,
perhaps, superficial instruction. Its scope has been chiefly
love and hope for all human beings, and among others for
thyself.

We have seen many fair poesies of human life, in which,
however, the tragic thread has not been wanting. We have
beheld the exquisite developments of childhood, and sunned
the heart in its smiles. But also have we discerned the evil
star looming up that threatened cloud and wreck to its future
years. We have seen beings of some precious gifts lost irrecoverably, as regards this present life, from inheritance of a
bad organization and unfortunate circumstances of early years.
The victims of vice we have observed lying in the gutter, com-
panied by vermin, trampled upon by sensuality and ignorance,
and saw those who wished not to rise, and those who strove
so to do, but fell back through weakness. Sadder and more
ominous still, we have seen the good man — in many impulses
and acts of most pure, most liberal, and undoubted goodness
— yet have we noted a spot of base indulgence, a fibre of
brutality canker in a vital part this fine plant, and, while we
could not withdraw love and esteem for the good we could
not doubt, have wept secretly in the heart for the ill we
could not deny. We have observed two deaths ; one of the
sinner, early cut down ; one of the just, full of years and
honor — *both* were calm ; both professed their reliance on the
wisdom of a heavenly Father. We have looked upon the
beauteous shows of nature in undisturbed succession, holy
moonlight on the snows, loving moonlight on the summer
fields, the stars which disappoint never and bless ever, the
flowing waters which soothe and stimulate, a garden of roses
calling for queens among women, poets and heroes among
men. We have marked a desire to answer to this call, and
genius brought rich wine, but spilt it on the way, from her

careless, fickle gait; and virtue tainted with a touch of the
peacock; and philosophy, never enjoying, always seeking,
had got together all the materials for the crowning experiment, but there was no love to kindle the fire under the furnace, and the precious secret is not precipitated yet, for the
pot will not boil to make the gold through your

> " Double, double,
> Toil and trouble,"

if love do not fan the fire.

We have seen the decay of friendships unable to endure the
light of an ideal hope — have seen, too, their resurrection in
a faith and hope beyond the tomb, where the form lies we once
so fondly cherished. It is not dead, but sleepeth; and we
watch, but must weep, too, sometimes, for the night is cold
and lonely in the place of tombs.

Nature has appeared dressed in her veil of snowy flowers for
the bridal. We have seen her brooding over her joys, a young
mother in the pride and fulness of beauty, and then bearing her
offspring to their richly ornamented sepulchre, and lately observed her as if kneeling with folded hands in the stillness of
prayer, while the bare trees and frozen streams bore witness
to her patience.

O, much, much have we seen, and a little learned. Such is
the record of the private mind; and yet, as the bright snake-
skin is cast, many sigh and cry, —

> " The wiser mind
> Mourns less for what Time takes away
> Than what he leaves behind."

But for ourselves, we find there is kernel in the nut, though
its ripening be deferred till the late frosty weather, and it
prove a hard nut to crack even then. Looking at the individual, we see a degree of growth, or the promise of such.
In the child there is a force which will outlast the wreck, and

reach at last the promised shore.   The good man, once roused
from his moral lethargy, shall make atonement for his fault,
and endure a penance that will deepen and purify his whole
nature.   The poor lost ones claim a new trial in a new life,
and will there, we trust, seize firmer hold on the good for the
experience they have had of the bad.

> " We never see the stars
> Till we can see nought else."

The seeming losses are, in truth, but as pruning of the vine
to make the grapes swell more richly.

But how is it with those larger individuals, the nations,
and that congress of such, the world?   We must take a
broad and superficial view of these, as we have of private life;
and in neither case can more be done.   The secrets of the
confessional, or rather of the shrine, do not come on paper,
unless in poetic form.

So we will not try to search and mine, but only to look over
the world from an ideal point of view.

Here we find the same phenomena repeated; the good
nation is yet somehow so sick at heart that you are not sure
its goodness will ever produce a harmony of life; over the
young nation, (our own,) rich in energy and full of glee, brood
terrible omens; others, as Poland and Italy, seem irrecoverably lost.   They may revive, but we feel as if it must be
under new forms.

Forms come and go, but principles are developed and displayed more and more.   The caldron simmers, and so great is
the fire that we expect it soon to boil over, and new fates
appear for Europe.

Spain is dying by inches; England shows symptoms of
having passed her meridian; Austria has taken opium, but
she must awake ere long; France is in an uneasy dream —
she knows she has been very sick, has had terrible remedies
administered, and ought to be getting thoroughly well, which

she is not. Louis Philippe watches by her pillow, doses and bleeds her, so that she cannot fairly try her strength, and find whether something or nothing has been done. But Louis Philippe and Metternich must soon, in the course of nature, leave this scene; and then there will be none to keep out air and light from the chamber, and the patients will be roused and ascertain their true condition.

No power is in the ascending course except the Russian; and that has such a condensation of brute force, animated by despotic will, that it seems sometimes as if it might by and by stride over Europe and face us across the water. Then would be opposed to one another the two extremes of Autocracy and Democracy, and a trial of strength would ensue between the two principles more grand and full than any ever seen on this planet, and of which the result must be to bind mankind by one chain of convictions. Should, indeed, Despotism and Democracy meet as the two slaveholding powers of the world, the result can hardly be predicted. But there is room in the intervening age for many changes, and the czars profess to wish to free their serfs, as our planters do to free their slaves, and we suppose with equal sincerity; but the need of sometimes professing such desires is a deference to the progress of principles which bid fair to have their era yet.

We hope such an era steadfastly, notwithstanding the deeds of darkness that have made this year forever memorable in our annals. Our nation has indeed shown that the lust of gain is at present her ruling passion. She is not only resolute, but shameless, about it, and has no doubt or scruple as to laying aside the glorious office, assigned her by fate, of herald of freedom, light, and peace to the civilized world.

Yet we must not despair. Even so the Jewish king, crowned with all gifts that Heaven could bestow, was intoxicated by their plenitude, and went astray after the most worthless idols. But he was not permitted to forfeit finally the position designed for him: he was drawn or dragged back to it; and so shall it be with this nation. There are trials in store which shall amend us.

We must believe that the pure blood shown in the time of our revolution still glows in the heart; but the body of our nation is full of foreign elements. A large proportion of our citizens, or their parents, came here for worldly advantage, and have never raised their minds to any idea of destiny or duty. More money — more land ! are all the watchwords they know. They have received the inheritance earned by the fathers of the revolution, without their wisdom and virtue to use it. But this cannot last. The vision of those prophetic souls must be realized, else the nation could not exist; every body must at least " have soul enough to save the expense of salt," or it cannot be preserved alive.

What a year it has been with us ! Texas annexed, and more annexations in store ; slavery perpetuated, as the most striking new feature of these movements. Such are the fruits of American love of liberty ! Mormons murdered and driven out, as an expression of American freedom of conscience ; Cassius Clay's paper expelled from Kentucky ; that is American freedom of the press. And all these deeds defended on the true Russian grounds, " We (the stronger) know what you (the weaker) ought to do and be, and it *shall* be so."

Thus the principles which it was supposed, some ten years back, had begun to regenerate the world, are left without a trophy for this past year, except in the spread of Ronge's movement in Germany, and that of associative and communist principles both here and in Europe, which, let the worldling deem as he will about their practicability, he cannot deny to be animated by faith in God and a desire for the good of man. We must add to these the important symptoms of the spread of peace principles.

Meanwhile, if the more valuable springs of action seem to lie dormant for a time, there is a constant invention and perfection of the means of action and communication which seems to say, " Do but wait patiently; there is something of universal importance to be done by and by, and all is preparing for it to be universally known and used at once." Else what avail magnetic telegraphs, steamers, and rail-cars traversing every rood of land and ocean, phonography and the mingling of all literatures, till North embraces South and Denmark lays her head upon the lap of Italy? Surely there would not be all this pomp of preparation as to the means of communion, unless there were like to be something worthy to be communicated.

Amid the signs of the breaking down of barriers, we may mention the Emperor Nicholas letting his daughter pass from the Greek to the Roman church, for the sake of marrying her to the Austrian prince. Again, similarity between him and us: he, too, is shameless; for while he signs this marriage contract with one hand, he holds the knout in the other to drive the Roman Catholic Poles into the Greek church. But it is a fatal sign for his empire. 'Tis but the first step that costs, and the Russians may look back to the marriage of the Grand Duchess Olga, as the Chinese will to the cannonading of the English, as the first sign of dissolution in the present form of national life.

A similar token is given by the violation of etiquette of which Mr. Polk is accused in his message. He, at the head of a government, speaks of governments and their doings straightforward, as he would of persons, and the tower, stronghold of the idea of a former age, now propped up by etiquettes and civilities only, trembles to its foundation.

Another sign of the times is the general panic which the decay of the potato causes. We believe this is not without a providential meaning, and will call attention still more to the wants of the people at large. New and more provident regulations must be brought out, that they may not again be left with only a potato between them and starvation. By another of these whimsical coincidences between the histories of Aristocracy and Democracy, the supply of *truffles* is also failing. The land is losing the "nice things" that the queen (truly a young queen) thought might be eaten in place of bread. Does not this indicate a period in which it will be felt that there must be provision for all — the rich shall not have their truffles if the poor are driven to eat nettles, as the French and Irish have in bygone ages?

The poem of which we here give a prose translation lately appeared in Germany. It is written by Moritz Hartmann, and contains the *gist* of the matter.

MISTRESS POTATO.

There was a great stately house full of people, who have been running in and out of its lofty gates ever since the gray times of Olympus. There they wept, laughed, shouted, mourned, and, like day and night, came the usual changes of joys with plagues and sorrows. Haunting that great house up and down, making, baking, and roasting, covering and waiting on the table, has there lived a vast number of years a loyal serving maid of the olden time — her name was Mrs. Potato. She was a still, little, old mother, who wore no bawbles or laces, but always had to be satisfied with her plain, every-day clothes ; and unheeded, unhonored, oftentimes jeered at and forgotten, she served all day at the kitchen fire, and slept at night in the worst room. When she brought the dishes to table she got rarely a thankful glance; only at times some very poor man would in secret shake kindly her hand.

Generation after generation passed by, as the trees blossom, bear fruit, and wither; but faithful remained the old housemaid, always the servant of the last heir.

But one morning — hear what happened. All the people came to table, and lo! there was nothing to eat, for our good old Mistress Potato had not been able to rise from her bed. She felt sharp pains creeping through her poor old bones. No wonder she was worn out at last! She had not in all her life dared take a day's rest, lest so the poor should starve.

Indeed, it is wonderful that her good will should have kept her up so long. She must have had a great constitution to begin with.

The guests had to go away without breakfast. They were a little troubled, but hoped to make up for it at dinner time. But dinner time came, and the table was empty; and then, indeed, they began to inquire about the welfare of Cookmaid Potato. And up into her dark chamber, where she lay on her poor bed, came great and little, young and old, to ask after the good creature. "What can be done for her?" "Bring warm clothes, medicine, a better bed." "Lay aside your work to help her." "If she dies we shall never again be able to fill the table;" and now, indeed, they sang her praises.

O, what a fuss about the sick bed in that moist and mouldy chamber! and out doors it was just the same — priests with their masses, processions, and prayers, and all the world ready to walk to penance, if Mistress Potato could but be saved. And the doctors in their wigs, and counsellors in masks of gravity, sat there to devise some remedy to avert this terrible ill.

As when a most illustrious dame is recovering from birth of a son, so now bulletins inform the world of the health of Mistress Potato, and, not content with what they thus learn, couriers and lackeys besiege the door; nay, the king's coach is stopping there. Yes! yes! the humble poor maid, 'tis about her they are all so frightened! Who would ever have believed it in days when the table was nicely covered?

The gentlemen of pens and books, priests, kings, lords, and ministers, all have senses to scent our famine. Natheless Mistress Potato gets no better. May God help her for the sake, not of such people, but of the poor. For the great it is a token they should note, that all must crumble and fall to ruin, if they will work and weary to death the poor maid who cooks in the kitchen.

19

She lived for you in the dirt and ashes, provided daily for poor and rich; you ought to humble yourselves for her sake. Ah, could we hope that you would take a hint, and *next time* pay some heed to the housemaid before she is worn and wearied to death!

So sighs, rather than hopes, Moritz Hartmann. The wise ministers of England, indeed, seem much more composed than he supposes them.   They are like the old man who, when he saw the avalanche coming down upon his village, said, " It is coming, but I shall have time to fill my pipe once more." *He* went in to do so, and was buried beneath the ruins.   But Sir Robert Peel, who is so deliberate, has, doubtless, manna in store for those who have lost their customary food.

Another sign of the times is, that there are left on the earth none of the last dynasty of geniuses, rich in so many imperial heads.   The world is full of talent, but it flows downward to water the plain.   There are no towering heights, no Mont Blancs now.   We cannot recall one great genius at this day living.   The time of prophets is over, and the era they prophesied must be at hand ; in its conduct a larger proportion of the human race shall take part than ever before. As prime ministers have succeeded kings in the substantials of monarchy, so now shall a house of representatives succeed prime ministers.

Altogether, it looks as if a great time was coming, and that time one of democracy.   Our country will play a ruling part. Her eagle will lead the van ; but whether to soar upward to the sun or to stoop for helpless prey, who now dares promise ? At present she has scarce achieved a Roman nobleness, a Roman liberty ; and whether her eagle is less like the vulture, and more like the Phœnix, than was the fierce Roman bird, we dare not say.   May the new year give hopes of the latter, even if the bird need first to be purified by fire.

Jan. 1, 1846.

NEW YEAR'S DAY.

IT was a beautiful custom among some of the Indian tribes, once a year, to extinguish all the fires, and, by a day of fasting and profound devotion, to propitiate the Great Spirit for the coming year. They then produced sparks by friction, and lighted up afresh the altar and the hearth with the new fire.

And this fire was considered as the most precious and sacred gift from one person to another, binding them in bonds of inviolate friendship for that year, certainly; with a hope that the same might endure through life. From the young to the old, it was a token of the highest respect; from the old to the young, of a great expectation.

To us would that it might be granted to solemnize the new year by the mental renovation of which this ceremony was the eloquent symbol. Would that we might extinguish, if cnly for a day, those fires where an uninformed religious ardor has led to human sacrifices; which have warmed the household, but, also, prepared pernicious, more than wholesome, viands for their use.

The Indian produced the new spark by friction. It would be a still more beautiful emblem, and expressive of the more extended powers of civilized men, if we should draw the spark from the centre of our system and the source of light, by means of the burning glass.

Where, then, is to be found the new knowledge, the new thought, the new hope, that shall begin a new year in a spirit not discordant with "the acceptable year of the Lord"? Surely there must be such existing, if latent — some sparks of new fire, pure from ashes and from smoke, worthy to be

offered as a new year's gift.   Let us look at the signs of the
times, to see in what spot this fire shall be sought — on what
fuel it may be fed.   The ancients poured out libations of the
choicest juices of earth, to express their gratitude to the Power
that had enabled them to be sustained from her bosom.   They
enfranchised slaves, to show that devotion to the gods induced
a sympathy with men.

Let us look about us to see with what rites, what acts of
devotion, this modern Christian nation greets the approach
of the new year; by what signs she denotes the clear morning of a better day, such as may be expected when the eagle
has entered into covenant with the dove.

This last week brings tidings that a portion of the inhabitants of Illinois, the rich and blooming region on which every
gift of nature has been lavished, to encourage the industry and
brighten the hopes of man, not only refuses a libation to the
Power that has so blessed their fields, but declares that the
dew is theirs, and the sunlight is theirs — that they live from
and for themselves, acknowledging no obligation and no duty
to God or to man.*

One man has freed a slave; but a great part of the nation
is now busy in contriving measures that may best rivet the
fetters on those now chained, and forge them strongest for
millions yet unborn.

Selfishness and tyranny no longer wear the mask; they
walk haughtily abroad, affronting with their hard-hearted
boasts and brazen resolves the patience of the sweet heavens.
National honor is trodden under foot for a national bribe, and
neither sex nor age defends the redresser of injuries from the
rage of the injurer.

Yet, amid these reports which come flying on the paper-
wings of every day, the scornful laugh of the gnomes, who

* [In refusing to repeal what are technically and significantly termed her
" Black Laws," relating to the settlement of colored men, and their rights
within that state. — ED.]

begin to believe they can buy all souls with their gold, was checked a moment when the aged knight * of the better cause answered the challenge — truly in keeping with the "chivalry" of the time — "You are in the wrong, and I will kick you," by holding the hands of the chevalier till those around secured him. We think the man of old must have held him with his eye, as physicians of moral power can insane patients. Great as are his exploits for his age, he cannot have much bodily strength, unless by miracle.

The treatment of Mr. Adams and Mr. Hoar seems to show that we are not fitted to emulate the savages in preparation for the new fire. The Indians knew how to reverence the old and the wise.

Among the manifestos of the day, it is impossible not to respect that of the Mexican minister for the manly indignation with which he has uttered truths, however deep our mortification at hearing them. It has been observed for the last fifty years, that the tone of diplomatic correspondence was much improved, as to simplicity and directness. Once, diplomacy was another name for intrigue, and a paper of this sort was expected to be a mesh of artful phrases, through which the true meaning might be detected, but never actually grasped. Now, here is one where an occasion being afforded by the unutterable folly of the corresponding party, a minister speaks the truth as it lies in his mind, directly and plainly, as man speaks to man. His statement will command the sympathy of the civilized world.

As to the state papers that have followed, they are of a nature to make the Austrian despot sneer, as he counts in his oratory the woollen stockings he has got knit by imprisoning all the free geniuses in his dominions. He, at least, only appeals to the legitimacy of blood ; these dare appeal to legitimacy, as seen from a moral point of view. History will class

* John Quincy Adams.

19 *

such claims with the brags of sharpers, who bully their victims about their honor, while they stretch forth their hands for the gold they have won with loaded dice. "Do you dare to say the dice are loaded? Prove it; *and* I will shoot you for injuring my honor."

The Mexican makes his gloss on the page of American honor; * the girl † in the Kentucky prison on that of her freedom; the delegate of Massachusetts, ‡ on that of her union. Ye stars, whose image America has placed upon her banner, answer us! Are not your unions of a different sort? Do they not work to other results?

Yet we cannot lightly be discouraged, or alarmed, as to the destiny of our country. The whole history of its discovery and early progress indicates too clearly the purposes of Heaven with regard to it. Could we relinquish the thought that it was destined for the scene of a new and illustrious act in the great drama, the past would be inexplicable, no less than the future without hope.

Last week, which brought us so many unpleasant notices of home affairs, brought also an account of the magnificent telescope lately perfected by the Earl of Rosse. With means of observation now almost divine, we perceive that some of the brightest stars, of which Sirius is one, have dark companions, whose presence is, by earthly spectators, only to be detected from the inequalities they cause in the motions of their radiant companions. It was a new and most imposing illustration how, in carrying out the divine scheme, of which we have as yet only spelled out the few first lines, the dark is made to wait upon, and, in the full result, harmonize with, the bright. The sense of such pervasive analogies should enlarge patience and animate hope.

---

* For her treatment of a sister republic in our late war with Mexico.

† Miss Delia Webster.

‡ Hon. Samuel Hoar, sent to Charleston, S. C., to test in the courts her laws, and driven thence with his daughter by a mob.

Yet, if offences must come, woe be to those by whom they come; and that of men, who sin against a heritage like ours, is as that of the backsliders among the chosen people of the elder day. We, too, have been chosen, and plain indications been given, by a wonderful conjunction of auspicious influences, that the ark of human hopes has been placed for the present in our charge. Woe be to those who betray this trust! On their heads are to be heaped the curses of unnumbered ages!

Can he sleep, who in this past year has wickedly or lightly committed acts calculated to injure the few or many; who has poisoned the ears and the hearts he might have rightly informed; who has steeped in tears the cup of thousands; who has put back, as far as in him lay, the accomplishment of general good and happiness for the sake of his selfish aggrandizement or selfish luxury; who has sold to a party what was meant for mankind? If such sleep, dreadful shall be the waking.

"Deliver us from evil." In public or in private, it is easy to give pain — hard to give pure pleasure; easy to do evil — hard to do good. God does his good in the whole, despite of bad men; but only from a very pure mind will he permit original good to proceed in the day. Happy those who can feel that during the past year, they have, to the best of their knowledge, refrained from evil. Happy those who determine to proceed in this by the light of conscience. It is but a spark; yet from that spark may be drawn fire-light enough for worlds and systems of worlds — and that light is ever new.

And with this thought rises again the memory of the fair lines that light has brought to view in the histories of some men. If the nation tends to wrong, there are yet present the ten just men. The hands and lips of this great form may be impure, but pure blood flows yet within her veins — the blood of the noble bands who first sought these shores from the

British isles and France, for conscience sake. Too many have come since, for bread alone. We cannot blame — we must not reject them; but let us teach them, in giving them bread, to prize that salt, too, without which all on earth must lose its savor. Yes! let us teach them, not rail at their inevitable ignorance and unenlightened action, but teach them and their children as our own; if we do so, their children and ours may yet act as one body obedient to one soul; and if we act rightly now, that soul a pure soul.

And ye, sable bands, forced hither against your will, kept down here now by a force hateful to nature, a will alien from God! It does sometimes seem as if the avenging angel wore your hue, and would place in your hands the sword to punish the cruel injustice of our fathers, the selfish perversity of the sons. Yet are there no means of atonement? Must the innocent suffer with the guilty? Teach us, O All-Wise, the clew out of this labyrinth; and if we faithfully encounter its darkness and dread, and emerge into clear light, wilt thou not bid us "go and sin no more"?

Meanwhile, let us proceed as we can, *picking our steps* along the slippery road. If we keep the right direction, what matters it that we must pass through so much mud? The promise is sure : —

Angels shall free the feet from stain, to their own hue of
    snow,
If, undismayed, we reach the hills where the true olives
    grow.
  The olive groves, which we must seek in cold and damp,
  Alone can yield us oil for a perpetual lamp.
Then sound again the golden horn with promise ever new;
The princely deer will ne'er be caught by those that slack
    pursue;
Let the " White Doe " of angel hopes be always kept in view.

Yes ! sound again the horn — of hope the golden horn !
Answer it, flutes and pipes, from valleys still and lorn ;
Warders, from your high towers, with trumps of silver scorn,
And harps in maidens' bowers, with strings from deep hearts
      torn, —
All answer to the horn — of hope the golden horn !

There is still hope, there is still an America, while private
lives are ruled by the Puritan, by the Huguenot conscien-
tiousness, and while there are some who can repudiate, not
their debts, but the supposition that they will not strive to
pay their debts to their age, and to Heaven, who gave them
a share in its great promise.

ST. VALENTINE'S DAY.

THIS merry season of light jokes and lighter love-tokens, in which Cupid presents the feathered end of the dart, as if he meant to tickle before he wounded the captive, has always had a great charm for me. When but a child, I saw Allston's picture of the "Lady reading a Valentine," and the mild womanliness of the picture, so remote from passion no less than vanity, so capable of tenderness, so chastely timid in its self-possession, has given a color to the gayest thoughts connected with the day. From the ruff of Allston's Lady, whose clear starch is made to express all rosebud thoughts of girlish retirement, the soft unfledged hopes which never yet were tempted from the nest, to Sam Weller's Valentine, is indeed a broad step, but one which we can take without material change of mood.

But of all the thoughts and pictures associated with the day, none can surpass in interest those furnished by the way in which we celebrated it last week.

The Bloomingdale Asylum for the Insane is conducted on the most wise and liberal plan known at the present day. Its superintendent, Dr. Earle, has had ample opportunity to observe the best modes of managing this class of diseases both here and in Europe, and he is one able, by refined sympathies and intellectual discernment, to apply the best that is known and to discover more.

Under his care the beautifully situated establishment at Bloomingdale loses every sign of the hospital and the prison, not long since thought to be inseparable from such a place.

It is a house of refuge, where those too deeply wounded or disturbed in body or spirit to keep up that semblance or degree of sanity which the conduct of affairs in the world at large demands, may be soothed by gentle care, intelligent sympathy, and a judicious attention to their physical welfare, into health, or, at least, into tranquillity.

Dr. Earle, in addition to modes of turning the attention from causes of morbid irritation, and promoting brighter and juster thoughts, which he uses in common with other institutions, has this winter delivered a course of lectures to the patients. We were present at one of these some weeks since. The subjects touched upon were, often, of a nature to demand as close attention as an audience of regular students (not college students, but real students) can be induced to give. The large assembly present were almost uniformly silent, to appearance interested, and showed a power of decorum and self-government often wanting among those who esteem themselves in healthful mastery of their morals and manners. We saw, with great satisfaction, generous thoughts and solid pursuits offered, as well as light amusements, for the choice of the sick in mind. For it is our experience that such sickness arises as often from want of concentration as any other cause. One of the noblest youths that ever trod this soil was wont to say, " he was never tired, if he could only see far enough." He is now gone where his view may be less bounded ; but we, who stay behind, may take the hint that mania, no less than the commonest forms of prejudice, bespeaks a mind which does not see far enough to correct partial impressions. No doubt, in many cases, dissipation of thought, after attention is once distorted into some morbid direction, may be the first method of cure ; but we are glad to see others provided for those who are ready for them.

St. Valentine's Eve had been appointed for one of the dancing parties at the institution, and a few friends from "the world's people" invited to be present.

At an early hour the company assembled in the well-lighted hall, still gracefully wreathed with its Christmas evergreens; the music struck up and the company entered.

And these are the people who, half a century ago, would have been chained in solitary cells, screaming out their anguish till silenced by threats or blows, lost, forsaken, hopeless, a blight to earth, a libel upon heaven!

Now, they are many of them happy, all interested. Even those who are troublesome and subject to violent excitement in every-day scenes, show here that the power of self-control is not lost, only lessened. Give them an impulse strong enough, favorable circumstances, and they will begin to use it again. They regulate their steps to music; they restrain their impatient impulses from respect to themselves and to others. The Power which shall yet shape order from all disorder, and turn ashes to beauty, as violets spring up from green graves, hath them also in its keeping.

The party were well dressed, with care and taste. The dancing was better than usual, because there was less of affectation and ennui. The party was more entertaining, because native traits came out more clear from the disguises of vanity and tact.

There was the blue-stocking lady, a mature belle and bel-esprit. Her condescending graces, her rounded compliments, her girlish, yet " highly intellectual " vivacity, expressed no less in her head-dress than her manner, were just that touch above the common with which the illustrator of Dickens has thought fit to heighten the charms of Mrs. Leo Hunter.

There was the travelled Englishman, *au fait* to every thing beneath the moon and beyond. With his clipped and glib phrases, his bundle of conventionalities carried so neatly under his arm, and his " My dear sir," in the perfection of cockney dignity, what better could the most select dinner-party furnish us in the way of distinguished strangerhood?

There was the hoidenish young girl, and the decorous,

elegant lady smoothing down " the wild little thing." There was the sarcastic observer on the folly of the rest; in that, the greatest fool of all, unbeloved and unloving. In contrast to this were characters altogether lovely, full of all sweet affections, whose bells, if jangled out of tune, still retained their true tone.

One of the best things of the evening was a dance improvised by two elderly women. They asked the privilege of the floor, and, a suitable measure being played, performed this dance in a style lively, characteristic, yet moderate enough. It was true dancing, like peasant dancing.

An old man sang comic songs in the style of various nations and characters, with a dramatic expression that would have commanded applause " on any stage."

And all was done decently and in order, each biding his time. Slight symptoms of impatience here and there were easily soothed by the approach of this, truly " good physician," the touch of whose hand seemed to possess a talismanic power to soothe. We doubt not that all went to their beds exhilarated, free from irritation, and more attuned to concord than before. Good bishop Valentine! thy feast was well kept, and not without the usual jokes and flings at old bachelors, the exchange of sugar-plums, mottoes, and repartees.

This is the second festival I have kept with those whom society has placed, not outside her pale, indeed, but outside the hearing of her benison. Christmas I passed in a prison ! There, too, I saw marks of the miraculous power of love, when guided by a pure faith in the goodness of its source, and intelligence as to the design of the creative intelligence. I saw enough of its power, impeded as it was by the ignorance of those who, eighteen hundred years after the coming of Christ, still believe more in fear and force : I saw enough, I say, of this power to convince me, if I needed conviction, that love is indeed omnipotent, as He said it was.

A companion, of that delicate nature by which a scar is felt

20

as a wound, was saddened by the thought how very little our partialities, undue emotions, and manias need to be exaggerated to entitle us to rank among madmen. I cannot view it so. Rather let the sense that, with all our faults and follies, there is still a sound spot, a presentiment of eventual health in the inmost nature, embolden us to hope, to *know* it is the same with all. A great thinker has spoken of the Greek, in highest praise, as " a self-renovating character." But we are all Greeks, if we will but think so. For the mentally or morally insane, there is no irreparable ill if the principle of life can but be aroused. And it can never be finally benumbed, except by our own will.

One of the famous pictures at Munich is of a madhouse. The painter has represented the moral obliquities of society exaggerated into madness ; that is to say, self-indulgence has, in each instance, destroyed the power to forbear the ill or to discern the good. A celebrated writer has added a little book, to be used while looking at the picture, and drawn inferences of universal interest.

Such would we draw ; such as this ! Let no one dare to call another mad who is not himself willing to rank in the same class for every perversion and fault of judgment. Let no one dare aid in punishing another as criminal who is not willing to suffer the penalty due to his own offences.

Yet, while owning that we are all mad, all criminal, let us not despair, but rather believe that the Ruler of all never could permit such wide-spread ill but to good ends. It is permitted to give us a field to redeem it —

> " to transmute, bereave
> Of an ill influence, and a good receive."

It flows inevitably from the emancipation of our wills, the development of individuality in us. These aims accomplished, all shall yet be well ; and it is ours to learn *how* that good time may be hastened.

We know no sign of the times more encouraging than the increasing nobleness and wisdom of view as to the government of asylums for the insane and of prisons. Whatever is learned as to these forms of society is learned for all. There is nothing that can be said of such government that must not be said, also, of the government of families, schools, and states. But we have much to say on this subject, and shall revert to it again, and often, though, perhaps, not with so pleasing a theme as this of St. Valentine's Eve.

FOURTH OF JULY.

The bells ring; the cannon rouse the echoes along the river shore; the boys sally forth with shouts and little flags, and crackers enough to frighten all the people they meet from sunrise to sunset. The orator is conning for the last time the speech in which he has vainly attempted to season with some new spice the yearly panegyric upon our country; its happiness and glory; the audience is putting on its best bib and tucker, and its blandest expression to listen.

And yet, no heart, we think, can beat to-day with one pulse of genuine, noble joy. Those who have obtained their selfish objects will not take especial pleasure in thinking of them to-day, while to unbiassed minds must come sad thoughts of national honor soiled in the eyes of other nations, of a great inheritance risked, if not forfeited.

Much has been achieved in this country since the Declaration of Independence. America is rich and strong; she has shown great talent and energy; vast prospects of aggrandizement open before her. But the noble sentiment which she expressed in her early youth is tarnished; she has shown that righteousness is not her chief desire, and her name is no longer a watchword for the highest hopes to the rest of the world. She knows this, but takes it very easily; she feels that she is growing richer and more powerful, and that seems to suffice her.

These facts are deeply saddening to those who can pronounce the words "my country" with pride and peace only so far as steadfast virtues, generous impulses, find their home in that country. They cannot be satisfied with superficial

(232)

benefits, with luxuries and the means of obtaining knowledge which are multiplied for them. They could rejoice in full hands and a busy brain, if the soul were expanding and the heart pure; but, the higher conditions being violated, what is done cannot be done for good.

Such thoughts fill patriot minds as the cannon-peal bursts upon the ear. This year, which declares that the people at large consent to cherish and extend slavery as one of our "domestic institutions," takes from the patriot his home. This year, which attests their insatiate love of wealth and power, quenches the flame upon the altar.

Yet there remains that good part which cannot be taken away. If nations go astray, the narrow path may always be found and followed by the individual man. It is hard, hard indeed, when politics and trade are mixed up with evils so mighty that he scarcely dares touch them for fear of being defiled. He finds his activity checked in great natural outlets by the scruples of conscience. He cannot enjoy the free use of his limbs, glowing upon a favorable tide; but struggling, panting, must fix his eyes upon his aim, and fight against the current to reach it. It is not easy, it is very hard just now, to realize the blessings of independence.

For what *is* independence if it do not lead to freedom? — freedom from fraud and meanness, from selfishness, from public opinion so far as it does not agree with the still, small voice of one's better self?

Yet there remains a great and worthy part to play. This country presents great temptations to ill, but also great inducements to good. Her health and strength are so remarkable, her youth so full of life, that disease cannot yet have taken deep hold of her. It has bewildered her brain, made her steps totter, fevered, but not yet tainted, her blood. Things are still in that state when ten just men may save the city. A few men are wanted, able to think and act upon principles of an eternal value. The safety of the country must lie in a

20 *

few such men; men who have achieved the genuine independence, independence of wrong, of violence, of falsehood.

We want individuals to whom all eyes may turn as examples of the practicability of virtue. We want shining examples. We want deeply-rooted characters, who cannot be
moved by flattery, by fear, even by hope, for they work in
faith. The opportunity for such men is great; they will not
be burned at the stake in their prime for bearing witness to
the truth, yet they will be tested most severely in their adherence to it. There is nothing to hinder them from learning
what is true and best; no physical tortures will be inflicted on
them for expressing it. Let men feel that in private lives,
more than in public measures, must the salvation of the
country lie. If that country has so widely veered from the
course she prescribed to herself, and that the hope of the
world prescribed to her, it must be because she had not men
ripened and confirmed for better things. They leaned too
carelessly on one another; they had not deepened and purified the private lives from which the public vitality must
spring, as the verdure of the plain from the fountains of the
hills.

What a vast influence is given by sincerity alone. The
bier of General Jackson has lately passed, upbearing a golden
urn. The men who placed it there lament his departure, and
esteem the measures which have led this country to her present position wise and good. The other side esteem them unwise, unjust, and disastrous in their consequences. But both
respect him thus far, that his conduct was boldly sincere. The
sage of Quincy! Men differ in their estimate of his abilities.
None, probably, esteem his mind as one of the first magnitude.
But both sides, all men, are influenced by the bold integrity
of his character. Mr. Calhoun speaks straight out what he
thinks. So far as this straightforwardness goes, he confers
the benefits of virtue. If a character be uncorrrpted, whatever bias it takes, it thus far is good and does good. It may

help others to a higher, wiser, larger independence than its own.

We know not where to look for an example of all or many of the virtues we would seek from the man who is to begin the new dynasty that is needed of fathers of the country. The country needs to be born again; she is polluted with the lust of power, the lust of gain. She needs fathers good enough to be godfathers — men who will stand sponsors at the baptism with *all* they possess, with all the goodness they can cherish, and all the wisdom they can win, to lead this child the way she should go, and never one step in another. Are there not in schools and colleges the boys who will become such men? Are there not those on the threshold of manhood who have not yet chosen the broad way into which the multitude rushes, led by the banner on which, strange to say, the royal Eagle is blazoned, together with the word Expediency? Let them decline that road, and take the narrow, thorny path where Integrity leads, though with no prouder emblem than the Dove. They may there find the needed remedy, which, like the white root, detected by the patient and resolved Odysseus, shall have power to restore the herd of men, disguised by the enchantress to whom they had willingly yielded in the forms of brutes, to the stature and beauty of men.

FIRST OF AUGUST.

Among the holidays of the year, some portion of our people borrow one from another land. They borrow what they fain would own, since their doing so would increase, not lessen, the joy and prosperity of the present owner. It is a holiday not to be celebrated, as others are, with boast, and shout, and gay procession, but solemnly, yet hopefully; in prayer and humiliation for much ill now existing; in faith that the God of good will not permit such ill to exist always; in aspiration to become his instruments for removal.

We borrow this holiday from England. We know not that she could lend us another such. Her career has been one of selfish aggrandizement. To carry her flag wherever the waters flow; to leave a strong mark of her footprint on every shore, that she might return and claim its spoils; to maintain in every way her own advantage, — is and has been her object, as much as that of any nation upon earth. The plundered Hindoo, the wronged Irish, — for ourselves we must add the outraged Chinese, (for we look on all that has been written about the right of that war as mere sophistry,) — no less than Napoleon, walking up and down, in his "tarred great-coat," in the unwholesome lodge at St. Helena, — all can tell whether she be righteous or generous in her conquests. Nay, let myriads of her own children say whether she will abstain from sacrificing, mercilessly, human freedom, happiness, and the education of immortal souls, for the sake of gains of money! We speak of Napoleon, for we must

ever despise, with most profound contempt, the use she made
of her power on that occasion. She had been the chief means
of liberating Europe from his tyranny, and, though it was for
her own sake, we must commend and admire her conduct and
resolution thus far. But the unhandsome, base treatment of
her captive, has never been enough contemned. Any private
gentleman, in chaining up the foe that had put himself in his
power, would at least have given him lodging, food, and
clothes to his liking, and a civil turnkey — and a great nation could fail in this! O, it was shameful, if only for the
vulgarity of feeling evinced! All this we say, because we
are sometimes impatient of England's brag on the subject
of slavery. Freedom! Because she has done one good
act, is she entitled to the angelic privilege of being the
champion of freedom?

And yet it is true that once she nobly awoke to a sense of
what was right and wise. It is true that she also acted out
that sense — acted fully, decidedly. She was willing to
make sacrifices, even of the loved money. She has not let
go the truth she then laid to heart, and continues the resolute
foe of man's traffic in men. We must bend low to her as we
borrow this holiday — the anniversary of the emancipation
of slaves in the West Indies. We do not feel that the extent
of her practice justifies the extent of her preaching; yet we
must feel her to be, in this matter, an elder sister, entitled to
cry shame to us. And if her feelings be those of a sister
indeed, how must she mourn to see her next of kin pushing
back, as far as in her lies, the advance of this good cause,
binding those whom the old world had awakened from its sins
enough to loose! But courage, sister! All is not yet lost!
There is here a faithful band, determined to expiate the
crimes that have been committed in the name of liberty.
On this day they meet and vow themselves to the service;
and, as they look in one another's glowing eyes, they read

there assurance that the end is not yet, and that they, forced
as they are

> "To keep in company with Pain,
> And Fear, and Falsehood, miserable train,"

> " Turn that necessity to glorious gain,"

> " Transmute them and subdue."

Indeed, we do not see that they "bate a jot of heart or
hope," and it is because they feel that the power of the Great
Spirit, and its peculiar workings in the spirit of this age, are
with them. There is action and reaction all the time ; and
though the main current is obvious, there are many little
eddies and counter-currents. Mrs. Norton writes a poem on
the sufferings of the poor, and in it she, as episode, tunefully
laments the sufferings of the Emperor of all the Russias for
the death of a beloved daughter. And it *was* a deep grief;
yet it did not soften his heart, or make it feel for man. The
first signs of his recovered spirits are in new efforts to crush
out the heart of Poland, and to make the Jews lay aside the
hereditary marks of their national existence — to them a sacrifice far worse than death. But then, — Count Apraxin is
burned alive by his infuriate serfs, and the life of a serf is
far more dog-like, or rather machine-like, than that of *our*
slaves. Still the serf can rise in vengeance — can admonish the autocrat that humanity may yet turn again and
rend him.

So with us. The most shameful deed has been done that
ever disgraced a nation, because the most contrary to consciousness of right. Other nations have done wickedly, but
we have surpassed them all in trampling under foot the principles that had been assumed as the basis of our national existence, and shown a willingness to forfeit our honor in the
face of the world.

The following stanzas, written by a friend some time since,

on the fourth of July, exhibit these contrasts so forcibly, that
we cannot do better than insert them here : —

Loud peal of bells and beat of drums
   Salute approaching dawn ;
And the deep cannon's fearful bursts
   Announce a nation's morn.

Imposing ranks of freemen stand
   And claim their proud birthright;
Impostors, rather ! thus to brand
   A name they hold so bright.

Let the day see the pageant show;
   Float, banners, to the breeze !
Shout Liberty's great name throughout
   Columbia's lands and seas !

Give open sunlight to the free ;
   But for Truth's equal sake,
When night sinks down upon the land,
   Proclaim dead Freedom's wake !

Beat, muffled drums ! Toll, funeral bell !
   Nail every flag half-mast ;
For though we fought the battle well,
   We're traitors at the last.

Let the whole nation join in one
   Procession to appear;
We and our sons lead on the front,
   Our slaves bring up the rear.

America is rocked within
   Thy cradle, Liberty,
By Africa's poor, palsied hand —
   Strange inconsistency !

We've dug one grave as deep as **Death**,
　For Tyranny's black sin ;
And dug another at its side
　To thrust our brother in.

We challenge all the world aloud, —
　"Lo, Tyranny's deep grave !"
And all the world points back and cries,
　"Thou fool !   Behold thy slave !"

Yes, rally, brave America,
　Thy noble hearts and free
Around the Eagle, as he soars
　Upward in majesty.

One half thy emblem is the bird,
　Out-facing thus the day ;
But wouldst thou make him wholly thine, —
　Give him a helpless prey !

This should be sung in Charleston at nine o'clock in the evening, when the drums are heard proclaiming "dead Freedom's wake," as they summon to their homes, or to the custody of the police, every human being with a black skin who is found walking without a pass from a white.   Or it might have been sung to advantage the night after Charleston had shown her independence and care of domestic institutions by expulsion of the venerable envoy of Massachusetts !   Its expression would seem even more forcible than now, when sung so near the facts, when the eagle soars so close above his prey.

How deep the shadow ! yet cleft by light.   There is a counter-current that sets towards the deep.   We are inclined to weigh as of almost equal weight with all we have had to trouble us as to the prolongation of slavery, the hopes that may be gathered from the course of such a man as Cassius

M. Clay, — a man open to none of the accusations brought to diminish the influence of abolitionists in general, for he has eaten the bread wrought from slavery, and has shared the education that excuses the blindness of the slaveholder. He speaks as one having authority; no one can deny that he knows where he is. In the prime of manhood, of talent, and the energy of a fine enthusiasm, he comes forward with deed and word to do his devoir in this cause, never to leave the field till he can take with him the wronged wretches rescued by his devotion.

Now he has made this last sacrifice of the prejudices of "southern chivalry," more persons than ever will be ready to join the herald's cry, "God speed the right!" And we cannot but believe his noble example will be followed by many young men in the slaveholding ranks, brothers in a new, sacred band, vowed to the duty, not merely of defending, but far more sacred, of purifying their homes.

The event of which this day is the anniversary, affords a sufficient guarantee of the safety and practicability of strong measures for this purification. Various accounts are given to the public, of the state of the British West Indies, and the foes of emancipation are of course constantly on the alert to detect any unfavorable result which may aid them in opposing the good work elsewhere. But through all statements these facts shine clear as the sun at noonday, that the measure was there carried into effect with an ease and success, and has shown in the African race a degree of goodness, docility, capacity for industry and self-culture entirely beyond or opposed to the predictions which darkened so many minds with fears. Those fears can never again be entertained or uttered with the same excuse. One great example of the *safety of doing right* exists; true, there is but one of the sort, but volumes may be preached from such a text.

We, however, preach not; there are too many preachers already in the field, abler, more deeply devoted to the cause.

21

Endless are the sermons of these modern crusaders, these ardent "sons of thunder," who have pledged themselves never to stop or falter till this one black spot be purged away from the land which gave them birth. They cry aloud and spare not; they spare not others, but then, neither do they spare themselves; and such are ever the harbingers of a new advent of the Holy Spirit. Our venerated friend, Dr. Channing, sainted in more memories than any man who has left us in this nineteenth century, uttered the last of his tones of soft, solemn, convincing, persuasive eloquence, on this day and this occasion. The hills of Lenox laughed and were glad as they heard him who showed in that last address (an address not only to the men of Lenox, but to all men, for he was in the highest sense the friend of man) the unsullied purity of infancy, the indignation of youth at vice and wrong, informed and tempered by the mild wisdom of age. It is a beautiful fact that this should have been the last public occasion of his life.

Last year a noble address was delivered by R. W. Emerson, in which he broadly showed the *juste milieu* views upon this subject in the holy light of a high ideal day. The truest man grew more true as he listened; for the speech, though it had the force of fact and the lustre of thought, was chiefly remarkable as sharing the penetrating quality of the "still small voice," most often heard when no man speaks. Now it spoke *through* a man; and no personalities, or prejudices, or passions could be perceived to veil or disturb its silver sound.

These speeches are on record; little can be said that is not contained in them. But we can add evermore our aspirations for thee, O our country! that thou mayst not long need to borrow a *holy* day; not long have all thy festivals blackened by falsehood, tyranny, and a crime for which neither man below nor God above can much longer pardon thee. For ignorance may excuse error; but thine — it is vain to deny it — is conscious wrong, and vows thee to the Mammon whose wages are endless remorse or final death.

THANKSGIVING.

"Canst thou give thanks for aught that has been given
　Except by making earth more worthy heaven ?
　Just stewardship the Master hoped from thee;
　Harvests from time to bless eternity."

THANKSGIVING is peculiarly the festival day of New England. Elsewhere, other celebrations rival its attractions, but in that region where the Puritans first returned thanks that some among them had been sustained by a great hope and earnest resolve amid the perils of the ocean, wild beasts, and famine, the old spirit which hallowed the day still lingers, and forbids that it should be entirely devoted to play and plum-pudding.

And yet, as there is always this tendency; as the twelfth-night cake is baked by many a hostess who would be puzzled if you asked her, "Twelfth night after or before what?" and the Christmas cake by many who know no other Christmas service, so it requires very serious assertion and proof from the minister to convince his parishioners that the turkey and plum-pudding, which are presently to occupy his place in their attention, should not be the chief objects of the day.

And in other regions, where the occasion is observed, it is still more as one for a meeting of families and friends to the enjoyment of a good dinner, than for any higher purpose.

This, indeed, is one which we want not to depreciate. If this manner of keeping the day be likely to persuade the juniors of the party that the celebrated Jack Horner is the prime model for brave boys, and that grandparents are chiefly to be respected as the givers of grand feasts yet a meeting in the spirit of kindness, however dull and blind, is not wholly without use in healing differences and promoting good intentions. The instinct of family love, intended by Heaven to make those of one blood the various and harmonious organs of one mind, is never wholly without good influence. Family love, I say, for family pride is never without bad influence, and it too often takes the place of its mild and healthy sister.

Yet where society is at all simple, it is cheering to see the family circle thus assembled, if only because its patriarchal form is in itself so excellent. The presence of the children animates the old people, while the respect and attention they demand refine the gayety of the young. Yes, it is cheering to see, in some large room, the elders talking near the bright fire, while the cousins of all ages are amusing themselves in knots. Here is almost all the good, and very little of the ill, that can be found in society, got together merely for amusement.

Yet how much nobler, more exhilarating, and purer would be the atmosphere of that circle if the design of its pious founders were remembered by those who partake this festival! if they dared not attend the public jubilee till private retrospect of the past year had been taken in the spirit of the old rhyme, which we all bear in mind if not in heart, —

> "What hast thou done that's worth the doing,
> And what pursued that's worth pursuing?
> What sought thou knew'st that thou shouldst shun,
> What done thou shouldst have left undone?"

A crusade needs also to be made this day into the wild places of each heart, taking for its device, "Lord, cleanse thou me from secret faults; keep back thy servant also from presumptuous sins." Would not that circle be happy as if music, from invisible agents, floated through it if each member of it considered every other member as a bequest from heaven; if he sup-

posed that the appointed nearness in blood or lot was a sign
to him that he must exercise his gifts of every kind as given
peculiarly in their behalf; that if richer in temper, in talents,
in knowledge, or in worldly goods, here was the innermost
circle of his poor; that he must clothe these naked, whether
in body or mind, soothing the perverse, casting light into the
narrow chamber, or, most welcome task of all! extending a
hand at the right moment to one uncertain of his way? It is
this spirit that makes the old man to be revered as a Nestor,
rather than put aside like a worn-out garment. It is such a
spirit that sometimes has given to the young child a ministry
as of a parent in the house.

But, if charity begin at home, it must not end there; and,
while purifying the innermost circle, let us not forget that it
depends upon the great circle, and that again on it; that no
home can be healthful in which are not cherished seeds of
good for the world at large. Thy child, thy brother, are given
to thee only as an example of what is due from thee to all
men. It is true that, if you, in anger, call your brother fool,
no deeds of so-called philanthropy shall save you from the
punishment; for your philanthropy must be from the love of
excitement, not the love of man, or of goodness. But then
you must visit the Gentiles also, and take time for knowing
what aid the woman of Samaria may need.

A noble Catholic writer, in the true sense as well as by
name a Catholic, describes a tailor as giving a dinner on an
occasion which had brought honor to his house, which, though
a humble, was not a poor house. In his glee, the tailor was
boasting a little of the favors and blessings of his lot, when
suddenly a thought stung him. He stopped, and cutting away
half the fowl that lay before him, sent it in a dish with the
best knives, bread, and napkin, and a brotherly message that
was better still, to a widow near, who must, he knew, be
sitting in sadness and poverty among her children. His little
daughter was the messenger. If parents followed up the

21 *

indulgences heaped upon their children at Thanksgiving dinners with similar messages, there would not be danger that children should think enjoyment of sensual pleasures the only occasion that demands Thanksgiving.

And suppose, while the children were absent on their errands of justice, as they could not fail to think them, if they compared the hovels they must visit with their own comfortable homes, their elders, touched by a sense of right, should be led from discussion of the rivalries of trade or fashion to inquiry whether they could not impart of all that was theirs, not merely one poor dinner once a year, but all their mental and material wealth for the benefit of all men. If they do not sell it *all* at once, as the rich young man was bid to do as a test of his sincerity, they may find some way in which it could be invested so as to show enough obedience to the law and the prophets to love our neighbor as ourselves.

And he who once gives himself to such thoughts will find it is not merely moral gain for which he shall return thanks another year with the return of this day. In the present complex state of human affairs, you cannot be kind unless you are wise. Thoughts of amaranthine bloom will spring up in the fields ploughed to give food to suffering men. It would, indeed, seem to be a simple matter at first glance. "Lovest thou me?" — "Feed my lambs." But now we have not only to find pasture, but to detect the lambs under the disguise of wolves, and restore them by a spell, like that the shepherd used, to their natural form and whiteness.

And for this present day appointed for Thanksgiving, we may say that if we know of so many wrongs, woes, and errors in the world yet unredressed; if in this nation recent decisions have shown a want of moral discrimination in important subjects, that make us pause and doubt whether we can join in the formal congratulations that we are still bodily alive, unassailed by the ruder modes of warfare, and enriched with the fatness of the land; yet, on the other side, we know of causes not so loudly proclaimed why we should give thanks. Abundantly and humbly we must render them for the movement, now sensible in the heart of the civilized world, although it has not pervaded the entire frame — for that movement of contrition and love which forbids men of earnest thought to eat, drink, or be merry while other men are steeped in ignorance, corruption, and woe; which calls the king from his throne of gold, and the poet from his throne of mind, to lie with the beggar in the kennel, or raise him from it; which says to the poet, " You must reform rather than create a world," and to him of the golden crown, " You cannot long remain a king unless you are also a man."

Wherever this impulse of social or political reform darts up its rill through the crusts of selfishness, scoff and dread also arise, and hang like a heavy mist above it. But the voice of the rill penetrates far enough for those who have ears to hear. And sometimes it is the case that " those who came to scoff remain to pray." In two articles of reviews, one foreign and one domestic, which have come under our eye within the last fortnight, the writers who began by jeering at the visionaries, seemed, as they wrote, to be touched by a sense that without a high and pure faith none can have the only true vision of the intention of God as to the destiny of man.

We recognized as a happy omen that there is cause for thanksgiving, and that our people may be better than they seem, the recent meeting to organize an association for the benefit of prisoners. We are not, then, wholly Pharisees. We shall not ask the blessing of this day in the mood of, " Lord, I thank thee that I, and my son, and my brother, are not as other men are, — not as those publicans imprisoned there," while the still small voice cannot make us hear its evidence that, but for instruction, example, and the " preventing God," every sin that can be named might riot in our hearts. The prisoner, too, may become a man. Neither his open nor our secret fault must utterly dismay us. We will treat him as if he had a soul. We will not dare to hunt him into a beast of prey, or trample him into a serpent. We will give him some crumbs from the table which grace from above and parental love below have spread for us, and perhaps he will recover from these ghastly ulcers that deform him now.

We were much pleased with the spirit of the meeting for the benefit of prisoners, to which we have just alluded. It was simple, business-like, in a serious, affectionate temper. The speakers did not make phrases or compliments — did not slur over the truth. The audience showed a ready vibration to the touch of just and tender feeling. The time was evidently ripe for this movement. We doubt not that many now darkened souls will give thanks for the ray of light that will have been let in by this time next year. It is but a grain of mustard seed, but the promised tree will grow swiftly if tended in a pure spirit; and the influence of good measures in any one place will be immediate in this province, as has been the case with every attempt in behalf of another sorrowing class, the insane.

While reading a notice of a successful attempt to have musical performances carried through in concert by the insane at Rouen, we were forcibly reminded of a similar performance we heard a few weeks ago at Sing Sing. There the female prisoners joined in singing a hymn, or rather choral, which describes the last thoughts of a spirit about to be enfranchised from the body; each stanza of which ends with the words, " All is well;" and they sang it — those suffering, degraded children of society — with as gentle and resigned an expression as if they were sure of going to sleep in the arms of a pure mother. The good spirit that dwelt in the music made them its own. And shall not the good spirit of religious sympathy make them its own also, and more permanently? We shall see. Should the *morally* insane, by wise and gentle care, be won back to health, as the wretched bedlamites have been, will not the angels themselves give thanks? And will any man dare take the risk of opposing plans that afford even a chance of such a result?

Apart also from good that is public and many-voiced, does not each of us know, in private experience, much to be thankful for? Not only the innocent and daily pleasures that we have prized according to our wisdom; of the sun and starry skies, the fields of green, or snow scarcely less beautiful, the loaf eaten with an appetite, the glow of labor, the gentle signs of common affection; but have not some, have not many of us, cause to be thankful for enfranchisement from error or infatuation; a growth in knowledge of outward things, and instruction within the soul from a higher source. Have we not acquired a sense of more refined enjoyments; clear convictions; sometimes a serenity in which, as in the first days of June, all things grow, and the blossom gives place to fruit? Have we not been weaned from what was unfit for us, or unworthy our care? and have not those ties been drawn more close, and are not those objects seen more distinctly, which shall forever be worthy the purest desires of our souls? Have we learned to do any thing, the humblest, in the service and by the spirit of the power which meaneth all things well? If so, we may give thanks, and, perhaps, venture to offer our solicitations in behalf of those as yet less favored by circumstances. When even a few shall dare do so with the whole heart — for only a pure heart can "avail much" in such prayers — then ALL shall soon be well.

OUR festivals come rather too near together, since we have so few of them ; thanksgiving, Christmas, new year's day, — and then none again till July. We know not but these four, with the addition of "a day set apart for fasting and prayer," might answer the purposes of rest and edification, as well as a calendar full of saints' days, if they were observed in a better spirit. But thanksgiving is devoted to good dinners; Christmas and new year's days, to making presents and compliments ; fast day, to playing at cricket and other games ; and the fourth of July, to boasting of the past, rather than to plans how to deserve its benefits and secure its fruits.

We value means of marking time by appointed days, because man, on one side of his nature so ardent and aspiring, is on the other so slippery and indolent a being, that he needs incessant admonitions to redeem the time. Time flows on steadily, whether he regards it or not ; yet unless *he keep time*, there is no music in that flow. The sands drop with inevitable speed, yet each waits long enough to receive, if it be ready, the intellectual touch that should turn it to a sand of gold.

Time, says the Grecian fable, is the parent of Power ; Power is the father of Genius and Wisdom ; Time, then, is grandfather of the noblest of the human family, and we must respect the aged sire whom we see on the frontispiece of the almanacs, and believe his scythe was meant to mow down harvests ripened for an immortal use.

Yet the best provision made by the mind of society, at large, for these admonitions, soon loses its efficacy, and re-

(250)

quires that individual earnestness, individual piety, should continually reanimate the most beautiful form. The world has never seen arrangements which might more naturally offer good suggestions, than those of the church of Rome. The founders of that church stood very near a history, radiant at every page with divine light. All their rites and ceremonial days illustrate facts of a universal interest. But the life with which piety, first, and afterwards the genius of great artists, invested these symbols, waned at last, except to a thoughtful few. Reverence was forgotten in the multitude of genuflections; the rosary became a string of beads, rather than a series of religious meditations, and " the glorious company of saints and martyrs" were not so much regarded as the teachers of heavenly truth, as intercessors to obtain for their votaries the temporal gifts they craved.

Yet we regret that some of these symbols had not been more reverenced by Protestants, as the possible occasion of good thoughts. And among others we regret that the day set apart to commemorate the birth of Jesus should have been stripped, even by those who observe it, of many impressive and touching accessories.

If ever there was an occasion on which the arts could become all but omnipotent in the service of a holy thought, it is this of the birth of the child Jesus. In the palmy days of the Catholic religion, they may be said to have wrought miracles in its behalf; and, in our colder time, when we rather reflect that light from a different point of view, than transport ourselves into it, — who, that has an eye and ear faithful to the soul, is not conscious of inexhaustible benefits from some of the works by which sublime geniuses have expressed their ideas in the adorations of the Magi and the Shepherds, in the Virgin with the infant Jesus, or that work which expresses what Christendom at large has not even begun to realize, — that work which makes us conscious, as we listen, why the soul of man was thought worthy and able to upbear a cross of such dreadful weight — the Messiah of Handel.

Christmas would seem to be the day peculiarly sacred to children, and something of this feeling here shows itself among us, though rather from German influence than of native growth. The evergreen tree is often reared for the children on Christmas evening, and its branches cluster with little tokens that may, at least, give them a sense that the world is rich, and that there are some in it who care to bless them. It is a charming sight to see their glittering eyes, and well worth much trouble in preparing the Christmas tree.

Yet, on this occasion as on all others, we could wish to see pleasure offered them in a form less selfish than it is. When shall we read of banquets prepared for the halt, the lame, and the blind, on the day that is said to have brought *their* Friend into the world? When will the children be taught to ask all the cold and ragged little ones, whom they have seen during the day wistfully gazing at the displays in the shop-windows, to share the joys of Christmas eve?

We borrow the Christmas tree from Germany. Would that we might but borrow with it that feeling which pervades all their stories about the influence of the Christ child ; and has, I doubt not, — for the spirit of literature is always, though refined, the essence of popular life, — pervaded the conduct of children there !

We will mention two of these as happily expressive of different sides of the desirable character. One is a legend of the Saint Hermann Joseph. The legend runs, that this saint, when a little boy, passed daily by a niche where was an image of the Virgin and Child, and delighted there to pay his devotions. His heart was so drawn towards the holy child, that, one day, having received what seemed to him a gift truly precious, — to wit, a beautiful red and yellow apple, — he ventured to offer it, with his prayer. To his unspeakable delight, the child put forth its hand and took the apple. After that day, never was a gift bestowed upon the little Hermann that was not carried to the same place. He needed nothing for himself, but dedicated all his childish goods to the altar.

After a while, grief comes. His father, who was a poor man, finds it necessary to take him from school and bind him to a trade. He communicates his woes to his friends of the niche, and the Virgin comforts him, like a mother, and bestows on him money, by means of which he rises, (not to ride in a gilt coach like Lord Mayor Whittington,) but to be a learned and tender shepherd of men.

Another still more touching story is that of the holy Rupert. Rupert was the only child of a princely house, and had something to give besides apples. But his generosity and human love were such, that, as a child, he could never see poor children suffering without despoiling himself of all he had with him in their behalf. His mother was, at first, displeased at this; but when he replied, "They are thy children too," her reproofs yielded to tears.

One time, when he had given away his coat to a poor child, he got wearied and belated on his homeward way. He lay down a while, and fell asleep. Then he dreamed that he was on a river shore, and saw a mild and noble old man bathing many children. After he had plunged them into the water, he would place them on a beautiful island, where they looked white and glorious as little angels. Rupert was seized with strong desire to join them, and begged the old man to bathe him, also, in the stream. But he was answered, "It is not yet time." Just then a rainbow spanned the island, and on its arch was enthroned the child Jesus, dressed in a coat that Rupert knew to be his own. And the child said to the others, "See this coat; it is one my brother Rupert has just sent to me. He has given us many gifts from his love; shall we not ask him to join us here?" And they shouted a musical "yes;" and the child started from his dream. But he had lain too long on the damp bank of the river, without his coat. A cold and fever soon sent him to join the band of his brothers in their home.

These are legends, superstitions, will you say? But, in casting aside the shell, have we retained the kernel? The image of the child Jesus is not seen in the open street; does his spirit find other means to express itself there? Protestantism did not mean, we suppose, to deaden the spirit in excluding the form?

The thought of Jesus, as a child, has great weight with children who have learned to think of him at all. In thinking of him, they form an image of all that the morning of a pure and fervent life should be and bring. In former days I knew a boy artist, whose genius, at that time, showed high promise. He was not more than fourteen years old; a slight, pale boy, with a beaming eye. The hopes and sympathy of friends, gained by his talent, had furnished him with a studio and orders for some pictures. He had picked up from the streets a boy still younger and poorer than himself, to take care of the room and prepare his colors; and the two boys were as content in their relation as Michael Angelo with his Urbino. If you went there you found exposed to view many pretty pictures: a Girl with a Dove, the Guitar Player, and such subjects as are commonly supposed to interest at his age. But, hid in a corner, and never shown, unless to the beggar page, or some most confidential friend, was the real object of his love and pride, the slowly growing work of secret hours. The subject of this picture was Christ teaching the doctors. And in those doctors he had expressed all he had already observed of the pedantry and shallow conceit of those in whom mature years have not unfolded the soul; and in the child, all he felt that early youth should be and seek, though, alas! his own feet failed him on the difficult road. This one record of the youth of Jesus had, at least, been much to his mind.

In earlier days, the little saints thought they best imitated the Emanuel by giving apples and coats; but we know not why, in our age, that esteems itself so enlightened, they should not become also the givers of spiritual gifts. We see in them, continually, impulses that only require a good direction to effect infinite good. See the little girls at work for foreign missions; that is not useless. They devote the time to a purpose that is not selfish; the horizon of their thoughts is extended. But they are perfectly capable of becoming home missionaries as well. The principle of stewardship would make them so.

I have seen a little girl of thirteen,—who had much service, too, to perform, for a hard-working mother,—in the midst of a circle of poor children whom she gathered daily to a morning school. She took them from the door-steps and the ditches; she washed their hands and faces; she taught them to read and to sew; and she told them stories that had delighted her own infancy. In her face, though in feature and complexion plain, was something, already, of a Madonna sweetness, and it had no way eclipsed the gayety of childhood.

I have seen a boy scarce older, brought up for some time with the sons of laborers, who, so soon as he found himself possessed of superior advantages, thought not of surpassing others, but of excelling, and then imparting — and he was able to do it. If the other boys had less leisure, and could pay for less instruction, they did not suffer for it. He could not be happy unless they also could enjoy Milton, and pass from nature to natural philosophy. He performed, though in a childish way, and in no Grecian garb, the part of Apollo amid the herdsmen of Admetus.

The cause of education would be indefinitely furthered, if, in addition to formal means, there were but this principle awakened in the hearts of the young, that what they have they must bestow. All are not natural instructors, but a large proportion are; and those who do possess such a talent are the best possible teachers to those a little younger than themselves. Many have more patience with the difficulties they have lately left behind, and enjoy their power of assisting more than those farther removed in age and knowledge do.

Then the intercourse may be far more congenial and profitable than where the teacher receives for hire all sorts of pupils, as they are sent him by their guardians. Here he need only choose those who have a predisposition for what he is best able to teach. And, as I would have the so-called higher instruction as much diffused in this way as the lower, there would be a chance of awakening all the power that now lies latent.

If a girl, for instance, who has only a passable talent for music, but who, from the advantage of social position, has been able to gain thorough instruction, felt it her duty to teach whomsoever she knew that had such a talent, without money to cultivate it, the good is obvious.

Those who are learning receive an immediate benefit by an effort to rearrange and interpret what they learn; so the use of this justice would be twofold.

Some efforts are made here and there; nay, sometimes there are those who can say they have returned usury for every gift of fate. And, would others make the same experiments, they might find Utopia not so far off as the children of this world, wise in securing their own selfish ease, would persuade us it must always be.

We have hinted what sort of Christmas box we would wish for the children. It would be one full, as that of the child Christ must be, of the pieces of silver that were lost and are found. But Christmas, with its peculiar associations, has deep interest for men, and women too, no less. It has so in their mutual relations. At the time thus celebrated, a pure woman saw in her child what the Son of man should be as a child of God. She anticipated for him a life of glory to God, peace and good will to man. In every young mother's heart, who has any purity of heart, the same feelings arise. But most of these mothers let them go without obeying their instructions. If they did not, we should see other children — other men than now throng our streets. The boy could not invariably disappoint the mother, the man the wife, who steadily demanded of him such a career.

And man looks upon woman, in this relation, always as he should. Does he see in her a holy mother worthy to guard the infancy of an immortal soul? Then she assumes in his eyes those traits which the Romish church loved to revere in Mary. Frivolity, base appetite, contempt are exorcised; and man and woman appear again in unprofaned connection, as brother and sister, the children and the servants of the one Divine Love, and pilgrims to a common aim.

Were all this right in the private sphere, the public would soon right itself also, and the nations of Christendom might join in a celebration, such as "kings and prophets waited for," and so many martyrs died to achieve, of Christ-Mass.

22 *

AMONG those whom I met in a recent visit at Chicago was Mrs. Z., the aunt of an old schoolmate, to whom I impatiently hastened, to demand news of Mariana. The answer startled me. Mariana, so full of life, was dead. That form, the most rich in energy and coloring of any I had ever seen, had faded from the earth. The circle of youthful associations had given way in the part that seemed the strongest. What I now learned of the story of this life, and what was by myself remembered, may be bound together in this slight sketch.

At the boarding school to which I was too early sent, a fond, a proud, and timid child, I saw among the ranks of the gay and graceful, bright or earnest girls, only one who interested my fancy or touched my young heart; and this was Mariana. She was, on the father's side, of Spanish Creole blood, but had been sent to the Atlantic coast, to receive a school education under the care of her aunt, Mrs. Z.

This lady had kept her mostly at home with herself, and Mariana had gone from her house to a day school; but the aunt being absent for a time in Europe, she had now been unfortunately committed for some time to the mercies of a boarding school.

A strange bird she proved there — a lonely one, that could not make for itself a summer. At first, her schoolmates were captivated with her ways, her love of wild dances and sudden

---

[* It is well known that in this sketch my sister gives an account of an incident in the history of her own school-girl life. I need scarcely say that only so far as this incident is concerned is the story of Mariana in any sense autobiographical. — ED.]

song, her freaks of passion and of wit. She was always new, always surprising, and, for a time, charming.

But, after a while, they tired of her. She could never be depended on to join in their plans, yet she expected them to follow out hers with their whole strength. She was very loving, even infatuated in her own affections, and exacted from those who had professed any love for her, the devotion she was willing to bestow.

Yet there was a vein of haughty caprice in her character; a love of solitude, which made her at times wish to retire entirely; and at these times she would expect to be thoroughly understood, and let alone, yet to be welcomed back when she returned. She did not thwart others in their humors, but she never doubted of great indulgence from them.

Some singular ways she had, which, when new, charmed, but, after acquaintance, displeased her companions. She had by nature the same habit and power of excitement that is described in the spinning dervishes of the East. Like them, she would spin until all around her were giddy, while her own brain. instead of being disturbed, was excited to great action. Pausing, she would declaim verse of others or her own; perform many parts, with strange catch-words and burdens that seemed to act with mystical power on her own fancy, sometimes stimulating her to convulse the hearer with laughter, sometimes to melt him to tears. When her power began to languish, she would spin again till fired to recommence her singular drama, into which she wove figures from the scenes of her earlier childhood, her companions, and the dignitaries she sometimes saw, with fantasies unknown to life, unknown to heaven or earth.

This excitement, as may be supposed, was not good for her. It oftenest came on in the evening, and spoiled her sleep. She would wake in the night, and cheat her restlessness by inventions that teased, while they sometimes diverted her companions.

She was also a sleep-walker; and this one trait of her case did somewhat alarm her guardians, who, otherwise, showed the same profound stupidity, as to this peculiar being, usual in the overseers of the young. They consulted a physician, who said she would outgrow it, and prescribed a milk diet.

Meantime, the fever of this ardent and too early stimulated nature was constantly increased by the restraints and narrow routine of the boarding school. She was always devising means to break in upon it. She had a taste, which would have seemed ludicrous to her mates, if they had not felt some awe of her, from a touch of genius and power, that never left her, for costume and fancy dresses; always some sash twisted about her, some drapery, something odd in the arrangement of her hair and dress; so that the methodical preceptress dared not let her go out without a careful scrutiny and remodelling, whose soberizing effects generally disappeared the moment she was in the free air.

At last, a vent for her was found in private theatricals. Play followed play, and in these and the rehearsals she found entertainment congenial with her. The principal parts, as a matter of course, fell to her lot; most of the good suggestions and arrangements came from her, and for a time she ruled masterly and shone triumphant.

During these performances the girls had heightened their natural bloom with artificial red; this was delightful to them — it was something so out of the way. But Mariana, after the plays were over, kept her carmine saucer on the dressing table, and put on her blushes regularly as the morning.

When stared and jeered at, she at first said she did it because she thought it made her look prettier; but, after a while, she became quite petulant about it — would make no reply to any joke, but merely kept on doing it.

This irritated the girls, as all eccentricity does the world in general, more than vice or malignity. They talked it over among themselves, till they got wrought up to a desire of punishing, once for all, this sometimes amusing, but so often provoking nonconformist.

Having obtained the leave of the mistress, they laid, with great glee, a plan one evening, which was to be carried into execution next day at dinner.

Among Mariana's irregularities was a great aversion to the meal-time ceremonial. So long, so tiresome she found it, to be seated at a certain moment, to wait while each one was served at so large a table, and one where there was scarcely any conversation ; from day to day it became more heavy to her to sit there, or go there at all. Often as possible she excused herself on the ever-convenient plea of headache, and was hardly ever ready when the dinner bell rang.

To-day it found her on the balcony, lost in gazing on the beautiful prospect. I have heard her say, afterwards, she had rarely in her life been so happy — and she was one with whom happiness was a still rapture. It was one of the most blessed summer days; the shadows of great white clouds empurpled the distant hills for a few moments only to leave them more golden; the tall grass of the wide fields waved in the softest breeze. Pure blue were the heavens, and the same hue of pure contentment was in the heart of Mariana.

Suddenly on her bright mood jarred the dinner bell. At first rose her usual thought, I will not, cannot go; and then the *must*, which daily life can always enforce, even upon the butterflies and birds, came, and she walked reluctantly to her room. She merely changed her dress, and never thought of adding the artificial rose to her cheek.

When she took her seat in the dining hall, and was asked if she would be helped, raising her eyes, she saw the person who asked her was deeply rouged, with a bright, glaring spot, perfectly round, in either cheek. She looked at the next — the same apparition! She then slowly passed her eyes down the whole line, and saw the same, with a suppressed smile distorting every countenance. Catching the design at once,

she deliberately looked along her own side of the table, at
every schoolmate in turn; every one had joined in the trick.
The teachers strove to be grave, but she saw they enjoyed the
joke.　The servants could not suppress a titter.

When Warren Hastings stood at the bar of Westminster
Hall; when the Methodist preacher walked through a line
of men, each of whom greeted him with a brickbat or a rot-
ten egg, — they had some preparation for the crisis, and it
might not be very difficult to meet it with an impassive brow.
Our little girl was quite unprepared to find herself in the
midst of a world which despised her, and triumphed in her
disgrace.

She had ruled like a queen in the midst of her companions; she had shed her animation through their lives, and
loaded them with prodigal favors, nor once suspected that a
powerful favorite might not be loved.　Now, she felt that she
had been but a dangerous plaything in the hands of those
whose hearts she never had doubted.

Yet the occasion found her equal to it; for Mariana had
the kind of spirit, which, in a better cause, had made the
Roman matron truly say of her death wound, " It is not painful, Pœtus." She did not blench — she did not change countenance.　She swallowed her dinner with apparent composure.
She made remarks to those near her as if she had no eyes.

The wrath of the foe of course rose higher, and the moment they were freed from the restraints of the dining room,
they all ran off, gayly calling, and sarcastically laughing, with
backward glances, at Mariana, left alone.

She went alone to her room, locked the door, and threw
herself on the floor in strong convulsions.　These had sometimes threatened her life, as a child, but of later years she had
outgrown them.　School hours came, and she was not there.
A little girl, sent to her door, could get no answer.　The
teachers became alarmed, and broke it open.　Bitter was
their penitence and that of her companions at the state in

which they found her. For some hours terrible anxiety was felt; but at last, Nature, exhausted, relieved herself by a deep slumber.

From this Mariana rose an altered being. She made no reply to the expressions of sorrow from her companions, none to the grave and kind, but undiscerning comments of her teacher. She did not name the source of her anguish, and its poisoned dart sunk deeply in. It was this thought which stung her so. — " What, not one, not a single one, in the hour of trial, to take my part! not one who refused to take part against me!" Past words of love, and caresses little heeded at the time, rose to her memory, and gave fuel to her distempered thoughts. Beyond the sense of universal perfidy, of burning resentment, she could not get. And Mariana, born for love, now hated all the world.

The change, however, which these feelings made in her conduct and appearance bore no such construction to the careless observer. Her gay freaks were quite gone, her wildness, her invention. Her dress was uniform, her manner much subdued. Her chief interest seemed now to lie in her studies and in music. Her companions she never sought; but they, partly from uneasy, remorseful feelings, partly that they really liked her much better now that she did not oppress and puzzle them, sought her continually. And here the black shadow comes upon her life — the only stain upon the history of Mariana.

They talked to her as girls, having few topics, naturally do of one another. And the demon rose within her, and spontaneously, without design, generally without words of positive falsehood, she became a genius of discord among them. She fanned those flames of envy and jealousy which a wise, true word from a third person will often quench forever; by a glance, or a seemingly light reply, she planted the seeds of dissension, till there was scarce a peaceful affection or sincere intimacy in the circle where she lived, and could not but rule, for she was one whose nature was to that of the others as fire to clay.

It was at this time that I came to the school, and first saw Mariana. Me she charmed at once, for I was a sentimental child, who, in my early ill health, had been indulged in reading novels till I had no eyes for the common greens and browns of life. The heroine of one of these, "the Bandit's Bride," I immediately saw in Mariana. Surely the Bandit's Bride had just such hair, and such strange, lively ways, and such a sudden flash of the eye. The Bandit's Bride, too, was born to be "misunderstood" by all but her lover. But Mariana, I was determined, should be more fortunate; for, until her lover appeared, I myself would be the wise and delicate being who could understand her.

It was not, however, easy to approach her for this purpose. Did I offer to run and fetch her handkerchief, she was obliged to go to her room, and would rather do it herself. She did not like to have people turn over for her the leaves of the music book as she played. Did I approach my stool to her feet, she moved away, as if to give me room. The bunch of wild flowers which I timidly laid beside her plate was left there.

After some weeks my desire to attract her notice really preyed upon me, and one day, meeting her alone in the entry, I fell upon my knees, and kissing her hand, cried, "O Mariana, do let me love you, and try to love me a little." But my idol snatched away her hand, and, laughing more wildly than the Bandit's Bride was ever described to have done, ran into her room. After that day her manner to me was not only cold, but repulsive; I felt myself scorned, and became very unhappy.

Perhaps four months had passed thus, when, one afternoon, it became obvious that something more than common was brewing. Dismay and mystery were written in many faces of the older girls; much whispering was going on in corners.

In the evening, after prayers, the principal bade us stay; and, in a grave, sad voice, summoned forth Mariana to answer charges to be made against her.

Mariana came forward, and leaned against the chimney-piece. Eight of the older girls came forward, and preferred against her charges — alas! too well founded — of calumny and falsehood.

My heart sank within me, as one after the other brought up their proofs, and I saw they were too strong to be resisted. I could not bear the thought of this second disgrace of my shining favorite. The first had been whispered to me, though the girls did not like to talk about it. I must confess, such is the charm of strength to softer natures, that neither of these crises could deprive Mariana of hers in my eyes.

At first, she defended herself with self-possession and eloquence. But when she found she could no more resist the truth, she suddenly threw herself down, dashing her head, with all her force, against the iron hearth, on which a fire was burning, and was taken up senseless.

The affright of those present was great. Now that they had perhaps killed her, they reflected it would have been as well if they had taken warning from the former occasion, and approached very carefully a nature so capable of any extreme. After a while she revived, with a faint groan, amid the sobs of her companions. I was on my knees by the bed, and held her cold hand. One of those most aggrieved took it from me to beg her pardon, and say it was impossible not to love her. She made no reply.

Neither that night, nor for several days, could a word be obtained from her, nor would she touch food; but, when it was presented to her, or any one drew near for any cause, she merely turned away her head, and gave no sign. The teacher saw that some terrible nervous affection had fallen upon her —that she grew more and more feverish. She knew not what to do.

23

Meanwhile, a new revolution had taken place in the mind of the passionate but nobly-tempered child. All these months nothing but the sense of injury had rankled in her heart. She had gone on in one mood, doing what the demon prompted, without scruple and without fear.

But at the moment of detection, the tide ebbed, and the bottom of her soul lay revealed to her eye. How black, how stained and sad! Strange, strange that she had not seen before the baseness and cruelty of falsehood, the loveliness of truth. Now, amid the wreck, uprose the moral nature which never before had attained the ascendant. "But," she thought, "too late sin is revealed to me in all its deformity, and sin-defiled, I will not, cannot live. The mainspring of life is broken."

And thus passed slowly by her hours in that black despair of which only youth is capable. In older years men suffer more dull pain, as each sorrow that comes drops its leaden weight into the past, and, similar features of character bringing similar results, draws up the heavy burden buried in those depths. But only youth has energy, with fixed, unwinking gaze, to contemplate grief, to hold it in the arms and to the heart, like a child which makes it wretched, yet is indubitably its own.

The lady who took charge of this sad child had never well understood her before, but had always looked on her with great tenderness. And now love seemed — when all around were in greatest distress, fearing to call in medical aid, fearing to do without it — to teach her where the only balm was to be found that could have healed this wounded spirit.

One night she came in, bringing a calming draught. Mariana was sitting, as usual, her hair loose, her dress the same robe they had put on her at first, her eyes fixed vacantly upon the whited wall. To the proffers and entreaties of her nurse she made no reply.

The lady burst into tears, but Mariana did not seem even to observe it.

The lady then said, "O my child, do not despair; do not think that one great fault can mar a whole life. Let me trust you, let me tell you the griefs of my sad life. I will tell to you, Mariana, what I never expected to impart to any one."

And so she told her tale: it was one of pain, of shame, borne, not for herself, but for one near and dear as herself. Mariana knew the lady — knew the pride and reserve of her nature. She had often admired to see how the cheek, lovely, but no longer young, mantled with the deepest blush of youth, and the blue eyes were cast down at any little emotion : she had understood the proud sensibility of the character. She fixed her eyes on those now raised to hers, bright with fast-falling tears. She heard the story to the end, and then, without saying a word, stretched out her hand for the cup.

She returned to life, but it was as one who has passed through the valley of death. The heart of stone was quite broken in her, the fiery life fallen from flame to coal. When her strength was a little restored, she had all her companions summoned, and said to them, " I deserved to die, but a generous trust has called me back to life. I will be worthy of it, nor ever betray the truth, or resent injury more. Can you forgive the past ? "

And they not only forgave, but, with love and earnest tears, clasped in their arms the returning sister. They vied with one another in offices of humble love to the humbled one; and let it be recorded as an instance of the pure honor of which young hearts are capable, that these facts, known to forty persons, never, so far as I know, transpired beyond those walls.

It was not long after this that Mariana was summoned home. She went thither a wonderfully instructed being, though in ways that those who had sent her forth to learn little dreamed of.

Never was forgotten the vow of the returning prodigal. Mariana could not resent, could not play false. The terrible crisis which she so early passed through probably prevented the world from hearing much of her. A wild fire was tamed in that hour of penitence at the boarding school such as has oftentimes wrapped court and camp in its destructive glow.

But great were the perils she had yet to undergo, for she was one of those barks which easily get beyond soundings, and ride not lightly on the plunging billow.

Her return to her native climate seconded the effects of inward revolutions. The cool airs of the north had exasperated nerves too susceptible for their tension. Those of the south restored her to a more soft and indolent state. Energy gave place to feeling — turbulence to intensity of character.

At this time, love was the natural guest; and he came to her under a form that might have deluded one less ready for delusion.

Sylvain was a person well proportioned to her lot in years, family, and fortune. His personal beauty was not great, but of a noble dscription. Repose marked his slow gesture, and the steady gaze of his large brown eye; but it was a repose that would give way to a blaze of energy, when the occasion called. In his stature, expression, and heavy coloring, he might not unfitly be represented by the great magnolias that inhabit the forests of that climate. His voice, like every thing about him, was rich and soft, rather than sweet or delicate.

Mariana no sooner knew him than she loved; and her love, lovely as she was, soon excited his. But O, it is a curse to woman to love first, or most! In so doing she reverses the natural relations; and her heart can never, never be satisfied with what ensues.

Mariana loved first, and loved most, for she had most force and variety to love with. Sylvain seemed, at first, to take her to himself, as the deep southern night might some fair star; but it proved not so.

Mariana was a very intellectual being, and she needed companionship. This she could only have with Sylvain, in the paths of passion and action. Thoughts he had none, and little delicacy of sentiment. The gifts she loved to prepare of such for him he took with a sweet but indolent smile; he held them lightly, and soon they fell from his grasp. He loved to have her near him, to feel the glow and fragrance of her nature, but cared not to explore the little secret paths whence that fragrance was collected.

Mariana knew not this for a long time. Loving so much, she imagined all the rest; and, where she felt a blank, always hoped that further communion would fill it up. When she found this could never be, — that there was absolutely a whole province of her being to which nothing in his answered, — she was too deeply in love to leave him. Often, after passing hours together beneath the southern moon, when, amid the sweet intoxication of mutual love, she still felt the desolation of solitude, and a repression of her finer powers, she had asked herself, Can I give him up? But the heart always passionately answered, No! I may be wretched with him, but I cannot live without him.

And the last miserable feeling of these conflicts was, that if the lover — soon to be the bosom friend — could have dreamed of these conflicts, he would have laughed, or else been angry, even enough to give her up.

Ah, weakness of the strong! of those strong only where strength is weakness! Like others, she had the decisions of life to make before she had light by which to make them. Let none condemn her. Those who have not erred as fatally should thank the guardian angel who gave them more time to prepare for judgment, but blame no children who thought at arm's length to find the moon. Mariana, with a heart capable of highest Eros, gave it to one who knew love only as a flower or plaything, and bound her heartstrings to one who parted his as lightly as the ripe fruit leaves the bough. The sequel could not fail. Many console themselves for the one

great mistake with their children, with the world. This was
not possible to Mariana. A few months of domestic life
she still was almost happy. But Sylvain then grew tired.
He wanted business and the world: of these she had no
knowledge, for them no faculties. He wanted in her the
head of his house; she to make her heart his home. No
compromise was possible between natures of such unequal
poise, and which had met only on one or two points. Through
all its stages she

> " felt
>   The agonizing sense
> Of seeing love from passion melt
>   Into indifference;
> The fearful shame, that, day by day,
>   Burns onward, still to burn,
> To have thrown her precious heart away,
>   And met this black return,"

till death at last closed the scene. Not that she died of one
downright blow on the heart. That is not the way such cases
proceed. I cannot detail all the symptoms, for I was not
there to watch them, and aunt Z., who described them, was
neither so faithful an observer or narrator as I have shown
myself in the school-day passages; but, generally, they were
as follows.

Sylvain wanted to go into the world, or let it into his house.
Mariana consented; but, with an unsatisfied heart, and no
lightness of character, she played her part ill there. The sort
of talent and facility she had displayed in early days were
not the least like what is called out in the social world by the
desire to please and to shine. Her excitement had been
muse-like — that of the improvisatrice, whose kindling fancy
seeks to create an atmosphere round it, and makes the chain
through which to set free its electric sparks. That had been
a time of wild and exuberant life. After her character became

more tender and concentrated, strong affection or a pure enthusiasm might still have called out beautiful talents in her. But in the first she was utterly disappointed. The second was not roused within her mind. She did not expand into various life, and remained unequal; sometimes too passive, sometimes too ardent, and not sufficiently occupied with what occupied those around her to come on the same level with them and embellish their hours.

Thus she lost ground daily with her husband, who, comparing her with the careless shining dames of society, wondered why he had found her so charming in solitude.

At intervals, when they were left alone, Mariana wanted to open her heart, to tell the thoughts of her mind. She was so conscious of secret riches within herself, that sometimes it seemed, could she but reveal a glimpse of them to the eye of Sylvain, he would be attracted near her again, and take a path where they could walk hand in hand. Sylvain, in these intervals, wanted an indolent repose. His home was his castle. He wanted no scenes too exciting there. Light jousts and plays were well enough, but no grave encounters. He liked to lounge, to sing, to read, to sleep. In fine, Sylvain became the kind but preoccupied husband, Mariana the solitary and wretched wife. He was off, continually, with his male companions, on excursions or affairs of pleasure. At home Mariana found that neither her books nor music would console her.

She was of too strong a nature to yield without a struggle to so dull a fiend as despair. She looked into other hearts, seeking whether she could there find such home as an orphan asylum may afford. This she did rather because the chance came to her, and it seemed unfit not to seize the proffered plank, than in hope; for she was not one to double her stakes, but rather with Cassandra power to discern early the sure course of the game. And Cassandra whispered that she was one of those

" Whom men love not, but yet regret ; "

and so it proved. Just as in her childish days, though in a different form, it happened betwixt her and these companions. She could not be content to receive them quietly, but was stimulated to throw herself too much into the tie, into the hour, till she filled it too full for them. Like Fortunio, who sought to do homage to his friends by building a fire of cinnamon, not knowing that its perfume would be too strong for their endurance, so did Mariana. What she wanted to tell they did not wish to hear; a little had pleased, so much overpowered, and they preferred the free air of the street, even, to the cinnamon perfume of her palace.

However, this did not signify; had they staid, it would not have availed her. It was a nobler road, a higher aim, she needed now; this did not become clear to her.

She lost her appetite, she fell sick, had fever. Sylvain was alarmed, nursed her tenderly; she grew better. Then his care ceased; he saw not the mind's disease, but left her to rise into health, and recover the tone of her spirits, as she might. More solitary than ever, she tried to raise herself; but she knew not yet enough. The weight laid upon her young life was a little too heavy for it. One long day she passed alone, and the thoughts and presages came too thick for her strength. She knew not what to do with them, relapsed into fever, and died.

Notwithstanding this weakness, I must ever think of her as a fine sample of womanhood, born to shed light and life on some palace home. Had she known more of God and the universe, she would not have given way where so many have conquered. But peace be with her; she now, perhaps, has entered into a larger freedom, which is knowledge. With her died a great interest in life to me. Since her I have never seen a Bandit's Bride. She, indeed, turned out to be only a merchant's. Sylvain is married again to a fair and laughing girl, who will not die, probably, till their marriage grows a "golden marriage."

Aunt Z. had with her some papers of Mariana's, which faintly shadow forth the thoughts that engaged her in the last days. One of these seems to have been written when some faint gleam had been thrown across the path only to make its darkness more visible. It seems to have been suggested by remembrance of the beautiful ballad, *Helen of Kirconnel Lee*, which once she loved to recite, and in tones that would not have sent a chill to the heart from which it came.

> " Death
> Opens her sweet white arms, and whispers, Peace;
> Come, say thy sorrows in this bosom ! This
> Will never close against thee, and my heart,
> Though cold, cannot be colder much than man's."

DISAPPOINTMENT.

"I wish I were where Helen lies."
A lover in the times of old,
Thus vents his grief in lonely sighs,
And hot tears from a bosom cold.

But, mourner for thy martyred love,
Couldst thou but know what hearts must feel,
Where no sweet recollections move,
Whose tears a desert fount reveal!

When "in thy arms bird Helen fell,"
She died, sad man, she died for thee;
Nor could the films of death dispel
Her loving eye's sweet radiancy.

Thou wert beloved, and she had loved,
Till death alone the whole could tell;
Death every shade of doubt removed,
And steeped the star in its cold well.

On some fond breast the parting soul
    Relies — earth has no more to give;
Who wholly loves has known the whole;
    The wholly loved doth truly live.

But some, sad outcasts from this prize,
    Do wither to a lonely grave;
All hearts their hidden love despise,
    And leave them to the whelming wave.

They heart to heart have never pressed,
    Nor hands in holy pledge have given,
By father's love were ne'er caressed,
    Nor in a mother's eye saw heaven.

A flowerless and fruitless tree,
    A dried-up stream, a mateless bird,
They live, yet never living be,
    They die, their music all unheard.

I wish I were where Helen lies,
    For there I could not be alone;
But now, when this dull body dies,
    The spirit still will make its moan.

Love passed me by, nor touched my brow;
    Life would not yield one perfect boon;
And all too late it calls me now —
    O, all too late, and all too soon.

If thou couldst the dark riddle read
    Which leaves this dart within my breast,
Then might I think thou lov'st indeed,
    Then were the whole to thee confest.

Father, they will not take me home;
    To the poor child no heart is free;
In sleet and snow all night I roam;
    Father, was this decreed by thee?

I will not try another door,
    To seek what I have never found;
Now, till the very last is o'er,
    Upon the earth I'll wander round.

I will not hear the treacherous call
    That bids me stay and rest a while,
For I have found that, one and all,
    They seek me for a prey and spoil.

They are not bad; I know it well;
    I know they know not what they do;
They are the tools of the dread spell
    Which the lost lover must pursue.

In temples sometimes she may rest,
    In lonely groves, away from men,
There bend the head, by heats distressed,
    Nor be by blows awoke again.

Nature is kind, and God is kind;
    And, if she had not had a heart,
Only that great discerning mind,
    She might have acted well her part.

But O this thirst, that nought can fill,
    Save those unfounden waters free!
The angel of my life must still
    And soothe me in eternity!

It marks the defect in the position of woman that one like Mariana should have found reason to write thus. To a man of equal power, equal sincerity, no more! — many resources would have presented themselves. He would not have needed to seek, he would have been called by life, and not permitted to be quite wrecked through the affections only. But such women as Mariana are often lost, unless they meet some man of sufficiently great soul to prize them.

Van Artevelde's Elena, though in her individual nature unlike my Mariana, is like her in a mind whose large impulses are disproportioned to the persons and occasions she meets, and which carry her beyond those reserves which mark the appointed lot of woman. But, when she met Van Arte-velde, he was too great not to revere her rare nature, without regard to the stains and errors of its past history; great enough to receive her entirely, and make a new life for her; man enough to be a lover! But as such men come not so often as once an age, their presence should not be absolutely needed to sustain life.

MEDITATION FIRST.

"And Jesus, answering, said unto them, Have faith in God." — *Mark* xi. 22.

O, DIRECTION most difficult to follow! O, counsel most mighty of import! Beauteous harmony to the purified soul! Mysterious, confounding as an incantation to those yet groping and staggering amid the night, the fog, the chaos of their own inventions!

Yes, this is indeed the beginning and the end of all knowledge and virtue; the way and the goal; the enigma and its solution. The soul cannot prove to herself the existence of a God; she cannot prove her own immortality; she cannot prove the beauty of virtue, or the deformity of vice; her own consciousness, the first ground of this belief, cannot be compassed by the reason, that inferior faculty which the Deity gave for practical, temporal purposes only. This consciousness is divine; it is part of the Deity; through this alone we sympathize with the imperishable, the infinite, the nature of things. Were reason commensurate with this part of our intellectual life, what should we do with the things of time? The leaves and buds of earth would wither beneath the sun of our intelligence; its crags and precipices would be levelled before the mighty torrent of our will; all its dross would crumble to ashes under the fire of our philosophy.

God willed it otherwise; WHY, who can guess? Why this planet, with its tormenting limitations of space and time, was ever created,—why the soul was cased in this clogging, stifling integument, (which, while it conveys to the soul, in a round-about way, knowledge which she might obviously acquire much better without its aid, tempts constantly to vice and indolence, suggesting sordid wants, and hampering or hinder-ing thought,)—I pretend not to say. Let others toil to stifle sad distrust a thousand ways. Let them satisfy themselves by reasonings on the nature of free agency ; let them imagine it was impossible men should be purified to angels, except by resisting the temptations of guilt and crime ; let them be *reasonably* content to feel that

> " Faith conquers in no easy war ;
>   By toil alone the prize is won ;
>   The grape dissolves not in the cup—
>   Wine from the crushing press must run ;
>   And would a spirit heavenward go,
>   A heart must break in death below."

Why an *omnipotent* Deity should permit evil, either as necessary to produce good, or incident to laws framed for its production, must remain a mystery to me. True, *we* cannot conceive how the world could have been ordered differently, and because *we*,—beings half of clay ; beings bred amid, and nurtured upon imperfection and decay ; beings who must not only sleep and eat, but pass the greater part of their tem-poral day in procuring the means to do so,—because WE, creatures so limited and blind, so weak of thought and dull of hearing, cannot conceive how evil could have been dis-pensed with, those among us who are styled *wise* and *learned* have thought fit to assume that the Infinite, the Omnipotent, could not have found a way ! " Could not," " evil must be incident "— terms invented to express the thoughts or deeds of the children of dust. Shall they be applied to the Omnipo-tent ? Is a confidence in the goodness of God more trying to faith, than the belief that a God exists, to whom these words, transcending our powers of conception, apply ? O, no,

no! *"Have faith in God!"* Strive to expand thy soul to
the feeling of wisdom, of beauty, of goodness; live, and act
as if these were the necessary elements of things; "live for
thy faith, and thou shalt behold it living." In another world
God will repay thy trust, and "reveal to thee the first
causes of things which Leibnitz could not," as the queen of
Prussia said, when she was dying. Socrates has declared that
the belief in the soul's immortality is so delightful, so elevat-
ing, so purifying, that even were it not the truth, "we should
daily strive to enchant ourselves with it." And thus with
faith in wisdom and goodness, — that is to say, in God, — the
earthquake-defying, rock-foundation of our hopes is laid; the
sun-greeting dome which crowns the most superb palace of
our knowledge is builded. A noble and accomplished man,
of a later day, has said, "To credit ordinary and visible
objects is not faith, but persuasion. I bless myself, and am
thankful, that I lived not in the days of miracles, that I never
saw Christ, nor his disciples; then had my faith been thrust
upon me, nor could I enjoy that greater blessing pronounced
upon those who believe yet saw not."

I cannot speak thus proudly and heartily. I find the world
of sense strong enough against the intellectual and celestial
world. It is easy to believe in our passionless moments, or
in those when earth would seem too dark without the guiding
star of faith; but to *live* in faith, not sometimes to feel, but
always to have it, is difficult. Were faith ever with us, how
steady would be our energy, how equal our ambition, how
calmly bright our hopes! The darts of envy would be blunted,
the cup of disappointment lose its bitterness, the impassioned
eagerness of the heart be stilled, tears would fall like holy dew,
and blossoms fragrant with celestial May ensue.

But the prayer of most of us must be, "Lord, we believe
— help thou our unbelief!" These are to me the most significant words of Holy Writ. I *will* to believe; O, guide,
support, strengthen, and soothe me to do so! Lord, grant me

to believe firmly, and to act nobly.   Let me not be tempted to
waste my time, and weaken my powers, by attempts to soar
on feeble pinions "where angels bashful look."   In *faith* let
me interpret the universe !

MEDITATION SECOND.

"Why is light given to a man whose way is hid, and whom God hath
hedged in ? " — *Job* iii. 23.

This pathetic inquiry rises from all parts of the globe, from
millions of human souls, to that heaven from whence the light
proceeds.   From the young, full of eager aspirations after
virtue and glory ; with the glance of the falcon to descry the
high-placed aim, — but ah! the wing of the wren to reach it !
The young enthusiast must often weep.   His heart glows, his
eye sparkles as he reads of the youthful triumphs of a Pom-
pey, the sublime devotion of an Agis ; * he shuts the book, he
looks around him for a theatre whereon to do likewise —
petty pursuits, mean feelings, and trifling pleasures meet his
eye ; the cold breeze of selfishness has nipped every flower ;
the dull glow of prosaic life overpowers the beauties of the
landscape.   He plunges into the unloved pursuit, or some despised amusement, to soothe that day's impatience, and wakes
on the morrow, crying, " I have lost a day ; and where, where
shall I now turn my steps to find the destined path ?"   The
gilded image of some petty victory holds forth a talisman
which seems to promise him sure tokens.   He rushes forward ; the swords of foes and rivals bar the way ; the
ground trembles and gives way beneath his feet ; rapid streams,
unseen at a distance, roll between him and the object of his
pursuit ; faint, giddy and exhausted by the loss of his best
blood, he reaches the goal, seizes the talisman, his eyes de-

[* Agis, king of Sparta, the fourth of that name. " One of the most
beautiful characters of antiquity." — ED.]

vour the inscription — alas! the characters are unknown to
him. He looks back for some friend who might aid him, —
his friends are whelmed beneath the torrent, or have turned
back disheartened. He must struggle onward alone and ignorant as before; yet in his wishes there is light.

Another is attracted by a lovely phantom; with airy
step she precedes him, holding, as he thinks, in her upward-
pointing hand the faithful needle which might point him to the
pole-star of his wishes. Unwearied he follows, imploring her
in most moving terms to pause but a moment and let him
take her hand. Heedless she flits onward to some hopeless
desert, where she pauses only to turn to her unfortunate captive the malicious face of a very Morgana.

The old, — O their sighs are deeper still! They have
wandered far, toiled much; the true light is now shown them.
Ah, why was it reflected so falsely through "life's many-colored dome of painted glass" upon their youthful, anxious
gaze? And now the path they came by is hedged in by new
circumstances against the feet of others, and its devious
course vainly mapped in their memories; should the light of
their example lead others into the same track, these unlucky
followers will vainly seek an issue. They attempt to unroll
their charts for the use of their children, and their children's
children. They feed the dark lantern of wisdom with the oil
of experience, and hold it aloft over the declivity up which
these youth are blundering, in vain; some fall, misled by the
flickering light; others seek by-paths, along which they hope
to be guided by suns or moons of their own. All meet at
last, only to bemoan or sneer together. How many strive
with feverish zeal to paint on the clouds of outward life the
hues of their own souls; what do not these suffer? What
baffling, — what change in the atmosphere on which they depend, — yet *not* in vain! Something they realize, something
they grasp, something (O, how unlike the theme of their
hope!) they have created. A transient glow, a deceitful thrill,

24 *

— these be the blisses of mortals. Yet have these given birth to noble deeds, and thoughts worthy to be recorded by the pens of angels on the tablets of immortality.

And this, O man! is thy only solace in those paroxysms of despair which must result to the yet eager heart from the vast disproportion between our perceptions and our exhibition of those perceptions. Seize on all the twigs that may help thee in thine ascent, though the thorns upon them rend thee. Toil ceaselessly towards the Source of light, and remember that he who thus eloquently lamented found that, although far worse than his dark presentiments had pictured came upon him, though vainly he feared and trembled, and there was no safety for him, yet his sighings came before his meat, and, happy in their recollection, he found at last that danger and imprisonment are but for a season, and that God is *good*, as he is great.

APPEAL FOR AN ASYLUM FOR DISCHARGED FEMALE CONVICTS.

THE ladies of the Prison Association have been from time to time engaged in the endeavor to procure funds for establishing this asylum.* They have met, thus far, with little success; but touched by the position of several women, who, on receiving their discharge, were anxiously waiting in hope there would be means provided to save them from return to their former suffering and polluted life, they have taken a house, and begun their good work, in faith that Heaven must take heed that such an enterprise may not fail, and touch the hearts of men to aid it.

They have taken a house, and secured the superintendence of an excellent matron. There are already six women under her care. But this house is unprovided with furniture, or the means of securing food for body and mind to these unfortunates, during the brief novitiate which gives them so much to learn and unlearn.

The object is to lend a helping hand to the many who show a desire of reformation, but have hitherto been inevitably repelled into infamy by the lack of friends to find them honest employment, and a temporary refuge till it can be procured. Efforts will be made to instruct them how to break up bad habits, and begin a healthy course for body and mind.

The house has in it scarcely any thing. It is a true Lazarus establishment, asking for the crumbs that fall from the rich man's table. Old furniture would be acceptable, clothes, books that are no longer needed by their owners.

[* In New York. — ED.]

This statement we make in appealing to the poor, though they are, usually, the most generous. Not that they are, originally, better than the rich, but circumstances have fitted them to appreciate the misfortunes, the trials, the wrongs that beset those a little lower than themselves. But we have seen too many instances where those who were educated in luxury would cast aside sloth and selfishness with eagerness when once awakened to better things, not to hope in appealing to the rich also.

And to all we appeal: to the poor, who will know how to sympathize with those who are not only poor but degraded, diseased, likely to be hurried onward to a shameful, hopeless death ; to the rich, to equalize the advantages of which they have received more than their share ; to men, to atone for wrongs inflicted by men on that " weaker sex," who should, they say, be soft, confiding, dependent on them for protection ; to women, to feel for those who have not been guarded either by social influence or inward strength from that first mistake which the opinion of the world makes irrevocable for women alone. Since their danger is so great, their fall so remediless, let mercies be multiplied when there is a chance of that partial restoration which society at present permits.

In New York we have come little into contact with that class of society which has a surplus of leisure at command ; but in other cities we have found in their ranks many — some men, more women — who wanted only a decided object and clear light to fill the noble office of disinterested educators and guardians to their less fortunate fellows. It has been our happiness, in not a few instances, by merely apprising such persons of what was to be done, to rouse that generous spirit which relieved them from ennui and a gradual ossification of the whole system, and transferred them into a thoughtful, sympathetic, and beneficent existence. Such, no doubt, are near us here, if we could but know it. A poet writes thus of the cities : —

Cities of proud hotels,
  Houses of rich and great,
A stack of smoking chimneys,
  A roof of frozen slate!
It cannot conquer folly,
  Time, and space, conquering steam,
And the light, outspeeding telegraph,
  Bears nothing on its beam.

The politics are base,
  The letters do not cheer,
And 'tis far in the deeps of history,
  The voice that speaketh clear.
Trade and the streets insnare us,
  Our bodies are weak and worn,
We plot and corrupt each other,
  And we despoil the unborn.

Yet there in the parlor sits
  Some figure of noble guise,
Our angel in a stranger's form,
  Or woman's pleading eyes.
Or only a flashing sunbeam
  In at the window pane,
Or music pours on mortals
  Its beautiful disdain.

These "pleading eyes," these "angels in strangers' forms," we meet, or seem to meet, as we pass through the thoroughfares of this great city. We do not know their names or homes. We cannot go to those still and sheltered abodes and tell them the tales that would be sure to awaken the heart to a deep and active interest in this matter. But should these words meet their eyes, we would say, " Have you entertained your leisure hours with the Mysteries of Paris, or the pathetic story of Violet Woodville?" Then you have some idea how innocence, worthy of the brightest planet, may be betrayed by want, or by the most generous tenderness; how the energies of a noble reformation may lie hidden beneath the ashes of a long burning, as in the case of " La Louve." You must have felt that yourselves are not better, only more protected children of God than these. Do you want to link these fictions, which have made you weep, with facts around you where your pity might be of use? Go to the Penitentiary at Blackwell's Island. You may be repelled by seeing those who are in health, while at work together, keeping up one another's careless spirit' and effrontery by bad association. But see them in the Hospital, — where the worn features of the sick show the sad ruins of past loveliness, past gentleness. See in the eyes of the nurses the woman's spirit still, so kindly, so inspiring. See those little girls huddled in a corner, their neglected dress and hair contrasting with some ribbon of cherished finery held fast in a childish hand. Think what " sweet seventeen " was to you, and what it is to them, and see if you do not wish to aid in any enterprise that gives them a chance of better days. We assume no higher claim for this enterprise. The dreadful social malady which creates the need of it, is one that imperatively demands deep-searching, preventive measures; it is beyond cure. But, here and there, some precious soul may be saved from unwilling sin, unutterable woe. Is not the hope to save here and there *one* worthy of great and persistent sacrifice?

THE RICH MAN.

An Ideal Sketch.

In my walks through this city, the sight of spacious and expensive dwelling-houses now in process of building, has called up the following reverie.

All benevolent persons, whether deeply-thinking on, or deeply-feeling, the woes, difficulties, and dangers of our present social system, are agreed that either great improvements are needed, or a thorough reform.

Those who desire the latter include the majority of thinkers. And we ourselves, both from personal observation and the testimony of others, are convinced that a radical reform is needed; not a reform that rejects the instruction of the past, or asserts that God and man have made mistakes till now. We believe that all past developments have taken place under natural and necessary laws, and that the Paternal Spirit has at no period forgotten his children, but granted to all generations and all ages their chances of good to balance inevitable ills. We prize the past; we recognize it as our parent, our nurse, and our teacher; and we know that for a time the new wine required the old bottles, to prevent its being spilled upon the ground.

Still we feel that the time is come which not only permits, but demands, a wider statement and a nobler action. The aspect of society presents mighty problems, which must be solved by the soul of man "divinely-intending" itself to the task, or all will become worse instead of better, and ere long the social fabric totter to decay.

Yet while the new measures are ripening, and the new men educating, there is still room on the old platform for some worthy action. It is possible for a man of piety, resolution, and good sense, to lead a life which, if not expansive, generous, graceful, and pure from suspicion and contempt, is yet not entirely unworthy of his position as the child of God, and ruler of a planet.

Let us take, then, some men just where they find themselves, in a mixed state of society, where, in quantity, we are free to say the bad preponderates, though the good, from its superior energy in quality, may finally redeem and efface its plague-spots.

Our society is ostensibly under the rule of the precepts of Jesus. We will then suppose a youth sufficiently imbued with these, to understand what is conveyed under the parables of the unjust steward, and the prodigal son, as well as the denunciations of the opulent Jews. He understands that it is needful to preserve purity and teachableness, since of those most like little children is the kingdom of heaven; mercy for the sinner, since there is peculiar joy in heaven at the salvation of such; perpetual care for the unfortunate, since only to the just steward shall his possessions be pardoned. Imbued with such love, the young man joins the active, — we will say, in choosing an instance, — joins the commercial world.

His views of his profession are not those which make of the many a herd, not superior, except in the far reach of their selfish interests, to the animals; mere calculating, money-making machines.

He sees in commerce a representation of most important interests, a grand school that may teach the heart and soul of the civilized world to a willing, thinking mind. He plays his part in the game, but not for himself alone; he sees the interests of all mankind engaged with his, and remembers them while he furthers his own. His intellectual discernment, no less than his moral, thus teaching the undesirableness of lying and stealing. he does not practise or connive at the falsities and meannesses so frequent among his fellows; he suffers many turns of the wheel of fortune to pass unused, since he cannot avail himself of them and keep clean his hands. What he gains is by superior assiduity, skill in combination and calculation, and quickness of sight. His gains are legitimate, so far as the present state of things permits any gains to be.

Nor is this honorable man denied his due rank in the most corrupt state of society. Here, happily, we draw from life, and speak of what we know. Honesty is, indeed, the best policy, only it is so in the long run, and therefore a policy which a selfish man has not faith and patience to pursue. The influence of the honest man is in the end predominant, and the rogues who sneer because he will not shuffle the cards in *their* way, are forced to bow to it at last.

But while thus conscientious and mentally-progressive, he does not forget to live. The sharp and care-worn faces, the joyless lives that throng the busy street, do not make him forget his need of tender affections. of the practices of bounty and love. His family, his acquaintance, especially those who are struggling with the difficulties of life, are not obliged to wait till he has accumulated a certain sum. He is sunlight and dew to them now, day by day. No less do all in his employment prize and bless the just, the brotherly man. He dares not, would not, climb to power upon their necks. He requites their toil handsomely, always; if his success be unusual, they share the benefit. Their comfort is cared for in all the arrangements for their work. He takes care, too, to be personally acquainted with those he employs, regarding them, not as mere tools of his purpose, but as human beings also; he keeps them in his eye, and if it be in his power to supply their need of consolation, instruction, or even pleasure, they find they have a friend.

25

"Nonsense!" exclaims our sharp-eyed, thin-lipped antagonist. "Such a man would never get rich,—or even *get along!*"

You are mistaken, Mr. Stockjobber. Thus far many lines of our sketch are drawn from real life ; though for the second part, which follows, we want, as yet, a worthy model.

We must imagine, then, our ideal merchant to have grown rich in some forty years of toil passed in the way we have indicated. His hair is touched with white, but his form is vigorous yet. Neither *gourmandise* nor the fever of gain has destroyed his complexion, quenched the light of his eye, or substituted sneers for smiles. He is an upright, strong, sagacious, generous-looking man ; and if his movements be abrupt, and his language concise, somewhat beyond the standard of beauty, he is still the gentleman ; mercantile, but a mercantile nobleman.

Our nation is not silly in striving for an aristocracy. Humanity longs for its upper classes. But the silliness consists in making them out of clothes, equipage, and a servile imitation of foreign manners, instead of the genuine elegance and distinction that can only be produced by genuine culture. Shame upon the stupidity which, when all circumstances leave us free for the introduction of a real aristocracy such as the world never saw, bases its pretensions on, or makes its bow to the footman behind, the coach, instead of the person within it.

But our merchant shall be a real nobleman, whose noble manners spring from a noble mind, whose fashions from a sincere, intelligent love of the beautiful.

We will also indulge the fancy of giving him a wife and children worthy of himself. Having lived in sympathy with him, they have acquired no taste for luxury ; they do not think that the best use for wealth and power is in self-indulgence, but, on the contrary, that " it is more blessed to give than to receive."

He is now having one of those fine houses built, and, as in other things, proceeds on a few simple principles. It is substantial, for he wishes to give no countenance to the paper buildings that correspond with other worthless paper currency of a credit system. It is thoroughly finished and furnished, for he has a conscience about his house, as about the neatness of his person. All must be of a piece. Harmony and a wise utility are consulted, without regard to show. Still, as a rich man, we allow him reception-rooms, lofty, large, adorned with good copies of ancient works of art, and fine specimens of modern.

I admit, in this instance, the propriety of my nobleman often choosing by advice of friends, who may have had more leisure and opportunity to acquire a sure appreciation of merit in these walks. His character being simple, he will, no doubt, appreciate a great part of what is truly grand and beautiful. But also, from imperfect culture, he might often reject what in the end he would have found most valuable to himself and others. For he has not done learning, but only acquired the privilege of helping to open a domestic school, in which he will find himself a pupil as well as a master. So he may well make use, in furnishing himself with the school apparatus, of the best counsel. The same applies to making his library a good one. Only there must be no sham; no pluming himself on possessions that represent his wealth, but the taste of others. Our nobleman is incapable of pretension, or the airs of connoisseurship; his object is to furnish a home with those testimonies of a higher life in man, that may best aid to cultivate the same in himself and those assembled round him.

He shall also have a fine garden and greenhouses. But the flowers shall not be used only to decorate his apartments, or the hair of his daughters, but shall often bless, by their soft and exquisite eloquence, the poor invalid, or others whose sorrowful hearts find in their society a consolation and a hope which nothing else bestows. For flowers, the highest expression of the bounty of nature, declare that for all men, not merely labor, or luxury, but gentle, buoyant, ever-energetic joy, was intended, and bid us hope that we shall not forever be kept back from our inheritance.

All the persons who have aided in building up this domestic temple, from the artist who painted the ceilings to the poorest hodman, shall be well paid and cared for during its erection; for it is a necessary part of the happiness of our nobleman, to feel that all concerned in creating his home are the happier for it.

We have said nothing about the architecture of the house, and yet this is only for want of room. We do consider it one grand duty of every person able to build a good house, also to aim at building a beautiful one. We do not want imitations of what was used in other ages, nations, and climates, but what is simple, noble, and in conformity with the wants of our own. Room enough, simplicity of design, and judicious adjustment of the parts to their uses and to the whole, are the first requisites; the ornaments are merely the finish on these. We hope to see a good style of civic architecture long before any material improvement in the country edifices, for reasons that would be tedious to enumerate here. Suffice it to say that we are far more anxious to see an American architecture than an American literature; for we are sure there is here already something individual to express.

Well, suppose the house built and equipped with man and horse. You may be sure my nobleman gives his "hired help" good accommodations for their sleeping and waking hours, — baths, books, and some leisure to use them. Nay, I assure you — and this assurance also is drawn from life — that it is possible, even in our present social relations, for the man who does common justice, in these respects, to his fellows, and shows a friendly heart, that thoroughly feels service to be no degradation, but an honor, who believes

"A man's a MAN for a' that;" —
"Honor in the king the wisdom of his service,
Honor in the serf the fidelity of his service," —

to have around him those who do their work in serenity of mind, neither deceiving nor envying him whom circumstances have enabled to command their service. As to the carriage, that is used for the purpose of going to and fro in bad weather, or ill health, or haste, or for drives to enjoy the country. But my nobleman and his family are too well born and bred not to prefer employing their own feet when possible. And their carriage is much appropriated to the use of poor invalids, even among the abhorred class of poor relations, so that often they have not room in it for themselves, much less for flaunting dames and lazy dandies.

We need hardly add that, their attendants wear no liveries. They are aware that, in a society where none of the causes exist that justify this habit abroad, the practice would have no other result than to call up a sneer to the lips of the most complaisant "milor," when "Mrs. Higginbottom's carriage stops the way," with its tawdry, ill-fancied accompaniments. *Will* none of their "governors" tell our cits the Æsopian fable of the donkey that tried to imitate the gambols of the little dog?

The wife of my nobleman is so well matched with him that she has no need to be the better half. She is his almoner, his counsellor, and the priestess who keeps burning on the domestic hearth a fire from the fuel he collects in his out-door work, whose genial heart and aspiring flame comfort and animate all who come within its range.

His children are his ministers, whose leisure and various qualifications enable them to carry out his good thoughts. They hold all that they possess — time, money, talents, acquirements — on the principle of stewardship. They wake up the seeds of virtue and genius in all the young persons of their acquaintance; but the poorer classes are especially their care. Among them they seek for those who are threatened with dying — "mute, inglorious" Hampdens and Miltons — but for their scrutiny and care; of these they become the teachers and pat-

25 *

rons to the extent of their power. Such knowledge of the
arts, sciences, and just principles of action as they have been
favored with, they communicate, and thereby form novices
worthy to fill up the ranks of the true American aristocracy.

And the house — it is a large one; a simple family does
not fill its chambers. Some of them are devoted to the use
of men of genius, who need a serene home, free from care,
while they pursue their labors for the good of the world.
Thus, as in the palaces of the little princes of Italy in a better day, these chambers become hallowed by the nativities of
great thoughts; and the horoscopes of the human births that
may take place there, are likely to read the better for it.
Suffering virtue sometimes finds herself taken home here, instead of being sent to the almshouse, or presented with half a
dollar and a ticket for coal, and finds upon my nobleman's
mattresses (for the wealth of Crœsus would not lure him or
his to sleep upon down) dreams of angelic protection which
enable her to rise refreshed for the struggle of the morrow.

The uses of hospitality are very little understood among
us, so that we fear generally there is a small chance of entertaining gods and angels unawares, as the Greeks and He-
brews did in the generous time of hospitality, when every
man had a claim on the roof of fellow-man. Now, none is
received to a bed and breakfast unless he come as "bearer of
despatches" from His Excellency So-and-so.

But let us not be supposed to advocate the system of all
work and no play, or to delight exclusively in the pedagogic
and Goody-Two-Shoes vein. Reader, if any such accompany
me to this scene of my vision, cheer up; I hear the sound of
music in full band, and see the banquet prepared. Perhaps
they are even dancing the polka and redowa in those airy,
well-lighted rooms. In another they find in the acting of ex-
tempore dramas, arrangement of tableaux, little concerts or
recitations, intermingled with beautiful national or fancy
dances, some portion of the enchanting, refining, and ennobling

influence of the arts. The finest engravings on all subjects
attend such as like to employ themselves more quietly, while
those who can find a companion or congenial group to converse with, find also plenty of recesses and still rooms, with
softened light, provided for their pleasure.

There is not on this side of the Atlantic — we dare our glove
upon it — a more devout believer than ourselves in the worship
of the Muses and Graces, both for itself, and its importance no
less to the moral than to the intellectual life of a nation.
Perhaps there is not one who has *so* deep a feeling, or so
many suggestions ready, in the fulness of time, to be hazarded
on the subject.

But in order to such worship, what standard is there as to
admission to the service? Talents of gold, or Delphian talents? fashion or elegance? "standing" or the power to move
gracefully from one position to another?

Our nobleman did not hesitate; the handle to his door bell
was not of gold, but mother-of-pearl, pure and prismatic.

If he did not go into the alleys to pick up the poor, they
were not excluded, if qualified by intrinsic qualities to adorn
the scene. Neither were wealth or fashion a cause of exclu-
sion, more than of admission. All depended on the person;
yet he did not *seek* his guests among the slaves of fashion, for
he knew that persons highly endowed rarely had patience
with the frivolities of that class, but retired, and left it to be
peopled mostly by weak and plebeian natures. Yet all depended on the individual. Was the person fair, noble, wise,
brilliant, or even only youthfully innocent and gay, or venerable in a good old age, he or she was welcome. Still, as simplicity of character and some qualification positively good,
healthy, and natural, was requisite for admission, we must say
the company was select. Our nobleman and his family had
weeded their "circle" carefully, year by year.

Some valued acquaintances they had made in ball-rooms
and boudoirs, and kept; but far more had been made through

the daily wants of life, and shoemakers, seamstresses, and graziers mingled happily with artists and statesmen, to the benefit of both. (N. B. — None used the poisonous weed, in or out of our domestic temple.)

I cannot tell you what infinite good our nobleman and his family were doing by creation of this true social centre, where the legitimate aristocracy of the land assembled, not to be dazzled by expensive furniture, (our nobleman bought what was good in texture and beautiful in form, but not *because* it was expensive,) not to be feasted on rare wines and highly-seasoned dainties, though they found simple refreshments well prepared, as indeed it was a matter of duty and conscience in that house that the least office should be well fulfilled, but to enjoy the generous confluence of mind with mind and heart with heart, the pastimes that are not waste-times of taste and inventive fancy, the cordial union of beings from all points and places in noble human sympathy. New York was beginning to be truly American, or rather Columbian, and money stood for something in the records of history. It had brought opportunity to genius and aid to virtue. But just at this moment, the jostling showed me that I had reached the corner of Wall Street. I looked earnestly at the omnibuses discharging their eager freight, as if I hoped to see my merchant. " Perhaps he has gone to the post office to take out letters from his friends in Utopia," thought I. " Please give me a penny," screamed a half-starved ragged little street-sweep, and the fancied cradle of the American Utopia receded, or rather proceeded, fifty years, at least, into the future.

THE POOR MAN.

AN IDEAL SKETCH.

THE foregoing sketch of the Rich Man, seems to require this companion-piece; and we shall make the attempt, though the subject is far more difficult than the former was.

In the first place, we must state what we mean by a poor man, for it is a term of wide range in its relative applications. A painstaking artisan, trained to self-denial, and a strict adaptation, not of his means to his wants, but of his wants to his means, finds himself rich and grateful, if some unexpected fortune enables him to give his wife a new gown, his children cheap holiday joys, and his starving neighbor a decent meal; while George IV., when heir apparent to the throne of Great Britain, considered himself driven by the pressure of poverty to become a debtor, a beggar, a swindler, and, by the aid of perjury, the husband of two wives at the same time, neither of whom he treated well. Since poverty is made an excuse for such depravity in conduct, it would be well to mark the limits within which self-control and resistance to temptation may be expected.

When he of the olden time prayed, " Give me neither poverty nor riches," we presume he meant that proportion of means to the average wants of a human being which secures freedom from pecuniary cares, freedom of motion, and a moderate enjoyment of the common blessings offered by earth, air, water, the natural relations, and the subjects for thought which every day presents. We shall certainly not look above this point for our poor man. A prince may be poor, if he has not means to relieve the sufferings of his subjects, or secure to them needed benefits. Or he may make himself so, just as a well-paid laborer by drinking brings poverty to his roof. So may the prince, by the mental gin of horse-racing or gambling, grow a beggar. But we shall not consider these cases.

Our subject will be taken between the medium we have spoken of as answer to the wise man's prayer, and that destitution which we must style infamous, either to the individual or to the society whose vices have caused that stage of poverty, in which there is no certainty, and often no probability, of work or bread from day to day, — in which cleanliness and all the decencies of life are impossible, and the natural human feelings are turned to gall because the man finds himself on this earth in a far worse situation than the brute. In this stage there is no ideal, and from its abyss, if the unfortunates look up to Heaven, or the state of things as they ought to be, it is with suffocating gasps which demand relief or death. This degree of poverty is common, as we all know; but we who do not share it have no right to address those who do from our own standard, till we have placed their feet on our own level. Accursed is he who does not long to have this so — to take out at least the physical hell from this world! Unblest is he who is not seeking, either by thought or act, to effect this poor degree of amelioration in the circumstances of his race.

We take the subject of our sketch, then, somewhere between the abjectly poor and those in moderate circumstances. What we have to say may apply to either sex, and to any grade in this division of the human family, from the hodman and washerwoman up to the hard-working, poorly-paid lawyer clerk, schoolmaster, or scribe.

The advantages of such a position are many. In the first place, you belong, inevitably, to the active and suffering par⁺

of the world. You know the ills that try men's souls and
bodies. You cannot creep into a safe retreat, arrogantly to
judge, or heartlessly to forget, the others.· They are always
before you; you see the path stained by their bleeding feet;
stupid and flinty, indeed, must you be, if you can hastily
wound, or indolently forbear to aid them. Then, as to yourself, you know what your resources are; what you can do,
what bear; there is small chance for you to escape a well-
tempered modesty. Then again, if you find power in yourself
to endure the trial, there is reason and reality in some degree
of self-reliance. The moral advantages of such training can
scarcely fail to amount to something; and as to the mental,
that most important chapter, how the lives of men are fashioned and transfused by the experience of passion and the
development of thought, presents new sections at every turn,
such as the distant dilettante's opera-glasses will never detect,
—to say nothing of the exercise of mere faculty, which,
though insensible in its daily course, leads to results of im-
mense importance.

But the evils, the disadvantages, the dangers, how many,
how imminent! True, indeed, they are so. There is the
early bending of the mind to the production of marketable
results, which must hinder all this free play of intelligence,
and deaden the powers that craved instruction. There is the
callousness produced by the sight of more misery than it is
possible to relieve; the heart, at first so sensitive, taking refuge in a stolid indifference against the pangs of sympathetic
pain, it had not force to bear. There is the perverting influence of uncongenial employments, undertaken without or
against choice, continued at unfit hours and seasons, till the
man loses his natural relations with summer and winter, day
and night, and has no sense more for natural beauty and joy.
There is the mean providence, the perpetual caution to guard
against ill, instead of the generous freedom of a mind which
expects good to ensue from all good actions. There is the

sad doubt whether it will *do* to indulge the kindly impulse,
the calculation of dangerous chances, and the cost between
the loving impulse and its fulfilment. Yes; there is bitter
chance of narrowness, meanness, and dulness on this path,
and it requires great natural force, a wise and large view
of life taken at an early age, or fervent trust in God, to
evade them.

It is astonishing to see the poor, no less than the rich, the
slaves of externals. One would think that, where the rich
man once became aware of the worthlessness of the mere
trappings of life from the weariness of a spirit that found itself entirely dissatisfied after pomp and self-indulgence, the
poor man would learn this a hundred times from the experience how entirely independent of them is all that is intrinsi-
cally valuable in our life. But, no! The poor man wants
dignity, wants elevation of spirit. It is his own servility that
forges the fetters that enslave him. Whether he cringe to, or
rudely defy, the man in the coach and handsome coat, the
cause and effect are the same. He is influenced by a costume
and a position. He is not firmly rooted in the truth that only
in so far as outward beauty and grandeur are representative
of the mind of the possessor, can they count for any thing at
all. O, poor man! you are poor indeed, if you feel yourself
so; poor if you do not feel that a soul born of God, a mind
capable of scanning the wondrous works of time and space,
and a flexible body for its service, are the essential riches of
a man, and all he needs to make him the equal of any other
man. You are mean, if the possession of money or other
external advantages can make you envy or shrink from a
being mean enough to value himself upon such. Stand
where you may, O man, you cannot be noble and rich if
your brow be not broad and steadfast, if your eye beam not
with a consciousness of inward worth, of eternal claims and
hopes which such trifles cannot at all affect. A man without
this majesty is ridiculous amid the flourish and decorations

procured by money, pitiable in the faded habiliments of poverty. But a man who is a man, a woman who is a woman, can never feel lessened or embarrassed because others look ignorantly on such matters. If they regret the want of these temporary means of power, it must be solely because it fetters their motions, deprives them of leisure and desired means of improvement, or of benefiting those they love or pity.

I have heard those possessed of rhetoric and imaginative tendency declare that they should have been outwardly great and inwardly free, victorious poets and heroes, if fate had allowed them a certain quantity of dollars. I have found it impossible to believe them. In early youth, penury may have power to freeze the genial current of the soul, and prevent it, during one short life, from becoming sensible of its true vocation and destiny. But if it *has* become conscious of these, and yet there is not advance in any and all circumstances, no change would avail.

No, our poor man must begin higher! He must, in the first place, really believe there is a God who ruleth — a fact to which few men vitally bear witness, though most are ready to affirm it with the lips.

2. He must sincerely believe that rank and wealth

> " are but the guinea's stamp ;
> The man's the gold ; " —

take his stand on his claims as a human being, made in God's own likeness, urge them when the occasion permits, but never be so false to them as to feel put down or injured by the want of mere external advantages.

3. He must accept his lot, while he is in it. If he can change it for the better, let his energies be exerted to do so. But if he cannot, there is none that will not yield an opening to Eden, to the glories of Zion, and even to the subterranean

26

enchantments of our strange estate. There is none that may
not be used with nobleness.

> " Who sweeps a room, as for Thy sake
> Makes that and th' action clean."

4. Let him examine the subject enough to be convinced
that there is not that vast difference between the employments
that is supposed, in the means of expansion and refinement.
All depends on the spirit as to the use that is made of an
occupation. Mahomet was not a wealthy merchant, and profound philosophers have ripened on the benches, not of the
lawyers, but the shoemakers. It did not hurt Milton to be
a poor schoolmaster, nor Shakspeare to do the errands of a
London play-house. Yes, "the mind is its own place," and
if it will keep that place, all doors will be opened from it.
Upon this subject we hope to offer some hints at a future
day, in speaking of the different trades, professions, and
modes of labor.

5. Let him remember that from no man can the chief
wealth be kept. On all men the sun and stars shine ; for all
the oceans swell and rivers flow. All men may be brothers,
lovers, fathers, friends ; before all lie the mysteries of birth
and death. If these wondrous means of wealth and blessing be likely to remain misused or unused, there are quite
as many disadvantages in the way of the man of money
as of the man who has none. Few who drain the choicest
grape know the ecstasy of bliss and knowledge that follows a
full draught of the wine of life. That has mostly been reserved for those on whose thoughts society, as a public, makes
but a moderate claim. And if bitterness followed on the joy,
if your fountain was frozen after its first gush by the cold
winds of the world, yet, moneyless men, ye are at least not
wholly ignorant of what a human being has force to know.
You have not skimmed over surfaces, and been dozing on

beds of down, during the rare and stealthy visits of Love and the Muses. Remember this, and, looking round on the arrangements of the lottery, see if you did not draw a prize in your turn.

It will be seen that our ideal poor man needs to be religious, wise, dignified, and humble, grasping at nothing, claiming all; willing to wait, never willing to give up; servile to none, the servant of all, and esteeming it the glory of a man to serve. The character is rare, but not unattainable. We have, however, found an approach to it more frequent in woman than in man.

DURING a late visit to Boston, I visited with great pleasure the Chinese Museum, which has been opened there.

There was much satisfaction in surveying its rich contents, if merely on account of their splendor and elegance, which, though fantastic to our tastes, presented an obvious standard of its own by which to prize it. The rich dresses of the imperial court, the magnificent jars, (the largest worth three hundred dollars, and looking as if it was worth much more,) the present-boxes and ivory work, the elegant interiors of the home and counting-room, — all these gave pleasure by their perfection, each in its kind.

But the chief impression was of that unity of existence, so opposite to the European, and, for a change, so pleasant, from its repose and gilded lightness. Their imperial majesties do really seem so " perfectly serene," that we fancy we might become so under their sway, if not " thoroughly virtuous," as they profess to be. Entirely a new mood would be ours, as we should sup in one of those pleasure boats, by the light of fanciful lanterns, or listen to the tinkling of pagoda bells.

The highest conventional refinement, of a certain kind, is apparent in all that belongs to the Chinese. The inviolability of custom has not made their life heavy, but shaped it to the utmost adroitness for their own purposes. We are now somewhat familiar with their literature, and we see pervading it a poetry subtle and aromatic, like the odors of their appropriate beverage. Like that, too, it is all domestic, — never wild. The social genius, fluttering on the wings of compliment, pervades every thing Chinese. Society has

(304)

moulded them, body and soul; the youngest children are more social and Chinese than human; and we doubt not the infant, with its first cry, shows its capacity for self-command and obedience to superiors.

Their great man, Confucius, expresses this social genius in its most perfect state and highest form. His golden wisdom is the quintescence of social justice. He never forgets conditions and limits; he is admirably wise, pure, and religious, but never towers above humanity — never soars into solitude. There is no token of the forest or cave in Confucius. Few men could understand him, because his nature was so thoroughly balanced, and his rectitude so pure; not because his thoughts were too deep, or too high for them. In him should be sought the best genius of the Chinese, with that perfect practical good sense whose uses are universal.

At one time I used to change from reading Confucius to one of the great religious books of another Eastern nation; and it was always like leaving the street and the palace for the blossoming forest of the East, where in earlier times we are told the angels walked with men and talked, not of earth, but of heaven.

As we looked at the forms moving about in the Museum, we could not wonder that the Chinese consider us, who call ourselves the civilized world, barbarians, so deficient were those forms in the sort of refinement that the Chinese prize above all. And our people deserve it for their senselessness in viewing *them* as barbarians, instead of seeing how perfectly they represent their own idea. They are inferior to us in important developments, but, on the whole, approach far nearer their own standard than we do ours. And it is wonderful that an enlightened European can fail to prize the sort of beauty they do develop. Sets of engravings we have seen representing the culture of the tea plant, have brought to us images of an entirely original idyllic loveliness. One long resident in China has observed that nothing can be more enchanting than the smile of love on the regular, but otherwise expressionless face of a Chinese woman. It has the simplicity and abandonment of infantine, with the fulness of mature feeling. It never varies, but it does not tire.

The same sweetness and elegance stereotyped now, but having originally a deep root in their life as a race, may be seen in their poetry and music. The last we have heard, both from the voice and several instruments, at this Museum, for the first time, and were at first tempted to laugh, when something deeper forbade. Like their poetry, the music is of the narrowest monotony, a kind of rosary, a repetition of phrases, and, in its enthusiasm and conventional excitement, like nothing else in the heavens and on the earth. Yet both the poetry and music have in them an expression of birds, roses, and moonlight; indeed, they suggest that state where "moonlight, and music, and feeling are one," though the soul seems to twitter, rather than sing of it.

It is wonderful with how little practical insight travellers in China look on what they see. They seem to be struck by points of repulsion at once, and neither see nor tell us what could give any real clew to their facts. I do not speak now of the recent lecturers in this city, for I have not heard them; but of the many, many books into which I have earlier looked with eager curiosity, — in vain, — I always found the same external facts, and the same prejudices which disabled the observer from piercing beneath them. I feel that I know something of the Chinese when reading Confucius, or looking at the figures on their tea-cups, or drinking a cup of *genuine* tea — rather an unusual felicity, it is said, in this ingenious city, which shares with the Chinese one trait at least. But the travellers rather take from than add to this knowledge; and a visit to this Museum would give more clear views than all the books I ever read yet.

The juggling was well done, and so solemnly, with the same concentrated look as the music! I saw the juggler afterwards at Ole Bull's concert, and he moved not a muscle while the nightingale was pouring forth its sweetest descant. Probably the avenues wanted for these strains to enter his heart had been closed by the imperial edict long ago. The resemblance borne by this juggler to our Indians is even greater than we have seen in any other case. His brotherhood does not, to us, seem surprising. Our Indians, too, are stereotyped, though in a different way; they are of a mould capable of retaining the impression through ages; and many of the traits of the two races, or two branches of a race, may seem to be identical, though so widely modified by circumstances. They are all opposite to us, who have made ships, and balloons, and magnetic telegraphs, as symbolic expressions of our wants, and the means of gratifying them. We must console ourselves with these, and our organs and pianos, for our want of perfect good breeding, serenity, and "thorough virtue."

THE poet had retired from the social circle. Its mirth was to his sickened soul a noisy discord, its sentiment a hollow mockery. With grief he felt that the recital of a generous action, the vivid expression of a noble thought, could only graze the surface of his mind. The desolate stillness of death lay brooding on its depths. The friendly smiles, the tender attentions which seemed so sweet in those hours when Meta was " crown of his cup and garnish of his dish," could give the present but a ghastly similitude to those blessed days. While his attention, disobedient to his wishes, kept turning painfully inward, the voice of the singer suddenly startled it back. A lovely maid, with moist, clear eye, and pleading, earnest voice, was seated at the harpsichord. She sang a sad, and yet not hopeless, strain, like that of a lover who pines in absence, yet hopes again to meet his loved one.

The heart of Klopstock rose to his lips, and natural tears suffused his eyes. She paused. Some youth of untouched heart, shallow, as yet, in all things, asked for a lively song, the expression of animal enjoyment. She hesitated, and cast a sidelong glance at the mourner. Heedlessly the request was urged: she wafted over the keys an airy prelude. A cold rush of anguish came over the awakened heart; Klopstock rose, and hastily left the room.

He entered his apartment, and threw himself upon the bed. The moon was nearly at the full: a tree near the large win-

---

* Meta, the wife of Klopstock, one of Germany's most celebrated poets, is doubtless well known to many of our readers through the beautiful letters to Samuel Richardson, the novelist, or through Mrs. Jameson's work, entitled the Loves of the Poets. It is said that Klopstock wrote continually to her even after her death.

dow obscured its radiance, and cast into the room a flickering shadow, as its leaves kept swaying to and fro with the breeze.

Vainly Klopstock sought for soothing influences in the contemplation of the soft and varying light. Sadness is always deepest at this hour of celestial calmness. The soul realizes its wants, and longs to be in harmony with itself far more in such an hour than when any outward ill is arousing or oppressing it.

"Weak, fond wretch that I am!" cried he. "I, the bard of the Messiah! To what purpose have I nurtured my soul on the virtues of that sublime model, for whom no renunciation was too hard? Four years an angel sojourned with me: her presence vivified my soul into purity and benevolence like her own. Happy was I as the saints who rest after their long struggles in the bosom of perfect love. I thought myself good because I sinned not against a bounteous God, because my heart could spare some drops of its overflowing oil and balm for the wounds of others: now what am I? My angel leaves me, but she leaves with me the memory of blissful years and our perfect communion as an earnest of that happy meeting which awaits us, if I prove faithful to my own words of faith, to those strains of religious confidence which are even now cheering onward many an inexperienced youth. And what are my deeds and feelings? The springs of life and love frozen, here I lie, sunk in grief, as if I knew no world beyond the grave. The joy of others seems an insult, their grief a dead letter, compared with my own. Meta! Meta! couldst thou see me in my hour of trial, thou wouldst disdain thy chosen one!"

A strain of sweet and solemn music swelled on his ear — one of those majestic harmonies which, were there no other proof of the soul's immortality, must suggest the image of an intellectual paradise. It closed, and Meta stood before him. A long veil of silvery whiteness fell over her, through which might be seen the fixed but nobly-serene expression of the large blue eyes, and a holy, seraphic dignity of mien. Klopstock knelt before her : his soul was awed to earth. "Hast thou come, my adored!" said he, "from thy home of bliss, to tell me that thou no longer lovest thy unworthy friend?"

" O, speak not thus!" replied the softest and most penetrating of voices. "God wills not that his purified creatures should look in contempt or anger on those suffering the ills from which they are set free. O, no, my love! my husband! I come to speak consolation to thy sinking spirit. When you left me to breathe my last sigh in the arms of a sister, who, however dear, was nothing to my heart in comparison with you, I closed my eyes, wishing that the light of day might depart with thee. The thought of what thou must suffer convulsed my heart with one last pang. Once more I murmured the wish I had so often expressed, that the sorrows of the survivor might have fallen to my lot rather than to thine. In that pang my soul extricated itself from the body ; a sensation like that from exquisite fragrance came over me, and with breezy lightness I rose into the pure serene. It was a moment of feeling almost wild, — so free, so unobscured. I had not yet passed the verge of comparison ; I could not yet embrace the Infinite : therefore my joy was like those of earth — intoxicating.

" Words cannot paint, even to thy eager soul, my friend, the winged swiftness, the onward, glowing hopefulness of my path through the fields of azure. I paused, at length, in a region of keen, pure, bluish light, such as beams from Jupiter to thy planet on a lovely October evening.

" Here an immediate conviction pervaded me that this was home — was my appointed resting place ; a full tide of hope and satisfaction similar to the emotion excited on my first acquaintance with thy poem flowed over this hour; a joyous confidence in the existence of Goodness and Beauty supplied for a season, the want of thy society. The delicious clearness of every emotion exalted my soul into a realm full of life. Some time elapsed in this state. The whole of my temporal existence passed in review before me. My thoughts, **my** actions, were placed in full relief before the cleared eye of my spirit. Beloved, thou wilt rejoice to know that thy Meta could then feel that her worst faults sprung from ignorance. As I was striving to connect my present state with my past, and, as it were, poising myself on the brink of space and time, the breath of another presence came across me, and, gradually evolving from the bosom of light, a figure rose before me, in grace, in sweetness, how excelling! Fixing her eyes on mine with the full gaze of love, she said, in flute-like tones, 'Dost thou know me, my sister?'

"'Art thou not,' I replied, 'the love of Petrarch? I have seen the portraiture of thy mortal lineaments, and now recognize that perfect beauty, the full violet flower which thy lover's genius was able to anticipate.'

"'Yes,' she said, 'I am Laura — on earth most happy, yet most sad; most rich, and yet most poor. I come to greet her whom I recognize as the inheritress of all that was lovely in my earthly being, more happy than I in her temporal state. I have sympathized, O wife of Klopstock! in thy transitory happiness. Thy lover was thy priest and thy poet; thy model and oracle was thy bosom friend. All that earth could give was thine; and I joyed to think on thy rewarded love, thy freedom of soul, and unchecked faith. Follow me now: we are to dwell in the same circle, and I am appointed to show thee thine abiding place.'

" She guided me towards the source of that light which I have described to thee. We paused before a structure of dazzling whiteness, which stood on a slope, and overlooked a valley of exceeding beauty. It was shaded by trees which had that peculiar calmness that the shadows of trees have below in the high noon of summer moonlight —

'. . . trees which are still
As the shades of trees below,
When they sleep on the lonely hill,
In the summer moonlight glow.'

It was decked with majestic sculptures, of which I may speak in some future interview. Before it rose a fountain, from which the stream of light flowed down the valley, dividing it into two unequal parts. The larger and farther from us seemed, when I first looked on it, populous with shapes, beauteous as that of my guide. But, when I looked more fixedly, I saw only the valley, carpeted with large blue and white flowers, which emitted a hyacinthine odor. Here, Laura, turning round, asked, 'Is not this a poetic home, Meta ?'

"I paused a moment ere I replied, 'It is indeed a place of beauty, but more like the Greek elysium than the home Klopstock and I were wont to picture to ourselves beyond the gates of Death.'

"'Thou sayest well,' she said; 'nor is this thy final home; thou wilt but wait here a season, till Klopstock comes.'

"'What,' said I, 'alone! alone in Eden ?'

"'Has not Meta, then, collected aught on which she might meditate? Hast thou never read, " While I was musing, the fire burned " ?'

"'Laura,' said I, 'spare the reproach. The love of Petrach, whose soul grew up in golden fetters, whose strongest emotions, whose most natural actions were, through a long life, constantly repressed by the dictates of duty and honor, she content might pass long years in that contemplation which was on earth her only solace. But I, whose life has all been breathed out in love and ministry, can I endure that my existence be reversed? Can I live without utterance of spirit? or would such be a stage of that progressive happiness we are promised ?'

"'True, little one !' said she, with her first heavenly smile; 'nor shall it be thus with thee. A ministry is appointed thee — the same which I exercised while waiting here for that friend whom below I was forbidden to call my own.'

"She touched me, and from my shoulders sprung a pair of wings, white and azure, wide and glistering.

"'Meta!' she resumed, 'spirit of love! be this thine office. Wherever a soul pines in absence from all companionship, breathe sweet thoughts of sympathy to be had in another life, if deserved by virtuous exertions and mental progress. Bind up the wounds of hearts torn by bereavement; teach them where healing is to be found. Revive in the betrayed and forsaken heart that belief in virtue and nobleness, without which life is an odious, disconnected dream. Fan every flame of generous enthusiasm, and on the altars where it is kindled strew thou the incense of wisdom. In such a ministry thou couldst never be alone, since hope must dwell with thee. But I shall often come and discourse to thee of the future glories of thy destiny. Yet more: Seest thou that marble tablet? Retire here when thy pinions are wearied. Give up thy soul to faith. Fix thine eyes on the tablet, and the deeds and thoughts which fill the days of Klopstock shall be traced on it. Thus shall ye not be for a day divided. Hast thou, Meta, aught more to ask?"

"'Messenger of peace and bliss!' said I, 'dare I frame another request? Is it too presumptuous to ask that Klopstock may be one of those to whom I minister, and that he may know it is Meta who consoles him?'

"'Even this, to a certain extent, I have power to grant. Most pure, most holy was thy life with Klopstock; ye taught one another only good things, and peculiarly are ye rewarded. Thou mayst occasionally manifest thyself to him, and answer his prayers with words, — so long,' she continued, looking fixedly at me, 'as he continues true to himself and thee!'

"O, my beloved, why tell thee what were my emotions at such a promise? Ah! I must now leave thee, for dawn is bringing back the world's doings. Soon I shall visit thee again. Farewell! Remember that thy every thought and deed will be known to me, and be happy!"

She vanished.

27

WHAT FITS A MAN TO BE A VOTER?

A Fable.

The country had been denuded of its forests, and men cried, "Come! we must plant anew, or there will be no shade for the homes of our children, or fuel for their hearths. Let us find the best kernels for a new growth." And a basket of butternuts was offered.

But the planters rejected it with disgust. "What a black, rough coat it has!" said they; "it is entirely unfit for the dishes on a nobleman's table, nor have we ever seen it in such places. It must have a greasy, offensive kernel; nor can fine trees grow up from such a nut."

"Friends," said one of the planters, "this decision may be rash. The chestnut has not a handsome outside; it is long encased in troublesome burs, and, when disengaged, is almost as black as these nuts you despise. Yet from it grow trees of lofty stature, graceful form, and long life. Its kernel is white, and has furnished food to the most poetic and splendid nations of the older world."

"Don't tell me," says another; "brown is entirely different from black. I like brown very well; there is Oriental precedent for its respectability. Perhaps we will use some of your chestnuts, if we can get fine samples. But for the present, I think we should use only English walnuts, such as our forefathers delighted to honor. Here are many basketsful of them, quite enough for the present. We will plant them with a sprinkling between of the chestnut and acorn."

"But," rejoined the other, "many butternuts are beneath

(314)

the sod, and you cannot help a mixture of them being in your wood, at any rate."

" Well, we will grub them up and cut them down whenever we find them. We can use the young shrubs for kindlings."

At that moment two persons entered the council of a darker complexion than most of those present, as if born beneath the glow of a more scorching sun. First came a woman, beautiful in the mild, pure grandeur of her look; in whose large dark eye a prophetic intelligence was mingled with infinite sweetness. She looked at the assembly with an air of surprise, as if its aspect was strange to her. She threw quite back her veil, and stepping aside, made room for her companion. His form was youthful, about the age of one we have seen in many a picture produced by the thought of eighteen centuries, as of one "instructing the doctors." I need not describe the features; all minds have their own impressions of such an image,

" Severe in youthful beauty."

In his hand he bore a white banner, on which was embroidered, " PEACE AND GOOD WILL TO MEN." And the words seemed to glitter and give out sparks, as he paused in the assembly.

" I came hither," said he, " an uninvited guest, because I read sculptured above the door 'All men born free and equal,' and in this dwelling hoped to find myself at home. What is the matter in dispute? "

Then they whispered one to another, and murmurs were heard — " He is a mere boy; young people are always foolish and extravagant; " or, " He looks like a fanatic." But others said, " He looks like one whom we have been taught to honor. It will be best to tell him the matter in dispute."

When he heard it, he smiled, and said, " It will be needful first to ascertain which of the nuts is soundest *within*." And with a hammer he broke one, two, and more of the English walnuts, and they were mouldy. Then he tried the other nuts, but found most of them fresh within and *white*, for they were fresh from the bosom of the earth, while the others had been kept in a damp cellar.

And he said, " You had better plant them together, lest none, or few, of the walnuts be sound. And why are you so reluctant? Has not Heaven permitted them both to grow on the same soil? and does not that show what is intended about it?"

And they said, " But they are black and ugly to look upon." He replied, " They do not seem so to me. What my Father has fashioned in such guise offends not mine eye."

And they said, " But from one of these trees flew a bird of prey, who has done great wrong. We meant, therefore, to suffer no such tree among us."

And he replied, " Amid the band of my countrymen and friends there was one guilty of the blackest crime — that of selling for a price the life of his dearest friend; yet all the others of his blood were not put under ban because of his guilt."

Then they said, " But in the Holy Book our teachers tell us, we are bid to keep in exile or distress whatsoever is black and unseemly in our eyes."

Then he put his hand to his brow, and cried in a voice of the most penetrating pathos, " Have I been so long among you, and ye have not known me?" And the woman turned from them the majestic hope of her glance, and both forms suddenly vanished; but the banner was left trailing in the dust.

The men stood gazing at one another. After which one mounted on high, and said, " Perhaps, my friends, we carry too far this aversion to objects merely because they are black. I heard, the other day, a wise man say that black was the color of evil — marked as such by God, and that whenever a white man struck a black man he did an act of worship to God.* I could not quite believe him. I hope, in what I am about to add, I shall not be misunderstood. I am no abolitionist. I respect above all things, divine or human, the constitution framed by our forefathers, and the peculiar institutions hallowed by the usage of their sons. I have no sympathy with the black race in this country. I wish it to be understood that I feel towards negroes the purest personal antipathy. It is a family trait with us. My little son, scarce able to speak, will cry out, ' Nigger! Nigger!' whenever he sees one, and try to throw things at them. He made a whole omnibus load laugh the other day by his cunning way of doing this.† The child of my political antagonist, on the other hand, says ' he likes *tullared* children the best.'† You see he is tainted in his cradle by the loose principles of his parents, even before he can say nigger, or pronounce the more refined appellation. But that is no matter. I merely mention this by the way ; not to prejudice you against Mr. ――, but that you may appreciate the very different state of things in my family, and not misinterpret what I have to say. I was lately in one of our prisons where a somewhat injudicious indulgence had extended to one of the condemned felons, a lost and wretched outcast from society, the use of materials for painting, that having been his profession. He had completed at his leisure a picture of the Lord's Supper. Most of the figures were well enough, but Judas he had represented as a black.† Now, gentlemen, I am of opinion that this is an unwarrantable liberty taken with the Holy Scriptures, and shows *too much* prejudice in the community. It is my wish to be moderate and fair, and preserve a medium, neither, on the one hand, yielding the wholesome antipathies planted in our breasts as a safeguard against degradation, and our constitutional obligations, which, as I have before observed, are, with me, more binding than any other ; nor, on the other

---

* Fact, that this is affirmed.　　　　† Facts,

27 *

hand, forgetting that liberality and wisdom which are the prerogative of every citizen of this free commonwealth. I agree, then, with our young visitor. I hardly know, indeed, why a stranger, and one so young, was permitted to mingle in this council; but it was certainly thoughtful in him to crack and examine the nuts. I agree that it may be well to plant some of the black nuts among the others, so that, if many of the walnuts fail, we may make use of this inferior tree."

At this moment arose a hubbub, and such a clamor of "dangerous innovation," "political capital," "low-minded demagogue," "infidel who denies the Bible," "lower link in the chain of creation," &c., that it is impossible to say what was the decision.

DISCOVERIES.

SOMETIMES, as we meet people in the street, we catch a sentence from their lips that affords a clew to their history and habits of mind, and puts our own minds on quite a new course.

Yesterday two female figures drew nigh upon the street, in whom we had only observed their tawdry, showy style of dress, when, as they passed, one remarked to the other, in the tone of a person who has just made a discovery, " *I* think there is something very handsome in a fine child."

Poor woman! that seemed to have been the first time in her life that she had made the observation. The charms of the human being, in that fresh and flower-like age which is intended perpetually to refresh us in our riper, renovate us in our declining years, had never touched her heart, nor awakened for her the myriad thoughts and fancies that as naturally attend the sight of childhood as bees swarm to the blossoming bough. Instead of being to her the little angels and fairies, the embodied poems which may ennoble the humblest lot, they had been to her mere " torments," who " could never be kept still, or their faces clean."

How piteous is the loss of those who do not contemplate childhood in a spirit of holiness! The heavenly influence on their own minds, of attention to cultivate each germ of great and good qualities, of avoiding the least act likely to injure, is lost — a loss dreary and piteous! for which no gain can compensate. But how unspeakably deplorable the petrifaction of those who look upon their little friends without any sympathy even, whose hearts are, by selfishness, worldliness, and vanity, seared from all gentle instincts, who can no longer appreciate their spontaneous grace and glee, that eloquence in every look, motion, and stammered word, those lively and incessant charms, over which the action of the lower motives with which the social system is rife, may so soon draw a veil!

We can no longer speak thus of *all* children. On some, especially in cities, the inheritance of sin and deformity from bad parents falls too heavily, and incases at once the spark of soul which God still doth not refuse in such instances, in a careful, knowing, sensual mask. Such are never, in fact, children at all. But the rudest little cubs that are free from taint, and show the affinities with nature and the soul, are still young and flexible, and rich in gleams of the loveliness to be hoped from perfected human nature.

It is sad that all men do not feel these things. It is sad that they wilfully renounce so large a part of their heritage, and go forth to buy filtered water, while the fountain is gushing freshly beside the door of their own huts. As with the charms of children, so with other things. They do not know that the sunset is worth seeing every night, and the shows of the forest better than those of the theatre, and the work of bees and beetles more instructive, if scanned with care, than the lyceum lecture. The cheap knowledge, the cheap pleasures, that are spread before every one, they cast aside in search of an uncertain and feverish joy. We did, indeed, hear one man say that he could not possibly be deprived of his pleasures, since he could always, even were his abode in the narrowest lane, have a blanket of sky above his head, where he could see the clouds pass, and the stars glitter. But men in general remain unaware that

> " Life's best joys are nearest us,
> Lie close about our feet."

For them the light dresses all objects in endless novelty, the rose glows, domestic love smiles, and childhood gives out with sportive freedom its oracles — in vain. That woman had seen beauty in gay shawls, in teacups, in carpets; but only of late had she discovered that "there was something beautiful in a fine child." Poor human nature! Thou must have been changed at nurse by a bad demon at some time, and strangely maltreated, — to have such blind and rickety intervals as come upon thee now and then!

POLITENESS TOO GREAT A LUXURY TO BE GIVEN TO THE POOR.

A FEW days ago, a lady, crossing in one of the ferry boats that ply from this city, saw a young boy, poorly dressed, sitting with an infant in his arms on one of the benches. She observed that the child looked sickly and coughed. This, as the day was raw, made her anxious in its behalf, and she went to the boy and asked whether he was alone there with the baby, and if he did not think the cold breeze dangerous for it. He replied that he was sent out with the child to take care of it, and that his father said the fresh air from the water would do it good.

While he made this simple answer, a number of persons had collected around to listen, and one of them, a well-dressed woman, addressed the boy in a string of such questions and remarks as these : —

" What is your name? Where do you live? Are you telling us the truth? It's a shame to have that baby out in such weather; you'll be the death of it. (To the bystanders :) I would go and see his mother, and tell her about it, if I was sure he had told us the truth about where he lived. How do you expect to get back? Here, (in the rudest voice,) somebody says you have not told the truth as to where you live."

The child, whose only offence consisted in taking care of the little one in public, and answering when he was spoken to, began to shed tears at the accusations thus grossly preferred against him. The bystanders stared at both; but among them all there was not one with sufficiently clear notions of

(322)

propriety and moral energy to say to this impudent questioner "Woman, do you suppose, because you wear a handsome shawl, and that boy a patched jacket, that you have any right to speak to him at all, unless he wishes it — far less to prefer against him these rude accusations? Your vulgarity is unendurable ; leave the place or alter your manner."

Many such instances have we seen of insolent rudeness, or more insolent affability, founded on no apparent grounds, except an apparent difference in pecuniary position ; for no one can suppose, in such cases, the offending party has really enjoyed the benefit of refined education and society, but all present let them pass as matters of course. It was sad to see how the poor would endure — mortifying to see how the purse-proud dared offend. An excellent man, who was, in his early years, a missionary to the poor, used to speak afterwards with great shame of the manner in which he had conducted himself towards them. "When I recollect," said he, "the freedom with which I entered their houses, inquired into all their affairs, commented on their conduct, and disputed their statements, I wonder I was never horsewhipped, and feel that I ought to have been ; it would have done me good, for I needed as severe a lesson on the universal obligations of politeness in its only genuine form of respect for man as man, and delicate sympathy with each in his peculiar position."

Charles Lamb, who was indeed worthy to be called a human being because of those refined sympathies, said, "You call him a gentleman: does his washerwoman find him so?" We may say, if she did, she found him a *man*, neither treating her with vulgar abruptness, nor giving himself airs of condescending liveliness, but treating her with that genuine respect which a feeling of equality inspires.

To doubt the veracity of another is an insult which in most *civilized* communities must in the so-called higher classes be atoned for by blood, but, in those same communities, the same men will, with the utmost lightness, doubt the truth of one who wears a ragged coat, and thus do all they can to injure and degrade him by assailing his self-respect, and breaking the feeling of personal honor — a wound to which hurts a man as a wound to its bark does a tree.

Then how rudely are favors conferred, just as a bone is thrown to a dog! A gentleman, indeed, will not do *that* without accompanying signs of sympathy and regard. Just as this woman said, "If you have told the truth I will go and see your mother," are many acts performed on which the actors pride themselves as kind and charitable.

All men might learn from the French in these matters. That people, whatever be their faults, are really well bred, and many acts might be quoted from their romantic annals, where gifts were given from rich to poor with a graceful courtesy, equally honorable and delightful to the giver and the receiver.

In Catholic countries there is more courtesy, for charity is there a duty, and must be done for God's sake; there is less room for a man to give himself the pharisaical tone about it. A rich man is not so surprised to find himself in contact with a poor one; nor is the custom of kneeling on the open pavement, the silk robe close to the beggar's rags, without profit. The separation by pews, even on the day when all meet nearest, is as bad for the manners as the soul.

Blessed be he, or she, who has passed through this world, not only with an open purse and willingness to render the aid of mere outward benefits, but with an open eye and open heart, ready to cheer the downcast, and enlighten the dull by words of comfort and looks of love. The wayside charities are the most valuable both as to sustaining hope and diffusing knowledge, and none can render them who has not an expansive nature, a heart alive to affection, and some true notion, however imperfectly developed, of the meaning of human brotherhood.

Such a one can never sauce the given meat with taunts,

freeze the viand by a cold glance of doubt, or plunge the man, who asked for his hand, deeper back into the mud by any kind of rudeness.

In the little instance with which we began, no help *was* asked, unless by the sight of the timid little boy's old jacket. But the license which this seemed to the well-clothed woman to give to rudeness, was so characteristic of a deep fault now existing, that a volume of comments might follow and a host of anecdotes be drawn from almost any one's experience in exposition of it. These few words, perhaps, may awaken thought in those who have drawn tears from other's eyes through an ignorance brutal, but not hopelessly so, if they are willing to rise above it.

28

CASSIUS M. CLAY.

THE meeting on Monday night at the Tabernacle was to us an occasion of deep and peculiar interest. It was deep, for the feelings there expressed and answered bore witness to the truth of our belief, that the sense of right is not dead, but only sleepeth in this nation. A man who is manly enough to appeal to it, will be answered, in feeling at least, if not in action, and while there is life there is hope. Those who so rapturously welcomed one who had sealed his faith by deeds of devotion, must yet acknowledge in their breasts the germs of like nobleness.

It was an occasion of peculiar interest, such as we have not had occasion to feel since, in childish years, we saw Lafayette welcomed by a grateful people. Even childhood well understood that the gratitude then expressed was not so much for the aid which had been received as for the motives and feelings with which it was given. The nation rushed out as one man to thank Lafayette, that he had been able, amid the prejudices and indulgences of high rank in the old *régime* of society, to understand the great principles which were about to create a new form, and answer, manlike, with love, service, and contempt of selfish interests to the voice of humanity demanding its rights. Our freedom would have been achieved without Lafayette; but it was a happiness and a blessing to number the young French nobleman as the champion of American independence, and to know that he had given the prime of his life to our cause, because it was the cause of justice. With similar feelings of joy, pride, and hope, we welcome Cassius M. Clay, a man who has, in like manner, freed himself from the prejudices of his position, disregarded selfish considerations, and quitting the easy path in which he might have walked to station in the sight of men, and such external distinctions as his State and nation readily confer on men so born and bred, and with such abilities, chose rather an interest in their souls, and the honors history will not fail to award to the man who enrolls his name and elevates his life for the cause of right and those universal principles whose recognition can alone secure to man the destiny without which he cannot be happy, but which he is continually sacrificing for the impure worship of idols. Yea, in this country, more than in the old Palestine, do they give their children to the fire in honor of Moloch, and sell the ark confided to them by the Most High for shekels of gold and of silver. Partly it was the sense of this position which Mr. Clay holds, as a man who esteems his own individual convictions of right more than local interests or partial, political schemes, that gave him such an enthusiastic welcome on Monday night from the very hearts of the audience, but still more that his honor is at this moment identified with the liberty of the press, which has been insulted and infringed in him. About this there can be in fact but one opinion. In vain Kentucky calls meetings, states reasons, gives names of her own to what has been done.* The rest of the world knows very well what the action is, and will call it by but one name. Regardless of this ostrich mode of defence, the world has laughed and scoffed at the act of a people professing to be free and defenders of freedom, and the recording angel has written down the deed as a lawless act of violence and tyranny, from which the man is happy who can call himself pure.

With the usual rhetoric of the wrong side, the apologists for this mob violence have wished to injure Mr. Clay by the epithets of "hot-headed," "visionary," "fanatical." But, if any have believed that such could apply to a man so

[* The destruction of Mr. Clay's press by a mob. —ED.]

clear-sighted as to his objects and the way of achieving them, the mistake must have been corrected on Monday night. Whoever saw Mr. Clay that night, saw in him a man of deep and strong nature, thoroughly in earnest, who had well considered his ground, and saw that though open, as the truly *noble* must be, to new views and convictions, yet his direction is taken, and the improvement to be made will not be to turn aside, but to expedite and widen his course in that direction. Mr. Clay is young, young enough, thank Heaven! to promise a long career of great thoughts and honorable deeds. But still, to those who esteem youth an unpardonable fault, and one that renders incapable of counsel, we would say that he is at the age when a man is capable of great thoughts and great deeds, if ever. His is not a character that will ever grow old; it is not capable of a petty and short-sighted prudence, but can only be guided by a large wisdom which is more young than old, for it has within itself the springs of perpetual youth, and which, being far-sighted and prophetical, joins ever with the progress party without waiting till it be obviously in the ascendant.

Mr. Clay has eloquence, but only from the soul. He does not possess the art of oratory, as an art. Before he gets warmed he is too slow, and breaks his sentences too much. His transitions are not made with skill, nor is the structure of his speech, as a whole, symmetrical; yet, throughout, his grasp is firm upon his subject, and all the words are laden with the electricity of a strong mind and generous nature. When he begins to glow, and his deep mellow eye fills with light, the speech melts and glows too, and he is able to impress upon the hearer the full effect of firm conviction, conceived with impassioned energy. His often rugged and harsh emphasis flashes and sparkles then, and we feel that there is in the furnace a stream of iron: iron, fortress of the nations and victor of the seas, worth far more, in stress of storm, than all the gold and gems of rhetoric.

The great principle that he who wrongs one wrongs all, and that no part can be wounded without endangering the whole, was the healthy root of Mr. Clay's speech. The report does not do justice to the turn of expression in some parts which were most characteristic. These, indeed, depended much on the tones and looks of the speaker. We should speak of them as full of a robust and homely sincerity, dignified by the heart of the gentleman, a heart too secure of its respect for the rights of others to need any of the usual interpositions. His good-humored sarcasm, on occasion of several vulgar interruptions, was very pleasant, and easily at those times might be recognized in him the man of heroical nature, who can only show himself adequately in time of interruption and of obstacle. If that be all that is wanted, we shall surely see him wholly; there will be no lack of American occasions to call out the Greek fire. We want them all — the Grecian men, who feel a godlike thirst for immortal glory, and to develop the peculiar powers with which the gods have gifted them. We want them all — the poet, the thinker, the hero. Whether our heroes need *swords*, is a more doubtful point, we think, than Mr. Clay believes. Neither do we believe in some of the means he proposes to further his aims. God uses all kinds of means, but men, his priests, must keep their hands pure. Nobody that needs a bribe shall be asked to further our schemes for emancipation. But there is room enough and time enough to think out these points till all is in harmony. For the good that has been done and the truth that has been spoken, for the love of such that has been seen in this great city struggling up through the love of money, we should to-day be thankful — and we are so.

28 *

THE stars tell all their secrets to the flowers, and, if we only knew how to look around us, we should not need to look above. But man is a plant of slow growth, and great heat is required to bring out his leaves. He must be promised a boundless futurity, to induce him to use aright the present hour. In youth, fixing his eyes on those distant worlds of light, he promises himself to attain them, and there find the answer to all his wishes. His eye grows keener as he gazes, a voice from the earth calls it downward, and he finds all at his feet.

I was riding on the shore of Lake Pontchartrain, musing on an old English expression, which I had only lately learned to interpret. " He was fulfilled of all nobleness." Words so significant charm us like a spell, long before we know their meaning. This I had now learned to interpret. Life had ripened from the green bud, and I had seen the difference, wide as from earth to heaven, between nobleness and the *fulfilment* of nobleness.

A fragrance beyond any thing I had ever known came suddenly upon the air, and interrupted my meditation. I looked around me, but saw no flower from which it could proceed. There is no word for it ; *exquisite* and *delicious* have lost all meaning now. It was of a full and penetrating sweetness, too keen and delicate to be cloying. Unable to trace it, I rode on, but the remembrance of it pursued me. I had a feeling that I must forever regret my loss, my want, if I did not return and find the poet of the lake, whose voice was such perfume. In earlier days, I might have disre-

(330)

garded such a feeling; but now I have learned to prize the
monitions of my nature as they deserve, and learn sometimes
what is not for sale in the market place. So I turned back,
and rode to and fro, at the risk of abandoning the object of
my ride.

I found her at last, the queen of the south, singing to herself in her lonely bower. Such should a sovereign be, most
regal when alone; for then there is no disturbance to prevent
the full consciousness of power. All occasions limit; a kingdom is but an occasion; and no sun ever saw itself adequately
reflected on sea or land.

Nothing at the south had affected me like the magnolia.
Sickness and sorrow, which have separated me from my kind,
have requited my loss by making known to me the loveliest
dialect of the divine language. "Flowers," it has been truly
said, "are the only positive present made us by nature."
Man has not been ungrateful, but consecrated the gift to
adorn the darkest and brightest hours. If it is ever perverted,
it is to be used as a medicine; and even this vexes me. But
no matter for that. We have pure intercourse with these
purest creations; we love them for their own sake, for their
beauty's sake. As we grow beautiful and pure, we understand them better. With me knowledge of them is a circumstance, a habit of my life, rather than a merit. I have lived
with them, and with them almost alone, till I have learned to
interpret the slightest signs by which they manifest their fair
thoughts. There is not a flower in my native region which
has not for me a tale, to which every year is adding new incidents; yet the growths of this new climate brought me new
and sweet emotions, and, above all others, was the magnolia
a revelation. When I first beheld her, a stately tower of
verdure, each cup, an imperial vestal, full-displayed to the
eye of day, yet guarded from the too hasty touch even of the
wind by its graceful decorums of firm, glistening, broad, green
leaves, I stood astonished, as might a lover of music, who, after

hearing in all his youth only the harp or the bugle, should be saluted, on entering some vast cathedral, by the full peal of its organ.

After I had recovered from my first surprise, I became acquainted with the flower, and found all its life in harmony. Its fragrance, less enchanting than that of the rose, excited a pleasure more full of life, and which could longer be enjoyed without satiety. Its blossoms, if plucked from their home, refused to retain their dazzling hue, but drooped and grew sallow, like princesses captive in the prison of a barbarous foe.

But there was something quite peculiar in the fragrance of this tree; so much so, that I had not at first recognized the magnolia. Thinking it must be of a species I had never yet seen, I alighted, and leaving my horse, drew near to question it with eyes of reverent love.

"Be not surprised," replied those lips of untouched purity, "stranger, who alone hast known to hear in my voice a tone more deep and full than that of my beautiful sisters. Sit down, and listen to my tale, nor fear that I will overpower thee by too much sweetness. I am, indeed, of the race you love, but in it I stand alone. In my family I have no sister of the heart, and though my root is the same as that of the other virgins of our royal house, I bear not the same blossom, nor can I unite my voice with theirs in the forest choir. Therefore I dwell here alone, nor did I ever expect to tell the secret of my loneliness. But to all that ask there is an answer, and I speak to thee.

"Indeed, we have met before, as that secret feeling of home, which makes delight so tender, must inform thee. The spirit that I utter once inhabited the glory of the most glorious climates. I dwelt once in the orange tree."

"Ah?" said I; "then I did not mistake. It is the same voice I heard in the saddest season of my youth. I stood one evening on a high terrace in another land, the land where 'the plant man has grown to greatest size.' It was an

evening whose unrivalled splendor demanded perfection in
man — answering to that he found in nature — a sky 'black-
blue' deep as eternity, stars of holiest hope, a breeze promis-
ing rapture in every breath. I could not longer endure this
discord between myself and such beauty; I retired within my
window, and lit the lamp. Its rays fell on an orange tree,
full clad in its golden fruit and bridal blossoms. How did
we talk together then, fairest friend! Thou didst tell me all;
and yet thou knowest, that even then, had I asked any part
of thy dower, it would have been to bear the sweet fruit,
rather than the sweeter blossoms. My wish had been expressed by another.

> ' O, that I were an orange tree,
>   That busy plant!
> Then should I ever laden be,
>   And never want
> Some fruit for him that dresseth me.'

Thou didst seem to me the happiest of all spirits in wealth of
nature, in fulness of utterance. How is it that I find thee now
in another habitation ? "

"How is it, man, that thou art now content that thy life
bears no golden fruit ? "

"It is," I replied, "that I have at last, through privation,
been initiated into the secret of peace. Blighted without,
unable to find myself in other forms of nature, I was driven
back upon the centre of my being, and there found all being.
For the wise, the obedient child from one point can draw all
lines, and in one germ read all the possible disclosures of
successive life."

"Even so," replied the flower, "and ever for that reason
am I trying to simplify my being. How happy I was in the
'spirit's dower when first it was wed,' I told thee in that
earlier day. But after a while I grew weary of that fulness
of speech; I felt a shame at telling all I knew, and challen-
ging all sympathies; I was never silent, I was never alone; I

had a voice for every season, for day and night; on me the merchant counted, the bride looked to me for her garland, the nobleman for the chief ornament of his princely hall, and the poor man for his wealth; all sang my praises, all extolled my beauty, all blessed my beneficence; and, for a while, my heart swelled with pride and pleasure. But, as years passed, my mood changed. The lonely moon rebuked me, as she hid from the wishes of man, nor would return till her due change was passed. The inaccessible sun looked on me with the same ray as on all others; my endless profusion could not bribe him to one smile sacred to me alone. The mysterious wind passed me by to tell its secret to the solemn pine, and the nightingale sang to the rose rather than me, though she was often silent, and buried herself yearly in the dark earth.

"I knew no mine or thine: I belonged to all. I could never rest: I was never at one. Painfully I felt this want, and from every blossom sighed entreaties for some being to come and satisfy it. With every bud I implored an answer, but each bud only produced an orange.

"At last this feeling grew more painful, and thrilled my very root. The earth trembled at the touch with a pulse so sympathetic that ever and anon it seemed, could I but retire and hide in that silent bosom for one calm winter, all would be told me, and tranquillity, deep as my desire, be mine. But the law of my being was on me, and man and nature seconded it. Ceaselessly they called on me for my beautiful gifts; they decked themselves with them, nor cared to know the saddened heart of the giver. O, how cruel they seemed at last, as they visited and despoiled me, yet never sought to aid me, or even paused to think that I might need their aid! yet I would not hate them. I saw it was my seeming riches that bereft me of sympathy. I saw they could not know what was hid beneath the perpetual veil of glowing life. I ceased to expect aught from them, and turned my eyes to the distant stars. I thought, could I but hoard from the daily expenditure of my juices till I grew tall enough, I might reach those distant spheres, which looked so silent and consecrated, and there pause a while from these weary joys of endless life, and in the lap of winter find my spring.

" But not so was my hope to be fulfilled. One starlight night I was looking, hoping, when a sudden breeze came up. It touched me, I thought, as if it were a cold, white beam from those stranger worlds.   The cold gained upon my heart; every blossom trembled, every leaf grew brittle, and the fruit began to seem unconnected with the stem; soon I lost all feeling; and morning found the pride of the garden black, stiff, and powerless.

" As the rays of the morning sun touched me, consciousness returned, and I strove to speak, but in vain. Sealed were my fountains, and all my heartbeats still. I felt that I had been that beauteous tree, but now only was — what — I knew not; yet I was, and the voices of men said, It is dead; cast it forth, and plant another in the costly vase. A mystic shudder of pale joy then separated me wholly from my former abode.

" A moment more, and I was before the queen and guardian of the flowers. Of this being I cannot speak to thee in any language now possible betwixt us; for this is a being of another order from thee, an order whose presence thou mayst feel, nay, approach step by step, but which cannot be known till thou art of it, nor seen nor spoken of till thou hast passed through it.

" Suffice it to say, that it is not such a being as men love to paint; a fairy, like them, only lesser and more exquisite than they; a goddess, larger and of statelier proportion; an angel, like still, only with an added power. Man never creates; he only recombines the lines and colors of his own existence: only a deific fancy could evolve from the elements the form that took me home.

" Secret, radiant, profound ever, and never to be known, was she; many forms indicate, and none declare her. Like all such beings, she was feminine. All the secret powers are "mothers." There is but one paternal power.

"She had heard my wish while I looked at the stars, and in the silence of fate prepared its fulfilment. 'Child of my most communicative hour,' said she, 'the full pause must not follow such a burst of melody. Obey the gradations of nature, nor seek to retire at once into her utmost purity of silence. The vehemence of thy desire at once promises and forbids its gratification. Thou wert the keystone of the arch, and bound together the circling year: thou canst not at once become the base of the arch, the centre of the circle. Take a step inward, forget a voice, lose a power; no longer a bounteous sovereign, become a vestal priestess, and bide thy time in the magnolia.'

"Such is my history, friend of my earlier day. Others of my family, that you have met, were formerly the religious lily, the lonely dahlia, fearless decking the cold autumn, and answering the shortest visits of the sun with the brightest hues; the narcissus, so rapt in self-contemplation that it could not abide the usual changes of a life. Some of these have perfume, others not, according to the habit of their earlier state; for, as spirits change, they still bear some trace, a faint reminder, of their latest step upwards or inwards. I still speak with somewhat of my former exuberance and over-ready tenderness to the dwellers on this shore; but each star sees me purer, of deeper thought, and more capable of retirement into my own heart. Nor shall I again detain a wanderer, luring him from afar; nor shall I again subject myself to be questioned by an alien spirit, to tell the tale of my being in words that divide it from itself. Farewell, stranger! and believe that nothing strange can meet me more. I have atoned by confession; further penance needs not; and I feel the Infinite possess me more and more. Farewell! to meet again in prayer, in destiny, in harmony, in elemental power."

The magnolia left me; I left not her, but must abide forever in the thought to which the clew was found in the margin of that lake of the South.

WHOEVER passes up Broadway finds his attention arrested by three fine structures — Trinity Church, that of the Messiah, and Grace Church.

His impressions are, probably, at first, of a pleasant character. He looks upon these edifices as expressions, which, however inferior in grandeur to the poems in stone which adorn the older world, surely indicate that man cannot rest content with his short earthly span, but prizes relations to eternity. The house in which he pays deference to claims which death will not cancel seems to be no less important in his eyes than those in which the affairs which press nearest are attended to.

So far, so good! That is expressed which gives man his superiority over the other orders of the natural world, that consciousness of spiritual affinities of which we see no unequivocal signs elsewhere.

But, if this be something great when compared with the rest of the animal creation, yet how little seems it when compared with the ideal that has been offered to him, as to the means of signifying such feelings! These temples! how far do they correspond with the idea of that religious sentiment from which they originally sprung? In the old world the history of such edifices, though not without its shadow, had many bright lines. Kings and emperors paid oftentimes for the materials and labor a price of blood and plunder, and many a wretched sinner sought by contributions of stone for their walls to roll off the burden he had laid on his conscience. Still the community amid which they rose knew little of these draw-

29 (337)

bncks. Pious legends attest the purity of feeling associated
with each circumstance of their building. Mysterious orders,
of which we know only that they were consecrated to brotherly love and the development of mind, produced the genius
which animated the architecture; but the casting of the bells
and suspending them in the tower was an act in which all
orders of the community took part; for when those cathedrals
were consecrated, it was for the use of all. Rich and poor
knelt together upon their marble pavements, and the imperial
altar welcomed the obscurest artisan.

This grace our churches want — the grace which belongs to
all religions, but is peculiarly and solemnly enforced upon the
followers of Jesus. The poor to whom he came to preach can
have no share in the grace of Grace Church. In St. Peter's,
if only as an empty form, the soiled feet of travel-worn disciples are washed; but such feet can never intrude on the fane
of the holy Trinity here in republican America, and the
Messiah may be supposed still to give as excuse for delay,
" The poor you always have with you."

We must confess this circumstance is to us quite destructive
of reverence and value for these buildings.

We are told, that at the late consecration, the claims of the
poor were eloquently urged; and that an effort is to be made,
by giving a side chapel, to atone for the luxury which shuts
them out from the reflection of sunshine through those brilliant
windows. It is certainly better that they should be offered
the crumbs from the rich man's table than nothing at all, yet
it is surely not *the* way that Jesus would have taught to provide for the poor.

Would we not then have these splendid edifices erected?
We certainly feel that the educational influence of good specimens of architecture (and we know no other argument in
their favor) is far from being a counterpoise to the abstraction
of so much money from purposes that would be more in fulfilment of that Christian idea which these assume to represent.

Were the rich to build such a church, and, dispensing with pews and all exclusive advantages, invite all who would to come in to the banquet, that were, indeed, noble and Christian. And, though we believe more, for our nation and time, in intellectual monuments than those of wood and stone, and, in opposition even to our admired Powers, think that Michael Angelo himself could have advised no more suitable monument to Washington than a house devoted to the instruction of the people, and think that great master, and the Greeks no less, would agree with us if they lived now to survey all the bearings of the subject, yet we would not object to these splendid churches, if the idea of Him they call Master were represented in them. But till it is, they can do no good, for the means are not in harmony with the end. The rich man sits in state while "near two hundred thousand" Lazaruses linger, unprovided for, without the gate. While this is so, they must not talk much, within, of Jesus of Nazareth, who called to him fishermen, laborers, and artisans, for his companions and disciples.

We find some excellent remarks on this subject from Rev. Stephen Olin, president of the Wesleyan University. They are appended as a note to a discourse addressed to young men, on the text, " Put ye on the Lord Jesus Christ, and make not provision for the flesh, to fulfil the lusts thereof."

This discourse, though it discloses formal and external views of religious ties and obligations, is dignified by a fervent, generous love for men, and a more than commonly catholic liberality ; and though these remarks are made and meant to bear upon the interests of his own sect, yet they are anti-sectarian in their tendency, and worthy the consideration of all anxious to understand the call of duty in these matters. Earnest attention of this sort will better avail than fifteen hundred dollars, or more, paid for a post of exhibition in a fashionable church, where, if piety be provided with one chance, worldliness has twenty to stare it out of countenance.

" The strong tendency in our religious operations to gather the rich and the poor into separate folds, and so to generate and establish in the church distinctions utterly at variance with the spirit of our political institutions, is the very worst result of the multiplication of sects among us; and I fear it must be admitted that the evil is greatly aggravated by the otherwise benignant working of the voluntary system. Without insisting further upon the probable or possible injury which may befall our free country from this conflict of agencies, ever the most powerful in the formation of national and individual character, no one, I am sure, can fail to recognize in this development an iffluence utterly and irreconcilably hostile to the genius and cherished objects of Christianity. It is the peculiar glory of the gospel that, even under the most arbitrary governments, it has usually been able to vindicate and practically exemplify the essential equality of man. It has had one doctrine and one hope for all its children; and the highest and the lowest have been constrained to acknowledge one holy law of brotherhood in the common faith of which they are made partakers. Nowhere else, I believe, but in the United States — certainly nowhere else to the same extent — does this anti-Christian separation of classes prevail in the Christian church. The beggar in his tattered vestments walks the splendid courts of St. Peter's, and kneels at its costly altars by the side of dukes and cardinals. The peasant in his wooden shoes is welcomed in the gorgeous churches of Notre Dame and the Madeleine; and even in England, where political and social distinctions are more rigorously enforced than in any other country on earth, the lord and the peasant, the richest and the poorest, are usually occupants of the same church, and partakers of the same communion. That the reverse of all this is true in many parts of this country, every observing man knows full well; and what is yet more deplorable, while the lines of demarcation between the different classes have already become sufficiently distinct, the tendency is receiving new

strength and development in a rapidly augmenting ratio.
Even in country places, where the population is sparse, and
the artificial distinctions of society are little known, the working of this strange element is, in many instances, made manifest, and a petty coterie of village magnates may be found
worshipping God apart from the body of the people.   But
the evil is much more apparent, as well as more deeply seated,
in our populous towns, where the causes which produce it
have been longer in operation, and have more fully enjoyed
the favor of circumstances.   In these great centres of wealth,
intelligence, and influence, the separation between the classes
is, in many instances, complete, and in many more the process is rapidly progressive.

"There are crowded religious congregations composed so
exclusively of the wealthy as scarcely to embrace an indigent
family or individual; and the number of such churches, where
the gospel is never preached to the poor, is constantly increasing.   Rich men, instead of associating themselves with their
more humble fellow-Christians, where their money as well as
their influence and counsels are so much needed, usually combine to erect magnificent churches, in which sittings are too
expensive for any but people of fortune, and from which their
less-favored brethren are as effectually and peremptorily excluded as if there were dishonor or contagion in their presence.   A congregation is thus constituted, able, without the
slightest inconvenience, to bear the pecuniary burdens of
twenty churches, monopolizing and consigning to comparative
inactivity intellectual, moral, and material resources, for want
of which so many other congregations are doomed to struggle
with the most embarrassing difficulties.   Can it for a moment
be thought that such a state of things is desirable, or in harmony with the spirit and design of the gospel?

"A more difficult question arises when we inquire after a
remedy for evils too glaring to be overlooked, and too grave
to be tolerated, without an effort to palliate, if not to remove

29 *

them. The most obvious palliative, and one which has already
been tried to some extent by wealthy churches or individuals,
is the erection of free places of worship for the poor. Such
a provision for this class of persons would be more effectual
in any other part of the world than in the United States.
Whether it arises from the operation of our political system,
or from the easy attainment of at least the prime necessaries
of life, the poorer classes here are characterized by a proud
spirit, which will not submit to receive even the highest benefits in any form that implies inferiority or dependence. This
strong and prevalent feeling must continue to interpose serious
obstacles in the way of these laudable attempts. If in a few
instances churches for the poor have succeeded in our large
cities, where the theory of social equality is so imperfectly
realized in the actual condition of the people, and where the
presence of a multitude of indigent foreigners tends to lower
the sentiment of independence so strong in native-born Americans, the system is yet manifestly incapable of general application to the religious wants of our population. The same
difficulty usually occurs in all attempts to induce the humbler
classes to worship with the rich in sumptuous churches, by reserving for their benefit a portion of the sittings free, or at a
nominal rent. A few only can be found who are willing to be
recognized and provided for as beneficiaries and paupers,
while the multitude will always prefer to make great sacrifices in order to provide for themselves in some humbler fane.
It must be admitted that this subject is beset with practical
difficulties, which are not likely to be removed speedily, or
without some great and improbable revolution in our religious
affairs. Yet if the respectable Christian denominations most
concerned in the subject shall pursue a wise and liberal policy
for the future, something may be done to check the evil.
They may retard its rapid growth, perhaps, though it will
most likely be found impossible to eradicate it altogether. It
ought to be well understood, that the multiplication of mag-

nificent churches is daily making the line of demarcation between the rich and the poor more and more palpable and impassable. There are many good reasons for the erection of such edifices. Increasing wealth and civilization seem to call for a liberal and tasteful outlay in behalf of religion; yet is it the dictate of prudence no less than of duty to balance carefully the good and the evil of every enterprise. It should ever be kept in mind, that such a church virtually writes above its sculptured portals an irrevocable prohibition to the poor—
'*Procul, O procul este profani.*' "

LATE ASPIRATIONS.

LETTER TO H——.

You have put to me that case which puzzles more than almost any in this strange world — the case of a man of good intentions, with natural powers sufficient to carry them out, who, after having through great part of a life lived the best he knew, and, in the world's eye, lived admirably well, suddenly wakes to a consciousness of the soul's true aims. He finds that he has been a good son, husband, and father, an adroit man of business, respected by all around him, without ever having advanced one step in the life of the soul. His object has not been the development of his immortal being, nor has this been developed; all he has done bears upon the present life only, and even that in a way poor and limited, since no deep fountain of intellect or feeling has ever been unsealed for him. Now that his eyes are opened, he sees what communion is possible; what incorruptible riches may be accumulated by the man of true wisdom. But why is the hour of clear vision so late deferred? He cannot blame himself for his previous blindness. His eyes were holden that he saw not. He lived as well as he knew how.

And now that he would fain give himself up to the new oracle in his bosom, and to the inspirations of nature, all his old habits, all his previous connections, are unpropitious. He is bound by a thousand chains which press on him so as to leave no moment free. And perhaps it seems to him that, were he free, he should but feel the more forlorn. He sees

(344)

the charm and nobleness of this new life, but knows not how to live it. It is an element to which his mental frame has not been trained. He knows not what to do to-day or to-morrow; how to stay by himself, or how to meet others; how to act. or how to rest. Looking on others who chose the path which now invites him at an age when their characters were yet plastic, and the world more freely opened before them, he deems them favored children, and cries in almost despairing sadness, Why, O Father of Spirits, didst thou not earlier enlighten me also? Why was I not led gently by the hand in the days of my youth? "And what," you ask, " could I reply?"

Much, much, dear H——, were this a friend whom I could see so often that his circumstances would be my text. For no subject has more engaged my thoughts, no difficulty is more frequently met. But now on this poor sheet I can only give you the clew to what I should say.

In the first place, the depth of the despair must be caused by the mistaken idea that this our present life is all the time allotted to man for the education of his nature for that state of consummation which is called heaven. Were it seen that this present is only one little link in the long chain of proba-tions; were it felt that the Divine Justice is pledged to give the aspirations of the soul all the time they require for their fulfilment; were it recognized that disease, old age, and death are circumstances which can never touch the eternal youth of the spirit; that though the "plant man" grows more or less fair in hue and stature, according to the soil in which it is planted, yet the principle, which is the life of the plant, will not be defeated, but must scatter its seeds again and again, till it does at last come to perfect flower, — then would he, who is pausing to despair, realize that a new choice can *never* be too late, that false steps made in ignorance can never be counted by the All-Wise, and that, though a moment's delay against conviction is of incalculable weight, the mistakes of forty years are but as dust on the balance held by an unerring hand. Despair is for time, hope for eternity.

Then he who looks at all at the working of the grand principle of compensation which holds all nature in equipoise, cannot long remain a stranger to the meaning of the beautiful parable of the prodigal son, and the joy over finding the one lost piece of silver. It is no arbitrary kindness, no generosity of the ruling powers, which causes that there be more joy in heaven over the one that returns, than over ninety and nine that never strayed. It is the inevitable working of a spiritual law that he who has been groping in darkness must feel the light most keenly, best know how to prize it — he who has long been exiled from the truth seize it with the most earnest grasp, live in it with the deepest joy. It was after descending to the very pit of sorrow, that our Elder Brother was permitted to ascend to the Father, who perchance said to the angels who had dwelt always about the throne, Ye are always with me, and all that I have is yours; but this is my Son; he has been into a far country, but could not there abide, and has returned. But if any one say, "I know not how to return," I should still use words from the same record: "Let him arise and go to his Father." Let him put his soul into that state of simple, fervent desire for truth alone, truth for its own sake, which is prayer, and not only the sight of truth, but the way to make it living, shall be shown. Obstacles, insuperable to the intellect of any adviser, shall melt away like frostwork before a ray from the celestial sun. The Father may hide his face for a time, till the earnestness of the suppliant child be proved; but he is not far from any that seek, and when he does resolve to make a revelation, will show not only the *what*, but the *how ;* and none else can advise or aid the seeking soul, except by just observation on some matter of detail.

In this path, as in the downward one, must there be the first step that decides the whole — one sacrifice of the temporal for the eternal day is the grain of mustard seed which may give birth to a tree large enough to make a home for the sweetest singing birds. One moment of deep truth in life, of choosing not merely honesty, but purity, may leaven the whole mass.

FRAGMENTARY THOUGHTS FROM MARGARET FULLER'S JOURNAL.

I gave the world the fruit of earlier hours:
O Solitude! reward me with some flowers;
Or if their odorous bloom thou dost deny,
Rain down some meteors from the winter sky!

Poesy. — The expression of the sublime and beautiful, whether in measured words or in the fine arts. The human mind, apprehending the harmony of the universe, and making new combinations by its laws.

Poetry. — The sublime and beautiful expressed in measured language. It is closely allied with the fine arts. It should sing to the ear, paint to the eye, and exhibit the symmetry of architecture. If perfect, it will satisfy the intellectual and moral faculties no less than the heart and the senses. It works chiefly by simile and melody. It is to prose as the garden to the house. Pleasure is the object of the one, convenience of the other. The flowers and fruits may be copied on the furniture of the house, but if their beauty be not subordinated to utility, they lose the charm of beauty, and degenerate into finery. The reverse is the case in the garden.

Nature. — I would praise alike the soft gray and brown which soothed my eye erewhile, and the snowy fretwork which now decks the forest aisles. Every ripple in the snowy fields, every grass and fern which raises its petrified delicacy above them, seems to me to claim a voice. A voice! Canst thou not silently adore, but must needs be doing? Art thou too good to wait as a beggar at the door of the great temple?

Woman — Man. — Woman is the flower, man the bee. She sighs out melodious fragrance, and invites the winged laborer. He drains her cup, and carries off the honey. She dies on the stalk; he returns to the hive, well fed, and praised as an active member of the community.

Action symbolical of what is within. — Gœthe says, "I have learned to consider all I do as symbolical, — so that it now matters little to me whether I make plates or dishes." And further, he says, "All manly effort goes from within outwards."

Opportunity fleeting. — I held in my hand the cup. It was full of hot liquid. The air was cold; I delayed to drink, and its vital heat, its soul, curled upwards in delicatest wreaths. I looked delighted on their beauty; but while I waited, the essence of the draught was wasted on the cold air: it would not wait for me; it longed too much to utter itself: and when my lip was ready, only a flat, worthless sediment remained of what had been.

Mingling of the heavenly with the earthly. — The son of the gods has sold his birthright. He has received in exchange one, not merely the fairest, but the sweetest and holiest of earth's daughters. Yet is it not a fit exchange. His pinions droop powerless; he must no longer soar amid the golden stars. No matter, he thinks; "I will take her to some green and flowery isle; I will pay the penalty of Adam for the sake of the daughter of Eve; I will make the earth fruitful by the sweat of my brow. No longer my hands shall bear the coal to the lips of the inspired singer — no longer my voice modulate its tones to the accompaniment of spheral harmonies. My hands now lift the clod of the valley which dares cling to them with brotherly familiarity. And for my soiling, dreary task-work all the day, I receive — food.

"But the smile with which she receives me at set of sun,
is it not worth all that sun has seen me endure? Can angelic
delights surpass those which I possess, when, facing the shore
with her, watched by the quiet moon, we listen to the tide of
the world surging up impatiently against the Eden it cannot
conquer? Truly the joys of heaven were gregarious and
low in comparison. This, this alone, is exquisite, because
exclusive and peculiar."

Ah, seraph! but the winter's frost must nip thy vine; a
viper lurks beneath the flowers to sting the foot of thy child,
and pale decay must steal over the cheek thou dost adore.
In the realm of ideas all was imperishable. Be blest while
thou canst. I love thee, fallen seraph, but thou shouldst not
have sold thy birthright.

"All for love and the world well lost." That sounds so
true! But genius, when it sells itself, gives up, not only the
world, but the universe.

Yet does not love comprehend the universe? The universe is love. Why should I weary my eye with scanning
the parts, when I can clasp the whole this moment to my
beating heart?

But if the intellect be repressed, the idea will never be
brought out from the feeling. The amaranth wreath will
in thy grasp be changed to one of roses, more fragrant indeed, but withering with a single sun!

The Crisis with Gœthe. — I have thought much whether
Gœthe did well in giving up Lili. That was the crisis in his
existence. From that era dates his being as a " Weltweise ; "
the heroic element vanished irrecoverably from his character ;
he became an Epicurean and a Realist ; plucking flowers and
hammering stones instead of looking at the stars. How
could he look through the blinds, and see her sitting alone in
her beauty, yet give her up for so slight reasons? He was
right as a genius, but wrong as a character.

The Flower and the Pearl. ——— has written wonders about the mystery of personality. Why do we love it? In the first place, each wishes to embrace a whole, and this seems the readiest way. The intellect soars, the heart clasps; from putting "a girdle round about the earth in forty minutes," thou wouldst return to thy own little green isle of emotion, and be the loving and playful fay, rather than the delicate Ariel.

Then most persons are plants, organic. We can predict their growth according to their own law. From the young girl we can predict the lustre, the fragrance of the future flower. It waves gracefully to the breeze, the dew rests upon its petals, the bee busies himself in them, and flies away after a brief rapture, richly laden.

When it fades, its leaves fall softly on the bosom of Mother Earth, to all whose feelings it has so closely conformed. It has lived as a part of nature; its life was music, and we open our hearts to the melody.

But characters like thine and mine are mineral. We are the bone and sinew, these the smiles and glances, of earth. We lie nearer the mighty heart, and boast an existence more enduring than they. The sod lies heavy on us, or, if we show ourselves, the melancholy moss clings to us. If we are to be made into palaces and temples, we must be hewn and chiselled by instruments of unsparing sharpness. The process is mechanical and unpleasing; the noises which accompany it, discordant and obtrusive; the artist is surrounded with rubbish. Yet we may be polished to marble smoothness. In our veins may lie the diamond, the ruby, perhaps the emblematic carbuncle.

The flower is pressed to the bosom with intense emotion, but in the home of love it withers and is cast away.

The gem is worn with less love, but with more pride; if we enjoy its sparkle, the joy is partly from calculation of its value; but if it be lost, we regret it long.

For myself, my name is Pearl.* That lies at the beginning, amid slime and foul prodigies from which only its un-
sightly shell protects. It is cradled and brought to its noblest
state amid disease and decay. Only the experienced diver
could have known that it was there, and brought it to the
strand, where it is valued as pure, round, and, if less brilliant
than the diamond, yet an ornament for a kingly head. Were
it again immersed in the element where first it dwelt, now
that it is stripped of the protecting shell, soon would it blacken
into deformity. So what is noblest in my soul has sprung
from disease, present defeat, disappointment, and untoward
outward circumstance.

For you, I presume, from your want of steady light and
brilliancy of sparks which are occasionally struck from you,
that you are either a flint or a rough diamond. If the former,
I hope you will find a home in some friendly tinder-box,
instead of lying in the highway to answer the hasty hoof of
the trampling steed. If a diamond, I hope to meet you in
some imperishable crown, where we may long remain together;
you lighting up my pallid orb, I tempering your blaze.

Dried Ferns about my Lamp-shade. — "What pleasure do
you, who have exiled those paper tissue covers, take in that
bouquet of dried ferns? Their colors are less bright, and their
shapes less graceful, than those of your shades."

I answer, "They grew beneath the solemn pines. They
opened their hearts to the smile of summer, and answered to
the sigh of autumn. *They* remind me of the wealth of nature;
the tissues, of the poverty of man. They were gathered by
a cherished friend who worships in the woods, and behind
them lurks a deep, enthusiastic eye. So my pleasure in seeing them is 'denkende' and 'menschliche.'"

"They are of no use."

"Good! I like useless things: they are to me the vouchers
of a different state of existence."

[* *Margaret* means *Pearl.* — ED.]

Light. — My lamp says to me, "Why do you disdain me, and use that candle, which you have the trouble of snuffing every five minutes, and which ever again grows dim, ungrateful for your care? I would burn steadily from sunset to midnight, and be your faithful, vigilant friend, yet never interrupt you an instant."

I reply, "But your steady light is also dull, — while his, at its best, is both brilliant and mellow. Besides, I love him for the trouble he gives; he calls on my sympathy, and admonishes me constantly to use my life, which likewise flickers as if near the socket."

Wit and Satire. — I cannot endure people who do not distinguish between wit and satire; who think you, of course, laugh *at* people when you laugh *about* them; and who have no perception of the peculiar pleasure derived from toying with lovely or tragic figures.

30 *

FAREWELL.*

FAREWELL to New York city, where twenty months have presented me with a richer and more varied exercise for thought and life, than twenty years could in any other part of these United States.

It is the common remark about New York, that it has at least nothing petty or provincial in its methods and habits. The place is large enough: there is room enough, and occupation enough, for men to have no need or excuse for small cavils or scrutinies. A person who is independent, and knows what he wants, may lead his proper life here, unimpeded by others.

Vice and crime, if flagrant and frequent, are less thickly coated by hypocrisy than elsewhere. The air comes sometimes to the most infected subjects.

New York is the focus, the point where American and European interests converge. There is no topic of general interest to men, that will not betimes be brought before the thinker by the quick turning of the wheel.

Too quick that revolution,—some object. Life rushes wide and free, but *too fast.* Yet it is in the power of every one to avert from himself the evil that accompanies the good. He must build for his study, as did the German poet, a house beneath the bridge ; and then all that passes above and by him will be heard and seen, but he will not be carried away with it.

Earlier views have been confirmed, and many new ones

[* Published in the New York Tribune, Aug. 1, 1846, just previous to sailing for Europe. — ED.]

opened. On two great leadings, the superlative importance of promoting national education by heightening and deepening the cultivation of individual minds, and the part which is assigned to woman in the next stage of human progress in this country, where most important achievements are to be effected, I have received much encouragement, much instruction, and the fairest hopes of more.

On various subjects of minor importance, no less than these, I hope for good results, from observation, with my own eyes, of life in the old world, and to bring home some packages of seed for life in the new.

These words I address to my friends, for I feel that I have some. The degree of sympathetic response to the thoughts and suggestions I have offered through the columns of the Tribune, has indeed surprised me, conscious as I am of a natural and acquired aloofness from many, if not most popular tendencies of my time and place. It has greatly encouraged me, for none can sympathize with thoughts like mine, who are permanently insnared in the meshes of sect or party; none who prefer the formation and advancement of mere opinions to the free pursuit of truth. I see, surely, that the topmost bubble or sparkle of the cup is no voucher for the nature of its contents throughout, and shall, in future, feel that in our age, nobler in that respect than most of the preceding ages, each sincere and fervent act or word is secure, not only of a final, but of a speedy response.

I go to behold the wonders of art, and the temples of old religion. But I shall see no forms of beauty and majesty beyond what my country is capable of producing in myriad variety, if she has but the soul to will it; no temple to compare with what she might erect in the ages, if the catchword of the time, a sense of *divine order*, should become no more a mere word of form, but a deeply-rooted and pregnant idea in her life. Beneath the light of a hope that this may be, I say to my friends once more a kind farewell!

PART III.

POEMS.

FREEDOM AND TRUTH.

TO A FRIEND.

THE shrine is vowed to freedom, but, my friend,
Freedom is but a means to gain an end.
Freedom should build the temple, but the shrine
Be consecrate to thought still more divine.
The human bliss which angel hopes foresaw
Is liberty to comprehend the law.
Give, then, thy book a larger scope and frame,
Comprising means and end in Truth's great name.

DESCRIPTION OF A PORTION OF THE JOURNEY TO TRENTON FALLS.

THE long-anticipated morning dawns,
Clear, hopeful, joyous-eyed, and pure of breath.
The dogstar is exhausted of its rage,
And copious showers have cooled the feverish air,
The mighty engine pants — away, away!

(357)

And, see! they come! a motley, smiling group —
The stately matron with her tempered grace,
Her earnest eye, and kind though meaning smile,
Her words of wisdom and her words of mirth.
Her counsel firm and generous sympathy;
The happy pair whose hearts so full, yet ever
Dilating to the scene, refuse that bliss
Which excludes the whole or blunts the sense of beauty.

Next two fair maidens in gradation meet,
The one of gentle mien and soft dove-eyes;
Like water she, that yielding and combining,
Yet most pure element in the social cup:
The other with bright glance and damask cheek,
You need not deem concealment there was preying
To mar the healthful promise of the spring.

Another dame was there, of graver look,
And heart of slower beat; yet in its depths
Not irresponsive to the soul of things,
Nor cold when charmed by those who knew its pass-word.

These ladies had a knight from foreign clime,
Who from the banks of the dark-rolling Danube,
Or somewhere thereabouts, had come, a pilgrim,
To worship at the shrine of Liberty,
And after, made his home in her loved realm,
Content to call it fatherland where'er
The streams bear freemen and the skies smile on them;
A courteous knight he was, of merry mood,
Expert to wing the lagging hour with jest,
Or tale of strange romance or comic song.

And there was one I must not call a page,
Although too young yet to have won his spurs;
Yet there was promise in his laughing eye,

That in due time he'd prove no carpet knight;
Now, bright companion on a summer sea,
With wingéd words of gay or tasteful thought,
He was fit clasp to this our social chain.

And now, the swift car loosened on its way,
O'er hill and dale we fly with rapid lightness,
While each tongue celebrates the power of steam;
O, how delightful 'tis to go so fast!
No time to muse, no chance to gaze on nature!
'Tis bliss indeed if " to think be to groan!"

The genius of the time soon shifts the scene:
No longer whirled over our kindred clods,
We, with as strong an impulse, cleave the waters.
Now doth our chain a while untwine its links,
And some rebound from a three hours' communion
To mingle with less favored fellow-men;
One careless turns the leaves of some new volume;
The leaves of Nature's book are too gigantic,
Too vast the characters for patient study,
Till sunset lures us with majestic power
To cast one look of love on that bright eye,
Which, for so many hours, has beamed on us.
The silver lamp is lit in the blue dome,
Nature begins her hymn of evening breezes,
And myriad sparks, thronging to kiss the wave,
Touch even the steamboat's clumsy hulk with beauty.
Then, once more drawn together, cheerful talk
Casts to the hours a store of gentle gifts,
Which memory receives from these bright minds
And careful garners them for duller days.

The morning greets us not with her late smile;
Now chilling damp falls heavy on our hopes,

And leaden hues tarnish each sighed-for scene.
Yet not on coloring, majestic Hudson,
Depends the genius of thy stream, whose wand
Has piled thy banks on high, and given them forms
Which have for taste an impulse yet unknown.
Though Beauty dwells here, she reigns not a queen,
An humble handmaid now to the Sublime.
The mind dilates to receive the idea of strength,
And tasks its elements for congenial forms
To create anew within those mighty piles,
Those "bulwarks of the world," which, time-defying
And thunder-mocking, lift their lofty brows.

Now at the river's bend we pause a while,
And sun and cloud combine their wealth to greet us.
Oft shall the fair scenes of West Point return
Upon the mind, in its still picture-hours,
Its cloud-capped mountains with their varying hues,
The soft seclusion of its wooded paths,
And the alluring hopefulness of view
Along the river from its crisis-point.
Unlike the currents of our human lives
When they approach their long-sought ocean-mother, —
This stream is noblest onward to its close,
More tame and grave when near its inland founts.
Now onward, onward, till the whole be known ;
The heart, though swollen with these new sensations,
With no less vital throb beats on for more,
And rather we'd shake hands with disappointment
Than wait and lean on sober expectation.

The Highlands now are passed, and Hyde Park flies, —
Catskill salutes us — a far fairy-land.
O mountains, how do ye delude our hearts !
Let but the eye look down upon a valley,

We feel our limitations, and are calm ;
But place blue mountains in the distant view,
And the soul labors with the Titan hope
To ascend the shrouded tops, and scale the heavens.

O, pause not in the murky, old Dutch city,
But, hasting onward with a renewed steam power,
Bestow your hours upon the beauteous Mohawk ;
And here we grieve to lose our courteous knight,
Just at the opening of so rich a page.

How shall I praise thee, Mohawk ?   How portray
The love, the joyousness, felt in thy presence ?
When each new step along the silvery tide
Added new gems of beauty to our thought,
And lapped the soul in an Elysium
Of verdure and of grace, fed by thy sweetness.
O, how gay Fancy smiled, and deemed it home !
This is, thought she, the river of my garden ;
These are the graceful trees that form its bowers,
And these the meads where I have sighed to roam.
I now may fold my wearied wings in peace.

———————

JOURNEY TO TRENTON FALLS.

I.

TO MY FRIENDS AND COMPANIONS.

IF this faint reflex from those days so bright
　　May aught of sympathy among you gain,
　　I shall not think these verses penned in vain ;
Though they tell nothing of the fancies light,

31

The kindly deeds, rich thoughts, and various grace
With which you knew to make the hours so fair,
   That neither grief nor sickness could efface
From memory's tablet what you printed there.
Could I have breathed your spirit through these lines,
   They might have charms to win a critic's smile,
   Or the cold worldling of a sigh beguile.
I could but from my being bring one tone ;
May it arouse the sweetness of your own.

II.

THE HIGHLANDS.

I saw ye first, arrayed in mist and cloud ;
   No cheerful lights softened your aspect bold ;
   A sullen gray, or green, more grave and cold,
The varied beauties of the scene enshroud.
Yet not the less, O Hudson ! calm and proud,
   Did I receive the impress of that hour
   Which showed thee to me, emblem of that power
Of high resolve, to which even rocks have bowed ;
   Thou wouldst not deign thy course to turn aside,
And seek some smiling valley's welcome warm,
   But through the mountain's very heart, thy pride
Has been, thy channel and thy banks to form.
   Not even the " bulwarks of the world " could bar
   The inland fount from joining ocean's war !

III.

CATSKILL.

How fair at distance shone yon silvery blue,
   O stately mountain-tops, charming the mind
   To dream of pleasures which she there may find,
Where from the eagle's height she earth can view !

Nor are those disappointments which ensue;
   For though, while eyeing what beneath us lay,
   Almost we shunned to think of yesterday,
As wonderingly our looks its course pursue.
   Dwarfed to a point the joys of many hours,
The river on whose bosom we were borne
Seems but a thread, of pride and beauty shorn;
   Its banks, its shadowy groves, like beds of flowers,
Wave their diminished heads; — yet would we sigh,
Since all this loss shows us more near the sky?

IV.

VALLEY OF THE MOHAWK.

Could I my words with gentlest grace imbue,
   Which the flute's breath, or harp's clear tones, can bless,
   I then might hope the feelings to express,
And with new life the happy day endue,
   Thou gav'st, O vale, than Tempe's self more fair!
With thy romantic stream and emerald isles,
Touched by an April mood of tears and smiles
   Which stole on matron August unaware;
The meads with all the spring's first freshness green,
   The trees with summer's thickest garlands crowned,
And each so elegant, that fairy queen
   All day might wander ere she chose her round;
No blemish on the sense of beauty broke,
But the whole scene one ecstasy awoke.

V.

TRENTON FALLS, EARLY IN THE MORNING.

The sun, impatient, o'er the lofty trees
   Struggles to illume as fair a sight as lies
   Beneath the light of his joy-loving eyes,
Which all the forms of energy must please;

A solemn shadow falls in pillared form,
Made by yon ledge, which noontide scarcely shows,
Upon the amber radiance, soft and warm,
Where through the cleft the eager torrent flows.
Would you the genius of the place enjoy,
In all the charms contrast and color give?
Your eye and taste you now may best employ,
For this the hour when minor beauties live;
Scan ye the details as the sun rides high,
For with the morn these sparkling glories fly.

VI.

TRENTON FALLS, (AFTERNOON.)

A calmer grace o'er these still hours presides;
Now is the time to see the might of form;
The heavy masses of the buttressed sides,
The stately steps o'er which the waters storm;
Where, 'neath the mill, the stream so gently glides,
You feel the deep seclusion of the scene,
And now begin to comprehend what mean
The beauty and the power this chasm hides.
From the green forest's depths the portent springs,
But from those quiet shades bounding away,
Lays bare its being to the light of day,
Though on the rock's cold breast its love it flings.
Yet can all sympathy such courage miss?
Answer, ye trees! who bend the waves to kiss.

VII.

TRENTON FALLS BY MOONLIGHT.

I deemed the inmost sense my soul had blessed
Which in the poem of thy being dwells,
And gives such store for thought's most sacred cells;
And yet a higher joy was now confessed.

With what a holiness did night invest
  The eager impulse of impetuous life,
  And hymn-like meanings clothed the waters' strife!
With what a solemn peace the moon did rest
  Upon the white crest of the waterfall;
The haughty guardian banks, by the deep shade,
In almost double height are now displayed.
  Depth, height, speak things which awe, but not appall.
From elemental powers this voice has come,
And God's love answers from the azure dome.

SUB ROSA, CRUX.

In times of old, as we are told,
  When men more child-like at the feet
    Of Jesus sat, than now,
A chivalry was known more bold
    Than ours, and yet of stricter vow,
Of worship more complete.

Knights of the Rosy Cross, they bore
Its weight within the heart, but wore
Without, devotion's sign in glistening ruby bright;
  The gall and vinegar they drank alone,
  But to the world at large would only own
The wine of faith, sparkling with rosy light.

They knew the secret of the sacred oil
  Which, poured upon the prophet's head,
Could keep him wise and pure for aye.
  Apart from all that might distract or soil,
    With this their lamps they fed,
Which burn in their sepulchral shrines unfading night and day.

31 *

The pass-word now is lost,
  To that initiation full and free ;
    Daily we pay the cost
  Of our slow schooling for divine degree.
We know no means to feed an undying lamp ;
Our lights go out in every wind or damp.

We wear the cross of ebony and gold,
  Upon a dark background a form of light,
A heavenly hope upon a bosom cold,
  A starry promise in a frequent night ;
The dying lamp must often trim again,
For we are conscious, thoughtful, striving men.

Yet be we faithful to this present trust,
Clasp to a heart resigned the fatal must ;
Though deepest dark our efforts should enfold,
Unwearied mine to find the vein of gold ;
Forget not oft to lift the hope on high ;
The rosy dawn again shall fill the sky.

And by that lovely light, all truth-revealed,
The cherished forms which sad distrust concealed,
Transfigured, yet the same, will round us stand,
The kindred angels of a faithful band ;
Ruby and ebon cross both cast aside,
No lamp is needed, for the night has died.

Happy be those who seek that distant day,
With feet that from the appointed way
      Could never stray ;
Yet happy too be those who more and more,
As gleams the beacon of that only shore,
      Strive at the laboring oar.

Be to the best thou knowest ever true,
    Is all the creed;
Then, be thy talisman of rosy hue,
    Or fenced with thorns that wearing thou must bleed,
Or gentle pledge of Love's prophetic view,
    The faithful steps it will securely lead.

Happy are all who reach that shore,
    And bathe in heavenly day,
Happiest are those who high the banner bore,
    To marshal others on the way;
Or waited for them, fainting and way-worn,
        By burdens overborne.

THE DAHLIA, THE ROSE, AND THE HELIO-TROPE.

In a fair garden of a distant land,
    Where autumn skies the softest blue outspread,
    A lovely crimson dahlia reared her head,
To drink the lustre of the season's prime;
    And drink she did, until her cup o'erflowed
    With ruby redder than the sunset cloud.

Near to her root she saw the fairest rose
    That ever oped her soul to sun and wind,
And still the more her sweets she did disclose,
    The more her queenly heart of sweets did find,
    Not only for her worshipper the wind,
But for bee, nightingale, and butterfly,
Who would with ceaseless wing about her ply,
    Nor ever cease to seek what found they still would find.

Upon the other side, nearer the ground,
  A paler floweret on a slender stem,
That cast so exquisite a fragrance round,
  As seemed the minute blossom to contemn,
Seeking an ampler urn to hold its sweetness,
And in a statelier shape to find completeness.

Who could refuse to hear that keenest voice,
Although it did not bid the heart rejoice,
And though the nightingale had just begun
His hymn ; the evening breeze begun to woo,
When through the charming of the evening dew,
The floweret did its secret soul disclose?
By that revealing touched, the queenly rose
Forgot them both, a deeper joy to hope
And heed the love-note of the heliotrope.

TO MY FRIENDS.

TRANSLATED FROM SCHILLER.

BELOVED friends ! Earth hath known brighter days
  Than ours ; we vainly strive to hide this truth ;
Would history be silent in their praise,
  The very stones tell of man's glorious youth,
In heavenly forms on which we crowd to gaze ;
  But that high-favored race hath sunk in night ;
  The day is ours — the living still have sight.

Friends of my youth ! In happier climes than ours,
  As some far-wandering countrymen declare,
The air is perfume ; at each step spring flowers.
  Nature has not been bounteous to our prayer ;

But art dwells here, with her creative powers,
  Laurel and myrtle shun our winter snows,
  But with the cheerful vine we wreathe our brows.

Though of more pomp and wealth the Briton boast,
  Who holds four worlds in tribute to his pride, —
Although from farthest India's glowing coast
  Come gems of gold to burden Thames' dull tide,
  And *bring* each luxury that Heaven denied, —
Not in the torrent, but the still, calm brook,
Delights Apollo at himself to look.

More nobly lodged than we in northern halls,
  At Angelo's gate the Roman beggar dwells;
Girt by the Eternal City's honored walls,
  Each column some soul-stiring story tells;
While on the earth a second heaven dwells,
  Where Michael's spirit to St. Peter calls;
Yet all this splendor only decks a tomb;
For us fresh flowers from every green hour bloom

And while we live obscure, may others' names
  Through Rumor's trump be given to the wind;
New forms of ancient glories, ancient shames,
  For nothing new the searching sun can find,
  As pass the motley groups of human kind;
All other living things grow old and die —
Fancy alone has immortality.

STANZAS.

WRITTEN AT THE AGE OF SEVENTEEN.

I.

COME, breath of dawn! and o'er my temples play;
   Rouse to the draught of life the wearied sense;
Fly, sleep! with thy sad phantoms, far away;
   Let the glad light scare those pale troublous shadows hence!

II.

I rise, and leaning from my casement high,
   Feel from the morning twilight a delight;
Once more youth's portion, hope, lights up my eye,
   And for a moment I forget the sorrows of the night.

III.

O glorious morn! how great is yet thy power!
   Yet how unlike to that which once I knew,
When, plumed with glittering thoughts, my soul would soar,
   And pleasures visited my heart like daily dew!

IV.

Gone is life's primal freshness all too soon;
   For me the dream is vanished ere my time;
I feel the heat and weariness of noon,
   And long in night's cool shadows to recline.

FLAXMAN.

WE deemed the secret lost, the spirit gone,
　Which spake in Greek simplicity of thought,
　And in the forms of gods and heroes wrought
Eternal beauty from the sculptured stone —
A higher charm than modern culture won,
　With all the wealth of metaphysic lore,
　Gifted to analyze, dissect, explore.
A many-colored light flows from our sun;
Art, 'neath its beams, a motley thread has spun;
　The prison modifies the perfect day;
But thou hast known such mediums to shun,
　And cast once more on life a pure white ray.
Absorbed in the creations of thy mind,
Forgetting daily self, my truest self I find.

THOUGHTS

ON SUNDAY MORNING, WHEN PREVENTED BY A SNOW
STORM FROM GOING TO CHURCH.

HARK! the church-going bell! But through the air
The feathery missiles of old Winter hurled,
Offend the brow of mild-approaching Spring;
She shuts her soft blue eyes, and turns away.
Sweet is the time passed in the house of prayer,
When, met with many of this fire-fraught clay,
We, on this day, — the tribe of ills forgot,

Wherewith, ungentle, we afflict each other, —
Assemble in the temple of our God,
And use our breath to worship Him who gave it.
What though no gorgeous relics of old days,
The gifts of humbled kings and suppliant warriors,
Deck the fair shrine, or cluster round the pillars;
No stately windows decked with various hues,
No blazon of dead saints repel the sun;
Though no cloud-courting dome or sculptured frieze
Excite the fancy and allure the taste,
No fragrant censor steep the sense in luxury,
No lofty chant swell on the vanquished soul.

Ours is the faith of Reason; to the earth
We leave the senses who interpret her;
The heaven-born only should commune with Heaven,
The immaterial with the infinite.
Calmly we wait in solemn expectation.
He rises in the desk — that earnest man;
No priestly terrors flashing from his eye,
No mitre towers above the throne of thought,
No pomp and circumstance wait on his breath.
He speaks — we hear; and man to man we judge.
Has he the spell to touch the founts of feeling,
To kindle in the mind a pure ambition,
Or soothe the aching heart with heavenly balm,
To guide the timid and refresh the weary,
Appall the wicked and abash the proud?
He is the man of God. Our hearts confess him.
He needs no homage paid in servile forms,
No worldly state, to give him dignity:
To his own heart the blessing will return,
And all his days blossom with love divine.

There is a blessing in the Sabbath woods,
There is a holiness in the blue skies;

The summer-murmurs to those calm blue skies
Preach ceaselessly.   The universe is love —
And this disjointed fragment of a world
Must, by its spirit, man, be harmonized,
Tuned to concordance with the spheral strain,
Till thought be like those skies, deeds like those breezes,
As clear, as bright, as pure, as musical,
And all things have one text of truth and beauty.

There is a blessing in a day like this,
When sky and earth are talking busily;
The clouds give back the riches they received,
And for their graceful shapes return they fulness;
While in the inmost shrine, the life of life,
The soul within the soul, the consciousness
Whom I can only *name*. counting her wealth,
Still makes it more, still fills the golden bowl
Which never shall be broken, strengthens still
The silver cord which binds the whole to Heaven.

O that such hours must pass away ! yet oft
Such will recur, and memories of this
Come to enhance their sweetness.   And again
I say, great is the blessing of that hour
When the soul, turning from without, begins
To register her treasures, the bright thoughts,
The lovely hopes, the ethereal desires,
Which she has garnered in past Sabbath hours.
Within her halls the preacher's voice still sounds,
Though he be dead or distant far.   The band
Of friends who with us listened to his word,
With throngs around of linked associations,
Are there; the little stream, long left behind,
Is murmuring still; the woods as musical;
The skies how blue, the whole how eloquent
With " life of life and life's most secret joy " !

32

TO A GOLDEN HEART WORN ROUND THE NECK.*

REMEMBRANCER of joys long passed away,
    Relic from which, as yet, I cannot part,
O, hast thou power to lengthen love's short day?
    Stronger thy chain than that which bound the heart?

Lili, I fly — yet still thy fetters press me
    In distant valley, or far lonely wood;
Still will a struggling sigh of pain confess thee
    The mistress of my soul in every mood.

The bird may burst the silken chain which bound him,
    Flying to the green home, which fits him best;
But, O, he bears the prisoner's badge around him,
    Still by the piece about his neck distressed.
He ne'er can breathe his free, wild notes again;
    They're stifled by the pressure of his chain.

[* Gœthe says, "A little golden heart, which I had received from Lili in those fairy hours, still hung by the same little chain to which she had fastened it, love-warmed, about my neck. I seized hold of it — kissed it." This was the occasion of these lines. The poet now was separated from Lili, and striving to forget her in journeying about. — ED.]

LINES

THESE pallid blossoms thou wilt not disdain,
   The harbingers of thy approach to me,
Which grew and bloomed despite the cold and rain,
   To tell of summer and futurity.

It was not given them to tell the soul,
   And lure the nightingale by fragrant breath:
These slender stems and roots brook no control,
   And in the garden life would find but death.
The rock which is their cradle and their home
Must also be their monument and tomb;
Yet has my floweret's life a charm more rare
Than those admiring crowds esteem so fair,
Self-nurtured, self-sustaining, self-approved:
Not even by the forest trees beloved,
As are her sisters of the Spring, she dies, —
Nor to the guardian stars lifts up her eyes,
But droops her graceful head upon her breast,
Nor asks the wild bird's requiem for her rest,
By her own heart upheld, by her own soul possessed.

Learn of the clematis domestic love,
   Religious beauty in the lily see;
Learn from the rose how rapture's pulses move,
   Learn from the heliotrope fidelity.
From autumn flowers let hope and faith be known;
Learn from the columbine to live alone,

To deck whatever spot the Fates provide
With graces worthy of the garden's pride,
And to deserve each gift that is denied.

These are the shades of the departed flowers,
My lines faint shadows of some beauteous hours,
Whereto the soul the highest thoughts have spoken,
And brightest hopes from frequent twilight broken.
Preserve them for my sake.   In other years,
When life has answered to your hopes or fears,
When the web is well woven, and you try
Your wings, whether as moth or butterfly,
If, as I pray, the fairest lot be thine,
Yet value still the faded columbine.
But look not on her if thy earnest eye,
Be filled by works of art or poesy ;
Bring not the hermit where, in long array,
Triumphs of genius gild the purple day ;
Let her not hear the lyre's proud voice arise,
To tell, "still lives the song though Regnor dies ; "
Let her not hear the lute's soft-rising swell
Declare she never lived who lived so well ;
But from the anvil's clang, and joiner's screw,
The busy streets where men dull crafts pursue,
From weary cares and from tumultuous joys,
From aimless bustle and from voiceless noise,
If there thy plans should be, turn here thine eye, —
Open the casket of thy memory ;
Give to thy friend the gentlest, holiest sigh.

DISSATISFACTION.

TRANSLATED FROM THEODORE KÖRNER.

"Composed as I stood sentinel on the banks of the Elbe."

FATHERLAND ! Thou call'st the singer
      In the blissful glow of day ;
He no more can musing linger,
    While thou dost mourn a tyrant's sway.
        Love and poesy forsaking,
    From friendship's magic circle breaking,
    The keenest pangs he could endure
        Thy peace to insure.

Yet sometimes tears must dim his eyes,
    As, on the melodious bridge of song,
The shadows of past joys arise,
    And in mild beauty round him throng.
In vain, o'er life, that early beam
Such radiance shed ; — the impetuous stream
Of strife has seized him, onward borne,
While left behind his loved ones mourn.

Here in the crowd must he complain,
    Nor find a fit employ ?
Give him poetic place again,
    Or the quick throb of warlike joy.
The wonted inspiration give ;
Thus languidly he cannot live ;
Love's accents are no longer near;
    Let him the trumpet hear.

32 *

Where is the cannon's thunder?
   The clashing cymbals, where?
While foreign foes our cities plunder,
   Can we not hasten there?
I can no longer watch this stream;
In prose I die! O source of flame!
O poesy! for which I glow, —
A nobler death thou shouldst bestow!

MY SEAL-RING.

MERCURY has cast aside
The signs of intellectual pride,
Freely offers thee the soul:
   Art thou noble to receive?
Canst thou give or take the whole,
   Nobly promise, and believe?
Then thou wholly human art,
A spotless, radiant, ruby heart,
And the golden chain of love
Has bound thee to the realm above.
If there be one small, mean doubt,
One serpent thought that fled not out,
Take instead the serpent-rod;
Thou art neither man nor God.
Guard thee from the powers of evil;
Who cannot trust, vows to the devil.
Walk thy slow and spell-bound way;
Keep on thy mask, or shun the day —
Let go my hand upon the way.

THE CONSOLERS.

TRANSLATED FROM GŒTHE.

" WHY wilt thou not thy griefs forget ?
　Why must thine eyes with tears be wet ?
　When all things round thee sweetly smile,
　Canst thou not, too, be glad a while ? "

" Hither I come to weep alone ;
　The grief I feel is all mine own ;
　Dearer than smiles these tears to me ;
　Smile you — I ask no sympathy ! "

" Repel not thus affection's voice !
　While thou art sad, can we rejoice ?
　To friendly hearts impart thy woe ;
　Perhaps we may some healing know."

" Too gay your hearts to feel like mine,
　Or such a sorrow to divine ;
　Nought have I lost I e'er possessed ;
　I mourn that I cannot be blessed."

" What idle, morbid feelings these !
　Can you not win what prize you please ?
　Youth, with a genius rich as yours,
　All bliss the world can give insures."

" Ah, too high-placed is my desire !
　The star to which my hopes aspire
　Shines all too far — I sigh in vain,
　Yet cannot stoop to earth again."

" Waste not so foolishly thy prime ;
    If to the stars thou canst not climb,
    Their gentle beams thy loving eye
    Every clear night will gratify."

" Do I not know it ?   Even now
    I wait the sun's departing glow,
    That I may watch them.   Meanwhile ye
    Enjoy the day — 'tis nought to me ! "

ABSENCE OF LOVE.

THOUGH many at my feet have bowed,
    And asked my love through pain and pleasure,
Fate never yet the youth has showed
    Meet to receive so great a treasure.

Although sometimes my heart, deceived,
    Would love because it sighed *to feel*,
Yet soon I changed, and sometimes grieved
    Because my fancied wound would heal.

MEDITATIONS.

SUNDAY, *May* 12, 1833.

THE clouds are marshalling across the sky,
Leaving their deepest tints upon yon range
Of soul-alluring hills. The breeze comes softly,
Laden with tribute that a hundred orchards
Now in their fullest blossom send, in thanks
For this refreshing shower. The birds pour forth
In heightened melody the notes of praise
They had suspended while God's voice was speaking,
And his eye flashing down upon his world.
I sigh, half-charmed, half-pained. My sense is living,
And, taking in this freshened beauty, tells
Its pleasure to the mind. The mind replies,
And strives to wake the heart in turn, repeating
Poetic sentiments from many a record
Which other souls have left, when stirred and satisfied
By scenes as fair, as fragrant. But the heart
Sends back a hollow echo to the call
Of outward things, — and its once bright companion,
Who erst would have been answered by a stream
Of life-fraught treasures, thankful to be summoned, —
Can now rouse nothing better than this echo;
Unmeaning voice, which mocks their softened accents.
Content thee, beautiful world! and hush, still busy mind!
My heart hath sealed its fountains. To the things
Of Time they shall be oped no more. Too long,
Too often were they poured forth: part have sunk
Into the desert; part profaned and swollen
By bitter waters, mixed by those who feigned
They asked them for refreshment, which, turned back,
Have broken and o'erflowed their former urns.

So when ye talk of *pleasure*, lonely world,
And busy mind, ye ne'er again shall move me
To answer ye, though still your calls have power
To jar me through, and cause dull aching *here*.

Not so the voice which hailed me from the depths
Of yon dark-bosomed cloud, now vanishing
Before the sun ye greet. It touched my centre,
The voice of the Eternal, calling me
To feel his other worlds; to feel that if
I could deserve a home, I still might find it
In other spheres, — and bade me not despair,
Though "want of harmony" and "aching void"
Are terms invented by the men of this,
Which I may not forget.
                              In former times
I loved to see the lightnings flash athwart
The stooping heavens; I loved to hear the thunder
Call to the seas and mountains; for I thought
'Tis thus man's flashing fancy doth enkindle
The firmament of mind; 'tis thus his eloquence
Calls unto the soul's depths and heights; and still
I deified the creature, nor remembered
The Creator in his works.
                              Ah now how different!
The proud delight of that keen sympathy
Is gone; no longer riding on the wave,
But whelmed beneath it: my own plans and works,
Or, as the Scriptures phrase it, my "*inventions*"
No longer interpose 'twixt me and Heaven.

To-day, for the first time, I felt the Deity,
And uttered prayer on hearing thunder. This
Must be thy will, — for finer, higher spirits
Have gone through this same process, — yet I think

There was religion in that strong delight,
Those sounds, those thoughts of power imparted. True,
I did not say, " He is the Lord thy God,"
But I had feeling of his essence.   But
" 'Twas pride by which the angels fell."   So be it !
But O, might I but see a little onward !
Father, I cannot be a spirit of power ;
May I be active as a spirit of love,
Since thou hast ta'en me from that path which Nature
Seemed to appoint, O, deign to ope another,
Where I may walk with thought and hope assured ;
" Lord, I believe ; help thou mine unbelief ! "
Had I but faith like that which fired Novalis,
I too could bear that the heart " fall in ashes,"
While the freed spirit rises from beneath them,
With heavenward-look, and Phœnix-plumes upsoaring !

RICHTER.

Poet of Nature, gentlest of the wise,
   Most airy of the fanciful, most keen
Of satirists, thy thoughts, like butterflies,
   Still near the sweetest scented flowers have been :
With Titian's colors, thou canst sunset paint ;
   With Raphael's dignity, celestial love ;
With Hogarth's pencil, each deceit and feint
   Of meanness and hypocrisy reprove ;
Canst to Devotion's highest flight sublime
   Exalt the mind ; by tenderest pathos' art
   Dissolve in purifying tears the heart,
Or bid it, shuddering, recoil at crime ;

The fond illusions of the youth and maid,
At which so many world-formed sages sneer,
    When by thy altar-lighted torch displayed,
Our natural religion must appear.
    All things in thee tend to one polar star;
    Magnetic all thy influences are;
A labyrinth; a flowery wilderness.
    Some in thy "slip-boxes" and honeymoons
Complain of — want of order, I confess,
    But not of system in its highest sense.
Who asks a guiding clew through this wide mind,
In love of nature such will surely find,
    In tropic climes, live like the tropic bird,
Whene'er a spice-fraught grove may tempt thy stray;
    Nor be by cares of colder climes disturbed:
No frost the summer's bloom shall drive away;
    Nature's wide temple and the azure dome
    Have plan enough for the free spirit's home.

THE THANKFUL AND THE THANKLESS.

With equal sweetness the commissioned hours
Shed light and dew upon both weeds and flowers.
The weeds unthankful raise their vile heads high,
Flaunting back insult to the gracious sky;
While the dear flowers, with fond humility,
Uplift the eyelids of a starry eye
In speechless homage, and, from grateful hearts,
Perfume that homage all around imparts.

PROPHECY AND FULFILMENT.

WHEN leaves were falling thickly in the pale November day,
A bird dropped here this feather upon her pensive way.
Another bird has found it in the snow-chilled April day;
It brings to him the music of all her summer's lay.
Thus sweet birds, though unmated, do never sing in vain;
The lonely notes they utter to free them from their pain,
Caught up by the echoes, ring through the blue dome,
And by good spirits guided pierce to some gentle home.

The pencil moved prophetic: together now men read
In the fair book of nature, and find the hope they need.
The wreath woven by the river is by the seaside worn,
And one of fate's best arrows to its due mark is borne.

VERSES

GIVEN TO W. C. WITH A BLANK BOOK, MARCH, 1844.

THY other book to fill, more than eight years
Have paid chance tribute of their smiles and tears;
Many bright strokes portray the varied scene —
Wild sports, sweet ties the days of toil between;
And those related both in mind and blood,
The wise, the true, the lovely, and the good,
Have left their impress here; nor such alone,
But those chance toys that lively feelings own
Weave their gay flourishes 'mid lines sincere,
As 'mid the shadowy thickets bound the deer.

Accept a volume where the coming time
Will join, I hope, much reason with the rhyme,
And that the stair his steady feet ascend
May prove a Jacob's ladder to my friend,
Peopled with angel-shapes of promise bright,
And ending only in the realms of light.

May purity be stamped upon his brow,
Yet leave the manly footsteps free as now ;
May generous love glow in his inmost heart,
Truth to its utterance lend the only art ;
While more a man, may he be more the child ;
More thoughtful be, but the more sweet and mild ;
May growing wisdom, mixed with sprightly cheer,
Bless his own breast and those which hold him dear ;
Each act be worthy of his worthiest aim,
And love of goodness keep him free from blame,
Without a need straight rules for life to frame.

Good Spirit, teach him what he ought to be,
Best to fulfil his proper destiny,
To serve himself, his fellow-men, and thee.
These pages then will show how Nature wild
Accepts her Master, cherishes her child ;
And many flowers, ere eight years more are done,
Shall bless and blossom in the western sun.

EAGLES AND DOVES.

GŒTHE.

A NEW-FLEDGED eaglet spread his wings
To seek for prey;
Then flew the huntsman's dart and cut
The right wing's sinewy strength away.
Headlong he falls into a myrtle grove;
There three days long devoured his grief,
And writhed in pain
Three long, long nights, three days as weary.
At length he feels
The all-healing power
Of Nature's balsam.
Forth from the shady bush he creeps,
And tries his wing; but, ah!
The power to soar is gone!
He scarce can lift himself
Along the ground
In search of food to keep mere life awake;
Then rests, deep mourning,
On a low rock by the brook;
He looks up to the oak tree's top,
Far up to heaven,
And a tear glistens in his haughty eye.

Just then come by a pair of fondling doves,
Playfully rustling through the grove.
Cooing and toying, they go tripping
Over golden sand and brook;
And, turning here and there,
Their rose-tinged eyes descry

The inly-mourning bird.
The dove, with friendly curiosity,
Flutters to the next bush, and looks
With tender sweetness on the wounded king.
" Ah, why so sad ?" he cooes ;
" Be of good cheer; my friend !
Hast thou not all the means of tranquil bliss
Around thee here ?
Canst thou not meet with swelling breast
The last rays of the setting sun
On the brook's mossy brink ?
Canst wander 'mid the dewy flowers,
And, from the superfluous wealth
Of the wood-bushes, pluck at will
Wholesome and delicate food,
And at the silvery fountain quench thy thirst?
O friend ! the spirit of content
Gives all that we can know of bliss ;
And this sweet spirit of content
Finds every where its food."
" O, wise one !" said the eagle, deeper still
Into himself retiring ;
" O wisdom, thou speakest as a dove !"

TO A FRIEND, WITH HEARTSEASE.

CONTENT in purple lustre clad,
Kingly serene, and golden glad ;
No demi hues of sad contrition,
No pallors of enforced submission ;
Give me such content as this,
And keep a while the rosy bliss.

ASPIRATION.

LINES WRITTEN IN THE JOURNAL OF HER BROTHER R. F. F.

FORESEEN, forespoken, not foredone, —
Ere the race be well begun,
The prescient soul is at the goal,
One little moment binds the whole;
Happy they themselves who call
To risk much, and to conquer all;
Happy are they who many losses,
Sore defeat or frequent crosses,
Though these may the heart dismay,
Cannot the sure faith betray;
Who in beauty bless the Giver;
Seek ocean on the loveliest river;
Or on desert island tossed,
Seeing Heaven, think nought lost.
May thy genius bring to thee
Of this life experience free,
And the earth vine's mysterious cup,
Sweet and bitter yield thee up.
But should the now sparkling bowl
Chance to slip from thy control,
And much of the enchanted wine
Be spilt in sand, as 'twas with mine,
Let blessings lost bring consecration,
Change the pledge to a libation.
For the Power to whom we bow
Has given his pledge, that, if not now,
They of pure and steadfast mind,
By faith exalted, truth refined,

33 *

Shall hear all music, loud and clear,
Whose first notes they ventured here.
Then fear not thou to wind the horn
Though elf and gnome thy courage scorn ;
Ask for the castle's king and queen,
Though rabble rout may come between,
Beat thee, senseless, to the ground,
In the dark beset thee round ;
Persist to ask, and they will come.
Seek not for rest a humbler home,
And thou wilt see what few have seen,
The palace home of king and queen.

THE ONE IN ALL.

THERE are who separate the eternal light
In forms of man and woman, day and night;
They cannot bear that God be essence quite.

Existence is as deep a verity :
Without the dual, where is unity ?
And the " I am " cannot forbear to be ;

But from its primal nature forced to frame
Mysteries, destinies of various name,
Is forced to give what it has taught to claim.

Thus love must answer to its own unrest ;
The bad commands us to expect the best,
And hope of its own prospects is the test.

And dost thou seek to find the one in two?
Only upon the old can build the new;
The symbol which you seek is found in you.

The heart and mind, the wisdom and the will,
The man and woman, must be severed still,
And Christ must reconcile the good and ill.

There are to whom each symbol is a mask;
The life of love is a mysteriou: task;
They want no answer, for they would not ask.

A single thought transfuses every form;
The sunny day is changed into the storm,
For light is dark, hard soft, and cold is warm.

One presence fills and floods the whole serene;
Nothing can be, nothing has ever been,
Except the one truth that creates the scene.

Does the heart beat, — that is a seeming only;
You cannot be alone, though you are lonely;
The All is neutralized in the One only.

You ask *a* faith, — they are content with faith;
You ask to have, — but they reply, "IT hath."
There is no end, and there need be no path.

The day wears heavily, — why, then, ignore it;
Peace is the soul's desire, — such thoughts restore it;
The truth thou art, — it needs not to implore it.

The Presence all thy fancies supersedes,
All that is done which thou wouldst seek in deeds,
The wealth obliterates all seeming needs.

Both these are true, and if they are at strife,
The mystery bears the one name of *Life*,
That, slowly spelled, will yet compose the strife.

The men of old say, " Live twelve thousand years,
And see the end of all that here appears,
And Moxen * shall absorb thy smiles and tears."

These later men say, " Live this little day.
Believe that human nature is the way,
And know both Son and Father while you pray;

And one in two, in three, and none alone,
Letting you know even as you are known,
Shall make the you and me eternal parts of one."

To me, our destinies seem flower and fruit
Born of an ever-generating root;
The other statement I cannot dispute.

But say that Love and ·Life eternal seem,
And if eternal ties be but a dream,
What is the meaning of that self-same *seem?*

Your nature craves Eternity for Truth;
Eternity of Love is prayer of youth;
How, without love, would have gone forth your truth?

I do not think we are deceived to grow,
But that the crudest fancy, slightest show,
Covers some separate truth that we may know.

In the one Truth, each separate fact is true;
Eternally in one I many view,
And destinies through destiny pursue.

This is *my* tendency; but can I say
That this my thought leads the true, only way?
I only know it constant leads, and I obey.

---

* Buddhist term for absorption into the divine mind.

I only know one prayer — " Give me the truth,
Give me that colored whiteness, ancient youth,
Complex and simple, seen in joy and ruth.

Let me not by vain wishes bar my claim,
Nor soothe my hunger by an empty name,
Nor crucify the Son of man by hasty blame.

But in the earth and fire, water and air,
Live earnestly by turns without despair,
Nor seek a home till home be every where ! "

A GREETING.

THOUGHTS which come at a call
Are no better than if they came not at all ;
Neither flower nor fruit,
Yielding no root
For plant, shrub, or tree.
Thus I have not for thee
One good word to say,
To-day,
Except that I prize thy gentle heart,
Free from ambition, falsehood, or art,
And thy good mind,
Daily refined,
By pure desire
To fan the heaven-seeking fire.
May it rise higher and higher,
Till in thee
Gentleness finds its dignity,
Life flowing tranquil, pure and free,
A mild, unbroken harmony.

LINES TO EDITH, ON HER BIRTHDAY.

If the same star our fates together bind,
Why are we thus divided, mind from mind?
If the same law one grief to both impart,
How couldst thou grieve a trusting mother's heart?

Our aspiration seeks a common aim ;
Why were we tempered of such differing frame ?
But 'tis too late to turn this wrong to right ;
Too cold, too damp, too deep, has fallen the night.

And yet, the angel of my life replies,
Upon that night a morning star shall rise,
Fairer than that which ruled thy temporal birth,
Undimmed by vapors of the dreamy earth.

It says, that, where a heart thy claim denies,
Genius shall read its secret ere it flies ;
The earthly form may vanish from thy side,
Pure love will make thee still the spirit's bride.

And thou, ungentle, yet much loving child,
Whose heart still shows the "untamed haggard wild,"
A heart which justly makes the highest claim,
Too easily is checked by transient blame.

Ere such an orb can ascertain its sphere,
The ordeal must be various and severe ;
My prayer attend thee, though the feet may fly ;
I hear thy music in the silent sky.

LINES

WRITTEN IN HER BROTHER R. F. F.'S JOURNAL.

" Mark the perfect man, and behold the upright, for the end of that man
is peace." — *Psalms* xxxvii. 37.

THE man of heart and words sincere,
　　Who truth and justice follows still,
Pursues his way with conscience clear,
　　Unharmed by earthly care and ill.
His promises he never breaks,
　　But sacredly to each adheres ;
Honor's straight path he ne'er forsakes,
　　Though danger in the way appears.
He never boasts, will ne'er deceive,
　　For vanity nor yet for gain ;
All that he says you may believe ;
　　For worlds he would not conscience stain.
If he desires what others do,
　　And they deserve it more than he,
He gives to them what is their due,
　　Happy in his humility.
Not to his friends alone he's kind,
　　But his foes too with candor sees ;
Not to their good intentions blind,
　　Though hopeless their dislike t' appease.
His eyes are clear, his hands are pure ;
　　To God it is his constant prayer
That, be he rich or be he poor,
　　He never may wrong actions dare.

If rich, he to the suffering gives
    All he can spare, and thinks it just,
That, since he by God's bounty lives,
    He should as steward hold his trust.
If poor, he envies not; he knows
    How covetousness corrupts the heart,
Whatever a just God bestows
    Receiving as his proper part.
O Father, such a man I'd be ;
    Like him would act, like him would pray :
Lead me in truth and purity
    To win thy peace and see thy day.

ON A PICTURE REPRESENTING THE DESCENT FROM THE CROSS.

BY RAPHAEL.

Virgin Mother, Mary mild !
It was thine to see the child,
    Gift of the Messiah dove,
    Pure blossom of ideal love,
Break, upon the " guilty cross,"
    The seeming promise of his life ;
Of faith, of hope, of love, a loss,
    Deepened all thy bosom's strife,
Brow down-bent, and heart-strings torn,
Fainting, by frail arms upborne.

All those startled figures show,
   That they did not apprehend
The thought of Him who there lies low,
   On whom those sorrowing eyes they bend.
They do not feel this holiest hour ;
Their hearts soar not to read the power,
    Which this deepest of distress
    Alone could give to save and bless.

Soul of that fair, now ruined form,
Thou who hadst force to bide the storm,
    Must again descend to tell
    Of thy life the hidden spell ;
Though their hearts within them burned,
The flame rose not till he returned.

Just so all our dead ones lie ;
Just so call our thoughts on high ;
Thus we linger on the earth,
And dully miss death's heavenly birth.

———•———

THE CAPTURED WILD HORSE.*

On the boundless plain careering,
By an unseen compass steering,
Wildly flying, reappearing, —

* This horse, Konick, was caught early, marked, and then let loose
agaiu. for a time, among the herd. He still retains a wild freedom and
beauty in his movements.

34

With untamed fire their broad eyes glowing,
In every step a grand pride showing,
Of no servile moment knowing, —

Happy as the trees and flowers,
In their instinct cradled hours,
Happier in fuller powers, —

See the wild herd nobly ranging,
Nature varying, not changing,
Lawful in their lawless ranging.

But hark! what boding crouches near?
On the horizon now appear
Centaur-forms of force and fear.

On their enslaved brethren borne,
With bit and whip of tyrant scorn,
To make new captives, as forlorn.

Wildly snort the astonished throng,
Stamp, and wheel, and fly along,
Those centaur-powers they know are strong.

But the lasso, skilful cast,
Holds one only captive fast,
Youngest, weakest — left the last.

How thou trembledst then, Konick!
Thy full breath came short and thick,
Thy heart to bursting beat so quick;

Thy strange brethren peering round,
By those tyrants held and bound,
Tyrants fell, — whom falls confound!

With rage and pity fill thy heart;
Death shall be thy chosen part,
Ere such slavery tame thy heart.

But strange, unexpected joy!
They seem to mean thee no annoy —
Gallop off both man and boy.

Let the wild horse freely go!
Almost he shames it should be so;
So lightly prized himself to know.

All deception 'tis, O steed!
Ne'er again upon the mead
Shalt thou a free wild horse feed.

The mark of man doth blot thy side,
The fear of man doth dull thy pride,
Thy master soon shall on thee ride.

Thy brethren of the free plain,
Joyful speeding back again,
With proud career and flowing mane,

Find thee branded, left alone,
And their hearts are turned to stone —
They keep thee in their midst alone.

Cruel the intervening years,
Seeming freedom stained by fears,
Till the captor reappears;

Finds thee with thy broken pride,
Amid thy peers still left aside,
Unbeloved and unallied;

Finds thee ready for thy fate;
For joy and hope 'tis all too late —
Thou'rt wedded to thy sad estate.

———

Wouldst have the princely spirit bowed?
Whisper only, speak not loud,
Mark and leave him in the crowd.

Thou need'st not spies nor jailers have;
The free will serve thee like the slave,
Coward shrinking from the brave.

And thy cohorts, when they come
To take the weary captive home,
Need only beat the retreating drum.

———

EPILOGUE TO THE TRAGEDY OF ESSEX.

SPOKEN IN THE CHARACTER OF THE QUEEN. — TRANS-
LATED FROM GŒTHE.

No Essex here! — unblest — they give no sign.
And shall such live, while earth's best nobleness
Departs and leaves her barren? Now too late
Weakness and cunning both are exorcised.
How could I trust thee whom I knew so well?

Am I not like the fool of fable?　He
Who in his bosom warmed the frozen viper,
And fancied man might hope for gratitude
From the betrayer's seed?　Away! begone!
No breath, no sound shall here insult my anguish.
Essex is dumb, and they shall all be so;
No human presence shall control my mood.
Begone, I say!　The queen would be alone!

(They all go out.)

Alone and still!　This day the cup of woe
Is full; and while I drain its bitter dregs,
Calm, queenlike, stern, I would review the past.
Well it becomes the favorite of fortune,
The royal arbitress of others' weal,
The world's desire, and England's deity,
Self-poised, self-governed, clear and firm to gaze
Where others close their aching eyes, to *dream.*

Who feels imperial courage glow within
Fears not the mines which lie beneath his throne;
Bold he ascends, though knowing well his peril —
Majestical and fearless holds the sceptre.
The golden circlet of enormous weight
He wears with brow serene and smiling air,
As though a myrtle chaplet graced his temples.
And thus didst *thou.*　The far removed thy power
Attracted and subjected to thy will,
The hates and fears which oft beset thy way
Were seen, were met, and conquered by thy courage.
Thy tyrant father's wrath, thy mother's hopeless fate,
Thy sister's harshness, — all were cast behind;
And to a soul like thine, bonds and harsh usage
Taught fortitude, prudence, and self-command,
To act, or to endure.　Fate did the rest.

34*

One brilliant day thou heard'st, " Long live the Queen!"
A queen thou wert; and in the heart's despite,
Despite the foes without, within, who ceaseless
Have threatened war and death, — a queen thou *art*,
And wilt be, while a spark of life remains.
But this last deadly blow — I feel it here!
Yet the low, prying world shall ne'er perceive it.
" Actress" they call me, — 'tis a queen's vocation!
The people stare and whisper — what would they
But acting, to amuse them? Is deceit
Unknown, except in regal palaces?
The child at play already is an actor.

Still to thyself, let weal or woe betide,
Elizabeth! be true and steadfast ever!
Maintain thy fixed reserve: 'tis just; what heart
Can sympathize with a queen's agony?
The false, false world, — it wooes me for my treasures,
My favors, and the place my smile confers;
And if for love I offer mutual love,
My minion, not content, must have the crown.
'Twas thus with Essex; yet to thee, O heart!
I dare to say it, thy all died with him!

Man must experience — be he who he may —
Of bliss a last, irrevocable day.
Each owns this true, but cannot bear to live
And feel the last has come, the last has gone;
That never eye again in earnest tenderness
Shall turn to him, — no heart shall thickly beat
When his footfall is heard, — no speaking blush
Tell the soul's wild delight at meeting, — never
Rapture in presence, hope in absence more,
Be his, — no sun of love illume his landscape!
Yet thus it is with me. Throughout this heart

Deep night, without a star ! What all the host
To me, — my Essex fallen from the heavens !
To me he was the centre of the world,
The ornament of time. Wood, lawn, or hall,
The busy mart, the verdant solitude,
To me were but the fame of one bright image ;
That face is dust, — those lustrous eyes are closed,
And the frame mocks me with its empty centre.

How nobly free, how gallantly he bore him,
The charms of youth combined with manhood's vigor !
How sage his counsel, and how warm his valor, —
The glowing fire and the aspiring flame !
Even in his presumption he was kingly !

But ah ! does memory cheat me ? What was all,
Since Truth was wanting, and the man I loved
Could court his death to vent his anger on me,
And I must punish him, or live degraded.
I chose the first ; but in his death I died.
Land, sea, church, people, throne, — all, all are nought,
I live a living death, and call it royalty.
Yet, wretched ruler o'er these empty gauds,
A part remains to play, and I will play it.
A purple mantle hides my empty heart,
The kingly crown adorns my aching brow,
And pride conceals my anguish from the world.

But in the still and ghostly midnight hour,
From each intruding eye and ear set free,
I still may shed the bitter, hopeless tear,
Nor fear the babbling of the earless walls.
I to myself may say, " I die ! I die !
Elizabeth, unfriended and alone,
So die as thou hast lived, — alone, but queenlike ! "

HYMN WRITTEN FOR A SUNDAY SCHOOL.

"And his mother said unto him, Son, why hast thou thus dealt with us? Behold, thy father and I have sought thee sorrowing.

"And he said unto them, How is it that ye sought me? Wist ye not that I must be about my Father's business?" — *Luke* ii. 48, 49.

I.

Thus early was Christ's course begun,
  Thus radiant dawned celestial day;
And those who such a race would run,
  As early should be on the way.

II.

His Father's business was his care,
  Yet in man's favor still he grew:
O, might we learn, by thought and prayer,
  Like him a work of love to do!

III.

Wisdom and virtue still he sought,
  Nor ignorant nor vile despised:
True was each action, pure each thought,
  And each pure hope he realized.

IV.

The empires of this world, in vain,
  Offered their sceptres to his hand;
Fearless he trod the stormy main,
  Fearless 'mid throngs of foes could stand.

V.

Yet with his courage and his power
  Combined such sweetness and such love,

He could revere the simplest flower,
   The vilest sinners firm reprove.

VI.

For all mankind he came, nor yet
   An infant's visit would deny;
Nor friend nor mother did forget
   In his last hour of agony.

VII.

O, children, ask him to impart
   That spirit clear and temper mild,
Which made the mother in her heart
   Keep all the sayings of her child.

VIII.

Bless him who said, of such as you
   His Father's kingdom is, and still,
His yoke to bear, his work to do,
   Study his life to learn his will.

DESERTION.

TRANSLATION OF ONE OF GARCILASO'S ECLOGUES.

WITH my lamenting touched, the lofty trees
Incline their graceful heads without a breeze;
The listening birds forego their joyous song,
For soft and mournful strains, which echoes faint prolong.

Lions and bears resign the charms of sleep
To hear my lonely plaint, and see me weep;

At my approaching death e'en stones relent.
   Yet though yourself the fatal cause you know,
Not once on me those lovely eyes are bent:
   Flow freely, tears! 'tis meet that you should flow!

Although for my relief thou wilt not come,
Leave not the place where once thou loved'st to roam!
Here thou mayst rove secure from meeting me;
With a torn heart forever hence I flee.
Come, if 'twere this alone thy footsteps stayed,
Here the soft meadow, the delightful shade,
The roses now in flower, the waters clear,
Invite thee to the valley once so dear.

Come, and bring with thee thy late-chosen love;
Each object shall thy perfidy reprove;
Since to another thou hast given thy heart,
From this sweet scene forever I depart.
And soon kind Death my sorrows shall remove,
The bitter ending of my faithful love.

SONG WRITTEN FOR A MAY DAY FESTIVAL.

TO BE SUNG TO THE TUNE OF "THE BONNY BOAT."

I.

O, BLESSÉD be this sweet May day,
   The fairest of the year;
The birds are heard from every spray,
   And the blue sky shines so clear!
White blossoms deck the apple tree,
   Blue violets the plain;

Their fragrance tells the wand'ring bee
   That Spring is come again.
We'll cull the blossoms from the bough
   Where robins gayly sing,
We'll wreathe them for our queen's pure brow,
   We'll wreathe them for our king.

II.

The winter wind is bleak and sad,
   And chill the winter rain;
But these May gales blow warm and glad,
   And charm the heart from pain.
The sick, the poor rejoice once more,
   Pale cheeks resume their glow,
And those who thought their day was o'er
   New life to May suns owe.
And we, in youth and health so gay,
   Sheltered by love and care,
How should we joy in blooming May,
   And bless its balmy air!

III.

We are the children of the Spring;
   Our home is always green;
Green be the garland of our king,
   The livery of our queen.
The gardener's care the seed has strown,
   To deck our home with flowers;
Our Father's love from high has shone,
   And sent the needed showers.
Barren indeed the plants must be,
   If they should not disclose,
Tended and cherished with such toil,
   The lily and the rose.

IV.

Meanwhile through the wild wood we'll rove,
　Where earliest flowerets grow,
And greet each simple bud with love,
　Which tells us what to do —
That, though untended, we may bloom
　And smile on all around,
And one day rise from earth's low tomb,
　To live where light is found.
A modest violet be our queen,
　Still fragrant, though alone,
Our king a laurel — evergreen —
　To which no blight is known.

V.

So let us bless the sweet May day,
　And pray the coming year
May see us walk the upward way —
　Minds earnest, conscience clear;
That fruit Spring's amplest hope may crown,
　And every wingéd day
Make to our hearts more dear, more known,
　The hope, the peace of May!
So cull the blossoms from the bough
　Where birds so gayly sing;
We'll wreathe them for our queen's pure brow,
　We'll wreathe them for our king.

CARADORI SINGING.

Let not the heart o'erladen hither fly,
Hoping in tears to vent its misery :
She soars not like the lark with eager cry,
Not hers the robin's notes of love and joy ;
Nor, like the nightingale's love-descant, tells
Her song the truths of the heart's hidden wells.
Come, if thy soul be tranquil, and her voice
Shall bid the tranquil lake laugh and rejoice ;
Shall lightly warble, flutter, hover, dance,
And charm thee by its sportive elegance.
A finished style the highest art has given,
And a fine organ she received from heaven :
But genius casts not here one living ray ;
Thou shalt approve, admire, not weep, to-day.

LINES

IN ANSWER TO STANZAS CONTAINING SEVERAL PASSAGES
OF DISTINGUISHED BEAUTY, ADDRESSED TO ME BY ———.

As by the wayside the worn traveller lies,
    And finds no pillow for his aching brow,
Except the pack beneath whose weight he dies, —
    If loving breezes from the far west blow,
Laden ·with perfume from those blissful bowers
Where gentle youth and hope once gilded all his hours,
As fans that loving breeze, tears spring again,
And cool the fever of his wearied brain.

35

Even so to me the soft romantic dream
  Of one who still may sit at fancy's feet,
Where love and beauty yet are all the theme,
  Where spheral concords find an echo meet.
To the ideal my vexed spirit turns,
But often for communion vainly burns.
Blest is that hour when breeze of poesy
From far the ancient fragrance wafts to me;
This time thrice blest, because it came unsought,
" Sweet suppliance," and *dear*, because *unbought*.

INFLUENCE OF THE OUTWARD.

THE sun, the moon, the waters, and the air,
The hopeful, holy, terrible, and fair;
Flower-alphabets, love-letters from the wave,
All mysteries which flutter, blow, skim, lave;
All that is ever-speaking, never spoken,
Spells that are ever breaking, never broken,—
Have played upon my soul, and every string
Confessed the touch which once could make it sing
Triumphal notes; and still, though changed the tone,
Though damp and jarring fall the lyre hath known,
It would, if fitly played, and all its deep notes wove
Into one tissue of belief and love,
Yield melodies for angel-audience meet,
And pæans fit creative power to greet.

O, injured lyre! thy golden frame is marred;
No garlands deck thee; no libations poured
Tell to the earth the triumphs of thy song;
No princely halls echo thy strains along;

But still the strings are there; and if at last they break,
Even in death some melody will make.
Mightst thou once more be strung, might yet the power
    be given,
To tell in numbers all thou hast of heaven!
But no! thy fragments scattered by the way,
To children given, help the childish play.
Be it thy pride to feel thy latest sigh
Could not forget the law of harmony,
Thou couldst not live for bliss — but thou for truth
    couldst die!

TO MISS R. B.*

A GRACEFUL fiction of the olden day
Tells us that, by a mighty master's sway,
A city rose, obedient to the lyre;
That his sweet strains rude matter could inspire
With zeal his harmony to emulate;
Thus to the spot where that sweet singer sat
The rocks advanced, in symmetry combined,
To form the palace and the temple joined.
The arts are sisters, and united all,
So architecture answered music's call.

In modern days such feats no more we see,
And matter dares 'gainst mind a rebel be;
The faith is gone such miracles which wrought;
Masons and carpenters must aid our thought;
The harp and voice in vain would try their skill
To raise a city on our hard-bound soil;

[* A sweet and beautiful singer. — ED.]

The rocks have lain asleep so many a year,
Nothing but gunpowder will make them stir;
I doubt if even for your voice would come
The smallest pebble from its sandy home;
But, if the minstrel can no more create,
For *building*, if he live a little late,
He wields a power of not inferior kind,
No longer rules o'er matter, but o'er mind.
And when a voice like yours its song doth pour,
If it can raise palace and tower no more,
It can each ugly fabric melt away,
Bidding the fancy fairer scenes portray;
Its soft and brilliant tones our thoughts can wing
To climes whence they congenial magic bring;
As by the sweet Italian voice is given
Dream of the radiance of Italia's heaven.

Whether in round, low notes the strain may swell.
As if some tale of woe or wrong to tell,
Or swift and light the upward notes are heard,
With the full carolling clearness of a bird,
The stream of sound untroubled flows along,
And no obstruction mars your finished song.
No stifled notes, no gasp, no ill-taught graces,
No vulgar trills in worst-selected places,
None of the miseries which haunt a land
Where all would learn what so few understand,
Afflict in hearing you; in you we find
The finest organ, and informed by mind.

And as, in that same fable I have quoted,
It is of that town-making artist noted,
That, where he leaned his lyre upon a stone,
The stone stole somewhat of that lovely tone,

And afterwards each untaught passer-by,
By touching it, could rouse the melody, —
Even thus a heart once by your music thrilled,
An ear which your delightful voice has filled,
In memory a talisman have found
To repel many a dull, harsh, after-sound ;
And, as the music lingered in the stone,
After the minstrel and the lyre were gone,
Even so my thoughts and wishes, turned to sweetness,
Lend to the heavy hours unwonted fleetness ;
And common objects, calling up the tone,
I caught from you, wake beauty not their own.

SISTRUM.*

Triune, shaping, restless power,
Life-flow from life's natal hour,
No music chords are in thy sound ;
By some thou'rt but a rattle found ;
Yet, without thy ceaseless motion,
To ice would turn their dead devotion.
Life-flow of my natal hour,
I will not weary of thy power,
Till in the changes of thy sound
A chord's three parts distinct are found.
I will faithful move with thee,
God-ordered, self-fed energy,
Nature in eternity.

[* A musical instrument of the ancients, employed by the Egyptians in the worship of Isis. It was to be kept in constant motion, and, according to Plutarch, was intended to indicate the necessity of constant motion on the part of men — the need of being often shaken by fierce trials and agitations when they become morbid or indolent. — Ed.]

IMPERFECT THOUGHTS.

THE peasant boy watches the midnight sky ;
He sees the meteor dropping from on high ;
He hastens whither the bright guest hath flown,
And finds — a mass of black, unseemly stone.
Disdainful, disappointed, turns he home.
If a philosopher that way had come,
He would have seized the waif with great delight,
And honored it as an aerolite.
But truly it would need a Cuvier's mind
High meaning in *my* meteors to find.
Well, in my museum there is room to spare —
I'll let them stay till Cuvier goes there !

SADNESS.

LONELY lady, tell me why
That abandonment of eye ?
Life is full, and nature fair ;
How canst thou dream of dull despair ?

Life is full and nature fair ;
A dull folly is despair ;
But the heart lies still and tame
For want of what it may not claim.

Lady, chide that foolish heart,
And bid it act a nobler part ;
The love thou couldst be bid resign
Never could be worthy thine.

O, I know, and knew it well,
How unworthy was the spell
In its silken band to bind
My heaven-born, heaven-seeking mind.

Thou lonely moon, thou knowest well
Why I yielded to the spell;
Just so thou didst condescend
Thy own precept to offend.

When wondering nymphs thee questioned why
That abandonment of eye,
Crying, " Dian,* heaven's queen,
What can that trembling eyelash mean ? "

Waning, over ocean's breast,
Thou didst strive to hide unrest
From the question of their eyes,
Unseeing in their dull surprise.

Thy Endymion had grown old;
Thy only love was marred with cold;
No longer to the secret cave
Thy ray could pierce, and answer have.

No more to thee, no more, no more,
Till thy circling life be o'er,
A mutual heart shall be a home,
Of weary wishes happy tomb.

[* Diana is represented as driving the chariot of the moon, as Apollo
that of the sun. Mythology states that while enlightening the earth as
Luna, the moon, she beheld the hunter Endymion sleeping in the forest.
With her rays she kissed the lips of the hunter — a favor she had never
before bestowed on god or man. — ED.]

No more, no more — O words which sever
Hearts from their hopes, to part forever!
They can believe it never!

LINES WRITTEN IN AN ALBUM.*

SOME names there are at sight of which will rise
Visions of triumph to the dullest eyes;
They breathe of garlands from a grateful race,
They tell of victory o'er all that's base;
To write them eagles might their plumage give,
And granite rocks should yield, that they may live.

Others there are at sight of which will rise
Visions of beauty to all loving eyes,
Of radiant sweetness, or of gentle grace,
The poesy of manner or of face,
Spell of intense, if not of widest power;
The strong the ages rule; the fair, the hour.

And there are names at sight of which will rise
Visions of goodness to the mourner's eyes;
They tell of generosity untired,
Which gave to others all the heart desired;
Of Virtue's *uncomplaining* sacrifice,
And holy hopes which sought their native skies.

If I could hope that at my name would rise
Visions like these, before those gentle eyes,
How gladly would I place it in the shrine

[* These lines were written without her signature attached. — ED.]

Where many honored names are linked with thine,
And know, if lone and far my pathway lies,
My name is living 'mid the good and wise.

It must not be, for now I know too well
That those to whom my name has aught to tell
O'er baffled efforts would lament or blame.
Who heeds a breaking reed? — a sinking flame?
Best wishes and kind thoughts I give to thee,
But mine, indeed, an *empty name* would be.

TO S. C.

Our friend has likened thee to the sweet fern,
  Which with no flower salutes the ardent day,
  Yet, as the wanderer pursues his way,
While the dews fall, and hues of sunset burn,
  Sheds forth a fragrance from the deep green brake,
  Sweeter than the rich scents that gardens make.
Like thee, the fern loves well the hallowed shade
  Of trees that quietly aspire on high;
Amid such groves was consecration made
  Of vestals, tranquil as the vestal sky.

Like thee, the fern doth better love to hide
  Beneath the leaf the treasure of its seed,
Than to display it, with an idle pride,
  To any but the careful gatherer's heed —
A treasure known to philosophic ken,
Garnered in nature, asking nought of men;
  Nay, can invisible the wearer make,
  Who would unnoted in life's game partake.

But I will liken thee to the sweet bay,
  Which I first learned, in the Cohasset woods,
To name upon a sweet and pensive day
  Passed in their ministering solitudes.

I had grown weary of the anthem high
  Of the full waves, cheering the patient rocks;
I had grown weary of the sob and sigh
  Of the dull ebb, after emotion's shocks;
My eye was weary of the glittering blue
  And the unbroken horizontal line;
My mind was weary, tempted to pursue
  The circling waters in their wide design,
Like snowy sea-gulls stooping to the wave,
  Or rising buoyant to the utmost air,
To dart, to circle, airily to lave,
  Or wave-like float in foam-born lightness fair:
I had swept onward like the wave so full,
Like sea weed now left on the shore so dull.

I turned my steps to the retreating hills,
  Rejected sand from that great haughty sea,
Watered by nature with consoling rills,
  And gradual dressed with grass, and shrub, and tree;
They seemed to welcome me with timid smile,
That said, "We'd like to soothe you for a while;
  You seem to have been treated by the sea
  In the same way that long ago were we."

They had not much to boast, those gentle slopes,
  For the wild gambols of the sea-sent breeze
Had mocked at many of their quiet hopes,
  And bent and dwarfed their fondly cherished trees;
Yet even in those marks of by-past wind,
There was a tender stilling for my mind.

Hiding within a small but thick-set wood,
I soon forgot the haughty, chiding flood.
The sheep bell's tinkle on the drowsy ear,
With the bird's chirp, so short, and light, and clear,
Composed a melody that filled my heart
With flower-like growths of childish, artless art,
And of the tender, tranquil life I lived apart.

It was an hour of pure tranquillity,
Like to the autumn sweetness of thine eye,
Which pries not, seeks not, and yet clearly sees —
Which wooes not, beams not, yet is sure to please.
Hours passed, and sunset called me to return
Where its sad glories on the cold wave burn.

Rising from my kind bed of thick-strewn leaves,
A fragrance the astonished sense receives,
Ambrosial, searching, yet retiring, mild:
Of that soft scene the soul was it? or child?
'Twas the sweet bay I had unwitting spread,
A pillow for my senseless, throbbing head,
And which, like all the sweetest things, demands,
To make it speak, the grasp of alien hands.

All that this scene did in that moment tell,
   I since have read, O wise, mild friend! in thee.
   Pardon the rude grasp, its sincerity,
And feel that I, at least, have known thee well.
Grudge not the green leaves ravished from thy stem,
   Their music, should I live, muse-like to tell;
Thou wilt, in fresher green forgetting them,
   Send others to console me for farewell.
Thou wilt see why the dim word of regret
Was made the one to rhyme with Margaret.

But to the Oriental parent tongue,
　　Sunrise of Nature, does my chosen name,
My name of Leila, as a spell, belong,
　　Teaching the meaning of each temporal blame;
I chose it by the sound, not knowing why;
　　But since I know that Leila stands for night,
I own that sable mantle of the sky,
　　Through which pierce, gem-like, points of distant light;
As sorrow truths, so night brings out her stars;
　　O, add not, bard! that those stars shine too late!
While earth grows green amid the ocean jars,
　　And trumpets yet shall wake the slain of her long
　　　century-wars.

LINES WRITTEN IN BOSTON ON A BEAUTI-
FUL AUTUMNAL DAY.

As late we lived upon the gentle stream,
　　Nature refused us smiles and kindly airs;
The sun but rarely deigned a pallid gleam;
　　Then clouds came instantly, like glooms and tears,
Upon the timid flickerings of our hope;
　　The moon, amid the thick mists of the night,
Had scarcely power her gentle eye to ope,
　　And climb the heavenly steeps. A moment bright
Shimmered the hectic leaves, then rudely torn
　　By winds that sobbed to see the wreck they made,
Upon the amber waves were thickly borne
　　Adonis' gardens for the realms of shade,
While thoughts of beauty past all wish for livelier life forbade.

So sped the many days of tranquil life,
    And on the stream, or by the mill's bright fire,
The wailing winds had told of distant strife,
    Still bade us for the moment yield desire
To think, to feel, the moment gave, — we needed not aspire !

Returning here, no harvest fields I see,
    Nor russet beauty of the thoughtful year.
Where is the honey of the city bee ?
    No leaves upon this muddy stream appear.
The housekeeper is getting in his coal,
    The lecturer his showiest thoughts is selling ;
I hear of Major Somebody, the Pole,
    And Mr. Lyell, how rocks grow, is telling ;
But not a breath of thoughtful poesy
    Does any social impulse bring to me ;
But many cares, sad thoughts of men unwise,
    Base yieldings, and unransomed destinies,
    · Hopes uninstructed, and unhallowed ties.

Yet here the sun smiles sweet as heavenly love,
    Upon the eve of earthly severance ;
The youthfulest tender clouds float all above,
    And earth lies steeped in odors like a trance.
The moon looks down as though she ne'er could leave us,
And these last trembling leaves sigh, " Must they too
        deceive us ? "
    Surely some life is living in this light,
    Truer than mine some soul received last night ;
I cannot freely greet this beauteous day,
    But does not *thy* heart swell to hail the genial ray ?
I would not nature these last loving words in vain should say.

TO E. C.

WITH HERBERT'S POEMS.

Dost thou remember that fair summer's day,
As, sick and weary on my couch I lay,
Thou broughtst this little book, and didst diffuse
O'er my dark hour the light of Herbert's muse?
The "Elixir," and "True Hymn," were then thy choice,
And the high strain gained sweetness from thy voice.
The book, before that day to me unknown,
I took to heart at once, and made my own.

Three winters and three summers since have passed,
    And bitter griefs the hearts of both have tried;
Thy sympathy is lost to me at last;
    A dearer love has torn thee from my side;
Scenes, friends, to me unknown, now claim thy care;
No more thy joys or griefs I soothe or share;
No more thy lovely form my eye shall bless;
The gentle smile, the timid, mute caress,
No more shall break the icy chains which may my heart
        oppress.

New duties claim us both; indulgent Heaven
Ten years of mutual love to us had given;
The plants from early youth together grew,
Together all youth's sun and tempests knew.
At age mature arrived, thou, graceful vine!
Didst seek a sheltering tree round which to twine;
While I, like northern fir, must be content
To clasp the rock which gave my youth its scanty nour-
        ishment.

The world for which we sighed is with us now;
No longer musing on the *why* or *how*,
What really does exist we now must meet;
Life's dusty highway is beneath our feet;
Life's fainting pilgrims claim our ministry,
And the whole scene speaks stern *reality*.

Say, in the tasks reality has brought,
Keepst *thou* the plan that pleased thy childish thought?
Does Herbert's " Hymn " in thy heart echo now?
Herbert's " Elixir " in thy bosom glow?
In Herbert's " Temper " dost thou strive to be?
Does Herbert's " Pearl " seem the true pearl to thee?
O, if 'tis so, I have not prayed in vain!—
My friend, my sister, we shall meet again.

I dare not say that *I* am always true
To the vocation which my young thought knew;
But the Great Spirit blesses me, and still,
Though clouds may darken o'er the heavenly will,
Upon the hidden sun my thoughts can rest,
And oft the rainbow glitters in the west.
This earth no more seems all the world to me;
Before me shines a far eternity,
Whose laws to me, when thought is calmly poised,
Suffice, as they to angels have sufficed.
I know the thunder has not ceased to roll,
Not all the iron yet has pierced my soul;
I know no earthly honors wait for me,
No earthly love my heart shall satisfy.
Tears, of these eyes still oft the guests must be,
Long hours be borne, of chilling apathy;
Still harder teachings come to make me wise,
And life's best blood must seal the sacrifice.

But He who still seems nearer and more bright,
Nor from my *seeking* eye withholds his light,
Will not forsake me, for his pledge is given ;
Virtue shall teach the soul its way to heaven.

O, pray for me, and I for thee will pray ;
And more than loving words we used to say
Shall this avail.   But little more we meet
In life — ah, how the years begin to fleet !
Ask — pray that I may seek beauty and truth ;
In their high sphere we shall renew our youth.
On wings of *steadfast faith* there mayst *thou* soar,
And *my* soul fret at barriers no more !

Jan. 24 1861.

www.ingramcontent.com/pod-product-compliance
Lightning Source LLC
Chambersburg PA
CBHW021330110726
47900CB00005B/1415